THE 13TH POWER
QUEST

Terry Wright

2016, TWB Press
www.twbpress.com

The 13th Power Quest
Copyright © 2016 by Terry Wright

Based on the original novel, "The 13th Power – The Most Dangerous Quest of All" (Gardenia Press 2001)

© Cover art by Terry Wright

ISBN: 978-1-944045-23-4

Foreword

American and European scientists have been building bigger and faster particle accelerators to smash atoms into smaller pieces. They are looking for the Higgs boson, the particle that gives matter mass, The God Particle. What if they find it?

Fermilab and CERN are the biggest players in this race for the Higgs boson, named after Peter Higgs who first proposed its existence in1964 as a way to explain why atoms have mass. Since then, tens of billions of dollars have been spent to prove the Higgs exists. Russia tried but failed in a catastrophic way.

However, in California, there's a smaller lab with an equally determined group of scientists in the hunt. Their motivations are as varied as the characters themselves. Whether it's love, money, power, fame, or revenge that drives them, they're about to set the world on a course of impending destruction.

This is their story.

Chapter 1

SKIMMING ABOVE the Borneo jungle in a Bell 47 helicopter, Melvin Anderson balled his fists. "You better lose those bastards," he shouted over the clattering engine and slapping rotor blades. Heart pounding with dread, he twisted in his seat and looked behind them. Three Malaysian Federation patrol choppers were flying a wedge formation several hundred yards back...and closing.

"Damn."

With white knuckles, Fred Jenkins worked the stick. "What the hell do they want?" Tracers streaked past the glass bubble. Faint gunfire rattled in the distance. "They're gonna kill us."

The radio crackled. "Control. Victor Eagle One," a chopper pilot reported to his base. "We have visual contact."

Melvin shuddered. "Those guys never give up."

"Good idea," Fred said. "Give up before they blow us out of the sky."

"Easy for you to say."

"Jesus. I've got kids at home."

"Hope you kissed 'em goodbye this morning."

"Damn it, man. We don't stand a chance against these guys."

Melvin gulped. Fred was right. This little two-seater was no match for those military choppers. Sure, it was risky chartering this copter to Ketapang, but there was no other way to escape. The Malaysian authorities were watching every transportation hub. He had to catch a fishing trawler to Jakarta. He had to get out of this godforsaken country.

The copter banked left and descended sharply. Melvin's stomach floated and dived. He glanced at Fred.

Beads of sweat trickled down the man's weathered face. He'd probably already pissed in his pants. Little did he know his high-dollar passenger would cause him so much trouble. Bad luck for Fred. "Hope you're a better pilot than a hero, watch out!"

Fred veered left, just missing a tree branch. "Think you can fly this thing any better?"

"I was flying crop dusters across Sumatra back when your mommy was powder-puffin' your ass."

Gunfire rattled again.

"What kind of trouble are you in?"

"Ahhh...they're just a bunch of sore losers."

"I didn't ask for none of this military shit, and I don't want in the middle of your squabble. I'm just running a flying service, for God's sake."

"You'll be flying with wings on your back if you don't shake these guys." Melvin turned around to check the squadron's position. Another volley of tracers streamed past, closer this time. There had to be a way to get out of this mess. He searched the leafy canopy whizzing by below. An opening appeared. "Go right, damn it. Go right!"

Copter blades strained in the turn.

"Down there!" Melvin pointed to the river that snaked below them, peeking out from under the forest canopy. "Go. Go."

"You gotta be nuts."

Melvin pushed the stick forward. The copter dove toward the river.

"Shit!" Fred pulled out of the dive and skimmed the skids over the frothy surface.

Jungle closed in around them. The riverbed turned dark as night, except for the occasional bursts of sunlight that flashed through scattered gaps in the canopy. Melvin swallowed hard. He'd really screwed up this time.

Fred flipped on the landing light switch. Halogens illuminated the eerie, forested tunnel. The skids clipped riverbank ferns. The rotors nicked low-hanging branches. One wrong move, they'd be swimming with the crocodiles.

White tracers flashed by like bright burning balls of magnesium.

Hot alarm pumped through Melvin's chest. He craned his neck to look back. The Federation choppers were flying single-file right behind them, their spinning rotor blades clipping tree branches as they rocked side to side in the air. He couldn't believe the balls on those pilots...following them into this treacherous tunnel. Another burst of gunfire shredded tree limbs on both sides of the copter.

"Warning shots." Fred dodged a fallen log. "They could've shot us down already. Don't you see? They're giving you a chance to surrender."

"No way in hell," Melvin snarled. "I'm not gonna spend the rest of my life in a Sumatra prison. I'd rather die, so keep this bird in the air."

"Sore losers, huh," Fred muttered and banked his copter through a sharp bend in the riverbed. Ahead, another large opening in the canopy appeared. "We're getting out of this deathtrap, right now."

"No don't."

The copter nosed up and broke out into sunlight. Melvin clenched his jaw. What a stupid move. Now they were out in the open again. "God damn you, Fred."

The Federation choppers flared out and flanked the copter on both sides, flying rotor tip to rotor tip. Melvin glared at the chopper on the left. The flight officer bared his teeth and pointed his gloved finger down while mouthing the word *land*. Melvin sneered at him and turned to the chopper flying starboard. He locked eyes with the pilot and flipped him a finger. "Bastard. You'll never take me alive."

The radio crackled. "Hail, Delta-Four-Niner-Echo. Melvin Anderson—you're under arrest."

Wide-eyed, Fred screamed, "Now what am I supposed to do?"

Melvin pulled up the pant leg of his jungle fatigues and reached into his boot. He fingered the cold steel of his .44 Magnum. *Risk nothing, gain nothing.* There'd be no prison in his future, even if he had to fly this damn thing himself—or die.

He snapped back the breach and pressed the muzzle against Fred's temple in plain view of the flanking officers.

"Say goodbye, Fred."

"What the fuck?"

Melvin squeezed the trigger.

Chapter 2

JANIS MACKEY, sweltering in his suit coat, stood on the bandstand of CU stadium in Boulder, Colorado, and scanned rows of gold and black banners hanging limp in the hot, still air. The CU Buffs were a great football team, but today was *his* day for glory, a day he'd worked toward for a long time.

Like warm spring-water, pride welled up inside. He looked over the crowd gathered for his induction ceremony: faculty, friends, and students, familiar faces, all smiling. They sat in bleachers set up on the fifty-yard line. Classes were out; the semester was over. Summertime had come to the Rockies. He pushed his wire-framed glasses up the bridge of his nose, wishing his mother could have been here to share in his moment of glory, but she didn't even know who he was anymore.

He hooked a finger under his collar, gave it a tug, and looked toward the foothills. A gray cloud hung over Flagstaff Mountain. Silent forks of lightning flashed to the ground. This heat wouldn't last much longer. The weather would provide a typical summer afternoon in Colorado: thunderstorms, wind, and hail, but he loved living here, the peaceful university life of Boulder.

Head Dean Dan Billings stepped up to the microphone. Sunshine glinted off the top of his bald head and his tie looked too tight.

"A-hum."

His voice reverberated around the stadium.

"As you all know, Dr. Mackey has been on the faculty here for twenty-two years. He's been a credit to the University of Colorado and an excellent teacher. Today he takes the big step up to administration."

The crowd applauded.

Janis showed them a smile. Had it really been twenty-two years? Teaching and researching the awesome power of numbers and the rules by which they existed had made him well revered in a small group of elite men. But the job didn't pay enough—just a notch above poverty—after his mother's expenses: medications, doctors, and the nursing home. Like leaches, they'd sucked her savings dry—and then his. After the money ran out, Medicaid kicked in, which helped some but not enough. He couldn't let her wilt away in some low-dollar state-run nursing home. A single mom, she'd sacrificed a lot for him in her lifetime. She deserved the best care his money could buy.

"As head of the Mathematics Department," Billings added. "He'll oversee the faculty and counsel students on their career goals."

Janis ran his fingers through pepper-gray hair. How many hundreds of kids had he seen graduate? Thousands maybe. He could take that accomplishment to his grave...but not to the bank.

"Dr. Mackey and I have been best of friends for the past ten years. I'm proud of his achievements and honored to have him on my staff."

Again, applause echoed around the stadium. Janis waved at the crowd. Finally, a promotion and a raise. Now, after taking care of his mother, he'd have money left over. He could junk that old Subaru and buy a new car. And that little house just off the turnpike—buying it was now within his financial reach.

Dan tapped the microphone. "And by the way, he's still single—in case any of you ladies might be interested."

Janis frowned. He didn't need any help finding the wrong women. He'd done just fine on his own—like with Donna. She was a nice gal but complained he didn't have enough time for her. She wasn't really mad when she left. She just left.

And then there was Jill—what a babe. But her cats stunk up the apartment. He told her she had to make a choice; it was him or the cats. She *was* mad when she left and took her damn cats with her.

Was he ever going to find the right woman?

"Ladies and gentlemen, Dr. Janis Mackey."

Chapter 3

THE MUZZLE BLAST was deafening. Fred's skull blew apart. Bullet and bone fragments shattered the copter's glass bubble. Blood gushed across the instrument panel. Fred fell on the controls and sent the copter into a spinning dive. Trying to pull back on the stick, Melvin struggled against centrifugal force and Fred's dead weight, but the forest canopy came up too quickly.

Belly first, the copter slammed into the treetops. Rotors ripped branches into splinters and scattered leaves in every direction. With a reverberating twang, the blades twisted, snapped, and whipped off into the foliage. The copter rolled over and tree limbs cracked.

Melvin's brain stopped working. Instinct kicked in. Survival mode made him unsnap his seatbelt and jump. Grabbing at thin air, he plummeted down with the copter. Sticks and leaves stung his face. His mouth hit a branch...hard. Everything flew by in a whirl. His legs snagged on a forked branch. Pain shot up his backbone, but he'd stopped falling. Blood spilled down his chin. He spit red.

What a rush.

Sucking in air, Melvin watched the copter crash down through the branches below him. Pieces flew off it like a Texas tornado. The bent fuselage hit black swamp water with a horrendous splash.

From the canopy above, Howler monkeys sounded the alarm. Hot engine parts sizzled in the water below. A hissing geyser of steam shot up from the wreckage. Melvin spit out a broken front tooth. His mouth throbbed. He was thankful to be alive.

The air-thumping sound of chopper blades thundered

overhead, whipping the trees mercilessly. He scrambled down the rickety limb toward a massive, worm-riddled tree trunk. Downdrafts pelted him with stinging splinters of wood and leaves that flew through the air like razor blades. He hung on tight and turned his face away from the onslaught.

Through the patchwork of sun and shadows below, crocodiles swam toward the wrecked copter. He counted three, four, five of the monsters. Their lumpy tails swayed in the water with a deadly grace.

Holding his breath, he watched the crocs nose into the broken copter bubble. One grabbed Fred. Then another. They yanked him out of the wreck, and twisting and thrashing around, they ripped his body apart. Pink and white strands of intestines floated in churning red-stained water. The beasts snapped and quarreled over the gruesome remains.

Melvin shut his eyes and fought off the nausea that threatened to expel his own guts into the swamp.

Fred had kids at home. He should've kept flying over the river, under the canopy, let the chopper pilots make a mistake and crash their bigger aircraft in the narrowing space. But no, he had to be a chicken shit. And look at him now; he paid the price for his cowardice.

The Federation choppers moved off, and the hammering subsided into the distance.

The radio crackled from inside the wrecked copter. "Control. Victor-Eagle-One," reverberated through the swamp. "Delta-Four-Niner-Echo crashed. No survivors."

Chapter 4

THE AFTERNOON Colorado sky grew dark and angry. Lightning forked to the ground. A clap of thunder battered the old Subaru. Janis mashed in the mushy clutch pedal and wrestled the shifter into second. The engine revved and knocked. He skipped third gear and went directly to fourth. Third made a lot of noise anyway. Raindrops the size of quarters pelted the windshield.

The wiper blades made thunky, creaky noises.

Janis hated the piece of junk he'd been driving for the past ten years. After a couple of paychecks, he'd get a new car. A Lexus would be nice, but he'd settle for a Camry.

Ahead, mailboxes cluttered the corner at the entrance to a parking lot off to the right. He'd driven this route home for the past five years, since he'd sold his house in *The Gardens* when his mother fell ill to Alzheimer's.

Then he called this place, Mission Meadows Apartments, his home. It may have been luxury living twenty years ago, but now, wind-driven litter flapped wildly in the untrimmed hedges. Busted old toys littered the weed-infested lawn. Out a third story window, neglected laundry flapped from makeshift clotheslines.

He parked next to a rusted Ford sitting on blocks. His Subaru was most likely the nicest car in the parking lot.

His life was going to change...after a couple of paychecks.

He shut off the ignition. The engine backfired. He swallowed his embarrassment along with his pride. On second thought, maybe his life would change after one paycheck. Car shopping. First thing on his list. He got out of the car. Hail started bouncing on the lawn.

He ran for the front doors. Rain angled down; thunder

clapped. He bounded into the lobby and stomped water off his shoes. Ten minutes from now, this storm would move east to pound Denver and Aurora.

He inserted the key to his door lock and heard the phone ringing inside his apartment. Pushing through the doorway, he rushed to answer the call. "Hello?"

Thunder boomed.

"Janis," Dan Billings said. "You got a minute?"

"What's up?"

"I didn't want to spoil your ceremony this morning, thought it best to save this 'til later. Bad news I'm afraid."

Janis's stomach tightened. Bad news? Mother?

"If there's anything I could do about it, I would."

"Give it to me straight, Dan."

"Those damn budget cuts...the Board of Trustees has been giving me fits."

"What's that got to do with me?"

"It's about your promotion."

"My promotion?" Janis felt like he'd been hit with a board. "You can't take my promotion away."

"Don't get all excited. You're still heading up the math department, but, well, your salary, Janis...it's been frozen. Six months...maybe a year...tops. You can hang in there that long, right?"

Janis dropped the phone.

Chapter 5

MELVIN CLUNG to the tree and struggled to catch his breath. Silence returned to the jungle. His body trembled; his broken tooth ached. The coppery taste of blood lingered in his mouth.

A bird cawed from somewhere. Made him jump.

He ripped off a piece of his shirttail, shoved it into the space where his tooth once was, and bit down hard. Pain shot up to his eyeballs. He peered across the sun-speckled darkness under the canopy. Crocodiles slithered into the shadows. Fine hell of a mess he'd gotten himself into this time. A violent death awaited him down there, but for the moment, he was satisfied to be in a tree. Alive.

He forced air through clenched teeth. That fishing trawler out of Ketapang would have to sail without him. The Malaysian authorities had ruined his plans for a quick getaway. Sure—stealing their ancient artifacts and selling them on the black market had been a profitable endeavor. He'd made a fortune as the world's most notorious grave robber, a reputation that he wore with pride. He couldn't be blamed for those crazy bastards going to war over that junk. It wasn't his fault they'd killed each other by the hundreds. The fools had to have somebody to blame. Scapegoat Melvin Anderson. He needed a new occupation.

Looking down from his sanctuary to the murky pool below, he thought about crocs, snakes, and quicksand. How much fun could one guy have? He spit out the bloody rag and began the treacherous descent.

He missed his .44. He'd dropped it during the crash. He had to do something to protect himself from the vermin that lurked about. A dead branch forking from the tree trunk gave him an idea. He broke it off and tested its weight. It would make a good poker, three-foot long, three inches thick, and sturdy. Something was better than nothing.

Straddling the last woody knot above the water, he carefully studied the swamp. Nothing stirred. Quietly, he slipped into the water, which rose to his waist and felt surprisingly warm. A fuel slick from the copter floated on the surface in rainbow-colored swirls.

He tried to take a step away from the tree but his boot was already stuck in the mud. Curling his toes, he strained harder, trying to pull his foot free without losing his boot. The swamp was determined to suck it off his sock. Struggling with this new dilemma, he soon realized the bottom wasn't going to yield him a single step. "Damn!" What else could go wrong in this fuckin' place?

With a mighty splash, the water surged upward, revealing the shiny pink throat of a monster croc. A million dagger-teeth glistened in the boil. Melvin squealed like a girl, it just came out that way, and thrust the poker upright between the gaping jaws. The croc bellowed and thrashed. The stick cracked...and snapped.

"Damn!" Melvin pulled his feet out of his boots and climbed the tree trunk to safety.

The angry croc roiled the water. In the canopy above, the Howlers howled in alarm.

Melvin hung on to a branch and shook from an adrenaline rush burning in his bloodstream. Gasping for air, he scouted the swamp again. There had to be another way out of here. He'd been in worse jams than this, though he couldn't remember when. Traversing this swamp wasn't an option; he'd surely die.

Above him, the Howlers clambered from tree to tree, honking and complaining. Vines dangled down from the canopy like the wavy tentacles of a jellyfish. Tarzan would be right at home here... Tarzan? He lived in the trees. That was the answer to Melvin's dilemma. The way through the rainforest was up there...

***

Melvin worked his way to the edge of the swamp. The sun cast long shadows to announce the day's end. He slid down a vine to a narrow dirt path and looked left and right. Not knowing which way to go, he chose to move downhill. Civilization had to be nearby. There would be no other reason for the path.

Between the copter crash and the jungle trees, his clothes were shredded to rags and soaked with sweat. Stinging scratches and aching bruises covered his body. His mouth hurt more than his muscles, which tortured him with every step. Darkness would soon envelop the jungle, so he plodded onward in haste, his tattered socks flopping in the dirt.

From the eerie shadows of nightfall, birds chirped and cawed. And other strange noises filled the night air: grunts of a wart hog family foraging in the bush, shrieks from a troop of monkeys swinging in the treetops, the faint strains of music. He stopped walking and cocked his head, trying to hone in on the sound's origin. Forward. Not far. Food. Water. Maybe a cold beer. Now that was wishful thinking. He started out again and picked up the pace.

A few minutes later, the jungle opened into a clearing. Light glowed from hut windows lining the path. Scattered campfires dotted the meadow and voices reached his ears. He strained to listen. The heady aroma of food drifted to his nostrils. He took in a deep breath. "Ahhh." When was the last time he'd eaten? Warily, he made his way down the path and into the little village.

A barking dog announced his arrival, but no one paid it any mind. The music was coming from a large hut with colorful lanterns flickering from the porch. A makeshift boardwalk stretched across a mud puddle and led to the doorway where an *OPEN* sign hung canted. The smell of food wafted from inside. He put on a stern face, threw his shoulders back, and pushed through swinging doors.

Every head turned toward him.

He stopped and looked around the hut. Small wooden tables cluttered the room. Most were vacant but all had a small candle burning in a glass orb. Shadows danced on the thatched walls. Stout wooden beams supported a rope net ceiling from which beer signs and banners hung. Behind the bar, a cassette recorder was playing an old Australian tune. A chubby-faced man wore a white apron and a look of surprise. "What duh hell happened ta you, mate?"

Melvin didn't reply. He walked to a corner table and pulled out a chair, which thudded on the wood-planked floor. Finally, he could sit down. What a relief. Through shredded socks, he rubbed his aching feet. The roomful of staring eyes made him nervous. With a sneer and a sharp jerk of his head, he motioned the curious onlookers to go about their business. Some did. Some didn't.

"Martha," the bartender called. "We've another guest for supper."

A moment later, the kitchen curtain parted and a stubby, overweight woman waddled out. She carried a heaping plate of food and looked at the bartender. He pointed at Melvin. "Over there."

Smiling, she made her way across the hut. The tattered hem of her blue flower-print dress dragged along the floor. She put the plate down in front of Melvin and handed him a big spoon. "Care for a spot of tea, or somethin' a bit stronger, sir?"

He didn't answer. He ate. Stew of some kind, but it smelled like prime rib, the meat melting in his mouth, the potatoes fat and soft, peas firm and fresh, all drowned in thick brown gravy. The pain of his broken tooth was numbed by the joy of eating.

The fat lady waddled off.

He quickly emptied his plate and pushed it aside. "Barkeep. Bring a bottle of whiskey and a glass." From a tattered pocket, he pulled out a wad of soggy cash and tossed it on the table.

The bartender was quick to respond.

Chapter 6

PEERING OUT from under bushy gray eyebrows, Boris ran his fingers across his lips and stared at the stranger's bottle of whiskey. Though his initial interest in the haggard man wasn't compelling, the thought of a free drink made his heart beat faster.

He stood, and slightly hunched over, shuffled across the hut with a discernible limp. Though his frizzy gray hair hadn't seen a comb in a while and his old wrinkled clothes smelled of sweat and soil, he truly believed he was in better shape than the stranger.

Grabbing a chair, Boris sat down with him. "What happen to you?" he asked in a broken Slavic accent while casting an obvious glance at the whiskey bottle.

At least he hoped it was obvious.

The man eyed him warily for a moment, then picked up the whiskey bottle and filled the glass. Nose-tantalizing vapor rose in the air. He lifted his drink and inspected the fill. "I fell off the turnip truck."

"Ha!" The stranger was a smart ass. Boris licked his lips. "Look like mighty fine whiskey you got."

The stranger threw down a gulp. "Where can I get some boots around here?" He grabbed the bottle and poured again.

"Tell bartender to bring another glass."

Glaring at him, the stranger stopped pouring.

Boris gulped. Perhaps he was being too pushy. However, his thirst for whiskey overpowered any common sense. He extended his hand to the man who was staring at him with gray eyes that had no soul.

"Name Boris. Boris Dagloskoff."

Chapter 7

MELVIN GLARED at Boris. The old man's clothes smelled like cat piss. "Go away!"

"I only try to be friendly."

"You're a beggar!"

"Things not always what they appear," Boris said, his hand still offered.

"Get out of my face."

"You want boots or not?"

Grinding his molars, Melvin finished filling his glass. Maybe the old man could be of some help. A little whiskey would be a small price to pay for a pair of boots. Without smiling, Melvin shook Boris's hand, which felt as smooth as a hooker's fanny. He hadn't seen a day of hard labor in his life. "Barkeep," Melvin called out. "Another glass for my friend."

Boris showed a smile full of perfectly white teeth. "What's your name?"

"Melvin." He decided to forgo his last name, just in case his notoriety had reached this far back in the boonies.

The bartender brought a glass and set it on the table. "Be careful of old Boris here. He'll drink you under the table."

Nearby patrons broke out in laughter.

Melvin wondered what was so funny.

"I from Russia where we drink vodka. They always make a joke."

Melvin didn't see any humor in stereotyping all Russian's as drunks. "Kind of far from home, aren't you?"

"Long story. But for you, I will tell." Boris placed the glass where Melvin could easily pour from the bottle.

With the old man's help, the booze was soon gone.

"Barkeep—another bottle," Melvin shouted. He started to relax, the whiskey numbing his ills of the day.

The bartender clunked down a new bottle, and as he sorted through the soggy cash for his fee, Melvin sized up Boris, a Russian out here in the middle of nowhere. The pristine condition of his hands meant he hadn't been living in this jungle very long. And his teeth had not longed for dental care. Melvin rubbed his chin, and aside from realizing he needed a shave, he found himself intrigued by the old man. He might be able to help him get more than a pair of boots...like maybe a gun. Or maybe a ride out of this shithole.

Boris swallowed whisky like it was afternoon tea. "What about this turnip truck you say?"

"Actually, it was a helicopter." Melvin took a slug of whiskey right from the bottle.

Boris laughed. "You fell out of helicopter? Turnip truck better bullshit."

"And a croc about bit my damn head off." He gave the bottle to Boris. "Came close to dying."

"What you do in jungle, anyway?"

Melvin didn't want anyone to know he was running from the law so he opted to lie. "Treasure hunting."

Boris cracked a bright smile. "Ah! You search for treasure. I too search for treasure. We do same thing." He slapped Melvin on the shoulder. "Comrades! Yes?"

"If you're an archeologist." *Aka grave robber.*

"Scientist," Boris whispered. "In Russia."

"What are you doing here?"

Boris glanced around like he feared prying ears. "Let's just say my employer and I have falling out."

Melvin didn't buy a bit of it but decided to play along. "What kind of treasure does a Russian scientist look for?"

"The God Particle." He guzzled from the bottle and handed it to Melvin.

Fisting the bottleneck, Melvin's interest spiked.

"What's the God Particle?"

"Higgs boson. Key to atom. Key to universe. Very much power...very much money."

Very much of those things interested Melvin very much. "Is it better than diamonds and gold, or something?"

"It is the atomic particle that gives matter mass."

"That's no treasure."

Boris leaned forward. "Control the Higgs, you control matter, how mass is put together. You know...stuff... Everything in universe." The excitement in his whisper caused the candle flame in the orb to flicker. "Think of possibilities. Change lead to gold, water to petro, or maybe if you like, salt to cocaine." He stared at Melvin and twitched his bushy eyebrows. "Make very famous man who finds what lies at the 13th Power."

"The 13th Power?" Sounded to Melvin like sci-fi gibberish.

Boris's eyes widened with awe. "Mathematically, the nucleus of atom is the 12th Power. The God Particle is very much smaller, the 13th Power, ten times smaller than quarks and mesons."

It was all Greek to Melvin. He glared at the Russian. Boris was definitely smarter than he acted, probably a ploy to dupe the locals into thinking he was crazy. A sympathy ploy, or was he trying to stay under his ex-employer's radar? The booze had definitely loosened his tongue, a dangerous thing for a man on the run, but was he telling the truth? Melvin's head felt woozy from the booze, but he wasn't drunk enough to believe Boris about turning lead into gold. "You're full of shit, old man."

Boris's eyes widened. "Oh yeah?" He sounded as though he'd been challenged to a duel. "Boris not full of shit."

"Yes you are, Boris," the bartender put in. "When the hell you gonna stop tellin' that old rag tale of yours?"

The other patrons howled and jeered, "Too dangerous.

Too dangerous."

Boris scowled at the bartender. "You I tell. Now him I tell. Quest for 13th Power very dangerous."

His mockers roared. "Too dangerous. Too dangerous."

Boris must've told this story many times. Nobody believed him, but what if there was something to it? With the right amount of money, personnel, and equipment invested, there'd be a fortune for the taking, unlike any other.

"Enough!" Melvin slapped the table with the palm of his hand, silencing the ridicule and laughter. "What's too dangerous, Boris?"

"It was very cold that day..."

***

A bitter wind hurled snow across the sprawling Siberian plains, due east of Novosibirsk, the only civilization for sixteen hundred kilometers. In the midst of this wilderness, a block building stood ten stories above the arctic terrain. High barbed wire surrounded the facility, and guard dogs barked from within. On the snow-choked road to the main gate, a weather-beaten sign read *Содержание вне*: Keep Out!

Inside the building, in a cram-packed room of consoles and monitors, Boris rushed in, buttoning his lab coat with hangover-clumsy fingers. Technicians and scientists seated at their stations bombarded him with scowls.

"You are late," Artur Petrov shouted, the senior member of the Institute of Nuclear Physics. He stood from his chair at a console stacked with computer monitors floor to ceiling. His scornful expression and frazzled hair made him look like the cover boy for Mad Scientist Journal. "There is no excuse for this delay."

"The heat, sir, in my apartment, it is on the fritz again."

Truth be told, Boris had overslept. The red-eyed evidence on his face easily revealed the reason. A night of heavy drinking. Imported Kentucky bourbon.

Vodka was for *kholops*.

He'd be lucky to see noon without puking.

"Take your position," Petrov ordered.

With a dull throb in his head, Boris scrambled to his threadbare swivel chair. He inhaled the aroma of hot electronics. The air vibrated to the hum of the Troitska particle accelerator, the largest in the world.

Petrov reseated himself in front of his monitors that displayed data from MAGGIE, Troitska's eight-story-high, fifty thousand ton particle detector, it too, the largest in the world. "Is everyone ready?"

Nods all around.

A few keystrokes brought up the Troitska status report. The massive atom-smashing machine circumvented twenty-nine kilometers of windswept tundra, two hundred feet below the permafrost. Super-cooled by liquid nitrogen, gargantuan electromagnets accelerated protons to the speed of light, eleven thousand revolutions per second around the collider ring.

Twenty-four hours a day. Seven days a week. At varying degrees of power. Until something broke. Then shut-down, repair, restart. Shut-down, repair, restart...

Chief mechanical engineer McClarence reported in. "Starting Higgs RUN 27-B."

A chill avalanched between Boris's shoulder blades. Today could be the day he would witness the elusive Higgs boson.

The God Particle.

There was danger delving into the beating heart of existence, the first pulse of the universe thirteen billion years ago, the spark of the Big Bang. Colliding protons at speeds high enough to reveal the Higgs would create mini black holes swirling inside the detector. Alarmists warned that these black holes could disintegrate the entire planet.

No one really knew the dangers. No one could ensure safety. Boris was prepared to shut down MAGGIE at the first sign of any abnormality.

Petrov's voice broke the din. "Engage the Scheduler."

Supercomputers initiated programs to control the experiment and record the outcome.

Never before had a harmless Xenon laser beam been introduced into a particle debris field at G-Zero, deep in MAGGIE's core where the protons collided. If the theory was correct, loosed Higgs bosons would give mass to the laser photons and create a superheated particle beam of unimaginable power.

Nobel prizes would surely be awarded.

Petrov pointed to Boris. "Begin."

His tongue felt like a flap of shoe leather. Wishing for whiskey to make it supple again, he keyed in the code for one hundred percent power.

High voltage surged through massive electromagnets, both in the accelerator ring and inside MAGGIE's detector field surrounding G-Zero. Ceiling lights dimmed.

An electronic female voice spoke from the intercom system: *"Two minutes to laser firing."*

Humming intensified, nippling the skin on Boris's arms.

"Ninety percent power," McClarence reported.

On Boris's display, opposing beams of protons and antiprotons crashed head-on. Luminosity readings at G-Zero shot off the scale, indicating a high number of proton collisions generating 12TeV. Twelve Trillion electron Volts. Impressive numbers, as MAGGIE was only running at ninety-percent power, but in reality, 12TeV equaled the energy of a dozen ants walking five feet across a level surface.

No Hiroshima here.

"Ninety seconds to laser firing."

McClarence again: "Ninety-five."

The supercomputers gathered data from MAGGIE and displayed each collision in a collage of images on dozens of monitors around the control room. The blossoming sprays and radiant swirls looked like fanciful works of abstract art. However, to Boris's trained eye, the patterns were nothing special. Nothing new.

"Ninety-seven."

Vibration seeped from the floor into the soles of Boris's shoes. MAGGIE began to sing under the strain of increased energy and speed.

"100TeV," McClarence shouted over the fierce hum.

One hundred walking ants.

"Ninety-nine percent."

Luminosity readings held high and strong.

"One minute to laser firing."

"One hundred percent power," McClarence shouted.

Rumbling came from the ground and shook the walls and the consoles.

"170TeV!"

Energy levels had never before reached these highs. The radiant displays streaming from MAGGIE revealed traces and patterns and colors never before recorded. It would take months, if not years, to decipher the data.

Pride consumed Boris. This would be a historic event, revered by Russian scientists for many generations to come.

"Forty-five seconds to laser firing."

A beep.

Alarm pumped through Boris's chest.

A message window appeared on his monitor:

CHANGES LOCKED OUT.

He shuddered. "Comrade Petrov, what is this?"

Petrov rose from his chair. "I have deleted the fail-safes. Vladimir Yzerman has ordered this. There will be no more delays."

"Bolvan!" How stupid! Boris had to shout over all the noise. "The Political Director knows nothing--"

"If we fail again, Moscow will stop our funding," Petrov shot back. "We cannot afford another shutdown. It is all or nothing for the glory of Mother Russia."

"It's too dangerous." The fool! Boris typed the code words that would shut MAGGIE down.

ACCESS DENIED

"Son of a *baruha!*" Whore! Boris felt hogtied.

"Thirty seconds to laser firing."

Petrov paced the control room like a caged squirrel. "We stand at the brink of a new frontier. Are we afraid? Yes. Are we cowards? No. Nothing will stop us now."

"Twenty seconds to laser firing."

MAGGIE could not be stopped. Data streams rose to never-before-seen levels.

Highest speeds.

Highest electron voltages.

"Ten seconds to laser firing."

Charging with energy, the Xenon laser resonator emitted a high-pitched squeal.

"200 TeV!" McClarence cheered. "Phenomenal!"

Error reports began scrolling down Boris's display.

DETECTOR CORE UNSTABLE

G-ZERO BREACH

Boris stiffened with fear. MAGGIE was going berserk.

BIOS OVERLOAD

CACHE FILES CORRUPT

The computers couldn't keep up with the high flow of data streaming from MAGGIE.

Numbers and letters morphed into gobbledygook.

✓♭⊘🖑⌧⊗⊘**&₢**⊗×⊗⌧⊘✓

Zigzags flickered across the screens.

"We're losing it," McClarence shouted, his face now gaunt.

Forcing calm, Boris typed in the code to deactivate the laser.

UNAUTHORIZED USER

Boris couldn't breathe.

"Laser firing in four seconds ... three ... two ... one."

A thump.

Sudden silence, no hum, no roar, no vibration.

"What was that?" Petrov squeaked out like a girl.

"Negative 200TeV," McClarence shouted. "The electron flow is reversed. Something is sucking the power out of MAGGIE."

Someone shouted, "Black hole."

The monitors blinked off.

Boris's heart sank. This was the end.

Emergency horns blared.

"Evacuate the building," Petrov ordered into the intercom. "Everyone evacuate at once."

Boris bolted for the door, his muscles fueled by hot adrenaline and stale alcohol. He beat the stampede of terrified technicians outside where it was freezing and snowing and windy, and he wished he had grabbed his coat.

Petrov ran ahead of him, McClarence to his right, the others falling behind. Thrashing through knee-deep snow, Boris made it as far as the tool shed when the ground lurched.

Cracked.

Rumbled.

He turned to look back.

Directly before his eyes an immense crater appeared. It was as if the earth had been scooped up and made invisible by a spectacular magician's trick. Sunlight beamed down through a domed opening in the overcast sky.

MAGGIE had disintegrated, creating an enormous

sphere devoid of all matter, every atom crushed to oblivion by a million billion mini black holes working as one. The resulting vacuum held for a heartbeat and then collapsed under the force of atmospheric pressure.

A clap of thunder, louder than any ever heard on earth, hammered the ground.

The concussion kicked the air from Boris's lungs and swept him away in a blinding white fury.

***

Melvin stared at Boris, seeing him now in a different light.

"I have this limp ever since." Boris rubbed his right knee.

"You survived and you ran."

"Petrov blamed the disaster on me, for not shutting down Maggie when ordered to do so. Lying bastard. I almost not escape Russia. Now I live in jungle, eat mangos and snake stew, and drink this cheap Aussie whiskey. Some life I have now, huh?"

Melvin swallowed. Snake stew? He looked at his empty plate. "So the Higgs exploded?"

"More like imploded. The 13th Power create a sphere of influence, like the earth's magnetic field, around the Troitska. All atoms in that sphere expelled Higgs bosons. Matter lost mass. Everything disintegrated. We lost enough Russian soil to bury Moscow." He swept both hands in a big circle. "We could have destroyed the world." Boris shook his head as if he didn't believe his own story. He grabbed the whiskey bottle from Melvin and took a face-contorting slug. "We should have left 13th Power alone. Too dangerous."

Melvin tongued the void where his tooth had once been, recalling how he'd lost it. Shooting his pilot didn't get much more dangerous than that.

Risk nothing, gain nothing.

His father had taught him that nothing worth having was too risky to pursue. The 13th Power could be the ultimate dig, an excavation deep into an atom to pluck out a key to the universe... The God Particle.

If he possessed such power, he could create his own riches and not steal from governments that chased him down with military choppers.

Too dangerous didn't frighten Melvin. Besides, he needed a new occupation. He downed the last of the whiskey. "Let's go get them boots."

Chapter 8

JOHN NATHAN WALKED into the Oval Office. Sunshine beamed through the windows, and the whole place smelled of fine leather and polished wood. His official title gave him access to this office, Deputy Director of the White House Chief of Staff. Only the President had any knowledge of his real title, his real job, and the reason he came here today.

Under his arm, he carried a red file folder, thick and heavy with *Directive Number 119* stamped on the jacket in bold black ink.

The silver-haired President looked up from the papers on his desk and spoke with a Southern accent. "Is it all there?"

"Everything you need to nail General Brigham."

"Let's have a look."

Nathan placed the file in front of the President and flipped it open.

Scanning the headers, the President grumped. "Just as I thought."

Nathan looked it over. The first report read:

From: Dr. Tracy McClarence, Cambridge, UK. Laser Physicist.

To: The Department of Defense, Ballistic Missile Defense Organization, Orbiting Laser Research Division.

Re: The latest series of particle beam tests failed. Request more funding.

"They're out of money again. Same old story." The President leaned back in his chair and folded his arms across his chest. "The Strategic Defense Initiative doesn't have a chance of succeeding with these crooks at the Department of Defense running the show." He pointed to

the second report on the facing page.
Congressional Report. Particle Beam Funding. Denied.

"All this bureaucratic bickering and the United States still sits vulnerable to a nuclear strike from anywhere around the globe. General Brigham and his cronies get away with grand larceny while the rest of us scramble for disarmament treaties."

"They've been working, so far," Nathan said.

The President leaned forward. "Did penned words on a piece of paper ever ensure peace or safety? Hell no. Ask our Native Americans. They know. Treaties aren't worth the ink they're written with." He stood and walked to the window. "Besides, there are too many crazies in this world. All it would take is one lunatic in Iran to push a button..."

"But they're not nuclear capable, sir. We're more worried about Korea—"

"Korea! Perfect example. They're out to kill us all, and we're sitting ducks just waiting for them to make the first move, fire the first shot."

"It'll be suicide if they do...we'll fire back."

"But how many cities will we lose in the process? How many Americans must die because we failed to implement SDI?"

"We're on top of it, sir."

"Why am I not relieved?" The President walked back to his desk and closed the file. "As of this afternoon, General Brigham and his boys are out of business. I'm giving Directive Number 119 to *The Ark*. I want you to handle it...personally."

"*The Ark*? Me? Are you sure?"

"Find another way to get the particle beam working." The President sat down and clasped his hands on the desk. "I expect you to work a miracle, John."

"How?"

The President pointed to the file. "Get a line on Dr.

Tracy McClarence for starters. Maybe she can help."

Nathan back-stepped toward the door. "Right away, Mr. President."

He walked out of the Oval Office. A chill skittered up his spine.

The Ark? Why did it have to be *The Ark?*

Chapter 9

BITING INTO A SLICE of mango, Melvin looked out the window of Boris's hut, searching the jungle path and the muddy jeep trail for any sign of the old man. Wispy rolls of fog bumped the treetops. Cattle and goats grazed in the meadow. Black-skinned children played in puddles left by the last downpour. But no Boris.

The air hung still as death, hot and muggy. A fly buzzed by his ear. He'd been stuck in this shithole for the last three weeks, and Boris's negative attitude was driving him crazy. *Too dangerous. Too dangerous.* The new boots fit nicely, but whether they were worth the aggravation or not, the jury was still out.

He spotted Boris limping out of the Aussie bar with a manila packet tucked under his arm. Melvin sat at the table and cut another slice of mango. What he wouldn't give for a McDonald's cheeseburger right now.

Boris appeared in the doorway, kicking mud from his boots. He clunked into the hut and tossed the packet on the table.

A chill skittered up the back of Melvin's neck.

"Your new papers," Boris said. "Melvin Anderson is officially deceased. Helicopter crash. Eyewitnesses certified crocs ate your body. I got that report from Singapore. Now you are Dr. Frank Curtis. I got that from your friend Smitty. Congratulations."

Melvin thumbed through the papers. Everything was there: passport, California driver's license, Social Security card, and even some credit references. "Smitty did a fine job."

Boris plucked a mango from a bowl on the table. "He told me to tell you, no more favors."

"He always says that. He got me in and out of a lot of countries." Melvin sorted the documents and slipped them back into the packet. "When's the Jeep coming?"

"Soon." Boris seemed distant, worried, with the long face of a man whose mother had just died.

Melvin squinted at him. "What's your problem?"

"You really are going to find the God Particle?"

"Yup."

Boris cut into his mango. "You need money, equipment, scientists. Where you find these things?"

"I've got enough money to buy all the equipment and scientists I need."

"Right, I forget. You a good grave robber."

"Archeologist."

"Of course."

Melvin bristled with confidence. "I have a friend in California who will help me with everything else. The 13th Power *will* be mine."

Boris looked at the floor. "Go to the USA and find the 13th Power. When California is a deep crater, don't say I didn't warn you."

Melvin smiled. "Meanwhile, you're going to keep your mouth shut, right?"

"Your secret safe with me." Boris walked out of the hut and didn't look back.

Chapter 10

A FOGHORN BLARED as a fishing trawler docked in a slip at the Port of Tanjung, Jakarta. Melvin had made it home at last. The Java Sea crossing had been rough, but it was more comfortable than the mud-slinging jeep ride through the jungle to Ketapang. Being dead afforded him a measure of invisibility. The authorities weren't looking for him anymore.

His body ached; his eyelids felt like boat anchors, but he had a plan, places to go and things to do.

Seawater rose up against the concrete harbor walls and slipped back down to the barnacles. Timing his jump, he leaped to the dock. Wooden planks creaked under his boots as he ran toward a cab idling at the end of the pier. Pelicans perched on the posts took startled flight. Seagulls sawed back and forth in the wind. He climbed into a dilapidated Toyota van. "Rangkayo Rasuna."

"Buckle your seatbelt," the driver replied.

The cab clunked along a rutted road toward the inner city. Melvin steadied himself against the window frame. An endless clutter of shanties with red-tiled roofs closed in around him.

On the Gunung Expressway, the cab weaved through heavy traffic, past Merkado Palace, Parliament, and the University of Indonesia. Melvin took in all the familiar sights with pride.

At Rangkayo Rasuna, the cab slowed and turned a corner where military jeeps surrounded his bungalow. His heart fell into his stomach. Barbwire curled across his front yard and armed soldiers stood at his door, eyeing the cab as it approached.

He ducked down. "Drive on. Drive on!"

A sweat broke out on his brow. The Malaysian government had seized his property. Had they found his secret bank accounts—stripped him of his wealth, his hoarded loot, and his prized possessions? What a rotten homecoming that would be. He tapped the driver's shoulder. "Bank National Indonesia."

In the bank lobby, Melvin's fingers trembled as he typed at a computer terminal. His list of accounts scrolled down the monitor. They were safe. He thought he would faint from relief. Working the keys again, he transferred several hundred million dollars to banks in the United States. He picked three that sounded good: First Industrial, United Bank and Trust, Empire. *TRANSFERS COMPLETED* scrolled across the screen.

Now for the toys.

The bank manager unlocked Melvin's safety-deposit vault. He stepped into the room and switched on a light. A musty odor assailed his nostrils, but everything appeared to be in its place: gold from Egypt, ivory from India, rubies and gems from the ancient kingdoms of Kediri and Mataram.

He looked over his treasures, his sights set on his prized golden staff, there, leaning in a corner, alone. An eagle's head of gold, with green emerald eyes, adorned the top of a golden shaft. Ramses III, King of Egypt, must have been proud of this walking stick.

Melvin took it in his hands, savored its weight, and caressed the cold and shiny gold, its beauty eclipsed only by its deadly secret.

In a box of gold jewelry, Melvin spotted a bracelet once worn by a Queen of Ethiopia. Because he didn't know exactly which Queen wore it, the World Society of Archeologists claimed it was just another gold bracelet. What did they know? He darted his tongue across the gap left from his missing tooth and thought of Sahib. Bracelet in hand, he locked his vault and left for his dental appointment.

***

Melvin stashed the packet of fake documents under his suit coat and boarded a 747 at Halim International Airport, bound for Los Angeles. In his first-class seat, he set the golden staff across his lap and laughed aloud for the joy of his new adventure.

"I'm glad you're having a good time, Dr. Curtis," the flight attendant said. Her voice floated in the air like classical music. "Would you like a drink?"

Dr. Frank Curtis smiled, showing her the bright shine of his new gold tooth.

Chapter 11

NATHAN PUSHED through the doors at Andrews Air Force Base and quickstepped down the concourse toward gate number seven. He hadn't bothered to shave, change into a clean shirt, or button his black suit coat. The briefcase he clutched in his right hand was all he needed. One phone call from Singapore had changed everything. It was the break he'd been hoping for.

He glanced around the concourse, looking for Bret Lawrence. The CIA Chief of Internal Affairs should've been here by now. Dr. McClarence was waiting for them in Atlanta. They had to get in the air as quickly as possible.

"Nathan," Lawrence shouted, running down the corridor, his long overcoat flapping behind him. His bald head shined under the ceiling lights and his striped tie whipped back and forth. "This is never going to work."

"You let me worry about that," Nathan said.

Breathing hard, Lawrence ran up beside him and matched his stride. "Let's just arrest the son of a bitch and be done with it."

"I want to hear what the Russian has to say, first. Tracy tells me it'll blow the lid off Star Wars."

"We're all gonna end up with our necks on the chopping block."

"You worry too much."

"When *The Ark* is involved, what do you expect?"

Nathan quickened his steps. He didn't want to talk about *The Ark*; he had enough problems.

A flight attendant waved them to come on at gate seven. He ran outside to a shiny Falcon jet, its turbine engines already whining.

Another flight attendant appeared in the oval

doorway. Dressed in a sharply-pressed blue uniform, her smile shined as bright as the silver bars on her collars.

Nathan climbed the steps. "Evening, Lieutenant. Sorry to drag you out like this."

"Glad to be of service, sir." Her smile didn't waver.

He ducked inside the plane. Perfume scented the air. Taking the executive seat halfway down the cabin, he stowed his briefcase underneath and cinched his seatbelt. Lawrence buckled up in a seat across the aisle.

The intercom crackled. "Ready when you are, sir."

Nathan said, "Let's go."

Ceiling lights dimmed. Engines revved. The jet began to roll. Nathan looked out the window. The aircraft rocked and thumped along a taxiway. As the jet turned, green runway lights came into view. He looked at Lawrence who was pulling on his seatbelt. Sweat beaded his forehead.

A chime echoed through the cabin. Nathan shifted his eyes to the Lieutenant as she strapped herself into the first seat behind the cockpit.

The engines revved to a thunderous roar. Inertia pushed Nathan against the seatback. As the nose pitched up, the runway lights dropped away, and the landing gear banged into their compartments. Inertia subsided into the floating sensation of flight.

Washington D.C. glowed below him like a carpet of Christmas tree lights, the city of his boyhood dreams: the President, the White House, the most powerful city in the world. The only place *The Ark* could function and get away with it.

Rolling left, the Falcon climbed into the night sky. Nathan turned his attention to Lawrence. He looked nervous. Was it because of the Russian or because of *The Ark*? Nathan glanced at his watch. Atlanta was more than an hour away. They had a lot to talk about. "Tell me what you've got on the Russian."

Lawrence wiped his brow. "Boris Dagloskoff. A

Russian nuclear physicist. He's clearing customs in Atlanta. Agent Stevens will run him through INS before we can see him."

"I hear he's not cooperating." Nathan reclined his seat.

"He wants the 13th Power experiments stopped...says they're too dangerous."

"Offer him a permanent resident visa to help us out."

"Political asylum in exchange for his story, that's all he wants. We stop Dr. Curtis and he stays out of prison in Russia."

"Not good enough." Nathan rubbed his chin. "Give him a choice: the visa or deportation."

"What if he's right?"

Nathan frowned. "The end of the world? Not likely."

"He knew about Solartech Labs. Dr. Curtis took control of the corporation, just like Boris had said."

"I've sent a team to Simi Valley."

"Oh? And who'd you get to lead this team?"

Nathan grinned. "Alex."

"Alex Gibson?"

"Only the best for *The Ark*."

The jet rolled right and continued to climb.

Nathan examined his fingernails, confident he'd done the right thing. "What did Boris say about Curtis?"

"He's an ex-archeologist named Melvin Anderson. He invited Boris to join him in California to help him on the 13th Power project. The old man never thought Curtis would actually go through with his quest for the Higgs, got scared, and turned himself in. Curtis doesn't know we're on to him."

"And we're going to keep it that way."

"For how long?"

"No telling." The thought of a lengthy operation settled in Nathan's stomach like a rock. "Dr. McClarence is due in Simi Valley tomorrow night. She's been hired as the laser tech. Curtis already has a nuclear physicist, some guy by the name of Ray Crawford. Nobody's ever heard of him. They're currently looking for a mathematician."

"What do you make of the disintegration problem Boris was talking about? Any evidence of an accident in Russia?"

"Nothing, so far."

The jet leveled off.

"Curtis won't have any better luck finding the Higgs boson than the Russians. The particle beam is all we want. When they've got it working, we'll move in and arrest Curtis for his past crimes."

Lawrence balled a fist. "Too risky. We should nail the bastard right now, before it's too late."

Nathan scowled. His CIA director didn't have the liver for this job. "We're not taking the easy way, Lawrence. Directive Number 119 is at stake, the security of the nation. Failure is not an option."

Lawrence gave him a sour look. "Failure is always an option."

"I'm counting on you to support the mission. Do your job. We'll get through it without a scratch."

Chapter 12

RAIN POUNDED DOWN on Los Angeles Boulevard, the main thoroughfare through Simi Valley, California. Tracy McClarence stood inside the door of Bennie's coffee shop and peered out at the rain-slicked street. Car headlights reflected off wet pavement and sloshed by in an endless rhythm, like the rain in the streetlights, an unending drizzle. Her eyes searched the shadows. He was out there somewhere, watching. Waiting.

Door glass reflected the fear in her eyes. She pulled the scarf over her head, wishing she hadn't let the cabbie drive away. Now she'd have to wait for another taxi to drive by.

It had seemed like a good idea. She'd left Solartech Labs to come into town for a magazine and a cup of coffee. She couldn't sleep anyway, worrying about the project. The operation. The sting. If she'd known she was going to be followed, she'd have stayed in her room. Obviously, Dr. Curtis didn't trust her. He seemed suspicious of every technician on the team.

Her breath fogged the glass. She wiped it away with the palm of her hand and stared out into the night. Curtis's bodyguard was out there spying on her. Everyone called him Judas. He'd rat out his own mother. She'd heard stories. True or not, one thing was for certain; if he knew about her complicity with *The Ark*, he'd kill her, for sure.

"We're closin' up, lady," the clerk shouted. "Ya can't stay here all night."

The ceiling lights went out.

"I was hoping for a cab."

"It's midnight. Good luck with that."

She zipped her jacket and tucked the magazine under

her arm. "Goodnight then." She pushed through the door and into the rain.

A horn honked. She looked toward the street where some drunk hung out the window of a red T-Bird, waving at her to come over to the car. He must've thought she was a hooker. Pretty and slim, yes. But sexy? Not tonight. Not with her long red hair tucked under a scarf and fatigue lines etched under her eyes. Ignoring him, she rushed around the corner. Bad move. Judas!

Her heart clutched.

He was leaning against the building like a mobster in a 1930's flick. His ashen and pockmarked face shown eerily under the streetlight. His hands were thrust deep into the pockets of his trench coat, the collar turned up against the rain, which dripped from the brim of his fedora. He stared at her with cold eyes.

"What do you want?" she managed to get out.

Judas walked toward her, breath vapors whisking from his nostrils. Her eyes shifted to his hidden hands. Did he have a gun? A knife? Her feet wanted to run. She told them *no*. Her knees trembled. "You stay away from me."

Judas kept walking. The rain kept coming down.

#

Down the block, a black four-door Ford idled in the shadows. Rivulets of rain trickled down the windshield. Behind the wheel, Alex Gibson tightened his grip on the binoculars he held to his eyes. The man in the trench coat was walking toward the woman. "He's getting closer."

"He's gonna kill her."

Alex glanced at his partner sitting in the passenger seat. Craig Stevens was a good agent. He had a sixth sense, like he knew when somebody was about to die. This time he was wrong. Alex felt it in his gut. "There's no way Judas can know who she is. He's trying to scare her, see if she has anything to hide."

"Look at her face. She's going to crack." Craig pulled

a gun from under his suit coat.

"No need for that. She's tough. She can handle him."

"I'm going to be ready." Stevens rolled the window down an inch and pushed the barrel through the crack.

Alex held his arm. "Shoot and the mission is over. Curtis will know we're on to him."

"We can't just let her die."

"*The Ark* said she's expendable. No one is more important than the 13th Power project."

"But…"

"Hold your fire, agent. That's an order."

\#

Tracy clenched her fists at her side. Judas was too close. Her knees felt like rubber, her head faint.

Judas glowered in her face. "What are you doin' sneakin' around this time of night?"

She inhaled, wondering why he hadn't killed her yet. He probably didn't know a damn thing about *The Ark*. *Come on, Tracy. Think. Say something.* "You scared the shit out of me, damn it."

His eyes narrowed. "You meetin' up with someone tonight?"

"Yeah. Bennie's. For an espresso. I cleared it with Security first. They called the cab for me. So don't start with this cloak and dagger stuff." She sidestepped to go around him.

He checked her move with a bump to the arm.

Her magazine fell to the sidewalk, landing in a big puddle. "Now look what you've done."

"Klutz," Judas said.

She glared at him. "Do you have to be so rude?"

"Somethin' don't seem right about you."

Tracy blinked raindrops from her eyelashes. She hoped the story she'd rehearsed wouldn't come out sounding rehearsed. "I'm an expert in laser technology. The Russian called me at Cambridge University, said he needed my help."

"Why you?"

"We worked together in Russia, before Moscow shut us down. Curtis needed help with his laser problems. Boris told him I was the best." She stared at Judas, hoping he wouldn't detect a lie in her eyes.

He stuck out his chin. Streams of water spilled from the brim of his hat. His eyes got big around. "I'll be watching you." He turned and walked away.

"Wait. Give me a ride back."

"Find your own ride."

She put her hands on her hips and watched him disappear into the drizzle. What a jerk.

A car pulled up to the curb, honking.

"Forget it, Buster!" She turned, thinking it was the fool in the red T-Bird again. Instead, a black four-door Ford idled in the rain, a staff car from Solartech Labs. She made out the silhouettes of two men sitting inside.

The man riding shotgun rolled down the window. "Get in."

She opened the rear door and slid onto the seat. The dome light lit Alex Gibson's handsome face. His square jaw and high cheekbones made him look sexy and fearsome. She'd heard he'd done a lot of killing in the war, but he didn't look fifty and his smile was the most beautiful thing she'd seen all night. "Thank God you're here."

"Are you all right?" Alex asked with a sharp edge to his voice.

"I thought I was going to have to walk back." She shifted her eyes to Agent Stevens. He had that country boy look, blond hair combed down over his forehead and freckles scattered across his nose and cheeks.

"You did great," Stevens said.

She pulled the door shut, snuffing the dome light. "No thanks to you guys."

"We had your back." Alex accelerated the car into

traffic.

"We shouldn't have let you go into town," Stevens said. "But we had to find out if Curtis was suspicious. When Judas followed your cab, we knew you were in trouble."

Tracy shivered, the cold rain soaking through to her bones. "They don't know anything. Tell *The Ark* we're in the clear."

Chapter 13

J ANIS MACKEY READ the note a Special Delivery courier had just handed him. It was from an old college pal.

Must meet with you at once. URGENT! The Balli Club. San Francisco, noon Friday. Ticket at United counter, Denver International Airport, 8:45 A.M.

He stashed the note in his coat pocket, drank the last splash of orange juice, and rinsed the glass in the sink. Ray Crawford had been working at that secret company in Nevada too long. The hot sun must've fried his brain. He could've emailed this information, or called him on the phone. *Special Delivery* went out with the Pony Express.

Walking to the picture window, Janis pushed his glasses up the bridge of his nose. He wondered if Ray was in some kind of trouble.

A yellow cab pulled into the parking lot and glistened in the early morning rays. The horn blared. He pushed through the front doors of Mission Meadows and, dodging busted toys on the sidewalk, headed toward the car.

"Beautiful day," the burley black cabby said, holding the rear door open for his fare.

Janis looked at a clear blue sky. "Too bad I won't be here to enjoy it." He slid into the car. "I have one hour to get to the airport. Can we make it?"

"If I can't get around the traffic, I'll go over it. They don't call me Captain Ben for nothin'." He shut the door and piled in behind the wheel, his weight rocking the car on its springs.

Janis groaned. *Just great. Another manic cab driver.*

Settling into the back seat, he noticed the lack of odors that usually linger in a taxi. Instead of stale cigar smoke, sour beer, and cheap perfume, the interior had that new-car smell. He buckled his seatbelt. "New cab?"

Captain Ben dropped the gearshift into reverse. "Since yesterday. Ain't she a beauty?" He twisted around, put his elbow over the seatback, and released the brake. "The old one was a wreck. I swear I keep my body shop boys stocked in beer and loose women."

"How's that?"

"Don't know what it is about my luck. Somethin' always happens to tear my shit up. But not with this one. No, sir." His wide smile showed off a mouthful of white teeth. "This one's not gonna get a scratch."

"Would be a shame," Janis assured him.

#

Captain Ben backed out of the parking lot and drove south on Rogers Lane. When he turned east on Baseline Road, a blue van pulled away from the curb, made a reckless U turn, and raced up behind him. Captain Ben paid it no mind and made a tire-squealing turn onto the freeway ramp. He merged the cab effortlessly onto the Boulder Turnpike. When he checked his rearview mirror to make a lane change, he saw the blue van speed up alongside him.

"Idiot," he grumbled under his breath and released the throttle. The van slowed. He accelerated. The van sped up. Ben shot the driver a frown. The driver flipped him a finger.

"What the hell is his problem?"

The side door of the van slid open, and he found himself looking down the black barrel of a machinegun attended by two masked men.

"Holy shit." He slammed on the brakes.

The tires squealed as the machinegun began its deadly report. Lethal rounds pummeled the fender and hood.

"Get down."

Shards of metal, ricocheting at random, shattered the windshield and spewed a crystalline mist into Ben's face. He spit.

"Hang on."

Stomping on the emergency brake, he yanked the steering wheel to the right. His pulverized cab spun in a circle and careened into the lane directly behind the van. Slamming the throttle to the floor, he released the brake and rammed the van's rear bumper. The jolt sent the hood ripping over the roof.

"You guys wanna play tough?" He kept his foot on the gas, hard to the floor. Engine roaring, he plowed the van into the concrete crash barrier. Sparks cascaded across the median. The sounds of crunching metal and breaking glass filled the air, but he kept the throttle down, bouncing and jerking, pushing the van along the barrier. Chunks of smoldering rubber slapped his shattered windshield. Ben gritted his teeth. Sons of bitches! He gave the steering wheel a quick jerk left, sending the van into a right-hand skid. Blue tire smoke pumped from the undercarriage as it careened across the highway and smashed into a sign pillar, head-on. The van crumpled and exploded into a yellow ball of fire. Ammunition went off like a fireworks display.

"Take that, you morons." He slammed on the brakes and turned to watch the fury of smoke and flame rise from the highway. The stink of rubber and gunpowder permeated the air.

He looked down at his passenger sprawled on the back seat. His face looked ghostly white. He sat up, staring over the frames of his crooked glasses.

"I'm alive!" Janis exclaimed. "We're okay." Wide-eyed, he looked around the car. "Oh shit. Your new cab is a mess!"

"Damn. My body man is gonna be delighted."

Sirens sounded in the distance.

"And here come the cops."

#

Janis pushed his glasses up and looked out the rear window. Distorted through the heat waves emanating from the burning van, he saw the flashing overheads of approaching emergency vehicles. "I don't have time to deal with them. I've gotta make that flight. Let's get out of here."

Captain Ben shrugged. "You're the boss." Returning his attention to the front he added, "Tell ya the truth. I've had more than my share of cops." He floored the accelerator.

Janis watched the smoking carnage fade in the distance. It was a miracle they'd survived, thanks to Captain Ben's driving. "How did you spin the car around like that?"

"Easy." Captain Ben cocked his head toward the back seat. "Just lock the emergency brake and crank the wheel. The rear end will slide around. Trick is to hit the brake release and the gas when you're pointed in the direction you want to go next. In this case, right up that damn van's ass."

"Doesn't sound very easy to me." Janis wiped glass dust from his slacks. "Sorry about your cab."

Captain Ben grunted. "Who were those guys?"

"I wish I knew." Janis was willing to bet the attack had something to do with Ray Crawford.

Chapter 14

RAY CRAWFORD STOOD under a stone archway and looked into the empty dining room of the Balli Club. A bearded man in tan coveralls was vacuuming the carpet around the tables. Ray noticed a hearing aid in his ear and felt a moment of gratitude for not having to wear one of his own.

The kitchen doors swung open. Jimmy rushed out. The tuxedo he wore fit his lanky frame perfectly. "Mr. Crawford, this way please."

Ray followed him to a reserved table against the back wall.

"This should do nicely."

The janitor wandered out. Jimmy disappeared through the swinging kitchen doors. Alone in the dining hall, Ray gathered his thoughts for the up-coming meeting; he assumed Janis would show.

Checking his view of the entrance, Ray adjusted his tie and flicked a piece of lint from the sleeve of his suit coat. He kept every detail of his appearance as neatly organized as his laboratory: his jet-black hair nicely cropped and combed and his thick mustache pruned to look like his mentor's, Albert Einstein. Satisfied nothing was out of place, he reached into his pocket and pulled out three folded newspaper clippings. The papers crackled with age as he laid them on the table.

Crawford-Mackey Team-up On Higgs Field Theory headlined the first article from the University Press. A surge of pride welled up inside as he read the text:

Ray Crawford's physics team joined forces today with Janis Mackey's mathematics team in an attempt to find the Higgs boson. Professor Yeager VanBlought predicts these *two students can crack the 13th Power mystery. However, the University Board of Trustees has limited their funding, which casts a shadow over all hopes of success.*

His jaw set as he turned to the next clipping: *Crawford-Mackey Fail On 13.*

"Damn it." He slapped the table. What did they expect with junk equipment and no money? The damn fools hadn't given them a fair chance. The memory rekindled his anger, an anger he had carried with him for twenty-seven years.

His stomach churned as he recalled his disgust with the penny-pinching Board of Trustees. He'd dropped out of college and never achieved his degree. Working at Atomtech, an atomic research and development company in Nevada, gave him little satisfaction. His boss there, Walter Devin, refused to take on the challenge of finding the Higgs. Ray's obsession only grew; his drive became more resolved. He justified his struggle by surmising that this was the price truly great scientists had to pay to grasp their place in history. A price *he* must pay.

He turned to the next clipping: *Dr. Janis Mackey Takes Top University Seat.*

Envy sliced through Ray's stomach like the blade of a knife. Twenty-seven years in the private sector had not brought him the fame he deserved for his dedication in the field of nuclear physics. What he wanted most eluded him. Recognition for breaching the 13th Power and finding the God Particle could be his reward for all those years of obscurity. And now, with this meeting, he had reached a turning point. If Janis joined the team, Ray had a chance. If not, he was finished.

"May I get something for you, sir?" Jimmy asked.

Ray quickly glanced around. Patrons had already begun to arrive before the lunch hour rush. A wave of anxiety rolled in his stomach. "Keep your eyes sharp for Dr. Mackey." He pointed to the man's picture in the newspaper clipping.

Jimmy gave him a two-fingered salute and walked away.

Ray carefully reorganized the old clippings and returned them to his pocket. He took a deep breath, but it didn't help quell the angst growing in his chest like a brewing storm.

Chapter 15

THE 737 STREAKED toward San Francisco. Janis stared out the window, but his mind wasn't on this flight or the sights to see below. Ray was up to something. In college he and Janis were inseparable. Aside from an occasional beer bash or Spring Break, they were immersed in their studies. While Janis spent his spare time boxing and playing chess, Ray hung out in the science labs, always tinkering.

"Drink, sir?" the flight attendant said. "Coffee, tea, soda?"

"N-no thanks," Janis replied, his voice still hoarse from his shaken nerves. He removed his glasses, rubbed his eyes, and returned to his thoughts. Ray had aced all his nuclear physics classes and went on to study the theory of relativity and the space-time continuum. He couldn't talk about anything else. The atomic force and the speed of light were making Ray a dull boy.

Word must've gotten out about his expertise. A company in Nevada offered him a job. Though his degree was only a few semesters away, he quit school. A couple years later, he'd called Janis with news of his marriage and subsequent birth of a daughter. Her name escaped Janis's memory. No wonder. That was twenty-plus years ago.

And now this note. He set his glasses back on and pulled the note from his suit coat pocket. A surge of panic welled up inside. The note was shredded, a hole ripped through it, the writing unreadable. He quickly examined his pocket and fingered the path of a bullet. His throat went dry. Those men who attacked his cab had damn near killed him.

***

The jet came to a stop at the gate. Passengers jumped up from their seats and grabbed their carry-ons, jammed the aisle and scrambled for the exit. Janis waited for the melee to subside then strolled down the gangway.

Walking onto the concourse, he spotted a young woman holding a sign.

Dr. Mackey.

His heart skipped a beat, not because of the written page, but because of the woman. Her blond hair hung straight down past her shoulders like beams of sunshine, and the dress she wore, a one-piece yellow miniskirt with white lace, looked a size too small for her curvaceous frame. He told his eyes to stop tracking those curves down her body, but they refused to obey, taking in her shapely hips, her long tan legs, and white high heels. Hand in the air, he could hardly spit out the words. "I—I'm Dr. Mackey."

She smiled and waved back.

Approaching her, he caught the fragrance of perfume, light and flowery. Her blue eyes sparkled, and her glossy lips begged to be kissed. A California girl, all right.

"I'm Lisa. Welcome to LA."

"I wasn't expecting anyone to meet me."

"The Balli Club sent me to escort you. Our limo is out front. Let's get your luggage."

"I'm going home this afternoon. I didn't pack anything."

Lisa's smile disappeared. "How unfortunate. My boss instructed me to show you the town tonight. Guess I'll miss the opportunity to party with you."

Janis gulped. Was California on earth or in heaven? *When in Rome* came to mind, but she wasn't much older than his students. "What a shame."

With a wink, Lisa took his hand. "This way," she

whispered and led the way out.

The limousine gleamed in the sunshine, a black Lincoln with tinted windows and elegant lines. Lisa opened the rear door to the spacious executive compartment. Janis started to get in but stopped. He didn't feel good about riding in the back by himself, a mistake he'd made in Captain Ben's cab. "Do you mind if I sit up front with you?"

"No problem." She closed the rear door and smiled again, those beautiful white teeth competing with the California sunshine.

Janis helped himself to the passenger door handle and climbed in. The cool air smelled of fresh pine. As she walked around the front of the limo, he eyed her fluid motion and confident stride. When she got in behind the wheel, his eyes went to work sweeping the area, looking for anything suspicious, especially blue vans.

Lisa accelerated away from the airport. He put his elbow over the seatback and peered at the large percentage of thigh exposed by her hiked miniskirt. The sight was inspiring—but why would a chauffeur be wearing something so provocative? She looked more like an executive's assistant than a limo driver. Something wasn't right about that. Adjusting his glasses and hoping not to show any special interest, he said, "Do you live around here?"

"Yes, of course." She giggled. "Do you?"

"N-no, of course not," he stumbled. "Colorado."

"Oh?" She looked intrigued. "A real cowboy?"

"Not exactly." Janis chuckled. He'd never thought of himself as a cowboy. "How long have you been working for the Balli Club?"

"You sure are full of questions, cowboy. Let's just say I'm a free woman in a free world and I'm into doing a lot of things. I know you're attracted to me. Most men are. They usually have one thing on their minds. Are you that kind of man?"

"I have students older than you." He wondered if all California women said exactly what was on their minds.

She glanced at him, "Of course you do, Dr. Mackey," and returned her eyes to the road.

"Please, call me Janis."

A few moments passed in silence. Her hair laid lazily over her shoulders, springing this way and that way as she attended to her driving duties. Judging from her figure, she looked very athletic, probably did some kind of California aerobics or Zumba or something. Occasionally, she would glance at him, so he didn't want to be caught gawking at her. Watching out the windshield, he recalled her invitation for this evening, which gave him a little flutter in his stomach.

"So, what's your story, cowboy?"

"An old college buddy needs me for something. I haven't heard from him in more than twenty years."

"Sounds boring." Again, the invitation surfaced, but he kept his mouth shut.

The limo pulled up under the Balli Club's marquee, its lights flashing: *Tango tonight with THE BOB MANSON BAND.*

"We're here." A smile lit up her eyes. "Call me on my cell when the meeting's over." She pulled a card from her purse. "I'll give you a ride back to the airport."

"Sure." Janis examined the card. The phone number was hand written on pink card stock, as if she'd prepared it for just this occasion. "Anytime?" he asked.

"Whenever you're ready."

He slipped the card into his shirt pocket. "California, what a great name for heaven."

He let himself out.

"Good luck with your friend, cowboy." She peeled off.

He watched her drive away, his head in a whirl. The

woman was dangerous. He'd better stay as far away from her as possible.

At the club entrance, the doorman squared his shoulders. "Good afternoon, sir." He opened the door.

"Thanks for sending your limo to pick me up at the airport."

The doorman frowned. "Sorry to say, sir. I've never seen that limo before."

Janis quickly looked down the street where the limo had disappeared. His blood felt hot, like it was boiling. He clenched his fists. Lisa, or whatever her name was, had a lot of explaining to do.

Chapter 16

THE BALLI CLUB was a rich man's paradise, the foyer adorned with beautiful tapestries from India and Tibet. Janis inhaled subtle smells of polished wood furniture and waxed hardwood floors. Strains of classical music drifted in the air.

A young man wearing a tuxedo greeted him. "Hello, Dr. Mackey. My name is Jimmy. Please allow me to show you to your table."

Janis wondered how many strangers knew he was coming to this meeting. His first instinct was to turn around, get himself a cab, and hightail it back to the airport, but he'd come this far, so reluctantly, he followed Jimmy under an archway and into a dining room. The aroma of food filled the air: roast beef, fresh bread, and garlic. Silverware clinked and plates clattered among the hubbub of conversation.

Walking, he scanned the crowd of diners at tables and patrons at the bar, searching for a familiar face. Someone near the back was waving at him. Suit and tie. Jet black hair. Ray Crawford. No doubt about it.

Janis clenched his jaw and followed Jimmy to Ray's table.

Ray stood. "Janis."

"I'll be back with you gentlemen shortly." Jimmy scurried off.

Ray patted Janis's shoulder and shook his hand. "Good to see you, old buddy."

Janis kept his demeanor cool, his smile restrained. "What's this all about, Ray?"

"Sit down. Sit down." Ray offered him a chair. "You look great."

Janis took a different chair, one directly across the table from Ray. It was obvious he wasn't going to talk business until the niceties were over. "How's the wife?"

"I divorced Kate twenty years ago. She was a complainer, always nagging about my long hours at work. You know the type."

"Can't say I do. And your daughter, how is she?"

"Who knows?" Ray twitched his mustache. "She hasn't called in a long time, probably still angry at me for one damn thing or another. Seems to be her favorite pastime."

"Angry?"

"She's in Europe. At school. It's a long story. Did you ever settle down? Wife? Kids?"

"No. I haven't found the right woman yet."

"Looks like you're sitting pretty on the Colorado U staff."

Janis shifted in his chair. "The peaceful life, the way I like it, until this morning."

Confusion eclipsed his face. "Something happen?"

"Damn right, Mr. Top Secret."

"What are you talking about?"

"I get one note from you in twenty years, and I'm suddenly up to my neck in trouble." He pulled a shredded piece of paper from his pocket and flipped it on the table. "Recognize this?"

Ray picked up the note. He looked visibly ill. "What happened?"

Janis showed him the bullet hole in his pocket. "Do you now anybody with a big machinegun?"

"What happened, damn it?"

"Goons attacked my cab this morning. They were driving a blue van. All hell broke loose on my way to the airport."

Ray seemed to be choking.

"Why would anyone want to stop us from meeting?"

"Hell if I know. You sure it wasn't some random gang violence?"

"Those guys were professional hit men. You'd better start talking, Ray. Right now."

Ray glared at him, not so much in anger, but more like shock. He shoved the note back at him. "I've got a proposition for you."

"Spit it out, or you'll be spitting out teeth."

Ray removed newspaper clippings from his pocket and unfolded them on the table. "Remember this?"

Janis leaned forward and studied the papers. *University Press. The 13th Power. God Particle.* He felt Ray's anxious stare.

"What do you think?"

Janis looked up at him over the rim of his glasses. "Yeah. I remember. We had fun until the money ran out. Came up with a good hypothesis, too." He glanced down at the clippings again, shaking his head. "I give up. What's this got to do with anything?"

"Look, Janis, back then, we didn't have the money or the proper equipment to give this experiment a fair shot. Now I've got everything we need to finish what we started. Everything, Janis. It'll be just like old times, you and me, only better."

"Now hold on...hold on one minute, Ray!" Janis glared at him, thinking he'd gone mad. "The Higgs? The God Particle? Are you out of your mind?"

"It's a race, Janis. Fermilabs and CERN are way ahead of us. I need your help."

"What a crock."

Ray stuck out his chin. "I can't crack the 13th Power alone."

"You're way out of your league, Ray. Still dreaming about that Nobel Prize?"

"A man's got to dream."

"About the center of matter's existence? What's

wrong with a hot blonde or—"

"Don't try to be funny, Janis. You're not very good at it."

"You know..." Janis glanced around for the waiter. "I'm hungry. I'm going to order lunch and head back to Colorado."

Ray's eyes grew to deer-in-the-headlight size. "Listen, Janis, please. Things are different for me now. My life has changed. I quit working at Atomtech...spent twenty-five years there, but they wouldn't listen to me. They couldn't see the possibilities of the 13th Power. I couldn't get their top mathheads to help me. My boss wasn't interested."

"You know why, Ray? It's worthless. You can't build a better toaster with the Higgs boson. Nobody cares."

"You're wrong. You're so so so wrong, Janis."

Where was a waiter when he needed one?

"The Higgs is the tiniest part of a field of energy that permeates the entire universe, goes way back to the Big Bang and keeps everything together. It's like a highway across space and time."

"String theory," Janis said. He'd heard the arguments on both sides. "It's not provable."

"Yes it is, and when we find it, harness it, and control it, we'll revolutionize transportation on a scale greater than the discovery of the wheel."

"Waiter," Janis shouted, though none were around.

"Space travel between planets in seconds, between galaxies in minutes. To the edge of the universe in an hour."

"Waiter!" McDonald's was sounding pretty good right now.

"We'll package it, sell it..."

"Stop!"

Ray blinked like he'd come out of a trance.

"Listen to yourself, ranting like a madman."

Leaning forward, Ray lowered his voice. "If CERN or Fermilabs get the Higgs first, the government will own it. The government will control it. If we get it first, we will have the power."

"You're certifiable. You know that?" Janis's jaw muscles twitched. "You brought me here for this bullshit? Didn't you consider I have a life of my own?"

"Life? What life? No family. You're hooked on your work. We're two of a kind. The quest for answers has been our whole life. This is like our Super Bowl, the big cohune, the whole ball of wax. Cut the crap and let's figure out how we're going to do it."

"You haven't changed a bit, still trying to make something out of nothing, chasing your silly obsession with nuclear space and time that doesn't exist. When are you going to grow up and join the real world?" Janis slid his chair back and stood. He'd had enough.

Ray grabbed his arm.

Janis stiffened. "Let go of me."

"I haven't brought you here for nothing, Janis. How does a million dollars sound?"

Janis swallowed, knocked a bit off kilter from the verbal blow. "You don't have that kind of money."

"No. I don't, but I know someone who does. He's on his way here. Right now. To speak with you."

Dollar signs flooded Janis's brain. His mother would be set for life. That house off the turnpike would be his. A new car. If it sounded too good to be true, it was. "Don't play games with me, Ray."

"A rich man approached me a few months ago, asked for my help. He believes in the Higgs. The possibilities. His organization has given me their full support. We keep getting error messages from the super computers. The math isn't working. We need your expertise to fix the problems."

Janis yanked his arm free of Ray's grasp. "All right. I'll talk to him."

"You won't regret it, Janis."

"If I didn't need the money, I'd be out of here by now."

#

Wearing a fake beard and dressed like a janitor, Steve Raven put his elbows on the bar and adjusted the hearing device in his ear. At 32, he was reputed to be a top-notch private eye. His eavesdropping microphone went unnoticed under the table where Ray and Janis held their conversation. Steve didn't know what they were talking about, but he was sure his client would.

He swallowed the last swig of beer in his mug and scratched his phony beard. "Barkeep. Another beer. And this time don't foam it up so bad." He flung another buck on the bar and turned when the front door suddenly opened with a rush of wind.

A tall man appeared under the stone archway. He wore a black suit and tie. A tuft of black hair fell over his forehead, partially covering one eye. He leaned on a glistening golden staff that could've come from the bowels of Egypt.

Steve shuddered. Happy Halloween. He turned back to his beer and the spying assignment at hand.

#

Janis spotted the man standing at the entrance. With that golden staff, he looked like he could be the richest man in the joint, but his dark form sent a chill up the back of Janis's neck. He nudged Ray's arm, directing his attention to the stone archway.

"That's him!" Ray said. "Dr. Curtis. He owns Solartech Labs. I tell you, this guy's our ticket to the Nobel Prize."

"He just came to you out of the blue?"

"With these newspaper clippings."

Janis drummed his fingers on the table. "This day keeps getting weirder by the minute."

Chapter 17

AN AFTERNOON BREEZE gusted into the Balli Club. Melvin Anderson, aka Dr. Frank Curtis, stood in the doorway and scanned the dining room. His long black coat whipped in the swirling wind and attracted the attention of several patrons seated nearby. He saw fear and shock in their eyes. Gave him a warm, fuzzy feeling inside.

Jimmy stepped up. "Good afternoon, Dr. Curtis. Your party is waiting. This way, please."

Walking into the room, he deliberately tapped the golden staff on the hardwood floor and leered at the curious patrons staring at him. They quickly turned their eyes away.

At a table in back, both his guests stood to greet him. *Excellent.* He retracted a gold watch from his vest pocket and flipped open the cover. "12:30. Right on schedule." He spoke to Jimmy. "My good lad, fetch me that bottle of wine, the one I've been saving for a special occasion such as this."

Jimmy nodded and rushed off.

"I'm happy to see you are here," he said to Ray but looked at the Mathematician. "And you must be Dr. Mackey."

"Ray says you have a job offer for me."

"All in good time." Curtis said, thinking the math man a bit pushy.

"Something about a million bucks," Dr. Mackey pressed.

Curtis smiled. "Pleased to meet you. I'm Frank Curtis."

"I'm Janis in Wonderland." Janis didn't smile. "Is Ray shittin' me, or what?"

"Please be seated," Curtis said in an attempt to keep control of the conversation.

Janis whispered to Ray, loud enough to show no regard for secrecy. "So this is your moneyman, huh?"

Curtis took a seat and set the golden staff across his lap. The atmosphere of tension surrounding the table seemed sulfuric, so for now he chose to ignore Janis's snide remark. "Sit," he ordered them with as much animosity as he could muster.

Both men took their seats, each glaring at the other with eyes casting blame.

Jimmy returned with a bottle of wine wrapped in white linen. In the other hand, he balanced a golden tray with three crystal glasses. One had a golden stem.

"Please do the honors, Jimmy." Curtis removed a golden corkscrew from his coat pocket. "With this."

Jimmy went to work opening the wine bottle.

Curtis passed out the glasses. The crystals he gave to his guests. The golden-stemmed glass he kept for himself.

Jimmy poured the wine.

Curtis figured these few minutes of wasted time were acceptable in the name of ceremony and pompousness, in neither of which he held any stock. He'd get to the point soon enough.

"Anything else?" Jimmy asked, cradling the empty wine bottle like a swaddled child.

"That will be all for now."

Jimmy left.

Curtis raised his glass to his guests. "Gentlemen, a toast to the 13th Power project. Salute."

He clinked his glass against Ray's, but the math man held his glass back.

"This is no time to be skeptical, Dr. Mackey. Drink up."

"What makes you think I'm skeptical?"

"If not, then you are stalling. May I suggest you are

not the type of man to waste your time?" He showed Janis a grin he hoped would say *you can't bullshit a bullshitter.*

"I'm a mathematician," Janis said. "Nothing is adding up. A million dollars for something worthless."

Curtis sipped his wine, eyeing Janis over the rim of his glass. The mathematician was determined to make this difficult? *Let him play his silly game.*

"Well, a million dollars or not, Mr. Curtis?"

"He's a doctor," Ray corrected him.

Janis tweaked an eyebrow. "Oh? A doctor of what?"

Curtis sat upright in the chair and set his glass on the table. "Archaeology, though not any longer. I made my fortune collecting ancient artifacts such as this golden Pharaoh's staff I have here." He raised it in evidence. "Truth is, fanatical government officials took back more artifacts than I kept. I'm disgusted with the whole business. So you see, I have retired from the *Doctor* occupation a long time ago, but you damn well better call me *doctor* anyway."

"I see." Janis's voice dripped with sarcasm. "Well, *Mister* Curtis, getting back to the original question, what about the million dollars?"

Staring at Janis, Curtis sipped his wine. "Dr. Mackey...or may I call you Janis?"

"Be my guest."

"Then Janis it is."

"Answer my question."

"Money can buy anyone or anything. I acquired Solartech Labs in a stock takeover. It may not be the best lab in the world, but it's a moneymaking machine, thanks to the government contracts we hold. However, its real purpose is to bring in new ideas and develop them through radical technology." He leaned forward. "The 13th Power is a radical concept, a vast inner-space where the God Particle resides, just out of reach, a problem without a solution. The rewards are hidden in the solution. The solution requires great minds and massive amounts of money. I have the money. You and Ray have the minds. It's a team project, gentlemen. We will solve the problem." He raised his wine glass and leaned back in his chair, his eyes keen on Janis, awaiting his reaction.

"Why the Higgs?" Janis asked. "Why not a cure for cancer, or AIDS, or any number of more pressing problems that need solutions?"

Curtis grumped. The old *there-are-better-things* argument, which he was prepared to counter. "Why fly a kite in a thunderstorm? Why send a man to Mars? Because it's something new, a new discovery to be made by those men brave enough to take on the challenge."

"Then why us?"

"You two worked well together in college. You have experience. You have a hypothesis. That puts us ahead of the game. You guys can make this happen. So here we are."

"That's all fine and dandy, *Mr.* Curtis, but what about the money?"

Curtis exhaled. "You confuse me, Dr. Mackey. Here you are, a prominent mathematician. Professional. Practical. I would expect a man of your caliber to care more about the science than the money."

"You're asking the impossible. I want to be sure I'm going to get paid."

"Perhaps Ray was wrong about you."

"I'm not one to waste my time, remember?"

"Or you just can't cut it."

Janis's face turned red. He stood, glaring. "I don't have to take any crap from you."

"What's the matter, Janis? The problem too tough for you?"

"You're crazy."

Ray butted in. "He believes in us, Janis."

"You're both crazy."

"Crazy or not, I'm prepared to pay a million dollars

for the 13th Power."

"Get one thing straight, Curtis."

"Dr. Curtis, please."

"I'm not signing on unless you guarantee payment, even when the project fails." Janis leaned forward. "And it will fail. I promise you that."

"I'll guarantee payment regardless of the outcome, but only if you don't invite failure and open your mind to the possibilities of the 13th Power."

"I'll open my mind to the lollipop power for a million bucks."

"Then we have a deal?"

Janis stared at him for a long moment.

Curtis could sense the math man calculating his next move.

Janis produced a pen, slid a napkin in front of him, and jotted something down. "Transferred to this account number." He pushed the napkin toward Curtis.

He grinned. Too easy. He took the napkin, folded it without looking at the numbers, and slipped it in his pocket. "Very good."

"On Monday," Janis added.

"On the first day of next month," Curtis replied. "I'm running this horse race. However, in case you are in a pinch for funds..." He produced a check for ten thousand dollars from his inside coat pocket, already made out to the mathematician. "This should hold you over."

Janis took the check, looked it over with bugged out eyes.

Curtis stood. "Enjoy your weekend, gentlemen. I expect to see both of you at Solartech on Monday."

"Wait!" Janis pocketed the check and produced a shred of paper. "What do you think of this?"

Curtis glanced at Ray.

The expression on Ray's face exuded concern. "Somebody attacked Janis's cab this morning, sir."

Janis folded his arms and leaned back in his chair. "Who would want to derail this meeting?"

A lump formed in Curtis's throat. Someone was screwing with his project. He'd have to get Judas on it right away. Meanwhile he had to keep his scientists appeased. "Seems you have some troublemaking enemies, Janis, as pushy as you are. Had nothing to do with us."

"I'd watch my back if I were you," Janis muttered.

"Don't worry about my back. Worry about your own. Tech-Com Control. Nine AM Monday. Be there on time."

He turned away and headed toward the exit, his golden staff thudding once again on the hardwood floor.

Chapter 18

JANIS DIDN'T THINK Curtis was telling the truth about this morning's attack. The shocked look on his face broke his air of calm, if only for a second.

Ray exhaled. "What do you think?"

"You don't want to hear it." Janis called to Jimmy. "Menus and ice tea all around, please."

"Right away, sir."

"What are you going to do with a million dollars?" Ray asked.

"My mother has Alzhiemers."

"Sorry."

"She'll be all right now, as long as Curtis comes through with the money."

"Don't worry," Ray said. "He has the money. Wait 'til you see his place in Simi Valley, you'll figure it like I did. He's a serious player."

"He'd better be." Janis calculated the costs. "Between Fermilabs and CERN, they've already spent over ten billion dollars in search of the Higgs. If he's got that kind of dough, what does he need the 13th Power for?"

"I don't know. He's dedicated to science. He's crazy. Who cares? I'm in it for the Nobel Prize."

"Get real."

"At least he listens to me. Devin wouldn't."

"Who's Devin?"

Jimmy brought the menus and ice tea. "I'll check back with you in a minute."

"Walter Devin, he's my ex-boss at Atomtech."

Janis's stomach was begging to be fed. He opened the menu. "Could Devin have anything to do with the attack on my cab this morning?"

"How could you be any threat to him?"

"Maybe he has it in for Curtis."

"Who knows?"

Who knows? Janis clenched his jaw. Lisa! Or whoever she was. Maybe she... "Did you send a limo to pick me up at the airport?"

"Not me." He looked puzzled." I figured you'd take a cab, same as all us working stiffs."

"Somebody sent a limo. Somebody knew my name. They had it written on a sign, for Christ's sake. What's going on around here, Ray?"

"How the hell should I know? Sounds to me like you brought the trouble with you."

Janis glared at his old friend. "My life was quiet and peaceful until you came back in it. This shit storm has to have something to do with you, and I'll bet that limo driver knows the connection."

"Look." Ray gave him a business card. "After lunch I'll make some calls, see what I can find out."

Janis read the card. "Super 8 Motel?"

"Yeah, the penthouse suite," he quipped.

"Take your orders now, gentlemen?" Jimmy seemed to pop in out of nowhere.

"I'll have the Deli Special Combo," Ray said.

"I'm not hungry." Janis produced the pink card from his coat pocket and waved it at Ray. "I've got a phone call to make."

#

At the bar, Steve pushed away his empty beer glass, dumbfounded by what he'd just heard. Devin had agreed to pay him a thousand dollars for this information. It had to be worth much more, say something with two more zeros.

Chapter 19

A GOLD ROLLS ROYCE PULLED up to the curb in front of the Balli Club. Sunbeams glistened off the silver lady poised on the hood prow. Curtis rushed out of the club, his long black coat too heavy for the hot California afternoon.

The doorman gave him a nod. "Enjoy your lunch, sir?"

Curtis didn't bother answering the peon and hurried toward the waiting car.

Standing six foot six, lanky and thin boned, Jonathan Kyles held open the rear door. His big blue eyes stared out from deep sockets, and though he looked a lot like the butler who did it, Jonathan was quick on his feet, fast-witted, and never backed down from a fight. "Done deal, sir?"

"Yeah. We got him." Curtis slid in on the leather seat. "Call the airport and have the jet prepared for takeoff to Dallas within the hour."

"Right away, sir." Jonathan got in behind the wheel, picked up his cell phone and drove away from the Balli Club.

As the Rolls maneuvered through traffic, Curtis cast a sober stare out the window, his mind playing with emotions he dared not reveal. The 13th Power experiments were finally on track, but Boris's warnings echoed in his mind: *Too dangerous.*

Were they about to make a scientific blunder into the unknown and destroy the world? He felt like a child playing with fire...frightened, yet bedazzled by the brilliance of it all. *Risk nothing, gain nothing.* Everything was in place for success.

However, the foreboding attack on Janis's cab meant an anonymous threat hung over the project. Was somebody onto him, or did someone have a grudge against Janis? Curtis huffed. That wasn't hard to figure, but he had to consider the threat real even though its source was a mystery.

Turning his attention to the backseat bar, he poured himself a Peach brandy. The aged wine he'd sipped earlier had left a foul taste in his mouth. He downed the brandy and pressed a button on the armrest. A black glass divider rose from the seatback, sealing his compartment in privacy. He lifted his laptop from the floor and opened the lid, revealing a Vidphone control panel.

Accessing Satellites scrolled across the display.

The engineers at Solartech Labs had designed this videophone to be untappable, its voice and video transmissions digitally coded and scrambled. He enjoyed being surrounded by high technology. A series of tones emitted from the speaker. *Ready.*

He tapped the keyboard.

"Hello, Dr. Curtis." The monitor revealed a young woman peering over her reading glasses at the web cam on her end.

"I'm on my way."

"I'll be ready," she said breathily.

He clicked disconnect. The monitor went blank. He pressed the intercom button. "Jonathan. Are we set?"

"The pilot just arrived, boss."

Curtis settled back into the plush leather seat. The 13th Power would soon be in his grasp.

Chapter 20

Lisa AIMED THE LIMO down an alley toward a three-story warehouse. Dust swirled in the air as she drove into the dark interior. Tires squealing, she headed up a ramp to the next level, turned into a brightly lit parking area, and parked in front of a door marked *Authorized Personnel Only*. Taking in a quick breath, she held it a moment to steel her resolve.

"You can pull this off," she whispered. "Just keep your cool, girl." She exhaled, blowing the air upward to stir her lofty bangs.

Glancing at the sign on the seat, the sign she'd held at the airport, she thought about Dr. Mackey. She'd expected a stuffed-shirt professor with the personality of an eraser. Instead, he had the good looks of a surfer dude, but clean cut and a million times more mature than any of the guys she knew. Her attraction for the mathematician surprised her, excited her, and scared the hell out of her, all at the same time.

"Colorado cowboy, huh?" She got out of the limo.

A blue Corvette was parked in a space marked, *Executive 1*, meaning Lo Chin was in his office. Smiling, she bolted through the door and dashed up the stairs.

"Lo," she sang, rushing into the office.

"How did it go, Miss Lisa?"

She plopped into a chair and propped her feet up on his desk, not caring what might be revealed under her short skirt. "I'm pretty sure he'll call. What red-blooded American scientist wouldn't want to know what makes this machine tick?" With a wave of her hand, she motioned to her outstretched shapely legs.

Lo returned to his paperwork, tamping a chuckle

under his breath.

Lisa set her purse on his desk and studied him for a moment. Lo Chin looked to be about sixty, had a stout frame and a face glowing with character, handsomely Asian. Fragile glasses sat low on the bridge of his nose. Lo ran a successful business, but she couldn't see any hint of what that business might be.

On the wall, he'd hung a diploma from UCLA, some kind of certificate from the National Guard, and a variety of photos in which he'd always posed alone, as if he had no family. No friends, no love of his life.

Lo had been a big help to her, gave her a place to stay in San Francisco, and let her use his limo. He was leery at first, thought she wouldn't be able to handle the big Lincoln, but after she'd told him how she'd driven a tractor-trailer rig in Canada, hauling logs to pay for her economics degree, he'd handed her the keys with a smile. Devin was right about Lo. He...

"Oh shit!" She jolted Lo from his work. "Devin!" Her feet hit the floor. She grabbed her purse and fished out the cell phone. "He's going to have a fit."

"It's only 1:00 in Nevada," Lo said. "You have time."

She brought up her address list and selected Walter Devin. After two rings, "Hello," came a voice over the line, growly as a Doberman guarding a bone.

"D-Devin?"

"Did Mackey show up at the airport?"

"Yes, he's in the meeting now..."

"Damn fools. Can't do anything right."

Hearing glass shatter on the other end of the line, she swallowed dryly. "Did I say something wrong?"

"What does he know about the meeting?"

"Nothing. Ray kept him in the dark. I'll find out what it was about when I see him later."

"I'll be waiting for your call." He hung up.

Lisa jacked the phone closed. "Lo, how long have *you*

known this creep?"

"I've been doing business with Atomtech for many years now. Devin is a hard man. He doesn't ask for favors, he demands favors, like now, with you and your little spy mission. You be careful of Devin, Miss Lisa."

She slumped back in the chair. "I still don't see how this charade is going to help me get back at my father for ruining my life?"

Lo took off his glasses and put them on top of his pile of papers. "Devin told me about your father. Not good for you to grow up without your mother."

"He kicked her out."

"Nanny okay, but real mother better."

"I hated my nannies."

"So he sent you away to private schools."

"Europe. Japan, Canada. He didn't want me around."

"Ah, but things are not always what they seem. Your father wanted only what is best for you, but you came back all mixed up, full of blame and hate."

"He's going to pay for what he did."

"Revenge have high price, Miss Lisa. Must sleep with enemy."

"Devin?"

"In a tiger den there are many tigers."

"I don't care."

"Maybe you will care before it's too late."

She managed an uneasy smile.

"How about a workout on the mats?" He stooped to the crouching tiger pose. "We can pass some time and burn up some of that bad energy inside you." He took a quick step forward and karate chopped the air twice. "Maybe I'll beat you this time."

She couldn't imagine that happening. They were both black belts, but she was younger and faster.

"What do you say?"

"No thanks, Lo. I'm saving my energy for Dr.

Mackey. Besides, you don't want to sleep with a hot pad again tonight."

Lo straightened. "Don't you know it's not right to beat up an old man?"

"It's not right to hit a girl."

"How did you get so good at karate?"

"Practice, Lo. Every time I kicked that damn bag, I saw my father's face. Bam! Bam! Bam! Over and over again until I thought the bag would bleed."

"Hate makes one strong, but stupid."

"I'm not stupid..." An electronic ring came from her phone. Heart fluttering, she let it ring two times as she reined in her emotions, and then flipped it open. "Hello," she said in a voice sweet and smooth as chocolate fudge.

"Lisa, I need to talk to you right away."

"Where are you, cowboy?"

"Meet me in front of the Balli club."

"I'll be right there." She stashed the phone in her purse and stood facing Lo. "Thanks for everything."

"You go quickly, pretty Miss Lisa, but go carefully. I need to see you again."

"Don't worry. I've got the tiger by the tail." She pecked him on the cheek.

"Ah, but tiger tail have teeth on the other end."

***

Janis paced the sidewalk in front of the Balli Club. The hot sun had stripped him of his suit coat. He'd slung it over his shoulder, loosened his tie, and unbuttoned the top button of his shirt. Sweat trickled down his neck. As long as he was staying in California for a while, he'd have to get some cooler clothes.

He stopped pacing and pulled the check from his back pocket. *$10,000.* Curtis's signature was smooth and simple with exaggerated capital letters.

Must be nice to be rich and eccentric.

The Pharaoh's walking staff seemed a bit overdone, even creepy. Scarier yet, Curtis wanted the impossible, the 13th Power. The Higgs boson. The God Particle. He was like a dog chasing a car. What would he do with it if he caught it?

Janis made note of the bank, *First Industrial*, and returned the check to his pocket. Come on Lisa!

He sat on the steps, waiting for the limo to appear. The doorman eyed him warily. It was a little cooler under the shaded awning, but not much. His mind wandered back to the incredible chain of events that led up to the meeting with Ray, Curtis, and the mysterious Lisa. Janis tried to find some logical way to explain why this was happening, but like Ray's obsession with the 13th Power, it defied reasoning.

"Looks like I'm in this up to my neck," he muttered to himself. "How did that go again?" The nucleus of an atom was the 12th Power negative. The Higgs boson could be ten times smaller, a galactic distance within the realm of nuclear dimensions. His brain couldn't imagine a place that small, but if he could stand there, the space around him would be as vast as the night sky.

Janis rubbed his chin and wondered if the laws of math and physics applied in a place so small. Would gravity function properly? Light? Numbers? And what good could come from finding out? The Higgs was worthless. "But it's got to be good for a Nobel Prize." He stood and began to pace again.

A stranger walked up, prickly-faced and smelling of sweat. An unlit cigarette dangled from his lower lip. "Do you have a light?"

Sidestepping the man, Janis said, "Sorry, I don't smoke."

A blue van screeched to the curb. The stranger grabbed Janis's arm. "You're going with us."

Hot adrenaline spilled into Janis's bloodstream. He spun around and tossed his suit coat over the stranger's head. The man released Janis's arm and flailed at the coat. Kicking into Golden Gloves Boxing mode, Janis delivered a left hook to the confused man's head, staggering him. Rubbing the sting from his knuckles, he drew back to throw another punch, but the van door flew open and regurgitated two big goons.

"You've gotta be shittin' me."

The goons balled their fists and grinned.

Janis delivered a swift kick to the stranger's left knee, buckling it backwards with a sharp crack. He hit the ground, screaming.

Janis gritted his teeth and turned to face the other two goons, fists cocked like a prizefighter. The goons must've sensed his boxing expertise and paused for a moment to glance at their comrade writhing on the sidewalk with a coat over his head.

Janis's adrenaline level peaked. "Come on. Let's get this over with."

The sound of screeching tires filled the air, spinning the goons around. They had to jump out of the way of the careening limo as it lurched to a stop at the curb.

"Thank God." Janis bolted to the limo's front door and flung it open. "Go. Go. Go," he shouted, fully prepared to hang on and ride the door down the block.

But the limo didn't move.

He dove into the car. "What the hell are you waiting for?"

The goons were rushing toward him. He slammed the door shut. "Go, damn it, go!"

Lisa smiled and shoved open the driver's door.

"What are you doing?"

She got out and stepped around the grill to the sidewalk.

The goons stopped, looked back and forth at each

other and Lisa.

Graceful as an exotic dancer, she discarded one high heel shoe, then the other. Standing in her bare feet, she gave the thugs a come-hither wave. "I wanna play, too."

The ugliest goon responded to her invitation first, launching his assault without warning. Lisa spun with a left kick, high to the bridge of the bad guy's nose, revealing a flash of white panties in the afternoon sunshine. Before the big oaf hit the ground, she recoiled a lovely knee and caught him in the throat on the way down.

Janis grimaced. That had to hurt. His mouth fell open as he watched the second man writhe on the sidewalk. Shifting his eyes to the Balli Club entrance, he noticed the doorman was nowhere in sight. Damn! Janis threw the door open to offer assistance with the last goon standing, but Lisa motioned him to stay back.

Crouched like some kind of Kung Fu master, elbows raised, hands stiff, she looked poised for an attack. "Come on, Mr. Tough Guy. It's your turn to see my panties." She took a step toward the scumbag.

The goon raised his hands. "Look, lady. We got no beef with you. We'll leave real quiet like. Okay?"

Lisa took another step forward.

"Please, lady," he cried, stepping backward. "Give me a break. Somebody has to be in one piece to drive the damn van."

She stood upright, blew the coward a kiss, and turned her attention to the big lug hacking on the ground. "Get this garbage off the sidewalk." She pivoted on her toes, stooped to pick up her shoes, and swayed her hips all the way back to the open limo door.

Feeling stun-gunned, Janis watched her slide in behind the wheel.

The injured goons crawled inside the van.

She tossed her shoes on the floor. "Check the license plate. Nevada."

Janis spotted his coat lying on the sidewalk. "Wait."

He started to push the door open when wailing sirens pierced the air.

"Damn!" The coat wasn't worth the delay. It had a bullet hole in it anyway. "Let's go. First Industrial Bank." He gave Lisa a suspicious glare. "Then you and I are going to have us a little chat."

Lisa bit her lower lip and sped away from the Balli Club.

Chapter 21

Ray DUG IN HIS POCKET for the key to his room. A vacuum cleaner was running somewhere down the hall, unseen. Once inside, he flung his coat on the bed, loosened his tie, and poured a glass of water from a pitcher on the dresser. The air conditioner under the window hummed softly. With drawn curtains, the dimly lit room felt cool. He settled into a recliner in the corner and took a moment to relax. The meeting had been a success—but not without complications. Now he had to solve some problems he hadn't counted on. Though he didn't want to believe the assault on Janis's cab had anything to do with the meeting, he had to be certain. He had too much at stake to let anyone ruin his chances of achieving his goal. Putting down his glass, he reached for the phone and dialed the labs in Simi Valley.

"Solartech Labs."

"Trish, get me Gibson right away."

"One moment, Mr. Crawford."

The phone went silent. Ray looked at the ceiling and thought about Alex Gibson. The Chief Security Officer of Solartech Labs had some powerful credentials, including a lengthy stint with the CIA from which he had retired. He seemed truly concerned about Curtis's quest for the 13th Power and had an uncanny knack of getting anything he needed to ensure security for the project. He had turned Solartech Labs into a military fortress.

"Mr. Crawford," Trish came back. "Alex is with the perimeter patrol at South Gate. Apparently they found some cut barbed wire out there. Can I get a phone number...?"

"Cut wire? What...what's going on?"

"All I know is they caught some guy in the mail room, day before yesterday. He was dressed in a lab coat and wearing a fake beard. He had your Special Delivery letter in his hand. Don't worry. The letter was sent."

The letter to Dr. Mackey. A lump formed in Ray's throat. "Tell Alex I want that guy held until I get there. And no cops."

"Sorry, Mr. Crawford, the guy got away. Alex went ballistic. He's heading up the investigation personally."

"So nobody knows who he was?"

"Nobody."

Ray hung up. He paced the floor. Now he was convinced that Janis was targeted. Someone was definitely interested in the 13th Power project. But who?

Knuckles rapped on the door. "Room Service." The voice sounded cold, like a construction worker, unlike the cordial tone of the room stewards.

"I didn't order room service."

The knock came again. "Room service."

"I said—"

The door exploded in a shower of splinters. A machinegun rattled from the hallway. Ray dove to the floor as murderous rounds ripped at curtains, walls, and mirrors, destroying everything in their paths and turning his room into a death chamber of flying debris. Glass exploded. Lamps threw sparks. The air-conditioner hissed gas. Throwing his hands over his head, he awaited the inevitable end of his life.

As suddenly as the onslaught began, it ended. Silence. His first fear was that someone was going to come in and finish him off, execution style. He strained to listen for approaching footsteps. A chunk of mirror fell and shattered on the floor. Almost gave him heart failure.

He peeked over the bed. No one was in sight. Dust swirled around the room, reflecting in beams of sunlight that shined through bullet-riddled curtains. The smell of gunpowder hung thick in the air. Fighting off an urge to panic, he slowly got to his feet and haphazardly brushed himself off. He felt dizzy from an overdose of adrenaline.

He grabbed his suit coat and pulled open the pulverized door. A wide-eyed maid stood in the hall, her white apron balled in her fists. She peered into the room then looked at him. "I'm not cleanin' up that mess." Shaking her head, she waddled away.

A steward rounded the corner in full stride. "What's going on up here?"

"I need another room."

In the distance, the wail of sirens filled the California air. Ray threw on his dusty jacket, tightened his tie, and prepared for the interrogation to come. He was stuck there, waiting for Janis. A sudden wave of horror crashed over him. Janis really was in danger.

Chapter 22

LISA ACCELERATED THE LIMO out of the bank teller lane. Janis counted his cash. Curtis's check had paid off like a slot machine. "I need clothes. Where's a Walmart?"

"Are you kidding? You're more the Executive Man type. It's on Vanness." Lisa aimed the limo toward the downtown section. "It's a high-class men's wear store..." She winked in his direction. "For high-class men like you."

Though the compliment was flattering, Janis didn't respond. He just stared at her, wondering if she was for real. Not knowing her intentions, he had to be careful. The mystery surrounding her involvement in this affair shot nagging questions through his mind, questions he wanted to confront her with, but he doubted he'd get any straight answers. However, if she were playing some kind of game, maybe playing along would get him to the truth. An idea came to him. He let a few minutes pass before he asked, "Will you help me pick out something with California flair, you know, cool and comfortable?"

She looked him up and down as if sizing him up. "Sure thing, cowboy." Her smile made his heart race. He hadn't expected to find someone like her in California.

He turned his attention to the sights of San Francisco. In the distance, the Golden Gate Bridge spanned the bay teeming with boats of all sizes. The afternoon sun hung low in the sky and cast shadows across the water. A light sea breeze swept in from the west, cooling the heated city. He reclined his seat and settled back to relax.

Lisa seemed to sense his weariness and tuned the radio to a soft music station. He glanced at her. Maybe she wasn't his adversary. Maybe she was his protector.

Smiling, he thought, what a beautiful protector, indeed.

Twenty minutes passed before Lisa swung the limo into a parking lot beside the prestigious men's store. With a yawn, Janis stretched the sleepiness from his arms and legs.

"Okay, Dr. Mackey. Let's get you some clothes."

Walking toward the store entrance, Janis took Lisa's hand and looked around the parking lot for anything that seemed suspicious, especially blue vans. His safety assured, they entered the lavish shop.

A balding clerk greeted them eagerly, like a puppy anticipating a treat. "How may I be of assistance?"

Lisa dragged them from one department to another, selecting shirts and pants, belts and ties, a sport coat and a shiny pair of black snakeskin shoes. Socks, underwear, a shaving kit, and a soft-side suitcase rounded off her shopping list.

Janis admired her eye for fashion and her ability to barter with the bewildered clerk. If it wasn't on sale, she insisted he put it on sale, constantly threatening to take their business to Walmart. Janis felt a little embarrassed but swallowed his pride and let her carry on with her harmless antics.

As he tried on clothes and paraded around the store in his stocking feet, he had to laugh at her enthusiasm and boundless energy. More than two hours had passed before she seemed satisfied that he'd be dressed properly for any occasion.

The clerk finished sacking the clothes.

Janis paid in cash.

Lisa said, "I'll bring the limo around to the front door."

Dusk had settled over San Francisco. The parking lot lights flickered to life. A breeze carried with it the briny scent of seawater.

Lisa headed toward the limo while Janis stood at the store entrance, watching her hourglass shape move gracefully away.

She walked around the limo and opened the driver door. Sliding in behind the wheel, she smiled at him and put the key in the ignition. The starter whined but the engine didn't start.

Janis frowned. That was all he needed. A broken down limo and a ride in a tow truck.

Lisa cranked the engine again. White sparks spewed from under the engine and bounced on the ground like hailstones. A spike of horror cut into his stomach, sharp as a knife. Something had gone wrong with the electrical system.

"Lisa, wait!"

A massive blast lifted the car off the ground, followed by a brilliant red and yellow fireball that billowed into the sky, turning dusk to daylight. The hood ripped off. The windows blew out. Fire rushed in. Glass and metal debris rained down in every direction.

The concussion knocked Janis to the ground. The plate glass store windows shattered. He ducked the shower of glass by covering his head with his arms. The boom rolled away like a clap of thunder.

Janis jumped to his feet. His ears ached. The limo was burning. He ran straight toward the inferno.

"Lisa!"

A tire exploded.

As he approached the fiery tomb, he could barely hear himself calling her name over the roar of the flames.

"Lisa!"

He tried to see beyond the flames and into the limo. The heat drove him back. He shielded his face with his arms and ran around to the driver's side of the inferno.

The door hung open on bent hinges. He turned to look away from the burning car. His chest felt as if it would burst.

"Lisa?"

Several yards away, she lay on the pavement, curled in a fetal position, motionless, her sooty hands covering her head, her blond hair singed and soiled. He ran to her and, fighting back tears, placed his fingers on the side of her neck. Felt a pulse.

"Yes. Lisa."

He scooped her up in his arms and carried her away from the inferno. As he ran, she opened her eyes and threw her arms around his neck. "Oh, Janis." She held him as if she would never let him go.

He felt his heart beating in his ears. So little he knew about her, so strongly he felt for her, and so nearly he had almost lost her.

Through the inferno's roar, wailing sirens pierced the night air. He dropped to the curb and just held her.

Chapter 23

JANIS PACED BEHIND the ambulance and occasionally stole glances into the back door windows. Paramedics were checking Lisa. He wanted to be with her, but they wouldn't let him in. Crowded around her, they went about their work, poking and prodding, their voices coming from the ambulance, but not their words. Lisa only looked to be scraped and singed. She had said her eardrums hurt. He hoped they wouldn't find anything more serious.

A chill ran through him as he glanced around the parking lot, the darkness flashing with emergency lights. Firemen, police, and curious onlookers were but silhouettes moving about erratically, like disco dancers under a strobe light. This wasn't his idea of a good time in California.

#

Chief Driskell watched his firemen douse stubborn flames. Only a black shell remained of the limo, twisted and disfigured. Black smoke swirled from the debris and leaned with the breeze. Several men wearing Arson Squad coats went about examining the wreckage. Flashes from their cameras lit the scene with an eerie contrast of gray and black shadows. Other investigators searched with flashlights and metal detectors. He hoped they would find some remnants of the bomb.

"Over here," one of his men called out.

Driskell rushed toward the fireman. "What is it?"

He displayed a handful of charred debris. "Crude device. Not very professional." He wiped his chin with a sooty glove. "A pipe bomb with a Swisher fuse. Puts out quite a sparkler show before it rips."

Taking the fragments in cupped hands, Driskell inspected pieces of twisted metal pipe and burnt packing, which were still warm and smelled of sulfur. "Has Michaels seen this yet?"

"No. He's over there." The fireman pointed toward a group of men in suits.

Michaels looked irritated as Driskell approached the detectives huddled in conversation.

"Never fails," Michaels said without a smile. "Mother's in town and this shit happens."

"Life's a bitch. Take a look at this stuff."

The detective examined the debris then tilted his head toward the ambulance. "What do you know about them?"

"The young lady is the limo driver. She damn near got killed. The gentleman is a professor from Colorado. She's got to answer some questions when the medical boys are done with her. If we—"

The back doors of the ambulance swung open with a creak. Two paramedics helped Lisa out. Her left elbow was wrapped in a white bandage and she looked wobbly on her feet.

"Now is as good a time as any." Michaels handed the evidence to one of his partners. "Bag this stuff." He turned to Driskell. "Let's go."

Together, they headed toward the group that had gathered behind the ambulance.

#

Janis hugged Lisa. "Are you okay?"

"My head is still ringing."

Firemen and paramedics clustered around. "Glad you're all right," one said. "Talk about a close call," said another. Others were jabbering among themselves about how lucky she was.

Two approaching officials caught Janis's attention. The taller man wore a helmet, an orange jump suit striped with reflective tape, and big brown boots. The other man walked with slouched shoulders and wore a black trench coat that hung unbuttoned down the front, revealing a white shirt with no tie. Faces pinched, they both looked ready to give someone the third-degree.

"I'm detective Michaels." He displayed a badge to Lisa. "And this is Fire Chief Driskell. Are you two all right?"

"We've been better," Janis said.

"Anybody here have a clue what this mess is all about?" Michaels pointed to the wreckage, now being loaded on a tow truck. The cable winch whined as it pulled the twisted hulk up the flat bed, metal on metal screeching.

Janis didn't like the cop's accusatory glare. "Look, officer, this day's been a disaster from the start, so lay off the girl. We don't know anything."

Michaels frowned. "Talk about a bad day. First I get a report of a street brawl at the Balli Club. Nobody's around when I get there. Seems the perps split in a limo. Funny thing about that. Now I've got a limo lookin' like a relic from Pearl Harbor."

He pointed to the tow truck and stared at Lisa. "An occupant of said limo is some kind of professor scientist or something. Funny thing about that, too. This afternoon some other scientist-type guy gets his hotel room redecorated by a machinegun assault force. Am I patrolling somewhere in the Twilight Zone or are these things connected somehow?" He switched his focus to Janis as if waiting for an enlightening reply.

But Janis was struggling to take his next breath, his mind reeling in the terror of the officer's words. Ray had been attacked in his hotel room. This deadly gauntlet was not computing for the mathematician, and Ray's fate became a burning question. "Is Ray all right?"

"Ray?" Lisa said, wide-eyed.

"Ah, so you do know something, after all," Michaels said. "He's in room 218 now. So let's have it." He eyed them back and forth. "What the hell's going on?"

"Ray?" Lisa said again, her voice an octave higher.

Janis looked at her as she trembled in his arms. "That's what I want to know, Lisa. You don't work for the Balli Club. You lied to me. Why?"

She pushed away from him and turned a full circle as if looking for an escape route, but officers, firemen, and paramedics were standing all around, blocking her way. Janis resisted the urge to grab her arm, thinking it best to let her work this dilemma out for herself.

Slowly, she came back to him, and with a look of despair in her eyes, took his hands, her lips quivering. "R-Ray who?"

"Ray Crawford. Why?"

Her face paled. "He's my father." She threw her arms in the air. "Walter Devin sent me to find out why you came to California. Why you were meeting my father. Don't you see? Devin is the one who's trying to kill us."

"Ray's ex-boss?" Janis remembered Ray mentioning him. "What does he care?"

"I don't know."

"What did you tell him?"

"Nothing. You haven't said a word about the meeting, but it's obvious he doesn't care anymore. He's just going to kill everybody that's connected to Curtis."

Janis felt a chill. "What does Devin have against Curtis?"

"Who cares?" Lisa turned to the cop. "Devin is pissed off. He's dangerous. Can you help us?"

"Sure, Missy. Just tell me where he is and we'll go arrest his ass, right after you two get an Oscar. Father! Devin! Curtis! Beam me up, Scotty! I should haul you both in right now."

"For what?" Janis asked, thinking the cop was being a bit over-dramatic.

"Disturbing the peace and felony littering." He motioned to the mess in the parking lot.

"It's not our fault Devin wants us dead," Lisa shouted.

Janis thought about that. They could use some protection. "Can you put us in jail for the night? Protective custody or something."

Driskell said to Michaels, "That's a good idea."

"It's not worth the paperwork. Besides, my mother's waiting for me to get home to dinner."

"You can't just leave us here," Janis said.

The cop nudged the Chief. "Let's get out of here. My meat loaf is getting cold."

They walked away.

Lisa sat on the back bumper of the ambulance. "They don't get it."

Sitting next to her, Janis looked into her eyes, started to speak, but she spoke first. "Janis, wait. Let me explain. I knew Devin was after us when I saw the Nevada plates on that blue van at the Balli Club. Atomtech is in Nevada and Devin uses a fleet of unmarked blue vans. He's convinced that Curtis is up to something and obsessed with finding out what it is. I thought all he wanted was information."

Her chin quivered as if she was about to cry, but she held her tears at bay. "Devin's known me since I was a little girl. He just tried to kill me, Janis. We need help...and I know just where to find it. I'm going to call him right now."

"Wait," Janis said. Questions ran through his mind, one more important than the others. If he was going to trust Lisa, he had to know the answer. "How did you get mixed up in this?"

Lisa squared her shoulders. "I agreed to help him find out what Curtis was planning by pushing myself on some old professor who was coming to a meeting at the Balli Club." A soft smile brightened her eyes. "Some *old professor* you turned out to be."

"So you lied to me."

Her gaze dropped. "I'm sorry, but I had to. Devin said he'd help me get back at my father for what he did."

"What did he do?" Janis asked, thinking the worst, sexual abuse. Rape.

"He ruined my life, so I agreed to help Devin."

"How did he ruin your life?"

"First he got rid of my mother, and then he sent me away to school, far away, clear around the world. And he was always moving me around from one school to another. I was never in one place long enough to make any friends. He made me a prisoner in those horrible places. He took away my mom. He took away my home. I was from nowhere, going nowhere."

"Why would he do that to you?"

"Because of his job, that's why. I was in the way, like my mother was in the way. His career was more important than his family. It hurt, Janis. I cried and I cried until the hurt turned to hate."

"And Devin took advantage of that."

"My dad quit working for him, took a job with Curtis at Solartech Labs. Devin's all paranoid about the competition, I guess, and asked me to help him. I certainly didn't think he'd try to kill anyone."

Janis rubbed her shoulder. "I wonder how he knew we were here."

"I don't know."

"And who would be so brazen as to rig a bomb in a car in broad daylight?"

"He has a bunch of goons working for him."

"Yeah, I know." He'd met them on the highway to the airport and at the Balli Club. "He must pay them pretty well to do his dirty work."

"My dad never liked him."

Janis glanced around the parking lot. Except for the ambulance and two cop cars, all the other emergency vehicles had left. If not for the smell of melted asphalt, the darkness would have given no hint of what had happened here. He brushed back a tangle of Lisa's hair. "What about that phone call?"

She got up from the bumper. "I'll call him right now."

"Who?"

"Lo Chin," she said with a smile. "You'll like him." She got out her cell phone and turned away to make the call.

As he watched her, he recalled Lisa's version of her childhood. Anger boiled up a storm in his stomach. He'd seen Ray's obsessive behavior in college. His studies took precedent over everything. And now his work, his job, his quest for the 13th Power had taken precedent over his family, his wife, and even his only daughter. Janis gritted his teeth. Ray had some explaining to do, by God!

#

Lisa punched the number into her cell phone. Lo Chin answered, "Hello, Miss Lisa."

"Lo, we need your help."

"What's the matter?"

"Devin is trying to kill us. He just blew up your limo and the cops aren't buying our story."

"Slow down, Miss Lisa. You talk too fast for old man's ears. What did you say is wrong with my limo?"

"It blew up. You know, ka-boom! A bomb. Lots of fire and smoke, pieces scattered all around."

"Devin bombed my limo? That no good son of a..." The line fell silent, then: "Are you okay?"

"I'm banged up some, Lo. I was trying to start the car when the next thing I knew, Janis was picking me up off the pavement. If I'd closed the driver door, I'd be dead right now."

"Why would Devin want you dead?"

"We're trying to make sense of it. Can you come and get us? We're at The Executive Man on Vanness."

"I'll be right there. You watch out for more trouble." Lo hung up.

Lisa clutched the phone to her chest. *Please hurry.*

Chapter 24

A RICKETY '52 Chevy pickup rattled into the parking lot of The Executive Man. Lo surveyed the scene of his limo's demise. The emergency vehicles were gone. Only a scorched and melted circle of asphalt remained. He put his forehead on the steering wheel, sadness sweeping over him: sadness for the loss of his friendship with Devin, who could have no excuse for this attack on Lisa.

Lo's sadness turned to anger and then to dread. What else did Devin have in store for her? How badly did he want her dead?

He scanned the parking lot. She was nowhere in sight. A big pile of packages by the store entrance caught his attention. He coaxed the old truck, popping and wheezing, to the curb and shut off the noisy engine. The night went silent.

Lisa ran out of the store toward him, her hair trailing behind her like a silken scarf. A distinguished-looking gentleman appeared in the doorway.

Lo jumped from the cab, his feet hitting the ground at the same time Lisa threw her arms around his neck.

"Lo."

"Lisa...it's okay now. Be careful of old man's bones."

"Thank God, you're here."

"And thank old truck, too. Corvette is good for picking up girls but not to carry gentlemen friend and half of the store you buy." He waved to the professor. "Come on. Load up and we go. Hurry. Hurry."

Lisa helped load the bagged clothes into the truck bed then took Janis's hand and led him to Lo. "This is Janis Mackey," she said with a glimmer of adoration in her eyes.

Lo shook the math man's hand. "Lo Chin. Nice to

meet you. But we better go before something else happen."

He helped Lisa into the truck. She sat in the middle. Janis rode shotgun. Lo fired up the engine, ground a couple of gears, and rumbled off into the California night.

As the rattletrap rattled down Vanness, Lisa took Janis's hand and rested her head on his shoulder. The sight warmed Lo's heart. "You two will be safe at my place tonight."

Lisa snuggled into Janis.

Lo worked the steering wheel back and forth as the old truck lumbered across the Golden Gate Bridge toward Marin County. A full moon hung on the horizon just below the spire of the Transtar Building. Ribbons of high clouds reflected silver moonbeams and appeared to wrap the city in silk. Lo sensed that Lisa felt safe. She'd fallen asleep in the crook of Janis's arm.

***

Janis yawned as the old truck rattled through the gate to Lo's luxurious estate and lumbered along a tree-lined drive that curved around to the front of his mansion. Lo parked next to a blue Corvette.

Janis gathered sleeping Lisa in his arms and carried her up granite steps to a door, which Lo held open for them.

"This way. Upstairs."

Janis followed him to an upper foyer that went around to a large bedroom.

Lo turned on a light.

In the middle of the room stood a round bed with high wooden posts and a silken canopy. Lo parted sheer pink veils that draped to the floor. Janis laid Lisa on plush bed covers, gently released her, and took a step back. Black soot spotted her yellow dress and tan face, her knees were scratched, and the white bandage on her elbow had already become soiled. Scorched blond hair lay in tangles on the pillow. Still, she looked beautiful. Ray's daughter, of all people, could she be the one he'd been looking for all his life? He didn't believe in love at first sight, but how could he ignore what his heart was telling him?

He turned to Lo. "Where's your phone? My cell battery's dead."

"Kitchen, where else?"

Janis followed him downstairs. A light scent of incense drifted in the air. At the end of a dimly lit hallway, Lo flicked on kitchen lights and headed straight for the refrigerator.

Taking the Motel 8 business card from his pocket, Janis dialed the phone number. Waiting, he watched Lo rummage through the refrigerator. A moment later, the front desk answered.

"Do you have a Ray Crawford in 218?"

"One moment."

Lo set out fixings for ham sandwiches, lettuce and cheese, pickles and olives and a big bag of chips.

"What? No Egg Foo Young?" Janis asked.

"You want Chinese food, you go to restaurant. I no like."

A frantic voice answered the phone. "Janis, that you?"

"In living color."

"Are you all right?"

"I hear your room got shot up."

"How did you know about that?"

"Word gets around."

Ray cleared his throat. "Where have you been?"

"Downtown. My limo got bombed."

"We gotta get out of here, Janis. Somebody's going to get killed."

"Pick us up tomorrow morning at 10:00 sharp."

"Us? Who's with you?"

Janis thought telling him wouldn't do any good. It was best he didn't know about Lisa. Not yet, anyway. "A woman I met."

"Come on, Janis. Can't you leave the damn women alone for one day?"

"Not this one."

"Where do I meet you?"

Janis asked Lo. "What's the address?"

"147 Willow Circle," Lo replied loudly, pressing down on the lid of a sandwich.

"Got it," Ray said.

"Don't be late."

"Watch your back, Janis. I called the lab. They had a security breach. A spy got in and found my letter to you. Somebody wants you dead."

"You too, Ray. And worse, Devin is the shooter. But I don't know why."

"Devin?" A gasp came over the line. "Devin must not want us to do the 13th Power experiments. He was adamantly against them when I worked for him."

"Why?"

"He thinks screwing with the Higgs can destroy the world."

"What do you think?"

"I'll bet he's trying to keep us from helping Curtis. Our only safe place is Solartech Labs. He can't get to us there. It's a fortress. Tomorrow we make a run for Simi Valley. It's our only hope."

"The three of us will go together."

"We're not taking the damn chick, Janis!"

"Yes we are," Janis yelled into the phone, his chest burning with rage. "I'm not letting her out of my sight." He slammed down the receiver. "Jerk."

He looked up. His heart missed a beat. Lisa was standing in the doorway, face cleaned, her hair brushed back into a ponytail, her smile a-gloss with fresh lipstick. A silky white gown replaced her soiled yellow miniskirt. She stared at him, looking as if she would explode with joy. Oh, no. Had she heard him? Did she know how he felt?

She ran to him and threw her arms around his neck.

She knew.

Holding her in his arms, he kissed her with breathy passion. Her tongue darted in and out of his mouth, sweet as candy, tempting him to play. Her perfume electrified the air. He caught quick breaths, short gasps between long kisses as he savored the taste of her mouth. But like a door slamming shut to heaven, his insides churned with a sudden regret. Not Ray's daughter. She was too young for him. Stop. Stop it now, before things get out of hand.

But he didn't stop kissing her until Lo interrupted. "Okay, you two. Eat first. Play later."

Janis released Lisa. A twinge of embarrassment warmed his cheeks. He had lost his head over this woman.

Lisa winked at him and took a seat at the table.

"Okay." Must be the way things were in California. Fast. Hot. Incredible.

He sat across from Lisa and grabbed a ham sandwich, glad he had something else to think about. "We're going to Solartech Labs tomorrow." He took a bite of sandwich. "I'll pack tonight. We'll get your things in the morning, Lisa. Where do you live?"

"I'm staying here. How did you like my room?"

Janis swallowed, a little set aback by the thought of her and Lo playing house. "Loved it."

Lo explained. "She needed a place to stay while in San Francisco on business for Devin, so I agreed to put her up for a few nights."

"My townhouse is in Santa Barbara," Lisa added, taking a napkin. "I love shopping on the pier, sunbathing on the beach, partying in the nightclubs. It's a fun place to live."

"California girl that you are," Janis added with a smile.

"And don't you forget it, cowboy."

He thought he'd better keep that in mind. California and Colorado were like two different worlds. He downed the last of his milk. After eating, he realized how heavy his eyelids felt.

Lo cleared the table, shuffling packages of meat and cheese to the fridge and clinking silverware into the sink. He finished and bowed from the doorway. "Goodnight." His silhouette disappeared down the hall.

Lisa smiled. "We're alone at last."

Trepidation clawed up Janis's backbone. "What do you mean by that?"

"You know." She puckered her lips.

"You're Ray's daughter."

"So?"

"It's late."

"It's early."

He slid his chair back. "I'm twice your age. Trust me. It's late."

Her lower lip curled. "I'll show you to your room."

"I'll find it myself. Which way?"

"Last door on the left." She pointed down the hall. "Sleep tight."

Janis made his way to the guest room. Thanks to Lo, his clothes were already laid out on the bed. He sorted through all his stuff and packed his suitcase.

After taking a shower, he slipped into a pair of California-style boxer shorts and admired them in the mirror. A tanned and bikini clad surfer-girl rode a yellow board on a big blue wave with a frothy crest, her blond ponytail trailing behind her. He imitated her pose and shifted his hips as if he were surfing. Gotta love California.

Chapter 25

AFTER TALKING WITH Janis, Ray wondered if his old college pal had gone nuts. What woman had he met? Why was he acting like an idiot? He couldn't waltz into Solartech Labs with some chick. And how did he know Devin was the shooter? A bad feeling dropped into Ray's stomach.

He got out of bed, turned on the table lamp, and paced. Why was Devin so violently opposed to the 13th Power experiments? He couldn't have resorted to shooting up cabs and motel rooms and blowing up limos. Did he really believe the fate of the world was at stake?

Ray pulled his loose underwear up a little higher as he paced. Would Devin stop at nothing to derail Curtis's project?

Opening the closet door, Ray pulled out his suitcase. He threw it on the bed and took out an electronic box, his Vidphone, an older model but just as secure as the fancy new ones. After setting it on the table, he flipped on a power switch. A green light blinked on the panel. The monitor chirped. Taking the hotel phone from its cradle on the nightstand, he placed the mouthpiece into a groove on the box. A series of tones emitted into the phone. It rang.

"Dallas Central," Jonathan said as his face came into focus on the monitor. "What do you want, Ray?" He looked angry.

"Is Curtis there?"

"This better be important."

"Just get him, Jonathan. It's serious."

A few moments later, Curtis's face appeared on the monitor. He looked angry, too. "What is your problem, Crawford?"

Ray glanced at the ceiling. *Well, hello, Ray. And how are you tonight? Oh, I'm fine, Dr. Curtis. Thank you for asking. I almost got shot to death today.* Did he have to be such a jerk? "We've got a problem, sir. Looks as though Devin doesn't want us to do the 13th Power experiments. According to Dr. Mackey, Devin is the one responsible for attacking the cab this morning in Denver. Since then, he's shot up my motel room and bombed Janis's limo."

"How does Janis know it was Devin?"

"He didn't say, but he sounded certain."

"I wondered if that ex-boss of yours would stick his fat finger into our pie."

"He's going to ruin everything."

Curtis huffed. "Not if I can help it."

"Tomorrow morning we're going to make a run for Simi Valley."

"You do that. In the meantime, I'll take care of Devin."

The phone line went dead, the monitor black.

Ray turned off the lamp and fell back into bed. Devin's *finger in the pie* was not a good thing. The man was powerful, resourceful, and determined, equally as much as Curtis. Each was a gladiator in the ring of technological competition. A chill ran down Ray's spine.

The gladiators were about to do battle.

Chapter 26

In DALLAS CENTRAL, Curtis keyed in a code on the Vidphone. Devin had become a dangerous threat to the project. He had to be stopped. The monitor blinked. *Waiting For Answer* scrolled across the screen. The message changed to *Transmitting* as Alex appeared, red-eyed, as if he hadn't slept in a while. "What's up, Frank?"

"Devin has endangered the lives of Ray and our new employee, Dr. Mackey. We can't afford to lose these people, and I'll not tolerate any interference in this highly prioritized project."

Rubbing his temples, Alex frowned. "I wonder if Devin sent that spy with the beard the other day. We found a breach in South Gate's perimeter. That's where he got in, jumpered the fence alarm circuits before he started cutting the wire. We're going to—"

"Never mind the snoop," Curtis cut in. "I want Devin dead and I don't care how you do it, just get on it right away. Lives depend on your success."

"No problem."

Curtis hung up. "Damn Devin. I never did like that son of a bitch."

***

Alex sat at his security desk in Solartech Lab's main administration building and contemplated Curtis's request. Though a need for sleep weighted his eyelids, the excitement of this new assignment spurred his imagination and stirred a second wind. After the embarrassing breach at South Gate, he needed the morale boost of a precision assault mission, just like in Vietnam. He knew it would take a lot of firepower to put Atomtech's security forces out of commission and get close enough to Devin to kill him. His people were first-rate. The compound was heavily defended. A military operation of that magnitude would require resources beyond those of Solartech Labs. And the use of those resources required authorization from a higher authority.

He went to his computer and typed *The Ark* along with a security code. The monitor turned bright blue with a silver CIA insignia embedded in the background. He typed: *Request authorization for military operations against Atomtech. Urgent. Mole.*

Leaning back in his chair, Alex knew *The Ark* was serious when he said the 13th Power project was to be protected at all costs, but would he go so far as ordering the death of American scientists and security guards? A few minutes later, a chime signaled a response. *Why? The Ark.*

Alex typed again: *Dr. Curtis believes Devin is trying to kill the scientists he has recruited to conduct the 13th Power experiments. The project is in jeopardy. We need to intervene. Mole.*

He clicked on the pulsating *Respond* button. The email window went blank except for the flashing curser. He stared at the screen, waiting for an answer.

Devin's interference is not tolerable. Authorization to eliminate the target is granted.

Alex felt a chill.

End Transmission scrolled across the screen.

He knew just the man for the job.

Chapter 27

ALEX HELD THE PHONE in his hand, thinking a moment before dialing James "Red" Colburn, a soldier he knew from Vietnam. Red had served twenty years in the Marine Corps and loved every minute of it. The nickname, *Red*, he earned while spilling the blood of his enemies. Sometimes killing wasn't enough for Red. He'd go berserk, leaving behind corpses disfigured and mutilated. They should've called him *Crazy Red*.

Retired with every medal a soldier could pin to his chest, he now commanded a paramilitary unit headquartered somewhere in the rugged terrain south of Chino Hills. His wife, Virginia, lived the life of suburbia, in comfort and style, while Red roughed it in the wilderness with his mercenaries. Alex had kept in touch with them over the years, mostly because of Virginia.

There was a time, before she even knew Red existed, when she was in love with Alex. But their life together wasn't meant to be. His heart sank with the memory. When Red came home from the war, rugged and tough, Alex had introduced him to Virginia, or more like showed her off. "He saved my life at the battle of Bien Hoa," Alex had told her.

Red took her hand. She smiled. From the look in their eyes, Alex knew it was the end for him and Virginia. The pain he felt on the day she married Red burned worse than the bullet he took in that stinking rice paddy.

But as the wound healed and painful memories faded, he eventually found solace in the fact that the woman he loved and his best friend were happy. These days, to get to Red, he had to go through Virginia. That was okay. It gave him a good excuse to call her. He dialed. The phone rang.

"Hello." Virginia's voice came over the line smooth as ice cream and blueberries.

"How are you, Virginia?"

"Alex. It's late."

"I need to talk to Red."

"He's right here, he'll be delighted."

"I'd rather talk to you."

"One moment, I'll get him." As he waited for Red to come to the phone, Alex wondered what the old soldier was up to. Being home on a weekend night seemed highly unusual. He should be busy with his men in the field, training for that possible Communist invasion or terrorist insurgency.

"Alex?" Red's voice blared like an old tuba, heavy, low and loud. "What's the matter?"

"Why are you home?"

"My men and I are going out on a training mission tomorrow. I'm spending the last night at home just in case I don't make it back. You know the way it goes."

Alex knew. Red always held to tradition. In Nam, before every mission, he and his men went into town for a night of wine, women, and song. For many, it would be their last night on earth, so it was time well spent. But a training mission seemed a rather lame excuse to uphold the tradition.

"Why are you calling?"

Alex shifted the phone to his other ear. "I need you for a dangerous mission."

"What are you talking about?"

"*The Ark.*"

Silence.

Alex knew it had been a long time since Red had heard that name. It must've sent a shiver up the old soldier's spine.

"What does he need?"

"We can't discuss it over the phone. Be at Solartech

Field in Simi Valley tomorrow morning. I'll fill you in then."

"We're flying out of Edwards on a C-130 transport. I can be there by 6:00 AM."

"How many men?"

"Thirty-nine troops, top notch, I tell ya, heavily armed." A hint of excitement radiated from his voice.

"Any C-4?"

"Enough to level Disneyland. Will that do?"

"Nicely. Tell Virginia I said goodbye."

"See you at six."

#

Red set the receiver down slowly, turned to his wife and held her close. If it weren't for Alex, he'd never have met her. Funny thing about love, how it takes its own course. There were winners and losers in war, winners and losers in love. Alex lost on both counts, a bullet knocked him out of the war, and his woman fell in love with his best friend. Maybe his luck would change. Maybe not. *The Ark* was certainly no guarantee.

Red put his hands on Virginia's shoulders and looked into her eyes. "The mission tomorrow is for real."

He didn't need to say any more. She took his hand and led the way upstairs.

Chapter 28

As THE EARLY MORNING SUN cast long shadows across Solartech Field, Alex leaned on the fender of a security bus, his eyes on a C-130 Hercules touching down on the rubber-scarred runway. Tires screeched; blue smoke swirled. With full flaps deployed and reverse thrusters roaring, the huge aircraft slowed and taxied to the tarmac. Four turboprop engines droned to a stop; the propellers coasted on their own momentum. The cargo ramp whined to the ground.

Red marched out of the plane, alone. His troops formed a double-file formation inside the fuselage, helmets on, rifles slung from their shoulders. Standing at attention, they were waiting for an order to disembark.

Treading toward the bus, Red didn't smile. The years had been hard on him. Though his stocky frame carried him upright, the wrinkles on his face gave away his age, maybe more than he deserved. His jowls hung lower than Alex remembered, but pride still glowed in the soldier's eyes. He was a strong man, a dangerous man.

Goose bumps climbed up Alex's arms as he remembered the chaos, the rapid fire of machineguns, the fecal smell of the rice paddy, men yelling, men moaning, men dying. Alex had never known fear like that before. It seemed like only yesterday when that AK-47 bullet slammed into his chest and ripped through a lung. It started leaking air like a punctured tire. Moments later, Red had hold of him, cursing, firing his M-16 wildly and dragging him through the muck to cover. Seeing Red brought it all back. Alex thought he'd be sick. He swallowed hard, greeted the old soldier with a salute, and followed him into the bus.

"What does *The Ark* want me to do?" Red asked.

On a makeshift table set up across the aisle, Alex laid out a map. "Dr. Curtis, the CEO of Solartech Labs, tells me that Devin, here at Atomtech in Nevada," he pointed to an *X* on the map, "is trying to kill two of our key personnel as they make their way toward Simi Valley." He traced his finger south from San Francisco. "It's our job to stop him."

Red looked over the map.

"Currently, Devin is inside the Atomtech compound directing operations against our people. We need to get in close, infiltrate, and eliminate him."

Red lifted his eyebrows. "A real live bad guy, huh?"

"Bad enough for *The Ark* to want him put out of commission."

"That's bad enough for me."

Alex folded the map. "I've laid out a model of the Atomtech facility in the main briefing room of C-Wing. We'll put together our mission teams and set a timetable for executing the assault. But we must be ready to go tonight."

"Then we'd better get started." Red jumped from the bus and headed back to his men. He barked commands; they filed down the cargo ramp and marched across the tarmac as if performing in a Veterans Day parade. The fully armed formation halted on command and stood at attention.

Red approached the C-130 pilots, saluted, and talked with them for a moment. After an about-face military turn, he marched back to his men. With a sharp command, the formation paraded toward the bus. Alex, his chest swelling with pride, stepped aside as the men boarded and took their seats.

"At ease, men," Red ordered. "We'll be moving into a briefing room to prepare for tonight's mission. No Smoking."

The bus rumbled toward C-Wing. Smiling, Red looked over the troops under his command and said to Alex, "Just like the good old days."

Alex didn't smile. He just watched the rocky hillside sweep by outside the windows and wondered if Red and his men could stop Devin before he killed Janis Mackey and Ray Crawford.

Chapter 29

IN THE GUEST ROOM of Lo Chin's mansion, knocking on the door rousted Janis from sleep. "Go away," he mumbled.

More knocking.

He suddenly remembered Lisa, Lo Chin, the mansion. A dinging chime sounded eight times from somewhere inside the house. Groping for his glasses, he checked the nightstand clock: *8:00 AM.* He yawned. The knocking persisted. "Okay. I'm awake."

Lisa rushed in and threw herself on his bed. "Good morning, cowboy." She tried to kiss him on the lips, but he turned his head and gave her a cheek instead.

After all, she was Ray's daughter.

Lying there, he allowed his arms to wrap around her, delighted by the softness of her silky nightgown pressed against his chest. Her body felt warm, smooth, and inviting. Too warm, smooth, and inviting. He rolled her onto her side. "Listen, Lisa, you have to understand—"

"What? We're both adults."

"I'm not used to women throwing themselves on me."

"With me around, you'd better get used to it."

He gazed into her blue eyes and took in the flowery scent of her perfume. There'd been worse things in his life he'd had to get used to. "Up you go, young lady," he forced himself to say. "Get dressed and packed."

She flashed him a crafty smile. "Can I stay a while longer?"

"No." He couldn't believe he'd said that word.

Her smile drooped into a sad puppy-dog face. "Okay." She sat up on the bed and stretched. By the light from the window, he could see the silhouette of her figure through her thin nightgown. It was obvious she was trying to make him regret his decision to send her out of the bedroom.

Leaning over him with her blond hair hanging down around his face like a shimmering curtain of sunshine, she kissed him, a soft hot kiss on the lips this time, the kind that made him want to surrender to her charms in spite of his convictions. He gathered his resistance and broke off the kiss. "Git along, little doggie." He chuckled. "Cowboy talk."

"Don't dally, cowboy." She slid off the bed and sauntered to the door, looked back, winked, and disappeared down the hall.

Though she was gone, her fragrance still lingered in the air and on the sheets. Janis climbed out of bed and shuffled into the bathroom. "I'm too old for this shit."

***

Sitting on the patio by the pool, Lo sipped his coffee.

Jeffries, Lo's butler of twenty years, set the coffee pot on the table. "Lovely morning, sir." His pudgy face always had a smile for his boss. "It's a shame about your limo."

"I called insurance company," Lo replied bitterly. "Bombing is an act of terrorism. They won't cover the loss."

"I told you not to sign the waiver, sir."

"Just show Dr. Mackey out here. We need to talk before he goes on trip today."

"Soon as I see him." Jeffries went back to the kitchen.

Lisa bounded onto the patio dressed in blue-jean shorts and a white blouse with the shirttails tied above her navel. Her sandals slapped the slate deck as she skipped around the tables and chairs to Lo. With a kiss to his cheek and a cheery, "Morning," she helped herself to a chair next to him.

"You look like cat that got the mouse this morning.

Were you a good girl last night?"

"I don't know what's gotten into me, Lo. Must be love."

"Ah, yes. About time Lisa find love. Now you must lose hate. Only then will you find happiness. Today is good day to start. Your father will be here. 10:00 sharp."

"No way. He's coming here?"

"I hear doctor Janis tell him on phone last night, before you rush in and get all mushy. He says you go on trip together. Bad time for bad feelings, Miss Lisa."

#

Lisa pulled her knees up to her chest and hugged her legs. She held no hope for changing her feelings for her father, too many years of hate and anger to erase, but she had to be strong. She had to keep the peace for Janis's sake. Gritting her teeth, she turned her attention to the calm surface of the pool, its crystal clear water relaxing her mind. She'd deal with her father in her own time, her own way.

#

"Whoa. Look at this layout," Janis said as he stepped onto the patio. "What do you do to deserve all this?" He took a seat at the table.

"Computers," Lo said. "I program the ones called 'Super.' They're all the same to me. Glad you like."

Janis glanced at Lisa. She winked.

The doorbell rang. Janis checked his watch. It was only 8:55, so it couldn't be Ray at the door. That showdown was coming at 10:00. He planned to confront his old college pal about the way he'd treated his daughter.

"Fed Ex," Jeffries announced as he opened the front door.

The courier's voice carried through the house. "Guaranteed delivery by nine AM and it's here with five minutes to spare. Sign right there."

"Have a nice day," Jeffries said. Moments later, he

appeared on the patio, carrying a package, which he set on the table in front of Lo then headed back to the kitchen.

Lo examined the box wrapped in brown paper. He seemed puzzled, his thin gray eyebrows taut, forehead furrowed. A message stamped in large black letters read: *Guaranteed Delivery by 9:00 AM.*

Janis didn't see a return address. That seemed odd.

The chime from the clock in the house began to sound the hour.

Ding. Ding. Ding.

Brown paper. Lo didn't look like the type of guy who ordered porn over the Internet.

"Say one thing," Lo said. "It's on time. I wonder..."

Ding. Ding. Ding.

Janis caught the look in Lo's eyes. It seemed as if he was locked in the terror of his own thoughts. Considering the events of the past twenty-four hours, anything was possible.

Ding. Ding...

At the risk of drowning a new blowup doll, Janis grabbed the package and pitched it into the pool.

Lo flung Lisa to the grass.

Janis hit the patio deck, belly first.

A numbing explosion erupted from the pool, blasting water into the air like a Yellowstone geyser. Windows on the backside of the house shattered and blew inside. The shock wave echoed into the distance, rolling away like thunder. Pool water rained down from the sky.

Ears ringing, Janis scrambled to his feet and ran to the pool. Most of the water was gone, the tiles cracked. He looked up to the twisted patio roof where water cascaded over the buckled eave.

Jeffries screamed.

Turning toward the back door, Janis saw the butler stagger out of the kitchen, blood gushing from his chest.

"Help me." He fell, his blood quickly pooling on the

gray patio slate.

Janis rushed to his side. It didn't look good. Hand shaking, Janis positioned it over the gushing wound and pressed down hard.

A blast of pain shrieked up his arm. He pulled his hand away and stared at a bloody gash in his palm. Shocked, he suddenly realized a jagged blade of glass was buried in Jeffries' chest, a shard of window that had been turned into deadly shrapnel by the blast. It glistened like a diamond wrapped in a scarlet shroud.

"Damn it." He squeezed his wrist. How stupid was that? He should have checked the wound for foreign objects. First Aid training 101, all the college professors were required to take it. Under the stress of the moment, he'd forgotten. "I need a towel."

Lo pointed to the pool room and Lisa ran.

"I'll Call 911." Lo disappeared inside the house as Lisa brought towels.

Janis pressed a towel to Jeffries' wound, but it quickly became soaked red. He grabbed another. Jeffries' body jerked. His breaths were but short erratic pants now. His blood pressure was probably zeroing out. Janis saw death in his face, which had turned ghostly white, his eyes wide open, pupils fixed and dilated. A moment later, he went still.

Lo ran to his side and knelt. "Hang on, Jeffries." He shook his aide's shoulder.

Janis stood and looked at his blood-soaked hands, not able to tell the difference between Jeffries' blood and his own. A rage swept over him. Devin had to be stopped.

California was again assailed by the wail of sirens approaching in the distance. Janis grabbed another towel, wrapped his hand, and then turned to find Lisa. She was lying on her back in the grass, her eyes staring up into a misty blue sky. Janis knelt at her side.

"I couldn't bear to watch him die." Her chin quivered

as she fought back tears.

Janis stroked her shoulder. "I know," he said softly. Looking around at the destruction, he suddenly realized that Lo Chin's life was in peril now, too.

As Lo directed paramedics to the patio, Janis could see sorrow etched deep in his face, his eyes shining from tears that didn't flow. Standing by Jeffries side, Lo watched the medical team attempt to revive him. Hope faded from their faces. All the medical technology in the world couldn't save him.

#

After homicide detectives took photos of the scene, the coroner laid Jeffries on a body bag and unceremoniously zipped it around him. Crime scene investigators lifted him to a gurney.

Detective Lieutenant Michaels walked out of the house and stood on the bloodied patio, his hair uncombed, his face unshaven. He looked annoyed. "Where's the owner of this place?"

Lo acknowledged with an index finger in the air.

Janis panicked when he caught Michael's glare. The cop had recognized him from last night. Lisa rushed to Janis's side.

"What's with you two?" Michaels strode toward them, the anger in his voice venomous. "How come I see you every time something gets blown up in this town?"

"Just lucky, I guess." Janis didn't care if he sounded sarcastic. "You weren't interested in what we had to say last night, so why should this morning be any different?"

"Last night we didn't have a customer for the morgue." Michaels sneered and turned a full circle while scanning the wrecked backyard. "What did this?"

"Mail bomb," Lo said.

"Sounds like a job for the Feds."

"That's right," Janis said. "You haven't got enough talent to find a firecracker on the Fourth of July. We told you Devin was dangerous. Have you got that now?"

"Look, Dr. Smart-Guy," Michaels growled, pointing a stiff finger at Janis. "Any more lip out of you and it'll be a night in county jail. Have you got that now?"

Janis stared at the officer, frustrated with his arrogant attitude but electing not to press his anger any further.

Michaels turned to Lo, put a hand on his shoulder. "What's this all about?"

"You guess, me guess. Same thing. I only know we're in trouble. Must find safe place."

"All four of us have to make a break for Simi Valley," Janis said.

Lo looked at Lisa, his eyes heavy with loss. "Devin will pay for this. I promise."

"But won't you have to sleep with the enemy to get your revenge?"

"Don't care no more."

Chapter 30

R<small>AY</small> ARRIVED in his Jeep Wagoneer. He spotted Detective Michaels walking out of the house on Willow Circle. "What's going on?"

"Your friend is out back," Michaels said. "I can't protect you people, you know." He walked backwards toward his squad car. "You better run for your lives."

Ray stood in the street and watched the police car start up and careen around the corner. What was that all about? He went into the house. Glass littered the floor. A coroner's gurney rattled through the dining room, complete with body bag. Janis followed behind. He looked ten years older than yesterday. Ray shivered. "What happened?"

"Your 13th Power just claimed another victim."

Ray followed Janis out to a patio strewn with broken glass and stained with blood. "How?"

"Devin struck again."

Ray saw the damaged pool. "He bombed the pool?"

"Something like that."

A blond woman turned to the sound of Ray's voice. His stomach knotted. "Lisa?" He couldn't believe his eyes. "What are you doing here?"

She glared at him for a moment then gave Janis a hug. "You're supposed to be in Europe."

She kissed Janis on the cheek. "Well, I'm home now."

Ray set his jaw. Though a hundred questions rushed through his mind, the sight of her and Janis smooching sent a rage burning through him. "Oh no you don't." He grabbed Janis by the shoulder and spun him around. "Not with my daughter!" He connected a right hook to Janis's jaw, sending him to the ground. His glasses flew off and clattered across the deck.

Flat on his back, Janis rubbed his jaw. "Fuck."

Ray leaned over him, grabbed his shirt, raised him off the ground, and slugged him in the mouth. Janis's shirt ripped, and he hit the ground again.

Before Ray could recoil and strike a third time, Lisa jumped on his back, her forearm cinched across his throat. He tried to get a breath, but her hold was strong, stronger than he'd thought possible. He spun around, trying to throw her off, but the pressure on his throat shot a blast of pain up behind his eyeballs. He gagged.

"You bastard." Lisa was a wild cat.

Struggling to free himself, he caught a glimpse of Janis getting to his feet, approaching with a fist balled and reared back. A sudden gush of pain across the bridge of his nose blackened his vision for a second then filled his head with swirling, flashing lights. His knees buckled, and he went down. Lisa landed on top of him. Everything was spinning.

"Lisa. Let him go," Janis shouted, wrestling with her grip. "Now!" But she wasn't listening. She wouldn't release the chokehold she had on her father. Ray's face was turning blue. "You're going to kill him."

"All right." She let him go. "You don't own me anymore."

Janis pulled her to her feet.

Ray rolled on the ground, coughing, his nose bleeding into the cup of his hand.

"Did he hurt you?" She touched Janis's swelling lip.

He rubbed his jaw. "My glasses?"

She found them quickly. "He didn't need to hit you." She handed Janis his glasses. "He's a jerk. I'm getting out of here." She headed toward the house.

As she walked away, Janis put his glasses on and looked down at Ray. "Are you out of your fucking mind?"

"You're damn right." Ray stood on wobbly legs. He wiped the back of his hand across his bloody nose and glared at Janis. "Don't ever touch my daughter again. I'll kill you."

"Take a reality check, Ray. You can go to hell if you think I'm worried about your stupid threats. Professionals have been trying to kill us for two days now, so cram it up your ass."

Ray spit. "You're too damn old for her."

Janis agreed but... "Since when does love have an age limit?"

"Then you admit it."

"Nothing happened between us, Ray."

"I'm just protecting her from the wrong people. First her mother, and now you."

"Protect her? Hell, you condemned her. Because of you she was isolated in misery. You call that protecting her? I call it abuse. Where is your heart, man, up your ass?" Janis felt the need to slug him again, but Ray just glared at him as if daring him to start round two.

"Don't judge me too quickly, Janis. I had good reason for what I did."

"Good enough to justify her hate for you now? I saw it in her eyes, Ray. She'd have killed you, just like that." He snapped his fingers.

"I don't think so."

Lo pushed his way between them and handed Ray a towel. "Fix bloody nose. Playtime over. Kiss and make up. We go now, before somebody else comes to kill us."

Janis backed away from Ray and rubbed his swollen lip. Lisa was right; Ray was a jerk.

#

Lo watched the coroner's wagon pull away with Jeffries' body inside. The other official vehicles followed behind it. Hanging his head as they drove off, he realized it was time to take a stand against Devin, and standing with Janis and Ray seemed the logical place to stand. He believed in the old saying, *every dog has its day*. Lo wanted to be there when Devin had his.

#

Janis changed out of his ripped shirt and collected his things then he helped load the Jeep Wagoneer. They were ready to go. He knew the sooner they got to Simi Valley, the sooner they'd be safe. Grabbing his arm, Lisa pulled him into the back seat. Ray climbed in behind the wheel. Janis looked toward the house. They were waiting for Lo.

"Ray..." Janis said. "This trip is going to be hard enough with Devin trying to kill us, so how about a truce?"

"Sure, a truce. Fuck you." Turning around, Ray looked at his daughter. "You hate me that much?"

"More," she said, her voice icy cold as she snuggled into Janis.

"Do you want a truce?"

"Never."

Ray looked at Janis and exhaled. "There. It's settled. It's going to be a long trip."

The door creaked open; Lo got in. "Let's go. Keep eyes open for more bad guys." He put his elbow on the seatback and said to Lisa, "Teeth on other end of tiger tail sharp."

Lisa cuddled into Janis as the Jeep accelerated down the driveway and into the city.

Chapter 31

STEVE RAVEN PITCHED his Cessna for sixty-five knots, dropped the flaps ten degrees, and reported into the radio mike, "Desert Rock traffic, Cessna niner-four-niner on downwind for two-zero, full stop, Desert Rock."

The wings of his blue and white airplane glistened in the Nevada morning sunshine. He banked left and lined up with the runway. Bumping and yawing in the convective air, the plane descended. In the distance, heat waves rose from the brick and concrete compound of Atomtech. A blue van raced down a dirt road toward the airfield, a plume of dust swirling in its wake. Steve grinned. His plan to put the squeeze on Devin for more cash was about to swing into action.

Tires barked as the Cessna touched down.

Parking his plane, he recalled the Balli Club meeting. Curtis was passing out millions and Devin was paying him peanuts. He shut off the engine. Now it would be a whole new soccer game.

The blue van pulled up beside the plane, and the front doors flew open. Two heavily armed goons stomped toward him. They wore baggy black pants, black shirts, and sour faces.

Steve's throat went dry but he wouldn't give them any hint of his anxiety. "Who the hell are you guys, the welcome wagon?"

"No funny stuff, Raven," the big goon bellowed. His belly overloaded his belt. "Devin is in a bad mood, and some of it's rubbed off on us."

Steve locked the plane. "I'm real scared, can't ya tell?" He headed for the van. "Swing by the fuel shed on our way out."

He helped himself to a captain's chair in the back and took a last look around the airfield. An eerie calm hung over the desert floor where cacti and sage basked under an intense sun. The serenity wouldn't last long. Afternoon winds would intensify and temperatures were expected to soar over one hundred degrees. Bad conditions for flying. He needed to finish his business with Devin before noon and get the hell out of here.

His escorts piled into the front seat. As the van headed for the fuel shed, the big goon riding shotgun turned around. "You better have the stuff on that meeting or Devin is gonna let *us* take care of you." The bad guy grinned, revealing a mouth full of missing teeth. "Personally, I hope you screw up. I never did like you pretty-boy private eyes."

"Don't take a bite out of something you can't chew, Toothless." Steve pulled his .45 and pointed it at the goon. "Turn that ugly mug around before I blow it off. Get the picture, bean brain?"

The runty driver turned a frightful look to the back seat, and Steve switched targets. "You too, Little Man."

The goons turned their attention forward as he guarded them from behind.

At the shed, Steve called out to an old man dressed in gray coveralls. "Fill up the Cessna and send the bill to Devin."

"Yes, sir." The old man headed for the fuel truck.

Rumbling down the dirt road toward Atomtech, the van creaked and rattled. Steve surveyed the vast desert around him. It offered solitude for Devin and his henchmen. The place was bleak and dusty, surrounded by bleak and dusty. A chain-link fence, laced with barbed wire and entangled with tumbleweeds, stretched for miles. Four fifty-foot sentry towers stood guard over a complex of metal sheds and hanger-sized Quonset huts. The main building was constructed of brick, stood three stories high, and looked as big as four football fields. A huge array of antenna and satellite dishes decorated the rooftop. Steve chuckled under his breath as the drawbar angled up for the speeding car.

Piece of cake.

Chapter 32

FROM A WINDOW in his third floor office, Walter Devin watched the blue van speed toward the main gate. He knew Raven's plane was coming, having tracked its approach on radar. Raven should have a recording of the meeting at the Balli Club. Now Curtis's plans would be revealed.

Puffing on a fat cigar, Devin turned to his intercom. "Miss Rivers, get Leonard up here."

Returning to the window to check on his approaching guest, he sucked on his cigar, the smoke thickening the air. When the van pulled up in front, the men got out and disappeared through doors below him.

Leonard ran in, breathless, sweat shining on the top of his balding head. A rim of brown hair hung down to his collar, uncombed. His white lab coat was stained with coffee. Wearing thick black-framed glasses, he was an aging nerd who often boasted about his position at Atomtech, being the lead technician in communications, heading up the satellite reconnaissance department. From his eye in the sky, he could win any game of hide-and-seek. "Yes, sir, you called for me?"

"What's the story from San Francisco this morning?"

"Crawford and his mathematician are headed for Simi Valley," he said with a nervous twitch. "We aren't having any luck stopping them."

"No shit. A pack of Boy Scouts could have done better than the boneheads you've been sending to do the job. They can't do anything right."

"They're trying, sir."

"Like hell. They couldn't manage to delay a stinking cab, detain Dr. Mackey for questioning, or even disable a limo without blowing it to bits."

"At least they didn't turn traitor, like Ray and Lisa."

Devin curled his upper lip. "I see now I shouldn't have trusted her."

"You should've left her out of this."

"And *you* should keep your mouth shut."

"So what should I do now?"

"Track their every move. I want hourly reports."

Leonard ran out and headed downstairs to his control center. Devin stood in the office doorway and grumbled, "Dumb bastard. Steve Raven had better have some answers."

Elevator doors slid open. Raven pushed the goons out in front of him, Toothless at gunpoint and Little Man cowering along. Devin could only shake his head as Raven paraded the humbled thugs past Miss Rivers sitting at her reception desk. Susan lifted a sleek eyebrow to Steve. She seemed impressed with the private eye's entrance.

Undaunted by the menacing weapon, Devin waved Raven into the office. He wasn't a big man, maybe five-foot-nine, a hundred sixty pounds, but gutsy for his size. Wavy brown hair hung down over his forehead. His eyes were dark and daring. He wore Dockers, a flight jacket, and a crafty smile. Devin had seen his type before, a sleeper. Didn't look like a bad ass, but he was.

"I certainly hope you didn't rough up my boys too much." Devin puffed on his cigar and motioned toward a chair in front of his massive desk. "Have a seat."

"No thanks," Steve said. "I don't dance sitting down." His voice carried an air of confidence with a touch of malice. "I'm tired of babysitting your bozos. Get rid of 'em."

Devin snapped his fingers. His goons backed out the door and slammed it shut.

After holstering the .45 under his leather flight jacket, Steve walked to the window and looked out. "I don't know what game you're playing with Curtis, but it's time to ante-up." Reaching into his pocket, he turned to Devin. "This tape I have here," he displayed the tiny reel, "is worth more than a lousy thousand bucks. I'd say a hundred thousand would be more like it."

Devin took a threatening step forward, glaring at the greedy private eye.

Raven reached for his .45 but didn't remove it from the holster. "Don't get cheap on me now."

Leering, Devin sat behind his desk, propped his feet up, and puffed on the cigar. He studied Raven for a moment. Did the clever sleuth have more guts than brains? Was he bluffing? Maybe. But it wouldn't be wise to call him on it, not yet anyway. "Let's hear the tape." He slid a recorder across the desk. "Then I'll decide what it's worth."

"A hundred-thousand, Devin, or I destroy the tape."

"You'll get shit if I don't hear it."

"It's worth a hundred grand, I tell ya."

"What do you know?"

Steve showed teeth, then backed down and inserted the tape.

The recorded conversation came through clearly. When it ended, Devin snatched the recorder and threw it against a wall. "Damn it." He stood and leaned forward, snarling at the astounded private eye. "You fool! Curtis wants the 13th Power. The Higgs boson. The God Particle. Do you have any idea what that means?" He walked to the window and looked out across the desert. "He has Ray Crawford and Janis Mackey, the best atomic physicist and the best mathematician this country has to offer. And he has Solartech Labs. The Higgs could be his."

Steve leaned back in his chair. "So what's the big deal about Curtis anyway, other than the fact that he's a bit eccentric?"

"He's a fraud. His real name is Anderson. Melvin Anderson. He's a world-renowned archeologist, along with his father. They had successful digs, in Mexico mostly, until his father was killed. That's when Melvin turned to stealing, became a goddamned grave robber, made Indonesia his specialty. He stole everything he discovered; horded the good stuff and sold the rest on the black market."

"He must be worth a fortune."

"The World Society of Archeologists banned him from digging. He was finished, but the damage was already done. Countries he defrauded tried to retrieve their lost artifacts from the black marketers. Battles sprouted like daisies in a cow pasture. Hundreds died in the conflict."

Steve sat up. "What does an archeologist want with the 13th Power?"

Devin didn't look away from the window. "The Higgs boson is part of a field of energy that permeates the universe, stronger than the strong force, the most powerful force in nature, the particle that gives matter mass. He wants the power that's hidden deep inside the atom. Whoever controls the Higgs has the power to control the building blocks of nature." He looked at Raven. "Trust me, Curtis won't use that power for anything good."

"Sounds a bit melodramatic to me."

"He could turn a rock into a gold nugget."

"Wow. I'd like in on some of that action."

"You idiot. Gold is precious because it's rare. Flood the market with counterfeit gold, the price goes down and the world economy tanks."

"So it's financial suicide to make fake gold."

"Curtis doesn't care. By the time the damage is done, he'll have raked in billions."

"You should call the cops."

Devin huffed. "I reported my concerns to Colonel Fallon about Curtis. But the Air Force Security Police Commander didn't believe the imposter posed a national security risk. He said he didn't give a shit *what* was going on at Solartech Labs. It's a free country. Hell, he even had the nerve to accuse me of whining about my competition getting an upper hand on Atomtech." Devin blew a cloud of cigar smoke into the air. "Fallon is my best friend. If *he* didn't believe me, why would anyone else?" A chill went down Devin's neck. "So you see, Curtis is *my* problem. If I don't stop him, life on earth will never be the same, if at all."

\#

The room fell silent. Steve sat back in his chair, thinking about Devin's last words. Life on earth was a bit heavy. Money was the only thing that interested Steve, and a new plan was already forming in his brain. Curtis would probably pay big bucks to keep his little secret quiet. "Let's get back to the price, Devin. Sounds like my offer of a hundred thou' is right on."

Padding back to his desk, Devin snuffed the cigar in an ashtray. "It's in a safe, behind that picture on the wall." He pointed to a painting of a lovely young lady dressed in rags. "Go ahead. It's unlocked."

Steve approached the picture cautiously, hesitated, then pulled on the frame. It came away from the wall like a cupboard door. Behind it, a safe, its door slightly ajar. His eyes went wide. He was rich. Piece of cake. He reached for the handle.

Something clanked. A horrific sinking sensation suddenly engulfed his body. The safe disappeared as the floor swallowed him. His chest tightened with terror. Devin's sinister laughter echoed in the distance as Steve plummeted into darkness.

\#

Devin released a hidden button under his desktop and laughed aloud for his clever dismissal of the troubling private eye. With a clank, the trapdoor closed. After plucking another fat cigar from its case, Devin turned to leave. Life was good.

Miss Rivers appeared in the doorway. "What's so funny?"

Devin lit the cigar with a silver Zippo. "Just another day at the office."

She batted cigar smoke and coughed. "Where's the private eye?"

"He had to leave all of a sudden." Devin chuckled.

"He didn't go past my desk."

"He didn't have to." Devin decided to let her chew on that thought. He headed downstairs to the communications control room and pushed through the double doors. Walking down the center of the room, he passed a row of super computers, cooling fans humming. Along the walls, lighted consoles with multiple monitors buzzed with activity. Flashing lights: green, yellow, and red, pulsed rhythmically. Technicians in white lab coats nursed the precious hardware like ever-vigilant mothers caring for their young.

Working a joystick, Leonard aimed the probing eye of his Sky Spy Satellite, the SSS, Atomtech's hottest government contract. Watching over Leonard's shoulder, Devin could see an image on the monitor, which had been transmitted from space to a dish on the roof, a Jeep Wagoneer speeding through traffic.

"Ah, ha!" With a mouse button click, Leonard locked the SSS on target.

"You sure that's them?"

"I'd recognize Ray's Jeep anywhere. The luggage rack is broken." Leonard reached for a headset and put it over his ears. He positioned the mouthpiece and pushed a button on his control panel. "Racer Ten, come in. Sand Trap calling. Racer Ten, come in."

Devin couldn't hear the reply.

"Target locked on. Coordinates coming to you on one-two-four-point-three. Redirect now." Leonard paused to listen. "Confirmed, Sand Trap." He pulled the headset off and said to Devin, "We'll get 'em this time."

"You'd better."

Several technicians gathered around Devin and Leonard at the monitor as the SSS tracked the speeding Jeep. Like watching a movie from the top down, they saw the Jeep careen onto southbound Interstate 5. No one spoke. The deadly game was on again.

Chapter 33

STEVE TRIED TO SCREAM but the sound lodged in his throat like the blade of a knife. Sliding downward, cold darkness surrounded him. He reached out, groping for something, anything to grab. But there was nothing but slimy walls entombing him in a speeding tunnel of black. He was going to die.

Suddenly, the sliding stopped and the falling began. His mind swelled with horror as he felt the emptiness of nothing around him.

"Shit!"

A bone-jarring impact knocked the wind out of him, but the immediate shock of landing in cold mud made him suck in air. Yuk! He groped the mire like a blind man. Thick slimy muck oozed through his fingers. Even the air tasted like mud, and worse, smelled like a sewer. God he hoped it was mud.

A rat squealed in the darkness. His senses went on full alert. He was alive, but for how long?

Where was he? Was there a way out?

Rolling to his knees in the goo, he struggled to his feet, but his boots stuck in the mud. When he tried to take a step, he tripped and fell face-first, back into the slop. He spit. Crawling seemed to have a distinct advantage in this goddamned pit of horror.

On his hands and knees, he slogged his way through the foul darkness and bumped into a wall, which crumbled when he ran his hands across its surface. Dirt? What kind of hellhole was this?

He went to the right, crawling along the wall. Feeling his way through the mire, he encountered an obstacle in his path. A pile of sticks? Curved sticks? Chunks of wood?

Bones? Human bones! He gagged. A scream surged up his throat. He gulped stagnant air and feared he'd go insane.

"Where's the damn light switch, Devin?" His words echoed away quickly. "You bastard, Devin!" It felt good to yell, stifled his fear, and tightened his resolve to find a way out.

He crawled onward, encountering other skeletons along the way. What had *they* done to deserve Devin's wrath? His chest heaved with a wave of panic. Had they searched for a way out, too, just as he was doing now? They had obviously failed. Maybe there was no way out. How long had it taken for them to die? Probably days: starving, freezing, and lying alone in this putrid black hell. It must've been a horrible way to go. His future started looking bleak.

A rattling sound shattered the silence and turned the darkness into a terror he'd never known. Chills rippled through his body without restraint. He'd heard that sound before. A rattlesnake. He froze. Where was it coming from? How close? How many? How big? His fears of a long, arduous death had just been nullified.

What happened to an old hunting buddy flashed through his mind. Bitten by a Diamond Back, the poison swelled his leg until it split wide open. He died screaming. Steve swallowed the lump in his throat. Did he dare move? If only he had a flashlight. A match. Anything. Ah, his trusty .45.

Slowly, he reached inside his mud-logged flight jacket and slipped the gun from its holster. The eerie rattling grated his nerves, made his hand shake. He aimed toward the sound. *Give it your best guess, Steve.* Was it in front of him and to the right? He squeezed the trigger. A deafening muzzle blast lit the chamber long enough to reveal the rattler's broad head, looming before him, well within striking range. Its shiny forked tongue slithered back into its mouth as darkness reclaimed the mud pit.

The rattling got louder, faster, like the snake was really pissed off now. Steve shivered. In the flash, he'd seen a ten-footer, maybe twelve, its thick body slick with mud. Its rattles were stacked on the tip of its tail, a lot of them. He was an old boy, but he was alone. Not good odds against Steve's .45.

He fired again and again, counting spent rounds and lighting the pit of horror like flashbulbs at a photo shoot, the reports blasting, echoing, his ears aching. The snake struck, its fangs glistening in the muzzle flashes, its mouth slamming into the sleeve of his leather jacket. Steve rolled in the mud, shaking with fear, waiting for the pain, the sting of poison.

Nothing.

Big boy had missed. Crouching on one knee in the muck, he held his .45 in both hands and locked his elbows. Two rounds left. He squeezed the trigger. The muzzle flash again revealed the snake's head and flicking tongue. Steve fixed his eyes on that spot in the darkness. Steady. Holding his breath so hard his lungs burned, he aimed on that fix in his mind. Steady. He fired.

The rattling stopped. Mud splattered as the rattler thrashed in its throes of death. Then silence. Devin's pet was dead. A sudden spasm took hold of his guts. Had he just condemned himself to a long and arduous death?

Steve grasped on to what was left of his sanity. He ejected the empty clip from his .45 and slapped in a new one. "I'm going to kill you, Devin." Yelling made him feel better.

Wiping gunk from his face with a mucky coat sleeve, his stomach knotted from the stench. He thought he was going to throw up, a reflex he resisted mightily; he hated the taste of vomit. His clothes were soaked and caked with muddy slime, which he tried to rinse off with fetid water from a puddle, but it was no use. He leaned his back against a dirt wall, like his skeletal pit-mates must've done to await their slow and soggy deaths.

Just then a noise, like footsteps, echoed through the pit, a light now piercing the darkness above cliff-like walls. He heard angry voices yelling. Crouched in the quagmire at the bottom of the pit, he waited, he watched, his .45 again in hand. Was it friend or foe up there?

Chapter 34

Susan Rivers watched Devin disappear downstairs towardward the control room. Sometimes he could be such a jerk. She returned her attention to his office. Where did the private eye go, the handsome man who had single-handedly muzzled Devin's goons? She wanted to congratulate him personally.

Inside the office, she spotted an open safe on the wall behind a strangely hung picture. She'd never seen it before. Was there anything in it? As she stepped forward, the floor creaked beneath her feet. She glanced down and spotted the telltale edges of a trapdoor in the carpet. Stomach clutching with a sudden fear, she jumped back to safer footing. Where did the trap door lead? Had the handsome man been dispatched to his death? *My God.*

She ran to her desk, grabbed the phone, and dialed maintenance. As the phone rang, she looked up and saw Toothless and Little Man coming up the stairwell, machineguns slung over their shoulders, pistols holstered. They eyed her suspiciously, like her brothers had done whenever she tried to sneak a cookie. The goons plopped on the couch in the reception area and made it obvious that they were there to keep an eye on her. Calmly, she hung up and sat at her desk as if nothing important was on her mind. She had to think of a way to distract them.

"Can I get you boys some coffee?" She smiled brightly.

They looked at each other and shrugged.

"Be right back, so don't go away." She walked to the elevator with a casual stride. Once inside, the doors slid shut and she hit the first-floor button for maintenance even though the cafeteria was on the second floor. She didn't have time to play musical elevators in order to fool the sentries upstairs. Though she'd been working for Devin ten years, his dopey bodyguards always treated her like an outsider. She guessed they needed someone to pick on, and she'd always been an easy target. The elevator stopped and she rushed down the hall to maintenance.

Pushing through heavy double doors, she called out, "Booie. Booie, where are you?" The cavernous room smelled of coal dust and floor wax. She walked past a furnace room door and headed down a corridor toward the main electrical substation. "Booie."

"Up here," came a raspy voice from a catwalk above. The janitor, black as pitch, had been around when this technical wonder was built and claimed to know every inch of the place. "What's all the fuss about?"

A wave of relief swept over her. "I need your help. The trapdoor in the floor of Devin's office, where does it lead to?"

"Hold on now. Never seen no trap door." He slowly negotiated his way down a metal ladder to the floor. Breathing hard, he hobbled up to her, his thin hair dripping sweat, the whites of his eyes glowing. "No trap door, I tell ya."

She placed her hand on his bony shoulder. "If I told you to build a trap door in Devin's office, where would it go?" She hoped to spark the old guy's memory of the building.

He scratched the stubble on his chin. "Don't rightly know. Need to check the blueprints." He motioned her to follow him down the corridor. "In here."

The storage room looked like a trash compacter that someone forgot to turn on. There had to be a floor somewhere under the piles of papers, books, and boxes that cluttered the dingy room. And what was that smell?

"Excuse the mess. Don't come in here much no more."

She didn't want to touch anything for fear a bug might jump out, or worse, a rat.

He opened a huge cabinet crammed full of important-looking papers. Dust swirled in the air. He shuffled from shelf to shelf, analyzing old documents, some bound, some rolled.

"Ah, here it is." He pulled a cardboard tube from a shelf. On a pile of boxes stacked against the wall, he rolled out the blueprints and pulled the chain on an overhead lamp, which swung back and forth, casting eerie shadows that swayed.

"Let's see. Here's Devin's office on the third floor." He pointed to one plot. "Below that, on the second floor, the cafeteria. See, a lot of air ducts and plumbing here."

She looked over his shoulder as he continued tracing downward with his bony finger. "First floor's the control room for the old particle accelerator that runs under the desert."

He turned to the next plot, pausing as he looked it over. "Here. Below the control room deep underground, the wastewater holding pit for the accelerator cooling system." He looked up. "'Fraid it hasn't been used in years."

"What's this?" Susan pointed to an area above the pit.

"Stairway, ma'am. Goes down to the upper deck…ah…looks like some thirty feet above the bottom. There's water valves up here, too." He pointed. "That's where I'd make my trapdoor go. A metal chute from Devin's office to the pit. Right there." Pride rang in his sandpaper voice.

"You're my hero, Booie." She kissed his sunken cheek. "Show me how to get down there."

She followed Booie out of maintenance to the other side of the building. The control room doors were locked. He fiddled with a big ring of keys and looked up. "I don't have no key for these doors. Been closed off for years."

A chime came from the elevator. The door slid open

and the two goons stepped out. They scowled when they spotted Susan and Booie standing at the locked doors.

"Hold it right there," Toothless ordered. "Hands up." He leveled his machinegun.

Susan swallowed her rising panic. She had to think fast. "Sorry about the coffee, boys, I got sidetracked." She took a step toward the goons. Little Man stood behind Toothless. He didn't seem anxious to get involved.

"Damn the coffee!" Toothless yelled. "What are you sneaking around here for?"

"Well...ah...Booie here, he thinks the guy you brought here today, the private eye, he's hiding in there." She pointed to the locked doors.

The big goon's chest swelled. "Raven? That son of a bitch. Get out of my way."

The crazed killer opened fire on the door, blasting away the locks as if they were made of papier-mâché. Susan pulled Booie to the floor. Gun smoke and dust swirled in the air. Both goons kicked in the pulverized doors, ran into the control room, and turned on the lights.

"Raven," Toothless screamed.

"Those guys are dumber than dirt," Susan whispered. "Let's go." She pulled Booie to his feet and they ran in after the goons, who were searching around the equipment, crouching, guns ready as though they expected a surprise attack.

"He ain't in *here*," Booie said. "He's down them stairs."

The enraged goons clunked down a dark stairwell. Booie flipped switches that lit the upper deck. Susan scrambled down after them. An awful stench hit her like a punch to the stomach.

"Whew-wee," Toothless said. "Even Raven don't smell this bad."

The goons tromped over to the edge of a pit and peered into an abyss. "Hey, Raven. You down there?"

Toothless fired his machinegun into the darkness.

Chapter 35

STEVE GOT THE ANSWER he was looking for...more bad guys, Toothless and Little Man, their silhouettes unmistakable. Raising his .45, he took careful aim at Toothless. Tightening his finger on the trigger, he was about to pick him off, when someone stepped up behind the goons and pushed them over the edge. Screaming, they tumbled into the pit. Steve jumped to the side, again diving into the sludge. The goons hit bottom with a splat, landing somewhere close-by, real close. He could hear them cursing and groaning and flinging mud in the darkness.

"Hey, Raven." A woman's voice rang out from above. "You okay?"

Spitting mud, Steve wondered what a woman was doing up there? The sound of her voice was much too sweet for this sour place. "I've had better days."

"I brought a couple of friends to play with you."

"Thanks, Miss. But now I'm gonna have to kill 'em."

"Behave yourselves, boys. You'll need all your energy for your swimming lesson today."

"What swimming lesson?"

"How long can you tread water?"

Rushing water cascaded into the pit with a sound like rolling thunder. "Oh, shit!" Steve barely had time to holster his .45 before the torrent engulfed him. The initial blast of cold water lasted only a few moments. The pit began to fill. Steve could hear the goons thrashing around in the darkness, but he wasn't worried about them killing him. Right now they were busy swimming for their lives.

The cold water sucked the heat from his body so fast, he started shivering, his chest constricting with each breath.

He swam in the rising boil, which began to wash the mud from his body, a relief he welcomed in spite of the chill. The water level finally reached light. He spotted the thugs. They saw him at the same time.

"Raven," Toothless roared. "I'm gonna kill you." The goon swam toward him. Steve could see only rage in the big man's eyes.

Treading water, Steve greeted Toothless with a quick right hook to the mouth, knocking out another one of his precious few teeth. "Keep it up and you'll be eating baby food, you dumb shit."

The goon backed off, one hand over his mouth, the other trying to keep him afloat. "Damn you, Raven."

Little Man kept his distance.

As the water reached the upper deck, Steve swam for the ledge, leaving the goons behind. A beautiful woman reached for his hand and pulled him out of the water. He recognized her from Devin's office.

"Raven?" she asked. "Like a crow?"

"Steve Raven, private eye, at your service and in your debt forever, ma'am," he said with all the charm he could muster for the lady who had just saved his life. "But I don't understand. Devin puts me in here and you get me out?"

"Devin's crazy. I'm Susan Rivers. I just work, or rather *worked* here." Her smile could have lit up the pit of horror.

Steve took her hand. "'Pleased to meet you would be an understatement."

She smiled. "I was very impressed with your entrance."

Dripping wet and shivering, he was unable to take his gaze from her face. Her deep brown eyes bedazzled him, and her black hair shined in the lights. His admiration for her went deeper than gratitude.

Booie turned the water valve off and opened the drain valve. The water level in the pit began to fall rapidly.

"Help us!" the goons yelled, dropping away in the swirling water.

Looking down at the goons going around and around, Steve shouted, "Now you know what a turd feels like when you flush it down the toilet."

"Not funny, Raven. Give us a break."

Booie turned the drain valve off. The water stopped receding. From an emergency cabinet on the platform, he removed a rescue rope and tossed it over the edge. "Can't leave 'em down there to die, but this'll buy you guys some time."

"Thanks, Booie."

"Glad I could help."

Miss Rivers waved goodbye and ran up the stairs. Steve followed close behind.

Outside, they climbed into the blue van. Steve grabbed the wheel.

"Where are we going?" Susan asked.

He twisted the ignition key. "Simi Valley, California." The engine fired.

"What are we going to do there?"

"Get rich." Steve dropped the gearshift into drive.

"How?"

"You just leave that to me."

The sour look on her face told him she wasn't satisfied with his answer, but he left it at that. She didn't have to know everything.

Accelerating, Steve headed for the main gate where the guard brandished his pistol. Steve floored the gas. "Get down," he told Susan. Engine roaring, he smashed through the drawbar as gunfire banged and bullets pinged off the van as it fishtailed down the road.

Susan sat up. "You're going to get us killed before we even get there."

"Not if I can help it."

A moment later, another blue van burst through the

main gate. Steve caught a glimpse of the approaching menace in the rearview mirror. "That didn't take them very long to get out of the pit."

He raced across the airfield to his plane. "Quick. Get in and buckle up."

Flipping switches, he started the engine. The propeller buzzed to life. No time for checklists. He pulled the mixture, pushed the throttle, and steered down the taxi ramp. Heat waves shimmered from the runway. Fuel gages read *Full*. Not good conditions for a fast take off.

As he swung the Cessna onto the runway, gunfire rang out. He pushed the throttle all the way in. The plane accelerated down the center line, the blue van careening up alongside, weaving back and forth, gunfire popping from open windows. Steve clenched his jaw. The bastards were aiming for his tires.

Hot afternoon air and gusty winds took a toll on his plane's performance. Because of the added weight of a passenger and full fuel tanks, he'd have to lengthen his takeoff roll. It now became a life or death drag race to the end of the runway, only a quarter mile away. He checked the airspeed indicator. 45 knots. Not fast enough. It would take 75 knots to get off the ground. His palms felt sticky. The airspeed needle climbed to 50 knots.

Tires squealing, the van fishtailed. Gunfire banged. A round tore through the fuselage, ripping into the back seat.

"Shit!"…55…

The engine roared; the propeller buzzed. …60…

At sixty-five knots, the van began to fall behind. Steve looked back, saw muzzle flashes but couldn't hear the gunshots. Bullets ricocheted, pinged off the plane. It wouldn't take much, one slug through a gas tank or control cable, and his plane would go down. Almost there…70…

He glanced at Susan. Her eyes were wide, her fists clenched in her lap. The end of the runway was dead ahead.

75.

He eased back on the yoke. The Cessna sliced into the Nevada sky. He quickly banked left, away from the speeding van, which skidded off the end of the runway and plowed the desert sand.

Susan smiled, her face awash with relief.

If she was impressed with his entrance, she must have been impressed with his exit, too.

Chapter 36

MANEUVERING HIS JEEP Wagoneer through heavy traffic, Ray glanced at his watch: 11:30. They should make Simi Valley by nightfall. He looked at Lo Chin's long face. He'd lost his friend and employee, Jeffries, and his house had been bomb damaged. What a rotten way to start the day. Ray had a bad feeling it wasn't going to get any better.

He checked his speedometer. Seventy-five seemed too slow for the urgency of this journey. In the rearview mirror, he could see his daughter snuggling up to Janis. Again, rage boiled inside. Ray wasn't about to let her take up with an older man. Resolving to end their little love affair, he returned his attention to the freeway.

#

Janis lifted the bloodstained towel from his cut hand. The bleeding had stopped. "Needs stitches."

Lisa took a closer look. "Does it hurt?"

Forcing his fingers to move, he made a fist a few times. The gash stayed closed but throbbed. "It'll be okay." The fat lip he had gotten from Ray hurt worse.

Lisa hugged him.

He felt better already, but he knew Ray wasn't going to allow them to continue being this close. It was just a matter of time before he blew a gasket and started wailing on him again.

The engine roared.

"We should make Solartech Labs by sundown." Ray careened the Jeep onto I-5.

Janis glanced at the speedometer. "You better watch your speed, Ray."

"Troopers thick like flies," Lo added. "Best slow

down not attract them."

Ray looked at Lo. "Got a fly swatter?"

Janis chuckled at Ray's arrogance. It would be his ticket.

Traffic congestion of the city gradually dwindled to a scattering of vehicles on the highway. Janis settled back in his seat. The humming engine and whining tires calmed his nerves.

Lisa kicked off her sandals and rested her head in his lap, eyes closed.

He stroked her shoulder while looking at Lo who seemed nervous, glancing repeatedly between Ray and the rear window. Ray looked edgy too, constantly checking the rearview mirror. Janis caught one of his quick glances. Ray was watching him and not the road.

#

As the Jeep roared under a viaduct, Ray spotted a cop car parked in the shadows. But it was too late. He blew by the California Highway Patrol trooper at ninety miles an hour. In the rearview mirror, Ray saw the cruiser light up like a Christmas tree, throw dirt from its rear tires, and speed after them.

"Shit. We've got company." He sat upright, pushed the accelerator to the floor, and grasped the steering wheel with both hands.

"What you gonna do, Ray, outrun radio, too?" Lo said. "Just stop, get ticket. Then we go on."

"A police escort may keep Devin off our backs so just hang on."

But his Jeep Wagoneer was no match for the powerful patrol car. The trooper pulled alongside, motioning Ray to pull over. Ignoring him, Ray pressed the Jeep over 100 miles an hour.

The wailing siren wrenched Lisa up from her nap. She glared at her father. "You're going to get us killed."

But Ray wasn't listening; he was watching the trooper

talk into his radio, probably calling for backup. Ray had to think fast. He had to do something, even if it was wrong.

"Hold on."

Giving the steering wheel a jerk left, he veered toward the trooper's car. Fishtailing, the trooper regained control of his car and pulled in behind the Jeep.

Janis pushed Lisa to the seat. "Get down."

Ray swerved from lane to lane, and the patrol car stayed on his rear bumper. That was exactly where he wanted the cop in case Devin had any nasty surprises for them.

Cresting a hill, he saw a helicopter rise into view directly in front of him, a Cobra attack helicopter, black and ominous. Bombs, missiles, and machineguns clung to its body like pollen on a honeybee. "What the hell?"

The Cobra's undercarriage erupted in smoke as a missile twisted toward his Jeep.

"Oh, shit." Ray yanked the steering wheel right and careened off the highway. The missile struck the patrol car, disintegrating it at 100 miles an hour. The blast blew out the Jeep's back window and pelted the interior with flying shards of glass.

Lisa screamed.

"Son of a bitch." Wrestling the Jeep back onto the highway, Ray looked all around, his chest throbbing so hard he thought it would burst.

"Where'd it go?" Janis shouted, looking out the windows in every direction, his voice filled with panic.

"Goddamn you, Devin!" Ray yelled.

"That thing belongs to Devin?"

"He keeps it at Edwards."

"What for?"

"The Pentagon wants nukes on the battlefield," Ray said, his eyes still scanning the sky. "Small ones capable of wiping out entire divisions. The Cobra is Devin's experimental delivery platform. Of course, he ordered it with all the options."

"What kind of pilot would use it against us?"

"His brat nephew, Burt. What a brown-noser."

"Bad blood run in family," Lo put in.

Ray steered onto the shoulder to get around a pack of slower cars. A horn blared. He looked up through the windshield, searching for the Cobra, saw nothing but hazy blue sky and smoke from the burning patrol car.

Up ahead, a column of California Highway Patrol troopers approached with lights flashing and sirens wailing. Heat waves, rising from the highway, distorted the procession like some kind of vision in a dream, a bad dream.

"Help's on the way," Ray trumpeted, but his elation was short-lived when the Cobra appeared again, this time circling around behind the line of patrol cars. "What's he doing?"

Another missile snaked from the chopper and blasted a patrol car off the highway. The other cars skidded and spun around. Gunfire rang out as officers tried to defend themselves against the military menace. A trooper frantically called out on the radio. "Dispatch! We're under attack. Scramble the National Guard right away..." The chopper from hell unleashed another missile. The squad car exploded in a ball of fire.

Other officers, crouched behind fenders and open doors, continued to fire their handguns at the Cobra, which answered with blazing machineguns. Exploding projectiles ripped the patrol cars to shreds, sending metal and glass flying in all directions. Several officers fell victim to the lethal debris and murderous rounds. Black smoke pumped skyward and drifted west on a lazy breeze.

"Those guys don't stand a chance against that Cobra," Ray said.

"W-why is he shooting the cops?" Lo shouted.

"Probably doesn't want any witnesses that can ID his

chopper."

"We need to get off this highway," Janis said. "How about that way?" He pointed to a road beyond a field.

"Quick, Dad, while the Cobra's busy."

Ray careened the Jeep off the highway, through a bumpy field, over an irrigation ditch, and onto a dirt road that curved west under the smoky veil. The Jeep bounced and fishtailed, but Ray managed to keep it on the road. In the distance, he spotted a forest, and hopefully, shelter from the airborne killer. He pushed the accelerator to the floor.

Passing a clump of bushes, the road made a sharp turn to the left. Ray wrestled with the steering but his tires lost traction. Loose gravel pummeled the undercarriage as the Jeep skidded off the road, slid down an embankment into a rocky ravine, and landed in a creek with a bone-jarring bang.

Undaunted, Ray floored the throttle and slammed the four-wheel-drive into gear. The tires spun wildly, slinging mud and rocks as the Jeep bounded up the creek bed, bouncing and jerking. Nobody said a word as he negotiated a couple of tight turns and headed into the forest where he encountered a bridge spanning the creek. He parked between the concrete bridge pylons and turned to check on his daughter. "Lisa, are you all right?"

She wouldn't even look at him.

He heaved a sigh of relief anyway. "This isn't much protection, but it'll have to do."

They were safe...for now.

#

Janis threw the door open and got out. In the distance, he could hear the battle raging on the highway: machineguns rattling, handguns popping. He climbed an embankment to the roadway above, hoping for a better view, but the trees were too thick to see what was going on.

He looked up the road, spotted a sign: *Hollister 42*. He slid back down the embankment, ran to the Jeep, and leaned in. "You got a map?"

Ray pulled one off the visor.

Spreading the map on the hood, Janis quickly figured out where they were. Lisa walked up beside him, her eyes scanning the underside of the bridge where chirping birds fluttered about. Ray approached. "What do you think?"

"Obviously, the highway is too wide open," Janis said. "We'll need to stick to these back roads, cut over to 101." He paused. "But there's something I don't understand."

"What?"

"How does Devin keep finding us?"

Ray looked up from the map and twitched his mustache. "It's gotta be Leonard."

"Who the hell is Leonard?"

"He operates Devin's SSS, his Sky Spy Satellite. It's a new Google Maps prototype, and he's damn good at using it. He can track our every move from orbit."

"How did Devin get a hold of a satellite?"

"The SSS is nuclear powered. Atomtech got the government contract. It's Devin's favorite toy."

"Is there a way to hide from it?"

"We'll need to switch vehicles." He pointed to the map. "Maybe here, in Hollister and hope Leonard doesn't see us doing it."

"What about the Cobra?" Lisa asked. "How are we going to hide from it all the way to Hollister?" She glanced back and forth between Ray and Janis.

Ray shrugged. "We may have to wait it out here. It'll need to refuel sometime."

For once, Janis agreed with Ray. He listened again for the sounds of battle but only heard leaves rustling in the breeze and water trickling from the creek. Smoke blotted out the sun overhead.

"Is it gone?" Lisa asked.

"We'll stay put for a while. In the meantime, let's

check the terrain upstream, see if we can find a way back up to the road." Janis took Lisa's hand. "Come on."

#

Ray folded the map, climbed back into his Jeep, and watched his daughter and Janis disappear around a bend. "What's with those two?" he asked Lo. "We're about to get blasted into eternity and they go for a stroll?"

Lo looked at Ray, like a father would look at his son. "Take time to smell roses."

"You think I care about roses?"

The whap of thumping rotor blades and whining turbine engines filled the air. Ray braced himself, hoping he'd hidden the Jeep well enough. The death machine hovered above the bridge, pivoting around as if hunting for a victim. Ray glanced at Lo then looked up the creek bed. Lisa and Janis were nowhere in sight. Panic rippled through him. Where were they? As if his worse nightmare had just materialized, the chopper flew upstream in the direction they had gone.

#

Janis held Lisa's hand as they made their way up the creek, looking for a suitable way out of this mess. He heard the Cobra approaching. His stomach knotted. Their stroll had left them with no cover; the nearest clump of bushes was too far away to run to. He searched the sky. Where was it? It had to be close by. Suddenly, the chopper came around a bend, flying low over the creek. The black and ugly machine looked heavy, cold, and deadly. He pulled Lisa under his arm and watched the awesome power approach. Adrenaline spilled into his veins. He felt suddenly dizzy.

Lisa yelled, "Run."

"No." Janis held her firmly. "Wave. Wave at him and smile. He doesn't know us. We're just a couple out for a walk. Act like we're lovers."

Lisa clutched his arm and mustered a smile. They

waved at the chopper. The roaring menace inched closer and closer. Turbulent winds from its rotating blades kicked up a wall of water from the creek, creating an eerie wave of power and fury. The noise was deafening but Janis stood his ground. He waved and smiled in spite of the terror swelling inside him. Again, the Cobra inched forward. Any wrong move and the chopper would unleash its arsenal of death.

He could see the pilot, a young man wearing sunglasses and a headset, staring down at them. Lisa smiled brightly and waved harder. A few heart-stopping moments later, the pilot smiled and waved back. Turbine engines throttled up, and the Cobra rose out of the ravine. Janis felt a wave of relief. He looked at Lisa and hugged her.

A screech ripped across the sky. He looked up just in time to see the Cobra explode into an expanding ball of red and yellow fire. The concussion from the blast knocked them into the creek. Like a flaming waterfall, burning jet fuel rained down; chopper wreckage crashed into the ravine. A big chunk of debris tumbled down an embankment, spewing black smoke and throwing off broken pieces, rolling toward them at breakneck speed. Janis leaped up and yanked Lisa to her feet.

"Run."

The wreckage slammed into the creek, just missing them. It hissed and spewed steam like some kind of demon.

Dripping wet, Janis pulled Lisa toward the bridge. He had to dodge clumps of smoldering debris and pools of burning fuel. The air reeked of fire and oil. At a bend in the ravine, he stopped and looked back. Only then did he realize he was shaking.

His eyes followed the smoke churning skyward. "What happened?" he yelled. As if answering his question, the sky boomed with the thundering wail of four National Guard F-15 Strike Eagles screaming above the treetops. The formation of fighters zoomed overhead, pitched upward, and disappeared in the sun's glare, their roaring engines resonating away.

Ray and Lo ran around the bend. They stopped abruptly, their wide eyes scanning the carnage in the ravine. Black smoke pumped from wreckage strewn along the creek bed. Nothing resembled the Cobra. Burning fuel flowed into the creek, and fire danced on the water. Mangled and flaming debris popped and groaned in its own kind of agony.

"Right on." Ray cheered. "Did you see those fighters blow that bastard away? Damn, that was awesome."

Lisa turned slowly toward her father, glaring. Janis saw the hate in her eyes, but he knew what she was feeling, for he too had felt sorry for the young pilot that waved them off with a smile and spared their lives. So quickly he was dead and gone. No doubt he deserved what he got for trying to kill them, and for killing those cops, but still...

"Let's get back to the Jeep." Janis turned Lisa away from another conflict with her father. Ray and Lo followed silently behind.

When Janis dropped the tailgate, broken glass scattered everywhere. He sat and looked at Lisa, then at her father. Though the Cobra was no longer a threat, he wished he could say the same for them. They were their own worst enemies. What a waste. But right now, getting to Simi Valley alive was more pressing than their feud.

"Let's head to Hollister. We'll need another vehicle to slip the SSS. I've got a bad feeling Devin has more dirty tricks up his sleeve."

Chapter 37

W HEN THE MISSILE STRUCK the patrol car, Devin went berserk. "Damn it." He threw his cigar on the floor and jumped up from his chair. A simple surprise attack on the Jeep had turned ugly. Now the authorities were involved. "Shit." The press was going to have a field day. He had no time for that kind of publicity. "Get Burt on the radio, now."

"Racer 10, come in," Leonard said into his mike.

A column of patrol cars suddenly appeared on the SSS monitor. "Christ. This thing is going from bad to worse. Give me that." Devin snatched the headset off Leonard's head.

"Racer 10, over," came the reply.

Devin adjusted the mouthpiece. "Squad cars approaching from the south. Eliminate them first, then go after the Jeep."

"Affirmative."

The chopper maneuvered around the troopers. Two patrol cars were destroyed, then another, but the carnage produced so much smoke that the view on the monitor became useless.

"Where are they?" Devin yelled at Leonard.

The SSS was frozen on the Jeep's last known fix.

"Maybe they've stopped," Leonard said as the Cobra continued its deadly assault on the California cops.

"Racer 10," Devin shouted. "Abort. Find that Jeep."

A few moments passed before the pilot reported back. "I don't see it around here. I'll sweep the area. Over."

The Cobra began circling under the drifting smoke, at times becoming completely obscured. As Devin and Leonard watched the monitor, the other technicians went back to their duties, not wanting to get in the middle of their boss's new problem.

Devin leaned on the console. "Move the SSS to the west."

The monitor's view changed as Leonard worked the joystick, but no Jeep came into sight.

"Racer 10, follow that dirt road," Devin ordered. The pilot didn't reply as the chopper flew over a winding road that came to a bridge just inside a forest.

"Got something there?"

The radio squelched. *"I don't know. Wait, I see someone."* The chopper flew up the ravine. *"Two people, by the creek. They're waving at me."*

"I can barely make them out," Leonard said.

"Witnesses." Devin growled. "Terminate them."

A few moments passed. The airborne assassin didn't fire.

"What are you waiting for?"

"Negative," came the pilot's response. *"They're harmless."* The chopper began to rise out of the ravine.

A warning horn suddenly sounded throughout the control room. Leonard checked his computer. *Radar Lock Detected*, flashed in red across the screen. Too late. An air-to-air missile had been launched from somewhere outside the SSS's view.

Devin watched his Cobra disintegrate in living color. "What?" He threw the headset down and glared at Leonard.

"Not my fault, boss," Leonard said, throwing up his hands.

But Devin must not have heard, or agreed. He grabbed Leonard by the lab coat and slammed him against a super computer, knocking the breath from his lungs. "That was your last stupid mistake, pea brain."

Leonard tried to protest, but Devin flung him to the floor like a ragdoll. As he struggled to crawl away, a boot slammed into his ribcage. Stabbing pain curled him into a fetal position. With an outstretched hand, he pleaded to his coworkers, but no one made a move in his defense.

Like a rabid dog, Devin attacked him again, punching and kicking until he felt numb. Then Devin grabbed Leonard's throat. Hacking and gagging, he tried to break free of Devin's fierce grip, but a dizzy blackness began to envelop him.

Just then, Devin's goons burst in, dripping wet. "Raven. He escaped," Toothless yelled.

Releasing Leonard's throat, Devin jerked his attention to his henchmen. "How the hell did that happen?" He showed them his balled fists. "Nobody's ever escaped the pit."

"Miss Rivers done it. We tried to stop 'em—"

"Bring her to me," Devin ordered in a slobbering rage.

But any faint flicker of sanity that he may have possessed disappeared as the goons explained how she and the slippery sleuth got away in his airplane.

"Fools." Devin turned to the main control console and flipped a switch. A round opening appeared, and an active radar screen blinked on. All the bleeping images were labeled with transponder codes from commercial airlines in the area, except one. The unidentified bleep had to be Raven's Cessna, close to the outer ring on the screen.

Devin pulled a lever that extended a radar-locking-beam antenna. He punched the plane's coordinates on a keyboard. A moment later, the computer beeped a solid tone.

TARGET LOCKED.

He lifted a cover that concealed a red key. "Raven, you're a dead man." He turned the key. An anti-aircraft missile streaked into the sky, bleeping on the radar screen with its trajectory homed in on the Cessna.

Devin cackled.

A dinging chime echoed through the control room. *Range* flashed in red on the screen. He quickly rechecked the coordinates. "What the hell?" Raven's Cessna had crossed the outer ring and was now out of the missile's range.

"Son of a bitch."

The missile arced back to earth and exploded on the desert floor. Bleeping weakly, the Cessna's fuzzy image faded off the radar screen. Devin slumped in a chair. Raven had to be the luckiest bastard on earth.

Leonard sat up, shaking and pale.

"Get back to work." Devin growled. "You've got a Jeep to find."

#

Leonard limped to his monitor and grabbed the joystick. He knew that once this problem with Curtis was resolved, they could all get back to business as usual. But right now, it hurt to breathe. If this were any other job, he would have walked out; he would have sued, but not this job. He'd never find another one like it anywhere. Besides, this was his home. He had a cushy suite in the employees' quarters, three square meals a day, and better than average pay. His whole life revolved around Atomtech, and he wasn't leaving, no matter what. He looked at Devin who was staring at the radar screen as though its rhythmic beeping had hypnotized him. Wincing from a sharp pain, Leonard wondered what was going on inside the madman's mind.

Chapter 38

ON THE MONITOR, Leonard spotted the Jeep Wagoneer speeding toward Hollister.

"There you are." A self-gratified smile formed on his lips as he locked the SSS on target with a click of his mouse button. As he watched the Jeep racing down the highway, he rubbed his side and hoped he didn't have any broken ribs. A plan came to him. RJ's Rock and Gravel Company, just outside Hollister, had bid on a construction contract coming up for Atomtech, a six million dollar deal. Leonard licked his lips. Maybe Pete could help. Switching to the mainframe computer, he brought up the phone book. After finding the number, he clicked the mouse to dial it.

"RJ's. Pete here."

"It's Leonard. I need your help with something important." He explained his plan, emphasizing that cooperation would assure them the contract they sought.

Pete was all ears.

***

The gravel road wound through the forest and came to a paved highway. Ray turned left and headed toward Hollister, heavy on the throttle again. The Cobra's demise had been a great relief. Now, the unknown awaiting them up ahead had him worried. He was sure Devin wouldn't stop until they were dead.

Lo smacked his lips. "Let's find burger joint in Hollister. What you guys say?"

"I'm thirsty," Lisa whimpered. "A soda would taste *so* good right now." She wiggled in her seat and showed Janis her lips.

He gave her a kiss.

"That'll have to hold you for a while," Janis said.

"It's gonna seem a lot longer now that you guys got me thinking about my stomach. Thanks a lot."

Ahead, a flagman stood on the center line. Behind him, rocks and boulders blocked the highway. Ray hit the brakes. "That's all we need, a rockslide."

The flagman waved his red flag. "Just pull behind the dump trailer over there. We'll have this thing cleared up in a few minutes." He pointed to a tractor-trailer rig parked near a pile of rocks. A huge front-end loader with a bucketful of rocks roared toward the truck's trailer.

Ray parked the Jeep as he was instructed.

Rumbling, the bucket dropped its load of rocks into the dump trailer. Dust swirled. Backing up, the big machine beeped loudly and bounced along on giant knobby tires. Hydraulics whined as the bucket came down then the loader turned toward the rock pile for another load.

Looking up the hill, Ray couldn't tell where all those rocks had come from. There was no sign of the rockslide's path, no broken trees, no rubble, just weeded ground and stands of young pine. It seemed to him as if the rocks had been dumped on the roadway. Deliberately.

He thought about backing up, turning around, and going back the way they came, but another big rig pulled up behind his Jeep. Brakes set with a shrill rush of air. A lump formed in his stomach, spurred by a feeling of being suddenly boxed in.

Again, the huge loader rolled toward the truck, its bucket of rocks raised high. But instead of maneuvering over the dump trailer, it suddenly changed direction and was now looming over the Jeep.

Ray shouted, "Duck!"

The bucket slammed down on the roof. Glass exploded. Metal crunched. Lisa screamed. Suddenly, they were trapped, entombed on the seats by the collapsed roof.

Lo was bent at the waist, his head up against the dash.

"Lo? You okay?" Terror choked Ray's words.

"It's a little cramped in here."

Ray wriggled around and looked out through an inch gap left between the roof and door. Backing up, the huge loader banged its bucket on the ground. The diesel engine roared like an angry monster, and as black smoke spewed from the exhaust stack, the loader lunged at the Jeep.

"Hang on."

The loader rammed the Jeep, picked it up in the bucket, and raised it high in the air. Lisa screamed again. A fatherly terror engulfed Ray. "Lisa."

God, please don't let anything happen to her.

Like an amusement park ride gone bad, the Jeep tilted, teetered, then plummeted upside down and impacted the bottom of the dump trailer with a gut-wrenching jolt. Fragmented glass pelted him. Something in his neck made a crunching sound, but he was less concerned about himself and more for his daughter. "Lisa! Are you all right? Are you hurt?" She didn't answer. "Lisa!" Oh, damn.

He twisted around and looked back between the bucket seats. Janis had already released his safety belt, and crawling on the ceiling, he brushed aside broken glass. Lisa was with him. They were making a path toward the tailgate. Gasoline vapors reached Ray's nostrils, burned his eyes. One spark, that was all it would take. They'd be toast.

"Let's go." Ray said to Lo.

"Hold on," Janis said. "Let me get this seatback unlatched." He tugged on the release lever, and the seat swung forward. Bracing it with a suitcase, he pushed aside the other luggage and crawled to the tailgate. After pulling the latch, he kicked it open. Wincing, he grabbed his bandaged hand.

"Must hurt," Ray said.

"Like hell."

A diesel engine roared and everything lurched into

motion. The Jeep teetered, slid on its roof, scraped across jagged rocks, and slammed into the trailer's steel wall.

Cringing, Ray braced for an explosion and fire.

Nothing happened.

As the tractor-trailer rig accelerated down the highway, the Jeep vibrated and creaked, sending shivers down Ray's spine. Another wave of fear rushed over him. If the wrecked Jeep shifted one more time, the back of the dump trailer would block the tailgate, their only exit. They'd be doomed. "Go."

Janis propped the tailgate up with his foot. "One at a time! Hurry!"

"How are we going to get out of this trailer?" Lisa asked, scurrying under the tailgate.

"We'll have to convince the driver to stop," Janis said.

"How?" Ray asked, crawling out after his daughter. "Making up a plan as you go?"

"Is there any other way?"

"You'd better hurry up." Ray grabbed the tailgate and held it for Janis. "This thing could blow any minute."

Janis helped Lo get out and then followed him.

It was tricky walking on rocks in a moving truck. Clumsily, Ray followed Janis to the front of the dump trailer, and with clasped hands, gave him a foothold and boosted him up to the rim. Janis peered over the edge, and then Ray lowered him back down. "What did you see?"

"The driver, through the back window of the cab. He's alone and no one's following behind us, at least not yet. They're probably busy cleaning up that mess they made on the road back there. We've got to hit this guy fast and hard."

"How?" Lo asked.

Janis rubbed his chin.

"Unhook the air hoses to the trailer," Lisa said. "Without air, the spring-loaded brakes will automatically engage."

"How do you know anything about truck brakes?" Ray asked harshly.

Lo said, "Lisa knows—"

"This rig will come to a screeching halt, Dad. Trust me." She glared at her father.

"It's worth a try." Janis braced himself against the rocking trailer. "I'll climb down to the tractor and unhook the air hoses." He looked at the Jeep. "But watch out for that Jeep. It may come flying up here."

"What are we gonna do when truck stop?" Lo asked.

"We'll make a run for it," Ray answered.

Janis said, "We wouldn't get far."

Lo put a hand on Janis's shoulder. "Don't look gift horse in mouth. We have truck."

"Lo's right." Janis smiled as if he'd read Lo's mind. "It's a long walk to Simi Valley. We need this truck...so..." He looked around. "When the driver gets out to see why his trailer brakes locked up, let's hit him with some of his own rocks." Janis crouched down, picked up a big one, and handed it to Ray. "Bomb him from up there." He pointed to the trailer's rim.

Ray knew he couldn't hit the broad side of a bus but thought Janis's idea might be their best shot. "Got it." He grabbed a couple more rocks.

Janis turned to Lisa. "Stay here and watch out for that Jeep."

She looked back at the wreck, wide-eyed.

Ray helped Janis over the rim. "Here goes nothing."

Lo said to Lisa, "Tiger no like it when you grab him by tail."

Chapter 39

Rushing air whistled. The truck brakes locked with a deafening bang. Ray braced himself against the trailer bed. Tires screeched and smoke billowed from both sides of the truck. He smelled burning rubber. The rig jerked to a halt and the Jeep lunged forward, spun sideways and jammed between the trailer's steel walls. Quickly, Lisa helped Ray and Lo climb up to the rim with their rocks in hand.

On rusty hinges, the cab door squealed open, and the driver jumped out. Ray shuddered at the sight of the trucker's big hairy arms, tattooed with skulls and snakes, and how dangerous he looked in that sleeveless shirt and baggy blue jeans. The top of his head reflected sunshine.

Ray took aim and threw the first rock, which hit the trucker's shoulder. He reeled around, but the look of confusion on his face melted into a smile when he spotted Janis standing on the tractor, a whistling air hose in hand. Before Ray could throw another rock, the trucker grabbed Janis and threw him to the pavement.

"You dumb shit!" the trucker bellowed and stomped on Janis's right leg like a WWF wrestler.

Janis hollered and rolled on the asphalt.

Ray hesitated to throw another rock for fear he'd hit Janis.

Lo reached down for Lisa's hand and pulled her up to the rim. "Janis need help with little guy down there."

She straddled the edge.

Ray gasped. "Where do you think you're going?"

"Just watch." She jumped to the tractor and onto the ground. The trucker was about to land another blow on Janis when she put her hands on her hips and wooed, "Hey, big boy. Wanna try a piece of this?"

The trucker spun around, a look of surprise on his face. His eyes scoped the little blonde up and down. He grinned. "Don't mind if I do." He started unzipping his pants. Janis jumped on his back, but the trucker threw him off like a bothersome child. Walking bull-legged toward Lisa, he said, "Come to Daddy, little girl. I'll—"

She didn't let him finish. A spinning left kick to his throat sent the trucker to his knees, gasping for air like a fish out of water. As he held his injured larynx she said, "You talk too much, fat boy." With a swift kick to his temple, she delivered the knockout blow. He fell over and lay motionless on the pavement.

Ray swallowed hard and stared at Lisa, speechless. His little girl was definitely capable of taking care of herself. Why hadn't he known that?

"Let's get out of here." Lisa brushed her hands together. She climbed into the cab and grabbed the big steering wheel while Janis reattached the air hose, recharging the brakes with a whoosh of air. Ray and Lo scrambled out of the trailer and into the cab. Janis joined them. Lisa slammed the transmission into gear and dropped the clutch. The truck lunged forward.

Lo smiled. "Look like we found new wheels for trip. Now get burger and fries."

Lisa shifted gears. The turbo diesel whined to her commands.

Ray rubbed his chin. "Lisa, I didn't know you could drive one of these things."

She ignored him.

"And how did you learn to fight like that?"

With an icy glare she said, "Isn't it fun to get to know someone?"

A wave of guilt rushed over Ray. She was right. He'd spent so much time trying to protect her that he'd never taken the time to get to know her. Lo's comment about smelling roses came to mind. Though he'd never given that old cliché any thought before, he now realized that only a fool would go through life without taking time to enjoy the gifts he'd been given. And right now, he was feeling damn foolish. What else would he learn about her on this flight to Simi Valley? In awe, he watched his daughter maneuver the big rig down the highway.

Hollister was just ahead.

Chapter 40

THE PIRATED TRACTOR-TRAILER rig idled in a
Burger Haven parking lot. Janis helped Ray pull bags and
suitcases from the wrecked Jeep and pass them down to Lo,
who stashed them in a storage compartment under the
semi's cab. Lisa ran in for burgers and drinks.

Janis broke the rhythm of their assembly-line-like
chore. "No telling when they'll show up looking for this
truck. We'll have to ditch the trailer and go on in the
tractor." He paused. "Too bad about your Jeep, Ray."

"Dr. Curtis will buy me a new one."

"*Mister* Curtis," Janis corrected him.

"Whatever." Ray huffed. "Truth is, if the SSS is still
locked on us, Leonard will see this switch anyway. We
could still end up dead."

Janis detected frustration in Ray's voice. Had
Atomtech's high technology suddenly become a formidable
foe? It had certainly turned Ray's pride into fear. Janis
could see it in his eyes. "We aren't dead yet."

Ray just shook his head and tossed another suitcase.

Pulling the bloodstained towel off his hand, Janis
winced and threw it down into the dump trailer with the
Jeep. The nasty bandage had become more of a nuisance
than anything medically useful. He caught a bag from Ray
and tossed it down to Lo.

The afternoon sun ducked behind a drifting cloud and
offered a little relief from the heat. Janis wiped his brow
with the back of his hand. What he wouldn't give for the
cool mountains of Colorado right now. Was this how
Dorothy felt when she was ripped away from her home and
dropped into a land of beauty and danger? Looking at his
feet, he almost expected to see the ruby slippers that would

send him back to Boulder. Was Devin the wicked witch of the West? Janis shuddered. *There's no place like home.* He tossed the last suitcase down to Lo.

After Lisa returned with three bags of food, she unhooked the air hoses and electrical cord from the dump trailer and pulled the fifth-wheel release rod. Without bothering to drop the trailer-tongue wheels, she joined the others who were already in the cab. "Let's go."

She popped the clutch. The truck lurched forward, dropping the trailer to the ground with a shattering bang. Startled birds took flight. The engine hammered as they headed for the junction just up ahead. From a bag on Lo's lap, Janis grabbed a burger; he felt as though he could eat a hundred of them.

A door panel rattled and suspension springs squeaked as Lisa pulled the high-range knob on the gearshift and negotiated the on-ramp. The turbo whined. Slamming another gear, she aimed the semi south on Highway 101.

Chapter 41

JANIS LOOKED AT his watch. Two hours had passed as the semi raced toward Simi Valley. The sun hung low, about to be extinguished behind a thick bank of clouds that hugged the ocean's horizon. Lisa scanned radio channels for another rock and roll station. Janis preferred country music but let Lisa have her way. He enjoyed watching her bebop in the seat.

The radio squelched through stations.

"And the Lord said unto Jesus…"

Lisa pushed the seek button.

"The big black brother told the little mother…"

Squelch.

"…on I-5 just south of Volta."

Janis put his hand on Lisa's hand. "Wait." The cut in his palm began to sting.

"Colonel Fallon, the Air Force Security Police Commander, is investigating the possibility that the pilot, Lieutenant Burt Evans of Edwards Air Force Base, was disgruntled over a promotion he hadn't received. Again, the California Highway Patrol suffered heavy losses in the attack."

Janis balled a fist. "Bullshit. They don't have a clue. Devin did it, you idiots."

"They'll figure it out, cowboy," Lisa said. "Give them some time." She pushed the seek button, again.

"For your love, for your love…"

Janis leaned back on the raggedy green seat, cramped with the four of them crammed together in the cab. The diesel droned under the hood, vibrating the floor and making his feet tingle. He curled his toes inside his shoes. How were they going to get out of this mess?

The traffic into King City moved along at seventy miles an hour, and the semi lumbered along with the flow. Janis caught Lisa trying to cover a sleepy yawn. The big truck was wearing the little woman down. Any wonder. He should insist she stop and rest but decided to let her voice her concerns if she felt the need.

#

Lo kept his eyes on the highway traffic and the flow on the frontage road where the speed limit was much slower. The truck always overtook vehicles bound in the same direction. Except one. For several miles, a four-door sedan had been keeping pace with the highway traffic, always behind his right shoulder whenever he looked back. Once, the traffic on the side road forced the sedan to run recklessly on the shoulder in an attempt to keep up. At first, he dismissed it, maybe a drunk driver or some clown in a hurry to get home. But given the events of the day, he finally succumbed to his fears and gave Ray a nudge with his elbow. "Check out that car."

The sedan passed a slower car and almost hit another head-on.

Ray tapped Janis on the shoulder. "I don't like the looks of this guy."

Janis eyed the sedan. "What's it say on the fender?" he asked, squinting. "I can't read it from here…Lisa, slow down to fifty-five."

Releasing the throttle, Lisa hit the Jake Brake and the truck slowed noisily. The sedan didn't react to the change in speed and was quickly within reading range.

"Sheriff," Lo said.

The number 2885 had been painted on the roof. Tinted windows hid the interior, so Lo couldn't tell if anyone inside was looking at them or not. As the sheriff continued on ahead without incident, Lo decided his worries were unfounded. "False alarm."

"Steady as you were, Lisa," Janis said with a sigh.

The turbo whined in acceleration.

#

A highway sign boasted King City, two miles ahead with gas, food, phone, and lodging at all exits. Janis noticed the tank gauges hanging on a quarter each. "Let's find a truck stop. We'll fuel up and get some dinner."

"I need pit stop, too," Lo said eagerly.

"Of course," Janis replied.

The flow of vehicles began to congest the freeway as day turned to dusk. Traffic slowed to fifty, then to forty. Lisa started downshifting and working the Jake Brake.

Janis looked behind them, worried that some fool might plow into their decelerating semi. For an instant, he thought he glimpsed the sheriff's sedan as it changed lanes and disappeared behind a delivery truck. When it didn't show itself again, he figured he'd been mistaken and returned his attention to the traffic in front.

A speeding blue van careened down an on-ramp, veered wildly into traffic and smashed into a pickup truck, which sent it slamming into several other cars. They all skidded and crashed into a pile. Flying metal, glass, and blue tire smoke filled the air. A tractor-trailer rig locked its brakes. The trailer jack-knifed across an inside lane, crushing a compact car, which burst into flames and plowed into the growing pile of twisted vehicles. Hungry flames fed voraciously on spilling fuel and grew into a brilliant wall of fire. Black smoke swirled skyward. Two Fords spun into the inferno; the fire billowed like a belching monster.

"Oh, shit." Janis braced himself against the dash. "Lisa."

She cranked the steering wheel right and nailed the throttle down. Tandem tires squawked in protest, but the wailing turbo-powered diesel battered them into submission. With vehicles sliding and spinning everywhere, the semi reigned to Lisa's command, bounced off the highway, plowed through a weed-belt, and careened around the pile of death.

"Holy shit!" Janis yelled as he turned to look at the carnage behind them. Several other vehicles had followed their escape route, headlights bouncing, but a second later, a city bus bashed its way through the flaming pile and rolled end over end across the weed-belt. A huge wall of yellow flames licked skyward, illuminating the California twilight. The highway was completely blocked.

"That was meant for us!" Ray shouted, his voice charged with hysteria. "You, you saw the blue van. Where did it go?"

"It rolled over, skidded on side," Lo said.

"A-a kamikaze van?" Ray said.

"I don't think on purpose, just ended up that way. Devin may be crazy and his henchmen run close second. But they're not that crazy. Odds of us get in pileup too great against."

"What do you think he was doing?"

"Devin wanted to stop us with wreck; block road. Attack come from behind."

Janis looked back at the distant fire's glow. Only three pairs of headlights dotted the highway behind them. Nothing seemed unusual. "Let's get some fuel and get the hell out of here."

Lisa turned off the highway at an exit advertising free showers at Don's Truck Plaza. One car followed them but pulled into a 7-11 store across the street. Lisa stopped in front of a diesel fuel pump where a young man wearing dirty coveralls and grease on his face greeted them.

"Fill both tanks," she said.

Everyone headed for the restrooms.

At a counter inside where customers paid for fuel, Janis looked out the big front window and noticed the suspicious car was still parked across the street, headlights on and facing the truck plaza.

Ray walked up to Janis. "Is he waiting for us?"

Janis wondered about that as he noticed Lisa and Lo walking across the brightly lit parking lot toward the semi. But before he could answer, the ominous car suddenly accelerated across the road. Dust swirled in the air as it careened into the truck plaza and headed straight for the semi. Janis's guts clenched when he recognized the 2885 car marked *Sheriff.*

"Goddamnit." He ran outside.

The sedan screeched to a stop beside the semi. Lisa and Lo stood in the middle of the lot, their eyes wide with fear. Janis ran to Lisa and tucked her under his arm. Lo and Ray stood next to them. They had nowhere to go. The sheriff had blocked their way to the truck.

Three more sheriffs' cars squealed around a corner and quickly surrounded them in a tire screeching display of stunt driving skills. Car doors flew open; a dozen guns came out. Janis wondered how many years would they get for grand theft semi truck.

Ray, Lisa, and Lo huddled around him as he stared through swirling dust at the tinted windows of the sheriff's sedan. The driver's door clicked and slowly opened. Janis swallowed. One shiny black boot appeared, then another. The sheriff stepped out, a big man, with a big belly, dressed in a sharply pressed blue uniform and sporting a brown Smokey-The-Bear hat. He puffed on a fat cigar as he approached his captives.

"Well, well. What do we have here?" His gruff voice chilled the air. Pacing, he eyed his prisoners through military-style sunglasses.

"Should we just shoot 'em here?" he asked his comrades. No one answered. The sheriff, puffing on his rank cigar, circled around his huddled captives, the heels of his boots clicking on the concrete.

A crowd gathered, whispering.

The big sheriff walked up to Ray, face to face, and

blew smoke in his eyes.

Without flinching, Ray just glared at him.

"You some kind of spies?" the Sheriff asked loud enough for everyone to hear. "We don't like spies."

Ray said nothing, his eyes locked on the lawman.

Janis gritted his teeth. What's with the spy crap? Maybe the sheriff knew all about them, and Devin. And why wasn't he concerned about the hijacked truck? Maybe he was just being an asshole cop. One way to find out. Janis cleared his throat. "Do spies drive semis around here?"

The sheriff jerked his attention to Janis. "I ask the questions around here," he barked then drew his service revolver from its holster. He poked the barrel against Janis's temple and snarled into his face. "You got that?"

Janis stiffened. He could feel the heat of the sheriff's cigar and smell tobacco on his breath, but Janis wasn't backing down. Lisa gripped his arm as if to restrain him from further conflict. Still, all his contempt was focused on the menacing lawman's face.

"Go ahead, shoot me. That's what Devin wants, some dumb cop to do his dirty work."

The sheriff twinged at the mention of Devin's name.

"Shoot me, damn it."

Pressing the muzzle against Janis's head, the sheriff cast a quick glance toward his comrades and the crowd. "Damn you," he grumbled.

Janis stared at him. There must have been too many witnesses to the murder he was about to commit.

The sheriff looked down at Lisa.

She cast up her eyes to the officer. "Please don't kill him."

He looked again at Janis, shoved him away, and dropped the revolver to his side. "I don't know what it is you people are up to, but I aim to find out." He turned to his deputies. "Cuff 'em," he ordered and walked toward his car.

The California evening air echoed with the clicking of cocking firearms. "Hands behind your head," the sergeant shouted in a voice filled with anger. "Do it now!"

Janis looked at Ray. He sneered and raised his hands. Janis turned to Lo who shrugged and put his hands behind his head. Lisa's hands were over her face, trembling. In defeat, Janis assumed the position.

"On your knees!"

They dropped to their knees and submitted to handcuffs dealt out by several officers. Janis watched a deputy climb into the semi. The brakes released with a whoosh of air, and the truck headed out of the plaza, speeding toward town.

"Shit!" Janis said under his breath. "There goes our ride."

The sheriff got into his sedan and closed the door, again hidden by tinted windows.

Roughly, a deputy pulled Janis to his feet and directed him to a waiting squad car. His wrists ached from the handcuffs. He saw Lisa and Lo being put into one car, and Ray in another.

"Watch your head," the officer said as he forced Janis to duck into the back seat.

The door slammed, and he fidgeted, trying to get comfortable sitting with his hands cuffed behind him, if that were possible. Two deputies got in front, shut their doors, and began talking quietly. A wire screen stretched across the car, caging him in the back seat like some kind of animal. The driver accelerated out of the truck plaza in the same direction the semi had gone. Looking out the back window, he saw the other patrol cars follow behind.

"Where are you taking us?" he asked, interrupting his captors' conversation.

"The station."

"Are we under arrest?"

"We're just following orders. Sheriff Doogan will

answer your questions later."

"Sheriff Doogan?"

"Shut up and enjoy the scenery."

Janis looked around the speeding patrol car. City lights whizzed by and a dark sky showed just a hint of where the sun had disappeared behind a cloudy horizon. Again, he looked back at the procession of squad cars and shivered. Lisa must have been terrified, as well as Ray and Lo, too. But there was nothing they could do to save themselves now. He felt a bleak hopelessness envelop him as the caravan of cars turned into a garage marked "County Sheriffs Only."

The line of patrol cars stopped in front of a set of double steel doors. Several deputies emerged, rushed to the squad cars, and plucked out their new prisoners. Janis clenched his jaw as a deputy yanked him from the car. Quickly, he noticed an oil-stained concrete floor, gray cinderblock walls, florescent ceiling lights, and video cameras mounted high in the corners. The place smelled like gasoline. As the garage door rattled down, he heard Ray yell, "Keep your filthy hands off her."

Lisa had attracted the deputies' attention. They acted like they'd never seen a woman before. Three grinning lawmen volunteered to restrain her. Respectful of the law, Lisa didn't resist, but grimaced when a big fat deputy with mustard on his mouth said, "I get to frisk her."

"Don't touch her." Ray struggled to break free of a deputy. Another rushed up. "Got a real fighter here, huh?"

The fat man approached Lisa with groping hands. When his blubberous body shielded her from view, Lisa cried out, "Daddy."

Ray kicked the deputy in the shin and yelled, "You bastards. Leave her alone."

The deputy hit Ray with a nightstick, right upside the head.

Ray staggered. "Goddamn it."

Janis watched in horror as the crazed deputies went about their gruesome work. Glancing up at a video camera, he wondered if the damn thing even worked. Or maybe the deputies didn't care if this atrocity was being recorded.

Lisa's screams echoed through the garage and landed on helpless ears. The hoggish man finally backed away. Her blouse was hanging open, her black bra crooked. Janis wanted to kill the fat bastard but couldn't get away from the deputies restraining him.

"Knock it off or you'll get a bashing like your buddy," one of them warned Janis.

The leader of the mob stepped out of his car. Janis spit. "Sheriff Doogan. Can't you control your men?"

The fat deputy flashed a sick smile at Janis and licked his tongue across his lips in defiance, smearing the mustard. Janis tried to lunge at him, but the deputies held him back.

Sheriff Doogan stepped up to the belligerent fat man, grabbed his flabby throat with one hand, and slammed him into a wall. "Enough foreplay, you pig." Doogan kneed him in the groin and dropped him to the ground.

Holding his crotch, the fat man writhed on the floor, wailing in agony.

Doogan turned to his deputies. "The rest of you idiots better pack up your hormones and get these prisoners into lockup. Right now."

Janis felt relieved.

The sheriff turned to a tall, stocky deputy with a scar on his face. "Lawson. You're the Sergeant in Command around here. Start acting like one."

Lawson sneered at his boss and mumbled something under his breath. He herded the captives, single file, through the double steel doors and into lockup.

Before the doors swung closed, Janis looked back at the sheriff who was now leaning against the front fender of his sedan, a short stub of cigar smoldering between his teeth. The big sheriff held their future in his hands. They were at his mercy. A burning fear seared through Janis's veins as the doors slammed shut with a bang.

At a cell door, deputies removed their handcuffs and shoved them inside. Someone tossed Ray an ice pack for the lump on his head. The heavily barred door squeaked as it swung, shutting with a clang that echoed ominously down the corridor.

Sergeant Lawson twisted the key. "End of the line for you guys."

Janis shuddered and sat on a steel bench bolted to the wall. Lisa cuddled up next to him. He wondered who was to blame for this predicament they were in. Was it Ray? He'd followed his lust for fame into this jail cell. Janis looked at Lisa. Her hate for her father had gotten her into this mess. And what about Lo? Revenge was his demise. Then Janis looked inward. Money. Curtis had bought him with a million-dollar deal. None of them could hide from the truth. Their own human frailties had put them in harm's way. Now, cast into this dingy cell, they awaited their punishment for persisting in the quest for self-gratification, the most dangerous quest of all.

Chapter 42

Jingling keys attracted Janis's attention to the cell door.

"Mackey," a deputy called out. "Doogan wants to see you." He led Janis, handcuffed again, down the hallway. Sergeant Lawson got up from his desk and followed them without saying a word.

Fighting off a nervous quiver in his stomach, Janis wondered what Doogan wanted. Was there anything Janis could say that would set them free?

A shove from behind sent him stumbling into an office where the sheriff sat at his desk, a cigar clenched in his teeth. His hat hung from an antler rack on the wall above his head. The room was dimly lit by a lamp shining above a metal folding chair set in the middle of the floor. The deputy pushed Janis into the chair.

Leaning against the doorframe, Lawson folded his arms over his chest, grinning.

Janis sat facing the man who had imprisoned him. The sheriff's cold eyes made him shiver. The bright light made him sweat. His glasses started sliding down his nose.

Doogan pointed a hairy-knuckled finger at Lawson. "Get back to your station."

Lawson said nothing, left the room and closed the door.

The deputy switched on a recorder.

Doogan seemed puzzled, looked Janis up and down and leaned forward. "Devin tells me you guys are enemy spies. What do you have to say about that?"

Janis glared at the officer. "Are we under arrest?"

The sheriff didn't answer.

"What are the charges against us?"

Again, Sheriff Doogan remained silent.

"I want to make a phone call, right now," Janis demanded though he didn't know how much help Dean Billings could be from Colorado.

"Dr. Mackey," the deputy said. "I suggest you cooperate with this investigation. We can hold you for seventy-two hours. Make it easy, make it hard, it's your choice."

Janis looked at the deputy and then the recorder. Satisfied it was running, he looked at Sheriff Doogan. "Devin is a liar. He's been trying to kill us since we met in San Francisco two days ago."

"Why?"

"He doesn't want us working for Dr. Curtis."

Sheriff Doogan squinted, closed one eye.

Janis wondered how he could explain their problem any better. He had to find a way to make him understand. But how…

Doogan blew cigar smoke. "You're a math professor, right?"

"So?"

"And Crawford is an atomic physicist?"

"The best."

"How do I know you're not using your expertise against our country?"

"It's Devin and Curtis you need to worry about."

Eyebrows raised, Doogan mouthed his stogie.

Janis leaned forward, wishing he wasn't handcuffed. "Ray and I made a deal with Curtis to do an experiment involving nuclear particle research, the 13th Power to be exact." He elaborated as if the sheriff would comprehend the science involved. "Devin doesn't want us to do the experiment, for whatever reason. We are not spies."

With the cigar clamped between his fingers, the sheriff motioned toward the recorder. The deputy turned it off. Frowning, Doogan said, "Is the 13th Power worth dying for?"

Hot adrenaline lit fires in Janis's bloodstream. Dying? "You're going to murder us?"

"That's right."

The deputy grinned. "How we gonna kill 'em, boss?"

"Later," the sheriff snapped. "Again, Dr. Mackey, is the 13th Power worth dying for?"

Janis's fear turned to anger. "No," he shouted. "But those people in your jail cell are. I gave my word to Ray, and I would die to keep it. I would die for my friend, Lo Chin, too. But most of all, I would not only die for Lisa, I would *kill* for Lisa."

The sheriff's eyebrows lifted. "Do you think they'd do the same for you?"

"I think the question here is whether *you* would die for Devin."

Looking at his deputy, Doogan snarled. "Get him out of here before I put a bullet in him myself."

The deputy pulled Janis to his feet and pushed him toward the door.

"Devin will have you burning in hell," Janis yelled as he was shoved into the hallway. "In hell, I tell ya."

#

Sergeant Lawson quickstepped down the hall. He was sure no one knew he'd been listening through the door. The conversation went as he had hoped. He ducked into the next office. The deputy and Janis passed by without seeing him. He rushed back to Doogan's office. The door was closed. As he reached for the doorknob, he heard Doogan's voice booming.

"Killing them won't solve anything, Devin."

Lawson stopped to listen.

"I don't care about the money. Murder was never an option."

A moment of silence.

"You're out of your mind." Doogan slammed down

the phone and kicked over the folding chair.

Lawson didn't like the way that conversation sounded. Retreating down the hall, he slipped back into the office and dialed Devin in Nevada.

***

The deputy keyed the handcuffs and pushed Janis back into the cell. His insides burning with anger, Janis noticed a tray of food on the table, mashed potatoes, roast beef, and something that looked like baby food. A small carton of milk sat next to it. Empty trays told him the others had eaten.

"Our last supper?" He sat down feeling defeated, out of hope.

Ray looked at him, concerned. "What was that all about?"

"Nothing." Janis didn't want to alarm them over what Doogan had said about killing them. "How's the lump on your skull?"

Ray lifted the ice pack and rubbed the side of his head. "Still there."

"The bastards will get theirs some day." Janis looked at Lisa. She was looking at her father, but not with her usual hateful glare. He saw a hint of pity in her eyes. Was she feeling sorry for him? Or was she impressed with his futile attempt to protect her from the crazed lawmen? Was her hate beginning to fade?

He looked at Lo who was sitting on a cot with his legs crossed and staring straight forward. "Lo. You okay?"

Lo didn't respond.

Janis shrugged and turned his attention to the meal in front of him. It tasted horrible. When he finished, he cuddled into Lisa, closed his eyes, and drifted into an uneasy sleep.

Tomorrow would be the last day of their lives.

Chapter 43

JANIS AWOKE TO a dreadful clanking, a nightstick striking the bars. Through sleep-laden eyes, he saw Lo and Ray standing by the cell door, which hung wide open. A second deputy stood behind them, his hand on his revolver. The sight triggered foggy memories of Doogan, this jail, and murders yet committed. Though he couldn't recall what he'd been dreaming, he knew it had to have been better than the nightmare into which he'd just awoke.

Lisa moaned. "Huh?"

"What time is it?"

"3:30," Ray said without checking his watch. "Looks like Doogan has decided what to do with us."

Janis and Lisa got in line.

The lead deputy said, "Let's go."

"What? No handcuffs?"

"Shut up," the trailing deputy said.

The line of the doomed shuffled out of the cell. Halfway down the hall, Janis caught a glimpse of Sergeant Lawson lurking around a corner. The procession turned down an intersecting hallway and passed through double steel doors into the parking garage where Sheriff Doogan stood by his squad car, engine running and headlights on.

"Looks like we're going for a ride," Janis said as sarcastically as he could.

"Shut up," the deputy barked behind him.

The column of prisoners approached the sheriff and stopped. The lead deputy spoke with him, but too softly for Janis to hear their words. As he strained to listen, he heard a sound behind him, a kind of scraping that drew his eyes toward the double doors, which were now teetering on their hinges. He saw Lawson slip behind a concrete pillar. Why was he sneaking around?

Doogan stepped aside. The deputy opened a rear door of the squad car. He motioned to Lo and Lisa. "You two, get in."

With wide eyes, they did as they were told.

Looking into the car, Janis noticed it had no wire partition between the seats. And why weren't they being handcuffed? What was Doogan doing? Did he really think he was going to get away with this?

The deputy shut the back door and opened the front passenger door. He motioned to Ray.

Ray got in, and the deputy shut the door. What? That left only Janis and the vacant driver's seat.

With a quick wave of his hand, the sheriff signaled the deputies to leave. They disappeared through the double doors. Doogan walked up to Janis. "Your belongings are in the trunk." With a firm grip, he shook Janis's hand then pointed to his squad car. "She's all yours."

Janis blinked. "Why?"

"Good luck. You've got a long way to go." A smile lit Doogan's face, a smile that surprised Janis, warm and sincere. He slid in behind the wheel and shut the door. *We're free.* He couldn't believe it.

Doogan backed away from the car. "Drive safely—"

Bang!

The blast of a firearm echoed through the garage. Janis whipped around. Out the rear window, he saw Lawson standing by a pillar, his gun held out, straight-armed. He yelled, "Double-cross Devin and die."

Two more shots rang out.

Lisa screamed and ducked down on the seat, clutching Lo. Janis looked at Sheriff Doogan, who lurched backwards from two rounds that tore into his chest. Blood spewed from his shirt, staining it red in an instant. The big man grimaced and grabbed for his gun.

"You think you're so tough," Lawson yelled. "Take

this." He fired again.

The slug tore mercilessly into Doogan's shooting arm, ripping away any chance he may have had to defend himself. Hunched over and holding his shattered arm, he glared at his killer. "Now Devin has your soul." Another round ripped into Doogan's throat. Blood gushed to the concrete floor. His eyes rolled back and he collapsed.

The next bullet hit the car.

Janis's stomach knotted. *He's gonna kill us all!* "Shit." Panic raced through his mind as he grabbed the gearshift and slammed the transmission into drive. He stomped the accelerator to the floor. Tires squealed. Several more shots rang out. Bullets pummeled the car. Janis ducked. Engine roaring, he steered toward the exit and, as if propelled by a force greater than the 13th Power, crashed the speeding car into the garage door. Aluminum panels exploded.

Lisa screamed.

The car careened out of the garage and into the early morning darkness.

Chapter 44

SIMI VALLEY LAY in sleepy darkness. Saturday night, the town had all but closed down. Only light traffic trickled through city streets, most of the residents having settled in for the night. At a local park, two teams slugged out a baseball game under bright lights. Roaring turboprop engines suddenly overpowered a group of cheering fans. At Solartech Field, Red stood in the glow of floodlights as the C-130 Hercules warmed up for takeoff. His small paramilitary army of professional soldiers boarded the big transport. A Jeep slid to a stop at the cargo ramp. Red saluted Alex.

"Get her aboard." The loadmaster waved him in.

As the Jeep rolled into the aircraft's belly, Red sprinted up after it. Buckled into webbed seating, his men secured their weapons in sling-holsters. He knew it had been a long day for his men, forming assault squads and mapping out individual phases of a difficult mission. Alex had supplied high-tech equipment that would enable them to sneak-up on Devin. The morale of his men was high; they talked and joked freely while awaiting takeoff.

Red made his way to the flight deck as the loadmaster pushed the ramp control lever up. Hydraulics whined and the ramp closed with a bang, sealing the soldiers inside a crimson-lit cargo hold.

"Ready when you are," Red informed the Captain with a sharp salute.

Seeing the green light glowing on his console, Captain Baine taxied his huge transport to the runway threshold.

"Flaps thirty," the copilot announced while sliding the control lever. "Go for takeoff."

Captain Baine pushed the brake pedals down and

shoved the throttle handles forward. Four huge turboprop engines revved to a thunderous roar, shaking the aircraft violently. At maximum power, he released the brakes. His aircraft began its deafening rumble down the runway. The airspeed indicator came alive.

A blinding light appeared directly in front of him, a hundred feet off the ground and heading straight for them. A landing aircraft was coming right at him.

Squinting, he yelled, "Abort," and yanked the throttle handles back, shutting down the massive engines, but the propellers were slow to respond. He feathered the props and jammed on the brakes. The blinding light came closer and closer, lower and lower. Transport tires squawked; smoke billowed from the brake casings.

"Brace yourselves." He careened the transport off the right side of the runway. The soft, grassy beltway helped slow the aircraft, and he regained complete control. Looking out his left window, he saw a blue and white Cessna settle on the runway. "Idiot," he screamed. "You trying to get us all killed?" He aimed the transport back onto the runway and swung it around to taxi back to the threshold. He'd need to start his takeoff run all over again.

But the Cessna made a U-turn and headed straight for them. "Now what?"

"Is this guy totally nuts?" the copilot shouted.

Again, the Captain applied the brakes and stopped the big transport in the middle of the runway.

The Cessna taxied up to the C-130, nose-to-nose. The single propeller clunked to a stop and a man jumped out. He signaled them to kill their engines with a slicing motion of his hand across his throat.

"Shut 'em down," Captain Baine ordered.

The turboprop engines whined to a stop and the California night fell silent. Satisfied, the Captain turned to find Red, but he was already out of his seat and scrambling for the jump door. He swung it open and leaped to the

runway, his Glock .40 drawn. Captain Baine watched him run around the left wingtip and approach the troublesome Cessna pilot.

#

Steve Raven gulped as a gun-wielding soldier ran toward him. Quickly, he pulled back the flap of his flight jacket, revealing his holstered .45. "Put the shooter away. We're both on the same side."

"What the hell do you think you're doing?" the old soldier yelled, still brandishing his weapon. Another soldier ran up from under the right wing. Steve recognized Alex Gibson from their encounter in the mailroom. Several other armed men followed behind him.

Steve felt out-numbered, but he held his ground. "I had to stop you bone-heads somehow. I heard your pilot's transmission to flight service, filing a flight plan to Desert Rock. I made the connection with Devin. In case you didn't know, he protects his airspace with ground-to-air missiles. You'll be scrap-metal within twenty-five miles." He looked at Alex. "Do you recognize me without my fake beard?"

"In the mailroom," Alex said with a huff. "You have a lot of nerve coming back here."

Steve spit on the runway. "I didn't come back to play patty cake with you guys. I want to know why a C-130 is going to Desert Rock."

"It's none of your business."

"I'm making it my business." He offered the old soldier a handshake. "Steve Raven, private eye, at your service."

Red holstered his Glock. "James Colburn." They shook hands. "But you can call me Red," he said with the proud tone of a patriot. "So you're the guy who beat Alex's security. You know, he's still a little touchy about your escapade, so let's not rub it in. If—" A movement on the Cessna caught Red's eye.

Steve looked toward his airplane. First one shapely

leg then another appeared under the open passenger door. Red's eyes narrowed and he cocked his head as Miss Rivers peered around the door.

"Is it safe to come out now?"

Red's eyes lit up. "Please, come join us."

Steve cleared his throat. "This is Susan Rivers. She saved my life."

Susan ducked under the Cessna wing strut and joined the group of men.

"It was nothing, really. Steve is the hero." She strolled to his side and took his hand. "He just saved your lives."

One of Red's soldiers had been examining the Cessna. "This aircraft has seen some action," he announced. "Looks like ground fire."

"That's right," Steve said. "Atomtech is under a full security alert."

Chapter 45

ALEX SWALLOWED a lump in his throat. If Steve Raven was right, their plan for a landing on the desert floor ten miles from Atomtech's compound would be a death sentence. The missile threat called for a change in plans. In order to neutralize that threat, the missile guidance and radar systems would have to be jammed within twenty-five miles of Atomtech. He turned to Red, motioned him to the side, and voiced his concerns.

Red touched his cheek. "How are we going to jam his airspace?"

"We'll need the Aircraft Advanced Sensor Eliminator aboard the C-130. With the AASE, Devin's radar won't be able to detect our approach nor will he be able to zero in on the aircraft if we're spotted visually. It's another one of Solartech's new hi-tech toys, on the cutting edge of stealth technology."

"Like the PASE units that our advance team, Jackal One, will wear for the tower assaults, only bigger?"

"You got it. The Personnel Advance Sensor Eliminator is just a smaller version of the AASE." He looked at his watch. "One call and about two hours. That's all we need to get it onboard."

"Do it!" Red spun around and marched to Steve. "Miss Rivers was correct. You saved our lives with that stunt you just pulled. The mission is on a two-hour hold."

Alex activated his wrist radio. "Station two, get the bus back here."

"Affirmative."

Red saluted Captain Baine and gave him new instructions, concluding with, "and don't file a flight plan this time."

"Clear the runway," Alex ordered.

Steve jumped in the Cessna, started the engine, and taxied to the parking area.

Whining hydraulics echoed as the cargo ramp dropped to the runway. A soldier backed the Jeep out. Alex, Red, and Susan climbed in. They sped after the Cessna to pick up Steve. In cadence, the soldiers marched down the ramp and paraded toward a gate where the bus would arrive. With a whine, the cargo ramp closed again. A tug drove up to the nose wheel, hooked a tether rod, and groaning defiantly, pulled the transport toward the tarmac.

As the Jeep approached Steve's parked Cessna, Alex turned to Red. "I don't know if our scientists will survive two more hours. With Devin having marked them for death, time is crucial."

"They're on their own until we can intervene." He looked at his watch. "We'll still make our predawn strike time. It's the best we can do."

Alex felt as though Red was just trying to ease his concerns. He might have succeeded if he could've hidden the worry in his eyes. Alex was sure that Curtis's new mathematician was crucial to the success of the project. He had to be protected, at all costs.

The Ark's orders.

Steve jumped into the Jeep's back seat with Susan. Speeding through the airfield gate toward C-Wing, Alex radioed the tech lab and ordered the AASE prepped and transported to the C-130. "Meet you on the flight line at 2300 hours sharp."

"Roger."

Arriving at C-Wing, the men jumped out. Alex offered Susan a hand.

She accepted with a smile. "Which way to the ladies room?"

"Just inside to the left." Alex pointed.

Steve watched her walk away and then said to Alex,

"So what are you soldier boys up to?"

Alex glanced at Red, looking for a hint of how to handle Steve's question.

Red just shrugged.

Steve persisted. "You're going to Atomtech. Is this some kind of raid?"

Alex didn't answer.

"Tell him," Red said. "Or he'll hound us to death."

Alex hesitated, thinking, then: "Yes, we're going to Atomtech."

"To get Devin?"

"That's right."

"Good," Steve said. "I'm going with you. Any luck, I'll be the one to pull the trigger on the bastard." He slapped his holstered .45. "He tried to kill me, twice."

Alex saw the hate in Steve's eyes. He wasn't going to take this news lightly. "You can't go."

"Like hell."

"Let *us* get him for you," Red said. "It's safer that way, for all of us."

"No way. I'm going."

"What about the lady?" Red pointed in the direction Susan had gone. "Stay here with her. My men are trained to do the dirty work."

"But…"

"I insist."

"Then I want to see his bloody carcass, dead at my feet."

"I'll take a picture with my cell phone," Red said. "Good enough?"

Alex patted Steve's shoulder. "Then it's settled." But Alex knew they had no plans to take pictures or document this raid in any way.

Red turned his attention to the busload of troops approaching C-Wing. The brakes squeaked; the door swung open. He clunked up the steps. "At ease men. We have two hours to kill. The phones are still off-limits. Cafeteria's open, but no smoking. We'll meet back here at 2200 hours. Any questions?"

"What's the delay about?" a young mercenary asked.

"Just an equipment change aboard the aircraft. Our plans are still the same. Remember, this is not a drill. Devin's security force will put up one hell of a fight." He smiled. "Just the way we like it, right men?"

"Yes, sir," came the response from his troops.

He saluted his men. How many of them wouldn't see tomorrow's sunrise? Should he tell them they were being sacrificed for *The Ark?*

No.

He thought it best they die without knowing.

Chapter 46

RED JOINED STEVE and Alex in the cafeteria. They had already found the coffee. A few minutes later, Susan strolled in, her hair freshly brushed. Steve offered her a chair. "Coffee?"

"With cream and sugar."

As Steve headed to the coffeemaker, she asked Alex, "What's next?"

"You'll be staying here tonight."

"With Steve?"

"If you like." Alex activated his wrist radio. "Housekeeping."

The speaker squawked. *"Yes, sir?"*

"We have a special guest for this evening. Pick her up at C-Wing in thirty minutes."

"An executive suite?"

"The best one you've got."

"Anything else, sir?"

"Take good care of her. First class all the way."

***

At 2300 hours, floodlights illuminated the C-130 as the AASE arrived in the arms of a forklift. A staff car pulled up; its doors flew open. Six technicians in white lab coats jumped out and surrounded the forklift with its beeping cargo. Alex watched the loadmaster wave them aboard.

The ensemble made its way up the ramp and into the cargo bay. Gently, the forklift set the AASE down and backed away. Technicians began hooking up electrical cables to the big box, the looms of wire stretching across the fuselage, into the power converter, and up to the cockpit.

At the flight engineer's seat, a supervisor secured a control terminal to an instrument panel with a Velcro strip. He typed a code on the keyboard. A red light started flashing and *Stand By* pulsed on the display screen.

"All set," he reported to Alex and left with his men.

"That's it. Let's go," Alex ordered.

The pilots strapped themselves in. A few minutes later, as the bus drove through the airfield gate, massive turboprop engines roared back to life. Black smoke drifted in the glowing floodlights. The troops buckled in and slung their weapons while payload specialists secured the Jeep with tie-down straps. "All secure."

The ramp closed with a bang. Crimson lighting illuminated the cargo bay and cast an eerie glow over the soldiers inside. Noticing they were in a more somber mood than earlier, Alex knew the reality was setting in. They would soon put their lives on the line for someone else's sake. No one spoke. Droning engines set an ominous tone over everyone onboard.

Red gave Alex a thumbs-up. He climbed into the cockpit and tapped Captain Baine on the shoulder. "Let her rip." Buckling into the engineer's seat, he watched the pilots go to work. A few moments later the roaring engines blew the massive aircraft down the runway and blasted it into a moonless California night sky.

***

From the window of their executive suite, Steve stood behind Susan, his hands on her hips, and watched the massive transport roar down the runway and rise into an ink-black sky. Sound waves shuddered the glass but subsided quickly as flashing navigation lights dimmed in the distance. When the plane was out of sight, he slid his hands around Susan and hugged her. In a few hours, his friends would be in grave danger. By dawn, the madman would be dead, his reign of terror over.

A tear ran down Susan's cheek. Steve wouldn't have noticed except for her sniffle. "What is it, babe?"

#

Susan relished the warmth she found in Steve's embrace. But she was thinking of a happier time at Atomtech, before Ray Crawford left on his relentless pursuit of the 13th Power, when her job had given her a great sense of pride. Sure, Devin had been a strict boss and a shrewd businessman, but he had always been good to her. Most of the time, he'd even been fun to be around. For a while, back then, she thought she might have been in love with him. Sometimes she had found it hard to keep her feelings professional. She remembered his laughter, before it became a sinister sort of cackle.

Now that same man must die. His life meant someone else's death. His death meant someone else's life. And her life had changed so suddenly that nothing was the same anymore. She turned to Steve, unafraid to let him see the stream of tears.

"Everything is happening so quickly." She buried her face in his chest. "Hold me until morning. Hold me until it's over."

Chapter 47

THE SHERIFF'S CAR SPED away from King City. Lisa and Lo hunkered down in the back seat. She'd used her body to shield him from the gunfire. Ray turned around, put his hand on her shoulder in an attempt to show her he cared for her safety. She'd seen more blood and death in the last two days than most people ever see in a lifetime. In her eyes, he saw the pain she felt for the victims of this deadly fiasco.

Lo looked at him. "When will the killing end?"

Ray didn't know the answer. He only wished everyone could've been spared this grief. It was his fault. His blind ambition, his obsession with the 13th Power, had put them all in danger. His stomach churned with guilt. He'd really made a mess of his daughter's life, and his own, for that matter, but he'd had no choice, back then, when Kate had forced him to do things he didn't want to do, things that he had now come to regret. They were in too deep to get out now.

He braced himself on the armrest as the car roared down Highway 101, the speedometer quivering at 120 miles an hour. Janis was driving like a man possessed. The gas gauge indicated someone had filled the tank. "Guess the sheriff wasn't a bad guy after all."

Janis clutched the steering wheel with both hands. Ray was right about Doogan. Though fully capable of carrying out Devin's wishes, he must have drawn the line when it came to murder. Janis admired his courage. By standing up to Devin, the sheriff had paid the ultimate price. He probably wasn't aware of Sergeant Lawson's allegiance to the madman.

Changing lanes to get around a slower car, Janis

glanced at Ray. "Doogan told me he was going to kill us."

Ray's eyes went wide.

"But for some reason he changed his mind. During the interrogation, I asked him if he would die for Devin. He must've decided the answer was *no*. How ironic, he died for us instead." A shiver ran up his neck, his concentration on the highway, its centerline racing along in the headlights like a yellow-striped snake.

Ray sat silent for a moment, as if digesting the sour truth. "We'd all be dead right now."

"That's right." Janis pushed his glasses up the bridge of his nose.

Again, Ray turned to his daughter in the back seat and reached for her hand. Janis watched her reaction in the rearview mirror. Without moving her cheek from Lo's shoulder she took her father's hand.

It was time to smell the roses.

***

In the parking garage under the King City police station, two deputies ran through the double steel doors with their revolvers drawn. They stopped and stared at the lifeless body of their leader, Sheriff Doogan, lying in a pool of blood. Lawson holstered his revolver, walked up to his victim and stooped to check for a pulse. Nothing. "Damn it."

"What happened?" one deputy asked as he dropped to his knees. The other deputy stood next to him, holding his pistol at his side, his eyes wide and mouth hanging open. Several more deputies ran to the scene of the sheriff's demise, reacting the same way. Lawson saw the terror in their eyes.

"What the hell happened?"

"Mackey jumped me," Lawson began. "He took my gun and shot Sheriff Doogan before I could wrestle it away from him. Then he tried to kill me. Hell, look at the skid marks. He tried to run me over. He's a cop killer."

"That doesn't make any sense," a deputy called out from the crowd of lawmen. He was the lead deputy who'd led the prisoners out to the car. "Sheriff Doogan was releasing them. He was giving them his car. Why would Mackey kill him?"

Lawson paused to think of an answer, then: "Mackey grabbed my gun before the sheriff could explain. He thought Doogan was going to kill them."

"That's right," another deputy put in. He had operated the recorder during the interrogation. "I was there when Mackey asked Doogan if he was going to murder them. Doogan said 'that's right'. I thought he was just trying to scare the professor. I played along."

The crowd of officers began talking among themselves as if trying to assess the information they were getting. Then the deputy added, "Mackey also said he would kill for Lisa."

"Let's get 'em," one officer yelled.

Lawson joined in. "Cop killers. Shoot 'em on sight." The mob of officers raced for their squad cars and peeled out of the garage. Like a horde of avengers, with sirens wailing and overheads flashing, they swarmed toward the highway. Sergeant Lawson transmitted his emergency to the world.

"Attention all cars, attention all precincts. This is an All Points Bulletin. Be on the lookout for a King City sheriff's sedan southbound on 101, headed for Simi Valley. Four suspects, three men and one woman. Use extreme caution. Wanted for the murder of Sheriff Doogan in King City. Repeat. Use extreme caution. Suspects are armed and dangerous."

With that, he ended his transmission. He knew he'd just issued their death sentences. Every lawman in California would be out to avenge the murder of a fellow officer. Mackey and his friends would surely die; they'd never make it to Simi Valley. More important to Lawson, the truth would be murdered along with them. He swerved around a patrol car, took over the lead, and grabbed his cell phone to call Devin.

A sleepy voice answered. "Atomtech, Devin."

"Doogan is dead, sir. The scientists you wanted escaped. We are pursuing them down 101. Can you help us out here?"

"Can't you do anything right?"

"They're driving a sheriff's car with 2885 painted on the roof, you know how they do that for the police choppers?"

"I'll get Leonard on it right away. How long before sunrise?"

"Another hour and a half," he replied. "Sky's clear. Nice morning to die."

"Enjoying your job, are you?" Devin interjected with a tone of approval. "Don't let me down, Lawson, or *you'll* be the one dying this morning."

"You just have Leonard call me when he's locked on the squad car. I'll take care of the rest." He hung up. Though he was paid well for his loyalty, he wasn't paid near enough to put up with Devin's threats. But Lawson's stomach tightened as Doogan's last words suddenly echoed back to him. *Now Devin has your soul.*

Leading his posse down Highway 101, Lawson strengthened his resolve to terminate the scientists.

Chapter 48

FROM A PLUSH APARTMENT adjacent to his third-floor office at Atomtech, Devin phoned the employee quarters. The phone rang several times before anyone awoke to answer it.

"Get Leonard up here right now!"

He threw on a pair of brown slacks, a t-shirt, and his boots, then made his way down to the main control room. Grumbling to one of the graveyard-shift technicians for a cup of coffee, he walked up to the SSS monitor, which revealed a vast span of dark ocean. The SSS wasn't locked on anything so it wandered with the rotation of the earth. Devin grabbed the joystick and yanked it to the right. An unfamiliar scene of city streets and buildings came into view. *Rochester, NY* scrolled across the bottom of the screen.

"Shit." He cranked the joystick a little to the left. A tractor appeared on the monitor, kicking up dust, plowing a field. *Russell, Kansas.*

"This is ridiculous. Where the hell is Leonard?" He backed away from the frustrating machine. At times like this, he appreciated an experienced man at the controls. It could take him all day to find King City, California.

A technician handed him a mug of steaming coffee. With it cupped in his hands, he sat down and tried to think, a hundred questions rolling through his mind. The news of Sheriff Doogan's death was unnerving enough on its own, without the added complication of Curtis's hired scientists on the loose again. How the hell had they gotten away? Sipping coffee, he watched the farmer plow his field in the early Kansas dawn.

With a bang, Leonard burst through the doors, still

buttoning his lab coat. "What is it now?" Pointing to the coffeemaker, he motioned a technician to get him a cup.

"Fix this piece of crap machine of yours." Devin flipped a finger at the monitor.

"What is Kansas doing here?" With the mouse, Leonard clicked the *Undo* command. That brought up New York instead of California. He grabbed a chair and scooted Devin out of the way. "This thing is a mess."

As Leonard cross-filed coordinates and type commands on the keyboard, Devin scowled. "What's taking you so long?"

Still typing, Leonard grumbled, "What the hell is going on now?"

"Crawford and his band of traitors got away from King City—"

"I'm sick of this shit," Leonard cut in. "Every time you get into trouble with this deal, you come screaming for me to bail you out. And when things go bad, you beat the crap out of me. When are you going to drop it and let us all get back to our real jobs?"

"When Curtis and his scientists are out of business."

Leonard said nothing, worked the keys and mouse until his hi-tech spy machine finally zeroed in on King City, California. "What am I looking for?"

"A car with 2885 on the roof. It should be southbound on 101. When you find it, we have to call Lawson on his cell phone."

Leonard worked the joystick, searching for his target, but there wasn't enough light. Sunrise was still an hour away. He had to strain his eyes to make out images on the screen.

Devin stood. "I need a cigar. Call me when you find them."

Leonard didn't look up until he heard the door close. Coffee cup in hand now, he stared into the screen, working the joystick, following 101 south. Suddenly, flashing

Terry Wright

emergency lights came into view, a dozen police cars barreling down the highway. Moving the SSS ahead of them, he came upon a lone sedan with 2885 painted on its roof. "Ah ha." With a click of his mouse, he snared his prey, then picked up the phone and dialed Lawson. "I found 'em, halfway between Bradley and San Miguel. They're really moving, one hundred twenty miles an hour."

"Let me know if they make any turns," Lawson ordered. "Hell, we must be thirty miles behind them." Lawson picked up his mike and pressed the button. "State Patrol, this is King City Sergeant Lawson. Come in."

The radio squelched. "*State Patrol dispatch. Go ahead.*"

"We need a roadblock as soon as possible on southbound 101, say somewhere around Paso Robles. The cop killers are approaching San Miguel. Can you help us out?"

"*Stand-by.*" A few minutes passed before the dispatcher returned. "*Okay, Sergeant. We'll roadblock at Atascadero.*"

Leonard said. "They're almost to Paso Robles. You guys had better hurry up."

Chapter 49

THROUGH THE DARK NEVADA night sky, the C-130 transport roared toward Atomtech's crucial twenty-five-mile mark. Captain Baine notified Alex of their position. "Time for you to work this contraption of yours."

Alex picked up the activation terminal, his heart beating faster. He pressed the *PROGRAM* button and typed in coordinates from the navigation computer. *READY* pulsed on the display. He turned the *ACTIVATE* knob. The device beeped three times, and the red light went out. *CLOAKING* glowed in green across the display. "This baby had better work."

The pilots glanced at each other uneasily.

"Start your descent to the landing zone." Alex switched on the intercom. "Red. We're going in."

Captain Baine eased back on the power. The engine drone subsided, and the transport began to sink in the air.

Alex looked out the front windows, saw nothing but blackness. "I hope you know what you're doing."

The Captain smiled. "Relax. Desert landing at night is tricky, but I've done it more times than I care to remember. This stretch of salt flats outside Desert Rock is a piece of cake compared to the sandy dunes of Iraq." He dimmed the cockpit lights. "Flaps?"

"Check," the copilot said. "Landing lights, off." He scanned the instruments. "Set her down, Captain."

The transport had descended to one hundred feet above the ground. The automatic night-landing system activated, firing flares from the aircraft to the ground. Alex squinted as they illuminated the desert floor, brightly.

"Okay, ease her down," the pilot said, coaxing his big bird back to earth. Massive tires rumbled on the desert floor as the giant aircraft flared out of the night sky. Clouded by dust, the burning flares glowed eerily in the wake of the landing plane. Reverse thrusters roared and slowed the aircraft to braking speed. A few moments later, the C-130 stopped, its mighty engines whining down. Hissing and spitting flares quickly burned out, returning the desert to darkness.

The cargo ramp whined as it came down. From the cargo hold's crimson glow, a Jeep backed out. Soldiers assembled into squads. In the dim light, Alex looked them over.

Lion One was his command team with Red. They would drive the Jeep, loaded with munitions and the radio isolator that would keep their transmissions hidden from detection.

Jackal One carried the PASE equipment. Each man had clipped cloaking devices on their belts, which rendered motion detectors and infrared sensors worthless. Undetectable, they would assault the guard towers first.

Jackal Two had the technical equipment required to circumvent perimeter security.

Jackal Three would destroy the main circuitry complex with C4 explosives and sever Devin's link to the outside world.

Jackal Four was prepared to storm the main building and eliminate Devin himself. With assault rifles, hand grenades, and bayonets, these soldiers would do battle with Devin's security force and end his reign of terror. The Desert Jackals executed an about-face and began a hike to their assigned positions.

Red, his face now blackened for combat, climbed into the Jeep. "See you at sunup," he said to the pilots. Alex hit the accelerator. The Jeep sped off toward Atomtech under a moonless, starlit sky.

Chapter 50

HARRY THALES SWALLOWED the last of his chicken sandwich and helped it down with a throat-burning gulp of soda. After a relieving belch, he glanced over the video monitors lining the wall in front of him. These monitors were linked to surveillance cameras and motion detectors positioned on electrified fences that encircled the Atomtech compound.

Below his tower, the main circuitry complex held the master terminals for all the wiring, computer links, and electronics used by technicians in the control center. All antenna and satellite dishes mounted on the roof were funneled through the main circuitry complex, fed into backup computers, and branched out to various departments within the compound. Harry felt proud to be the protector of such a great technological wonder.

After crumpling the paper bag that his wife had packed his dinner in, he tossed it into a wastebasket, thinking how long it had been since he'd eaten a home-cooked meal with his family and wondering how long it would be before he'd have dinner with them again. He missed his wife and three kids.

He stood from his chair and stretched, relieving the stiffness in his muscles. After a few knuckle-pops and cracks, he decided some fresh air would do him good and walked to the window. As he opened it, a cool breeze swept across his face. He closed his eyes and took in the scent of desert sage. Satisfied, he looked out toward the other guard towers. Automatic spotlight turrets swept the perimeter. Should the motion detectors activate, the computer would sound an alarm, and all the lights would automatically zero-in on the movement.

Harry saw something move. The system must not be working right. A dark figure was climbing up the adjacent guard tower, yet no alarm sounded. How could that be? Shaking, he grabbed his binoculars and focused on the ascending figure, a helmeted soldier with a rifle slung across his back and a knife clenched between his teeth. He was almost up to the guard's cabin.

Fred! I gotta warn Fred!

He tossed the binoculars on the table and reached for a walkie-talkie on his belt strap. Sudden blackness engulfed him as a bullet penetrated his brain.

Chapter 51

ALEX SPIT. "Why didn't you shoot him when I said shoot?"

Red, lying prone on the ground, lowered his rifle and turned onto one shoulder, glaring at Alex. "If I *had* fired, that guard might have dropped his binoculars from the window. The motion detectors would've sounded an alarm and brought every damn security guard in the compound down on us. All our asses would have been nailed. So I waited until the binoculars were out of the picture."

"You were taking too big a risk. What if you had missed."

Red shot him a stern look. The last man who had said *missed* to Red took the butt of his rifle in the teeth. Red never missed. Alex relented. "Nice shot."

"Damn right." Red looked down the fence line at his closest soldier. All his men were in position. Jackal One had taken out the other guard towers, as planned.

"Phase two. Open the bridge," Red ordered into his wrist radio.

Jackal Two went to work on the perimeter fence, bypassing ten-thousand volts and the alarm system. Then they cut out a large section of the chain-link.

A few minutes later: *"Jackal Two to Lion One, the bridge is open."*

"Phase three," Red commanded. "Cross the river."

Jackal One and Jackal Two teamed up, man for man, so they could enter the motion detection zone under the cloak of a PASE. In pairs, they slipped through the breached perimeter fence and ran across an open area toward the main circuitry complex. Alex held his breath for an alarm that never sounded. He exhaled when they reached the building.

Jackal One entered and eliminated the only graveyard-shift worker in the control room. With a slash across his throat from behind, the execution was silently carried out.

Jackal Two went to work disabling the motion sensor system. Bypassing this system without alerting the main control room required some sophisticated electronics and several well-placed jumper wires.

A few minutes later, the next transmission came. *"Jackal Two to Lion One. The river is crossed."*

"Jackal Three. Phase four. Plant 'em," Red ordered.

The explosive experts quickly crossed the compound without sounding an alarm. They carried satchels of C4, wiring, and detonators into the doomed main circuitry complex. The lethal C4 was deployed, wired, and armed.

A few minutes passed before the next transmission was received. *"Jackal Three to Lion One. We're hot."*

"Jackal Four, Phase five. Huntin', Fishin'."

Soldiers funneled through the hole in the fence and stormed the main building. Red turned to Alex. "Let's go get him." As they followed their men into battle, Red went to his wrist radio again. "Jackal Three. Blow it!"

A second later, the Nevada desert rocked from a mighty blast that tore the main circuitry complex from its foundation and shattered every window in the compound. A fireball billowed into the night sky. Walls fell. The roof collapsed. Debris flew in every direction and rained down around the compound.

Jackal Four infiltrated the main building. Gunfire marked their first encounter with Devin's security forces.

Red stopped running a moment to take it all in. The explosion and gunfire made his blood boil with excitement, the rush of adrenaline like a drug-induced high.

Alex called out. "Come on!"

Red sprinted toward the action. Jackal One joined forces with Jackal Four. The fighting escalated.

***

As Leonard watched the 2885 car speeding toward Paso Robles, he wondered about the roadblock at Atascadero. Moving the joystick, the SSS tracked ahead of the sheriff's car. The monitor soon revealed a dozen patrol cars parked across 101, lights flashing.

"All right," he said into the phone. "They're dead meat." As Lawson's laugh echoed in his ear, Leonard worked the joystick, returning to the place where he had last seen the 2885 car. A surge of panic rippled through him. Something was wrong. 2885 wasn't there. It must have turned off 101. But where? Frantically, he worked the joystick, sweat now trickling down his neck. They have to be around there somewhere...

The SSS monitor went black followed by a deafening blast that rocked the building. Leonard hit the floor. Ceiling plaster rained down and dust choked the air. He put the phone to his ear. "Lawson!"

The line was dead.

"Oh, shit!"

***

When Devin left Leonard in front of the SSS monitor, he went upstairs to his office for a fresh cigar. He found his faithful goons hanging out in the darkened foyer that once was Susan Rivers' office. Toothless lay awake. Little Man, his shadow of a partner, slept snoring on the couch.

"You're up early, boss," Toothless said.

"What are you doing up here?" Devin turned on the light and plucked a plump cigar from its case on the desk. The light beamed sharply off the foyer floor.

Toothless got up and shambled to Susan's desk. "Figured sackin' out here was no harm..." He picked up Susan's nameplate and waved it at Devin. "...seein' as how you don't got no use for this office anymore."

"No thanks to you." Devin snatched the nameplate from Toothless and set it back down on the desk, nice and neat. "Touch this again and I'll kill you."

"Sorry, boss. Didn't mean no disrespect."

"Raven got away with more than just his life yesterday, the bastard."

"Raven will get his," Toothless roared. "Our time will come,"

Devin mouthed the end of his stogie, lighter in hand. "Yeah, yeah, yeah, you and whose army? Raven has more dumb luck than the two of you have brains."

"Luck don't last forever, boss. Raven is going to screw up, and I'm gonna be there to cash in, with blood." He clenched his fist in the air.

Devin, liking the hate in Toothless's voice, flicked the lighter into flame and lit his cigar. The smoke was like nectar to his nostrils. He really didn't have much respect for his goons, but they were loyal as puppy dogs. He liked having followers around him; leaders always made waves.

Little Man stirred on the couch. "What are you bellyaching about now?" he mumbled.

Toothless fluffed him off with a swipe of his hand. "Ah, nothin'." He plopped back on the couch, propped his feet on the coffee table, settled back, and closed his eyes.

The light in Devin's office went out.

A horrendous boom blasted the darkness into a flash of yellow light. The concussion busted windows into lethal shards of flying glass. The walls shook. Like a clap of thunder, the explosion rolled off across the desert. The night glowed in a raging fire.

Toothless found himself lying on the floor, shaking. In the eerie yellow glow that painted the walls, he spotted Little Man sprawled on the floor, his forehead bleeding.

"Little Man." Toothless pushed away a broken end table and pulled a shredded curtain off his partner.

"What hit me?"

"Hell if I know." Toothless crawled toward the wall where the window had been and peered over the jagged edge. "We got big problems." Panic laced his words. He turned back to the disheveled room. "There's a whole fricken army out there…and…they're comin' this way." Gunfire echoed through the building. "We gotta get out of here."

Devin crawled from his office, pushing debris out of his way with his arms, the glowing cigar still clamped in his teeth. He looked angry as hell. "Security will deal with them. Meantime, get your weapons." He got to his feet, grabbed hold of the couch, and started muscling it toward the stairwell. "Make a barricade. We'll blast anyone who comes up."

Toothless started to help him but paused. "Boss, I hate to tell you, this furniture ain't gonna stop no military ammunition—"

The building shuddered from the blast of a grenade.

"Or explosives. We have to get out." He grabbed his machinegun, locked in a clip, and headed toward the stairs. "Come on."

***

"What was that?" Leonard shouted.

The control room lights flickered. With a sound like popping popcorn, sparks spewed from computers, and the room went dark. A second later, emergency lighting blinked on; its piercing glow revealed a haze of acrid electrical smoke swirling in the air.

Coughing, a technician yelled, "Let's get the hell out of here."

Leonard scrambled to his feet but froze in terror at the sounds he heard next. "Wait. Listen." *Gunfire?*

Again, he heard the reports of automatic weapons

coming closer and closer.

"Everybody get down."

The room fell silent. Every man found a spot under a table or counter, somewhere to hide. Horrified, Leonard listened to the battle raging outside the doors: rattling machineguns, banging rifles and pistols, yelling and screaming voices. The din would get louder and closer, then quieter, as if moving away, only to return louder than ever until the doors busted open. A grenade thudded across the floor.

Leonard covered his head.

Like being hit by a truck, the explosion slammed him into the wall under the SSS console, knocking him senseless. He couldn't breathe. His eardrums ached, and a burning pain skewered his body. Rancid sulfur laced the air. Choking, his throat burned. Blood streamed down his face. The sound of gunfire became muffled and distant like the pounding of his heart in his head.

Suddenly, men appeared above him, their faces clouded by smoke, blurry. They wore helmets and carried rifles. Either something was wrong with his eyes or he had been dropped into the middle of a war. He tried to scream but only gurgled. He tried to breathe but only gagged.

Footsteps clunked. He felt movement. Was he being dragged across the floor? *What's happening to me? What are they doing? Stop! Let me go!*

Someone lifted him up by his belt. Burning air rushed into his lungs. His stomach ejected a wave of nausea. He coughed up vomit and blood. *Is this what it feels like to die? No! I don't want to die! What have you bastards done to me?*

Soldiers were leaning over him now, yelling at him. "Where is Devin?"

Leonard strained to focus but only saw the blurry faces of two soldiers, identical twins.

"Where is Devin?"

He could barely hear the words. The soldiers shook him repeatedly.

"Where is Devin?"

"Upstairs," was all he could manage to say, but he didn't recognize the sound of his own voice. His consciousness started slipping away in a dizzying swirl.

#

Alex stood, the balding technician at his feet now jerking with spasms, an eyeball half out of its socket.

Red approached, Glock in hand, and looked down at the man hacking on the floor. "Poor bastard doesn't even know his leg is gone." Red raised his gun, pulled the trigger, and put an end to Leonard's suffering with a fatal blast that echoed down the battle-scarred corridor.

Alex stepped back. "Devin's upstairs."

Chapter 52

LOCKING A CLIP INTO his machinegun, Little Man followed Toothless down the stairwell. Devin stopped short of following them. He leaned on the couch, trembling from a sudden wave of shock. Why was this happening? Had Curtis struck back? How did he come up with a goddamned army?

A fierce gun battle erupted from the stairwell. Cursing voices mixed with rapid gunfire. Someone screamed. Devin shook with fear. Backing away from the stairwell, he retreated to his office and closed the door. There was no way out. Crouching behind his desk in the fire-lit darkness, he thought about the end of his life. "Stopping Curtis wasn't worth all this," he mumbled in disbelief and took a drag off his cigar as if it would be his last. "The bastard!"

Rage boiled in his stomach. He leaped to his feet and paced the floor, kicking broken glass and debris out of his way. As gunfire became more intense in the stairwell, he walked to the window and looked out across the desert, which flickered in the glow of the burning circuitry complex. The eastern horizon was ablaze with the start of a new day. A chill went through his bones. "Damn it. It's not going to end like this."

The door flew open.

He whipped around, muscles taut.

Toothless bolted in. "Little Man's holding them off."

"Jesus. You scared the shit out of me."

"We gotta jump, boss. It's the only way." He ran to the window with desperation in his eyes. He didn't seem to care that a three-story fall to concrete could be fatal. And there were soldiers with guns down there.

Devin grabbed his arm. "Wait," he said, suddenly

remembering how Raven had left his office earlier. "The pit. Didn't you say it was full of water? Is the rope still there?"

Toothless looked at him blankly. He didn't answer. Just stared.

Devin shook him. "Think, man."

His face contorted into an ugly smile. "Yes. The pit."

"I'll be a son of a bitch." Feeling like a condemned man getting a last minute reprieve from the Governor, he ran to his desk, stabbed his cigar into the ashtray, and pressed the hidden button. The trapdoor released with a clank in the dark. "Over here." He led Toothless to the opening.

The fearless goon stood there for a moment, looking into the black abyss. "It'll be like a ride at the water park." He sat down on the edge. "Geronimo." He pushed off and was gone. The trapdoor began to close but Devin caught it with his foot. After taking a deep breath, he followed his faithful goon down into the pit. The trapdoor snapped shut as darkness swallowed him.

***

Little Man had taken several rounds in the battle of the stairwell. He lay on the floor of the second landing, back propped against a wall, shooting short bursts down the steps, his last clip loaded and half gone. Blood covered his sleeve and hand, his fingers now sticky on the rifle grip and trigger. As soldiers pressed their relentless attack and bullets ricocheted around him, he thought of Devin and Toothless. What would become of them? He had to hold his position, hold off the attack, give them time to get away. It was getting harder to move, more painful by the second. Either his machinegun was getting heavier or he was getting weaker. The pool of blood around him was getting bigger. Feeling light headed, he could smell baked bread from his mother's kitchen, and he could hear music, music that floated in the air, violins, flutes, and harps. Everything seemed so peaceful. He squeezed off the last rounds in his clip. Somehow nothing mattered anymore.

***

Alex stood next to Red as his soldiers battled for the stairwell. It seemed brutally defended. The smell of burnt gunpowder spoiled the air.

"He's up there," Red said, his voice as cold as an executioner's. "I can feel it."

The battle raged for several minutes until finally, there was no more gunfire coming down the steps. Soldiers rushed the stairwell, firing as they went. But a lone defender, lying on the second landing in a pool of blood, was already dead. They stepped over his body and systematically swept the upstairs offices and attached suite. Finding no more resistance, they gave the all-clear signal.

"Let's get up there," Red yelled.

As they scrambled up the smoky, battle-scarred stairwell, Alex got a creepy feeling that Red was wrong about Devin being up here. Something about this siege didn't seem right. It was too easy.

Reaching the foyer, a team leader, sweating and breathing hard, reported to Red. "Nobody in the elevator shaft, sir." Another soldier ran up. "Nobody on the other end, either."

"Nobody hell. Find the son of a bitch."

The soldiers ran back to their search as Alex walked into an office he presumed to be Devin's. He looked around the flickering darkness. On the desk, he spotted the glow of a crushed cigar still smoldering in an ashtray. He picked it up. "Red, check this out. It's still hot."

"Devin was here, damn it," Red shouted. His face had the look of a man who'd been cheated at poker.

Alex looked out the window and saw a glowing horizon. "We can't stay any longer. One more sweep and we're out of here." Walking out of Devin's office, he noticed the nameplate on the receptionist's desk. *Susan Rivers*. He picked it up. "Souvenir for the lady. She'll know how close we came to Devin."

As he put it in his pocket, he saw anger rising in Red's coal black eyes. A sudden chill rippled down Alex's back. He'd seen that look before, in that Vietnamese rice paddy.

"The rat has a hole to hide in," Red snorted in a voice rasping with rage. "But he has to come out sometime. I'll make him wish he never had."

With a warrior-like cry, Red snatched the bayonet from its sheath on his belt and ran downstairs to the bullet-riddled body on the second landing.

Puzzled and concerned, Alex ran after him.

Red grabbed Little Man's corpse by the hair.

"What are you doing?" But even Alex's worse nightmares had not prepared him for what he saw next. A sudden wave of nausea gripped his guts as Red slashed the bayonet through the dead man's neck with the force of a butcher. He sawed back and forth through the neck bones. The torso fell away with a thud, its severed head now dangling in Red's grasp, blood dripping.

Alex's stomach cramped with a dry heave.

Holding the gruesome decapitation out in front of him, Red ran upstairs and into Devin's office.

Alex scrambled after him. "Are you crazy?"

"Just watch this," Red said, his voice reeking with insanity. He set the head on the desk, raised his bayonet, and slammed it through the skull like a toothpick through an olive. The steel blade embedded in the desktop with a thunk. Blood and brain matter spurted out and oozed.

"Take that, you bastard," Red yelled and stepped back, now folding his arms across his chest and cocking his head slightly, like an artist admiring his work. In the shadowy glow of the burning circuitry complex, the message he left for Devin looked like it could have come directly from hell.

Alex, shaking, raised his wrist radio. "All t-teams assemble and disperse," he ordered. Grabbing Red's arm, he pulled him toward the door. "Let's go, soldier. You've had enough fun for one day." Red's snarl turned into a smile. Not a happy smile, a satisfied smile that didn't reach his eyes.

Without finding the man they sought, the soldiers regrouped at the transport. Sunup was in ten minutes. The fiery horizon announced its coming as black smoke billowed into the Nevada sky.

Alex looked back toward the war-torn compound and tried to justify what they had done. The killing was necessary. To prevent death, he had to cause death. Devin had taken many lives and he could have taken many more. This morning, they'd avenged those he had murdered and saved countless others. But where was the madman now? Would he leave the 13th Power project alone, or would he come back with a vengeance?

Alex had a bad feeling this wasn't over yet.

Chapter 53

Janis DROVE THE SHERIFF'S CAR down Highway 101. He felt the hum of the powerful Chevy in the palms of his hands as the speedometer hit 130. Determined to put the most distance between themselves and King City in the least amount of time, he pressed his meager driving skills to the limit. Through every curve and straightaway he was thankful the traffic was light in the twilight hours of this California Sunday morning.

"They're coming after us, aren't they?" Ray said.

Janis thought that was a possibility. "Try the radio."

Ray fiddled with the knobs. The radio only squelched. "Nothing. Maybe that's good news."

"I doubt it." Janis passed two trucks laden with cargo. "We saw Lawson kill Doogan. You can bet he's made up some bullshit story to cover up the murder."

"What kind of story?"

Lo said, "Crooked cop will blame us. Tell comrades we did it. Get help to kill us that way. Witnesses no good alive."

Ray turned to the back seat. "Now that's a chilling thought. Can't you think of something else that would put us in a *bigger* jam?"

"No."

"If you're right, every cop in the country will hunt us down like mad dogs."

"Mad, rabid dogs."

Janis felt a cold shiver seep through his veins. "That's what I'd do. Try changing frequencies. Maybe we can get something."

Lisa leaned over the seatback. "Look in the glove box. Maybe there's a directory of some kind."

Ray hit the latch. In the glow of the glove box lamp, the blue steel of a service revolver glistened. The smell of fresh cleaning oil rose in the air. He stared at it, his silence attracting Janis's attention.

"What is it?"

Reaching in, Ray took hold of the gun, slowly removing it as if it were a vile of nitroglycerine.

"It's a gun." Janis saw silver bullets shining in the cylinder. "Loaded too, so don't shoot anybody."

"Very funny," Ray said. "Watch the road or we won't need one of these to get killed."

Janis concentrated on the highway again. Had Doogan put that gun in the glove box deliberately? He didn't seem the type of man who'd forget it was in there.

"Let me see it," Lisa said.

Ray gave her the gun. "It won't fire unless the hammer is cocked back." Returning to the glove box, he pulled out a lot of loose papers, half filled-out forms, a map, and some receipts from various places. After discarding the stuff on the floor, he kept digging and found a couple of pens, a comb, some toothpicks, and a handful of ketchup packs.

"Why do they always give you too many of these?"

Janis shrugged and, on a hunch, reached up and pulled the sun visor down. Taped to it, neatly typed on a piece of paper, was a list of frequencies, the California Highway Patrol's frequency on top. "Here we go. Try this one."

Ray twisted the dial. The radio remained quiet.

"Leave it there." Janis looked at the rearview mirror and caught a glimpse of Lisa examining the gun.

Chapter 54

Ray SAID, "San Miguel is up ahead."

Janis saw a police car pull onto the highway in front of them. He blew around it. Shifting his eyes to the rearview mirror, he saw the overheads come on and the cruiser speed up behind him. "Damn it."

"Janis?" Ray was looking back, as well. "Why would one cop chase another cop? He must know who we are."

"Guess we're back to Lo's theory," Janis said. "I can—"

The radio crackled. *"…Cop killers…approaching San Miguel…Can you help us out…? Stand-by…"*

Janis looked at Ray. His face was white as a ghost. Lisa and Lo leaned forward. Janis glanced at the rearview mirror. The cruiser was on his bumper. Visions of spending the rest of his life in jail raced through his mind, or worse, if Lo was right, a bullet to the back of his head.

"…Lawson…roadblock at Atascadero. San Miguel…in pursuit…We're on it…"

Ray slapped the dashboard. "Shit! Leonard's locked the SSS on us again."

The San Miguel cruiser pulled up beside Janis and shined a spotlight into the car. It nearly blinded him.

"What are we going to do now?" Ray shrieked. "They're waiting for us with a roadblock."

"Get rid of tail. Take different road," Lo said as if it were an easy solution.

"We can't outrun this guy," Janis said. "Hell, all he has to do is hang with us 'til we hit the roadblock. If we change routes, he'll radio the others. We're…"

Captain Ben came back to mind. How did that go, emergency brake, yank the steering wheel? That's it. He looked at Ray and gritted his teeth. "You know the saying, the best defense is a good offense?"

"So?"

"So, hang on."

Janis stomped on the emergency brake pedal and cranked the steering wheel hard to the right, spinning the car around. He clutched the wheel so tight his knuckles burned. Centrifugal force plastered him against the driver's door. Darkness swirled past his windshield until the taillights of the cruiser came around into view. Now. He pulled the brake release and floored the gas. The car fishtailed. He wrestled the steering wheel back and forth and raced up behind the cruiser so fast bumpers collided with a violent jolt.

The cruiser skidded sideways in front of him. Smoke swirled from its tires, forming a blue cloud that glowed in the headlights. Janis clenched his jaw. He could see the officer struggle with his steering wheel, but it was no use. The car was out of control. It veered off the highway and slammed into a tree.

"Wow!" Ray said. "Where did you learn that?"

"From a cab driver I know. Look. Up ahead. Highway 55. That's our way out."

"Until Leonard gets 'em headed in the right direction again," Ray said with the sarcasm of a condemned man. "Remind me to kill that little shit next time I see him."

"Want to use this gun?" Lisa asked, holding the weapon in the palm of her hand.

Ray pursed his lips, seemingly in agreement with her suggestion.

The thought made Janis shiver. Killing only led to more killing. Would it ever end? He turned off Highway 101 onto 55, a southbound side road out of Paso Robles.

They were going to need a miracle.

Chapter 55

LAWSON AND HIS BAND of enraged lawmen raced toward the roadblock at Atascadero. He drove with the cell phone pressed to his ear. When he heard Leonard say, "dead meat," he laughed, his confidence soaring. He looked in the rearview mirror at his pack of misinformed followers and grinned.

Suddenly, a muffled sound came over the cell phone, a short commotion, and then silence.

"What the hell? Leonard, you there?"

Nothing.

He pulled the phone from his ear and examined the display. The *in-use* light was out.

"Damn cell phones."

He re-dialed Leonard. It rang and rang with no answer.

"Shit!" He tossed the phone on the seat. *We got 'em anyway.* He leaned forward on the steering wheel. *They're dead meat. Remember?*

Just past San Miguel, Lawson and his speeding posse of patrol cars came upon the flashing lights of emergency vehicles along the highway. A fire truck and ambulance blocked his view of a crash on the shoulder. In spite of flares and warning lights, he didn't slow down. As his formation blew past the accident scene, Lawson caught a glimpse of a San Miguel officer standing by an ambulance with a white bandage around his head.

"What's the matter, dumb ass? Can't drive?"

Paso Robles was quickly in his rearview mirror. He passed two loaded semis like they were running on flat tires. His radio squawked.

"Sergeant Lawson, change to tack-two. Officer

Snyder at the roadblock wants a word with you."

"10-4." Lawson twisted the tack switch. "Lawson here. You got 'em? Are they dead? Over."

The voice on the radio sounded gruff and irritated. *"What are you King City boys up to? Over."*

Lawson swallowed hard. "The stolen sheriff's car should've reached your position by now. Over."

"What makes you so sure they were headed this way? Over."

"Never mind that," Lawson replied, his mouth turning dry as sandpaper. He didn't want to tell anyone about Devin's eye in the sky. Where had the scientists gone? He pushed the mike button. "San Miguel was in pursuit. They have to be somewhere between the crash and your roadblock." He paused a moment. What if they'd figured out how to use the radio? Damn it. "They might have ducked around you. Hold your position. We're six minutes out. Over."

"There must be a dozen side roads between Paso Robles and here. They could be anywhere by now. I'm calling for the helicopter. Out."

Lawson reached for the cell phone and re-dialed Leonard but got nothing. "Damn it," he muttered to himself. An idea came to him. Repositioning the switch to tack-one, he radioed again. "Mackey, I know you can hear me. We *will* find you. You can't kill a cop and get away with it." He hoped that would get a response. But the radio remained silent.

***

Ray reached for the mike. "That son of a bitch—"

Janis grabbed his arm. "No! Let him sweat. Lawson must've lost us. That means Leonard has lost us, too. Suddenly we're invisible. It's just what we needed."

"A fuckin' miracle," Ray said.

Looking at the sky, Janis saw a new day dawn in blazing yellow. He glanced at Ray, then to the back seat at Lisa. The revolver was still in her lap.

Chapter 56

LAWSON SKIDDED his patrol car up to the roadblock at Atascadero, his band of faithful followers right behind him. Putrid tire smoke permeated the air and lingered in the breezeless morning. Early rays of sunshine cast long tree shadows across the highway. Before getting out of his car, Lawson re-dialed Leonard. Again, nothing.

He tossed the phone down and climbed out of the car. With overheads flashing behind him, he walked toward the troopers huddled around their command car. Officer Snyder stepped forward, an open pouch of chewing tobacco in his hand. His belly hung over his belt and heavy jowls drooped from his cheeks. Double chins made him look like he had no neck. Lawson ignored the cold look in his eyes. "When's the helicopter going to be here?" Looking skyward, he turned a full circle.

Officer Snyder pinched a plug of tobacco and tucked it under his lower lip. "Five minutes."

Lawson felt the trooper's icy stare and didn't like it.

Snyder stashed the pouch in his pocket, tucked his thumbs under his belt, and puffed out his chest. "You know, Doogan and I go back a long way," he said with a huff of pride. "As Military Police, we served in the same infantry division in Vietnam. Pulled two tours, back to back." He spit a slug of spittle on the pavement.

Lawson scowled at the officer's gross behavior.

"After that, we attended the California Highway Patrol Academy. Graduated top of our class."

"Congratulations." Lawson was in no mood for a history lesson, but Snyder seemed intent on continuing his story. His eye contact was unnerving. What was the point?

"Then we spent several years together patrolling

California highways before he became Sheriff."

"What are you getting at?"

"His murder hit me pretty hard."

"I'll bet. It hit us pretty hard, as well," Lawson lied.

Snyder spit again. "What happened in King City that got my best friend killed?"

As Lawson trolled out his account of the events that led up to Doogan's death, Officer Snyder hung his head. An experienced cop, gunned down by a lowly math professor from Colorado. What an insult to Doogan's career. Anger boiled inside Snyder. He glared at Sergeant Lawson. "You must be the biggest pantywaist cop in California," he growled. "How could you let a pencil-pushing professor take your gun away from you? How tough can a mathematician be for Christ's sake?" He pointed his finger, shaking it in Lawson's face. "As far as I'm concerned, you're responsible for Doogan's death. Your gun killed him."

Lawson took a step forward. "Damn you. He jumped me—"

The air-slapping sound of helicopter blades interrupted Lawson. Snyder turned his attention to the landing aircraft. Noisily, the Bell D-47 copter settled on the roadway in a whirl of dust several yards away. The pilot motioned through the doorway of the glass bubble, a signal for Snyder to come forward. He and two other troopers ran under the rotating blades, ducking the blast of air.

"We need a search pattern around Paso Robles," Snyder shouted to the pilot.

"I can stretch the fuel two hours, tops."

Snyder turned to Lawson. "I'll finish with you later," he yelled over the clattering copter and climbed aboard. The other troopers ran back to their command car. With a rush of swirling wind, the helicopter ascended into the sky, vibrating, hammering. When it cleared the treetops, Snyder signaled his troopers to open the highway. A few moments later, all the patrol cars were lined up on the shoulder. Snyder gave them a thumbs-up sign and pointed the pilot toward Paso Robles. Something stunk about Lawson's story. Snyder needed to find the mathematician and get his side of the story. Just how tough could the professor be?

Lawson stormed back to his squad car, got in, and slammed the door shut. He noticed his deputies gathered together, one of them bounded over to the car and signaled him to roll down the window.

"What is it?"

"M-me and the boys think we should get back to the station," he said. "It'll be way past shift change by the time we get there, and the duty captain will need to be filled in on this. You know, paperwork."

"Just go," Lawson said with a huff. "I'll stay here and see to it those bastards pay for what they did to Doogan." He rolled his window up in the deputy's face and slammed the transmission into drive. In a swirl of tire smoke, he spun the squad car in a circle and headed toward Paso Robles.

Anger at Snyder festered inside him as he drove in the direction the helicopter had flown. *Pantywaist?* "I'll show you," he yelled. That smart-ass Snyder had just pissed off the wrong man.

In the distance, east of Paso Robles, he spotted the circling helicopter. He set his radio on tack-two and cranked up the volume. When they find the 2885 car and radio its position, he'd be closer than the others, faster to respond. It was now apparent he'd have to do the killing himself. His future depended on the witnesses being dead. Again, he went to the cell phone, but there was still no connection with Leonard and his high-flying spy machine.

Chapter 57

JANIS BACKED OFF the throttle. Highway 55 was a two-lane road that wound its way through the hilly California countryside. No room for a mistake. Tires squealing through a right-hand curve, Janis gripped the wheel like a racecar driver, both hands sweating. Roadside trees, posts, and signs whizzed by at a dizzying pace. The world seemed to be spinning by out of control. At any moment, their perilous flight could be terminated, probably with deadly force. The safety of Simi Valley seemed far away.

He glanced at Ray. "We have to call Solartech Labs," he said and quickly returned his attention to a left-hand curve. "Curtis needs to know we're in trouble out here."

"Use mine." Lisa offered Ray her cell phone.

"No. It's not safe. They can triangulate on a cell signal. My Vidphone will reach Curtis no matter where he is, and it's untraceable."

"Vidphone, cell phone, I don't give a damn what phone," Janis said. "We need help."

"Let's find a pay phone. Pull into that gas station up ahead."

Janis drove into the dirt lot of an old countryside fuel stop. Two antique gas pumps fronted a log cabin store. A big black Lab lying on the porch lifted a brow to the visitors, growled instinctively, and returned to his nap. Janis hit the trunk release button. Ray pulled out his suitcase. With Vidphone in hand and juggling cords, he headed across the parking lot to a phone booth by the fence. Janis followed him, pulling change from his pocket. Ray activated the box and set the payphone receiver into its cradle. Janis dropped in a quarter and the box began to emit tones.

Curtis answered, his voice filled with excitement. "Ray. You should've been here last night. Where the hell are you?"

"We're in a big mess, sir. Every cop in the world is after us. They think we killed the sheriff of King City."

"We didn't do it," Janis interjected into the phone.

"We're about twenty miles south of Paso Robles on Highway 55," Ray said. "Devin seems to have lost us for the moment."

"You won't need to worry about Devin anymore," Curtis said. "But those cops are a big problem. Keep moving south on 55. I'll find Alex and send help right away. Get moving."

"Yes, sir."

"We didn't do anything wrong," Janis expounded.

The connection terminated. Ray unplugged the Vidphone and turned back toward the car.

"What kind of help can he send?" Janis asked.

"A helicopter would be nice."

As if words could turn to sound, a helicopter appeared, hovering over the fuel store. Janis stopped and stared. Was it friend or foe? The helicopter rotated sideways, revealing a California Highway Patrol emblem. Foe!

Janis thought his heart had stopped. "Lawson!" But the aircraft just hovered there, it didn't approach to land, it didn't move toward them. What was it waiting for?

***

Sergeant Lawson followed the State Patrol helicopter as it circled search patterns around Paso Robles. Trees and hills hindered his view from time to time, but he was able to guess its position, never losing sight of it for long. The helicopter worked its way south of Paso Robles. He tailed it down highway 55.

Snyder's voice came over tack-two. *"Okay, boys. We've got 'em here on five-five about twenty miles out. Roll 'em!"*

Lawson sneered. They were just around the next bend. He switched off his radio and floored the accelerator. *They're dead meat.*

***

Over the racket of the engine and whipping rotor blades, Officer Snyder heard his name called on the radio. Keeping his eyes on the men standing in the parking lot looking up at him, he grabbed his mike.

"Snyder, here."

"Switch to tack-three, sir."

The emergency frequency? He twisted the dial. "What is it?"

"This is the duty captain at King City. You there, Snyder?"

"I'm kind-a busy right now. What can I do for you?"

The radio squawked. *"Doogan was shot to death, all right, but Dr. Mackey didn't do it. Video surveillance cameras in the police garage revealed that Lawson did it. So tell your boys to leave those people alone. And find Lawson. He's wanted for first degree murder."*

"The son of a bitch."

"That's dumb *son of a bitch, sir. He forgot about the cameras."*

"Roger. Out."

Officer Snyder gritted his teeth in anger. He switched the radio back to tack-two. He had to call off his men. Those people down there had to be scared to death.

"Put her down," he said to the pilot and keyed the radio to call his troopers.

A squad car careened into the parking lot below him,

~233~

throwing gravel. It was a King City car. Snyder grinned. *I just found the dumb son of a bitch.*

***

Screeching tires jerked Lisa's attention out the back window of the car. The revolver in her lap tumbled to the floor. She saw a sheriff's car slide to a dirt-flinging stop. Wide-eyed, she looked for her father who was standing with Janis between the car and the phone booth, their eyes on the King City cruiser, their faces flushed with surprise.

She looked back as Lawson got out. He had a gun in his hand. Without warning, he shot her father. The round ripped into his right shoulder, spinning him around and dropping him to his back.

She stifled a scream. *Oh, God, no!*

"Lisa, get down," Lo said.

She watched the Vidphone smash on the ground. Janis dove for cover behind the car. Hovering overhead, the helicopter's downdraft swirled dust around her fallen father and his attacker. Ray looked helpless. This couldn't be happening.

"Drop your weapon, Lawson!" Officer Snyder ordered over the helicopter's loudspeaker. "You're under arrest."

Lawson looked up. Through the cockpit door, he saw Snyder pull a service revolver out of its holster.

"Damn you," he yelled and stepped back to his car. He grabbed a flare gun from the seat pouch, turned quickly, and fired a flare at the hovering helicopter. The projectile ignited into a white-hot ball and twisted a trail of smoke into the copter's glass bubble. The interior became a fireball. The helicopter pitched and yawed in the air, then nose-dived into the fuel pumps.

The explosion rocked the country store. A bright yellow and red ball of fire churned skyward, fueled by severed pipes that fed gas to the pumps. Flying aircraft debris pummeled the 2885 car. The black Lab lit out, tail between its legs as black smoke billowed into the California morning sky.

Lawson turned his back to the inferno and walked up to Ray. With hell's fury burning behind him, he aimed the gun at Ray's forehead. "Time to die, motherfucker."

Chapter 58

Paralyzed with fear, Ray begged his muscles to move. To scoot him away from Lawson. To get to his feet and run. Anything, but all he could do was look up at the crazed lawman looming over him, his eyes narrow slits of anger, his teeth bared. Heat from the roaring inferno hit his face like a devil's wind. With his shoulder burning from the bullet, he realized there was no way out. Numbed by fear and resigned to his fate, he closed his eyes. This was how his life would end, a bullet to the brain.

The hammer clicked.

Bang!

The handgun's report echoed away. If he'd been shot, he shouldn't have heard anything. He'd expected to be swallowed by darkness and silence, but the fire still roared in his ears; his shoulder still burned from the bullet. It took a split second for him to realize that the blast had not come from the cop's gun. He popped his eyes open in time to see Lawson buckle over.

Ray looked toward Doogan's car. Lisa was standing at the open back door with a gun clasped in both hands, elbows locked, face aglow from the billowing inferno, and her hair whipping about in the hot wind.

Again, the gun spit fire as she squeezed off another round. The bullet jarred Lawson's body as it tore into his chest. His handgun clunked on the ground, and he dropped to his knees, his arms hanging limply at his side. With a wide-eyed look of disbelief on his face, blood spurted from his mouth and gushed down his chin.

Another blast from Lisa's gun knocked him to the dirt.

Janis bolted around the car, grabbed Lisa's arm and

pushed it down, pointing the gun to the ground. Again, she squeezed the trigger. The round struck the dirt, and as if she were locked in a fit of rage, she fired again and again until the revolver resounded only hollow clicks from empty chambers.

"Lisa. It's over."

She dropped the gun and looked at him with ice blue eyes. "I had to kill him. I had no choice."

"I know."

Ray started shaking. He got to his knees. He couldn't believe his eyes. His daughter had saved him. Holding his wounded shoulder, he looked up at a wall of fire towering into the sky. It seemed as though he'd passed through the gates of hell. The heat was like a blast furnace. Why did he feel so cold and numb? He looked back and forth between Lisa and the inferno, unable to move, his mind locked in the horror of his scrape with eternity.

The King City cop lay sprawled beside him, blood pooling underneath the lifeless body of Devin's secret henchman. Were there any more around here? Was the whole damn country infested with them?

Dazed, he suddenly realized Lo had come to his aide to check his wound. "Hang on, Ray. It's not too bad," he said unreassuringly. "Must hurt like hell." He pulled on Ray's other arm. "Let's go. More cops coming to kill us."

But Ray couldn't move. He just stared at Lo's face.

Lo looked at Lisa, standing in Janis's embrace. "This not good, you guys. We gotta run, now." He slapped Ray's face.

The sudden sting on his cheek yanked him back to reality. Shaking his head to clear the fog, he staggered to his feet and scrambled to Lisa. She threw her arms around his neck.

His shoulder burned and throbbed, but he hugged her anyway.

Chapter 59

CROSSING IN FRONT OF the car to get behind the wheel, Janis spotted a chunk of black helicopter wreckage stuck in the grill. Dripping green liquid made a small puddle under the radiator. Though he knew nothing about car mechanics, he was sure of one thing: that drip didn't look good.

Sirens wailed in the distance.

"Let's go," Ray yelled.

Janis jumped in behind the wheel. Doors slammed. "Buckle up." He gunned the engine and spun the car around the inferno, squealing tires onto southbound 55 just as a horde of State troopers rounded the curve. He floored the accelerator and looked in the rearview mirror. It seemed like there were a million flashing lights behind him.

Gripping the wheel, he raced down the winding road, pushing Doogan's car to its limit. Life or death hung on every curve. But it became obvious very quickly; he wasn't going to shake his relentless pursuers. Dogging him blindly and oblivious to the truth, they had but one thing on their minds: revenge. He could only hope to stay out of their grasp long enough for Curtis to intervene.

Winding its way down from the hills, Highway 55 finally broke out across the Carrizo Plain where the road became straight and flat. Humming under the hood, the powerful V-8 engine pulled the car ahead of the police. Janis counted nine cars in his mirror. God only knew how many more lay in wait up ahead. Another roadblock would mean disaster. The chatter coming over the radio sounded like a foreign language of code numbers and meaningless jabber, giving him no hint of what the troopers were planning.

Lo studied a map on Lisa's cell phone. "No side roads for sixty miles. No way out."

Janis glanced at Ray and Lisa in the back seat. She was wrapping her father's shoulder with a piece of his shirt. Her cheeks glistened from streaks of tears, happy tears, that her father was still alive.

The car surged; the engine bucked and jerked. "Oh, oh." He scanned the instruments. The temperature gauge read overheated. Again, the engine bucked. But this time a vibration shook the car so bad he could feel it in his teeth. Though he had the gas pedal pressed to the floor, the engine was losing power, laying out a trail of smoke so thick he thought the engine had caught fire. The car began to slow down. He glanced at the rearview mirror. The patrol cars were getting closer. His stomach sank. "We're not going to make it."

Everybody looked out the back window.

From out of the misty California sky, an aircraft appeared, flying low and slow over the highway. It over-flew the posse of State troopers.

"Look at that," Lisa said, pointing.

In the rearview mirror, Janis saw a C-130 Hercules rocking in the air, its cargo ramp hanging down and wing-flaps deployed as it dropped lower and lower, heading straight toward them.

Ray's eyes got big around. "What's he doing?"

Janis backed off the throttle. "Landing."

The massive transport roared over the squad car's roof. Turbulence buffeted the car violently. Flaring out of the sky, the plane settled on the highway in front of them, the cargo ramp dragging on the pavement and throwing up sparks like a curtain of glittering rain. An oncoming car swerved into the ditch.

"That's our ride out of here," Janis said. Heart pounding, he floored the gas pedal again, aiming for the ramp. The car, bucking and lurching, veered through the shower of sparks and hit the cargo ramp with a bone-jarring bang. Janis slammed on the brakes. The car screeched to a stop inside the plane's cargo hold. Steam spewed from under the hood. The overheated engine squealed and seized. Janis clung to the steering wheel, a cold sweat on his forehead.

He thought his chest would burst.

Chapter 60

As THE SUN ROSE above the Texas horizon, a shiny white and gold Learjet cruised toward Simi Valley at thirty-five thousand feet. The sleek aircraft cut effortlessly through a frozen sky, leaving a white ice-crystal contrail behind it. Whining engines hummed softly inside a cozy cabin where Curtis sipped a Bloody Mary that Jonathan had prepared in the aft-cabin bar. They'd spent the weekend partying in Dallas, though his mind wasn't entirely on the frivolities. Devin's relentless assault on the 13th Power project had made Dallas an uneasy respite. During the night, Curtis had tried to reach Alex on his Vidphone but there was no answer. Something big was going down and he wanted to get back to Solartech Labs as soon as possible.

Curtis eyed the concoction in Jonathan's glass. An umbrella protruded over the brim, shading what appeared to be a fruit salad floating in a pink slush. "What kind of drink is that?"

Jonathan plunged a straw into the swill. "A cross between a Daiquiri and a Kamikaze. Looks pretty. Tastes sweet." He took a swig. "But it's lethal."

Shaking his head, Curtis returned his attention to his own drink. Jonathan wasn't much of a drinking man, but the morning booster seemed appropriate, if not necessary. Though Curtis had a tendency to make spur-of-the-moment plans, Jonathan never complained. He was paid well for his tolerance.

Bright sunlight glared in through the windows. Curtis looked out beyond the wing. A thick bank of clouds hung over the mountains. Lake Powell snaked across the landscape ahead. He pulled the shade down, sat back in his seat, and sipped his drink again.

Jonathan handed him the morning paper. "Early edition of the Dallas News," he said. "It's the Captain's."

"Be sure to thank him for me."

As the paper unfolded in Curtis's hands, the headlines quickened his pulse. *Nevada Desert Atomic Plant Explodes.* Excitement bubbled up inside Curtis's chest, a warm and satisfying feeling that deserved another swig on his Bloody Mary. Devin was out of business. The 13th Power was close at hand.

Curtis turned the front page toward Jonathan. "Listen to this: *Fearing radiation leaks, officials are cautious about rushing to the remote area. No communications have been received from the site.*"

Raising his drink to Jonathan, Curtis said, "A toast to Devin's demise." They drank to the good news.

Curtis downed the rest of his Bloody Mary and picked up his golden staff, caressing its smooth surface and eagle-head handle, taking care not to exert too much pressure on its emerald eyes for fear of accidentally unleashing its deadly secret weapon. Nothing could stop him now...unless his scientists hadn't made it to Simi Valley. He wondered where they were now.

Lifting the window shade, he looked out his speeding aircraft. Were they safe somewhere out there? The 13th Power project depended on them. His new wealth, his new power. Ray and Janis had to be safe. Leaning back in his seat, he closed his eyes and let his mind savor the possibilities of controlling the Higgs boson. Gold... lots and lots of gold.

Two hours later, the sleek corporate jet turned on final approach to Solartech Field. "Buckle up," the copilot said over the intercom.

Curtis tugged on his seatbelt and turned his attention out the window. The descending jet's shadow raced along the valley floor, rippling over burnt orange grasslands strewn with boulder fields and scrub oak, which soon gave way to city streets, rows of houses and lines of traffic. Sifting through a chain-link fence, the shadow danced over an array of approach-light towers and slid across the runway threshold, finally converging with the jet, its tires squawking and reverse thrusters roaring as it slowed to taxi speed.

"Welcome home, boss," Jonathan said.

The executive car, a long black Lincoln with Solartech flags flapping from its fenders, raced toward the tarmac as the jet swung around and stopped. A chime echoed through the cabin. An auxiliary power unit hummed to life. The copilot opened the door, and steps dropped down to the pavement. A gold carpet unrolled automatically.

Curtis donned his long black coat and grabbed his golden staff.

Jonathan gave him a two-fingered salute. "See you later, sir. I'll clean up around here first."

"As you wish." Curtis turned to the copilot. "Great flight."

"Enjoy your day, sir."

Curtis deplaned and headed for the executive car where an attendant greeted him. "Good morning, Dr. Curtis."

"Security Central, right away."

Chapter 61

Down in the pit under Atomtech, Devin swam in darkness, shivering from the cold water. Anger kept his adrenaline pumping as he battled panic and a fear of drowning in the dark. Gulping air, he heard Toothless treading water nearby. "Over here, boss. I've got the rope."

Devin dogpaddled toward the voice. His strength was dwindling. His water-soaked clothes and boots kept trying to pull him under. Seemed as if his age had become a handicap. "Over where?" He swam right into a muddy wall. "Shit. Talk to me, you bonehead."

"To your left, boss. Keep coming. You can make it."

Devin reached out toward the voice. A strong hand grabbed his arm.

"Take the rope," Toothless said, guiding Devin's hand. "Follow me."

Toothless climbed the rope to the upper deck and pulled himself out of the pit. Dripping and shivering, he lay on the concrete floor, gasping air. "Come on."

Devin clung to the rope, his hands weak from the cold and burning from the strain. "Pull me up. I don't have enough strength to climb the rope."

"Who do you think I am, Mister Universe? I can't pull your fat ass up here."

"Fat ass?" Devin spit. "Who are you calling a fat ass?" If he didn't need his goon so badly, he'd have killed him for that. "Turn the water on."

Toothless sloshed over to the water valves sticking out of the wall. "Which one is it?"

"Hell if I know. Just pick one, damn it."

"Okay, boss. Eenie, meenie, minie, moe." He turned the valve.

Devin let out a scream as a sudden whirlpool nearly dragged him off the rope. "Wrong one, you idiot."

"Oops." Toothless shut the valve quickly and opened the other valve. The pit filled with water. He reached out a hand and helped Devin climb out. Together, they sat on the cold wet floor, shivering and dripping. Devin stared up the stairwell, listening for any portentous sounds, like screaming and gunfire. He heard nothing.

An hour passed. Devin trembled the whole while, thinking pneumonia was setting in and fearful of what he would find when he went up those stairs. Should they risk leaving the sanctuary of this hole? Were the soldiers gone? Could the silence be a trap? He ordered Toothless to go upstairs and see if it was safe to get out of this sewer.

While Toothless clunked up the stairs, Devin wondered how much damage Curtis had done. In a mental rage, he damned Curtis's quest for the Higgs, damned Ray Crawford's blind obsession over the 13th Power, and damned his daughter, too, the traitorous little bitch.

"Boss, you better get up here."

Shivering, Devin walked the wracked halls of Atomtech. He felt numb, stunned with disbelief. The place looked like a war zone, his company in shambles. Scattered throughout the debris lay the bodies of his workers and security men. Painful moans of the wounded echoed eerily down desecrated corridors. The stink of gunpowder and sulfur hung heavy in the air. Lingering dust and smoke burned his throat.

In the main control room, he came to realize the magnitude of his loss. The nerve center of all his technological wonders lay in ruins around his mangled technicians. Atomtech could no longer function. It would take years to repair the damage to his empire. He could never replace the professionals he had lost. Seeing one-legged Leonard lying in a pool of coagulating blood left him racked with nausea. Disbelief collided with reality.

Curtis had to be stopped. Somehow.

A scream from the stairwell sent a chill down his spine. Toothless. What would make the big goon scream like that?

Devin ran up the bullet-scarred stairwell. What he saw on the second landing made him reel in horror. The headless corpse of Little Man lay in a pool of blood. And the stench was something awful.

Toothless pounded his fist on the wall. "Why? Why did I let him stay here alone?"

"Come on," Devin said, his guts churning. "Keep going. Upstairs."

"What kind of animal would do this?"

"The worst kind. The *human* animal." Devin stepped over Little Man's torso and climbed the remaining stairs to the third floor foyer. Early morning sunbeams shined through blown out windows.

"Somebody's going to pay for this, boss," Toothless pledged as he shuffled through the room, dust swirling from his footsteps.

As he approached his office, Devin saw the bulging eyeballs of Little Man's severed head staring out from the shadows. Blood streaked his face like tears. A bayonet held his skull upright on the desk. Devin's stomach cramped. "The bastards."

Toothless ran to the doorway. "Little Man." The big goon buckled over, fell to his hands and knees and vomited on the floor.

Devin turned his head away, his stomach heaving from the smell of bile. Fighting a reflex to expel his guts, he swallowed hard and looked back into his office.

Like a wraith in flesh, the hideous image of Little Man's decapitation reflected the haunting truth about this real-life nightmare. There was no limit to what men would do to each other. Devin slammed his fist into the wall. He had been condemned and punished for trying to end

Curtis's quest for the 13th Power. If Colonel Fallon had believed him, maybe all of this destruction and death could have been avoided.

Devin felt like a lone soldier in a war the world knew nothing about. Curtis was winning; the world was losing. Something had to be done to turn the tide. Maybe *now* Fallon would help him stop the impostor.

"Get up." He yanked on Toothless's arm.

The burly goon rose, snorted in his sleeve, and spit on the floor. "Where we goin', boss?"

Devin walked into his office, ignoring the gruesome head skewered to his desk. "Indian Springs to find Colonel Fallon. Any objections?"

Toothless didn't answer.

"Make yourself useful and find us a van."

Scooping up a handful of cigars, he watched Toothless disappear down the stairs. A glance at Susan River's desk spurred him to be thankful she wasn't here during the attack. She too could have been killed. He noticed her nameplate was missing from her desk. Toothless and Little Man wouldn't have taken it, but somebody did.

Devin turned his attention to the severed head on his desk. Lower lip trembling, he felt the sorrow of losing his faithful aide. He couldn't find the words to thank Little Man for saving his life, for making the ultimate sacrifice, but he did promise to avenge his death in a bloodbath like no bloodbath the country had ever seen.

Chapter 62

STEAM SWIRLED AROUND the overheated sheriff's car, giving Janis an eerie sense of entombment in a crimson mist. A droning vibration shook the car violently as the massive aircraft climbed under full power. Clinging to the steering wheel, he felt as if he'd jumped on a fast elevator. His stomach turned queasy. The shaking slowly subsided, and his vertigo relented as the plane leveled off. He quickly turned his attention to the back seat.

Ray grimaced as he held his daughter. "Nice driving."

Janis reached back to touch Lisa's shoulder. "We're safe now..." Hesitating, he scanned the tinted windows. "I think." He looked at Lo. "You all right?"

Lo just stared straight forward in his usual trance.

Janis turned to Ray. "Curtis pulled off the impossible. I have to say I may have misjudged the man."

A thumping sound came from the driver's door window.

"Time to meet our rescuers," he said, noticing the steam dissipate. A soldier was rapping on the glass with a gloved hand.

Janis rolled down his window. "I'll have the burger and fries combo, please."

"Welcome aboard," the soldier said.

"Alex," Ray shouted, his voice beaming in surprise. "Where the hell did you come from?"

Alex stooped, looked in, and steadied himself on the doorframe as the aircraft rocked. "Ray! Are you all right?"

"I'm shot, damn it. Get me a doctor."

"Looks like you're in good hands." He smiled at Lisa. "Is she your nurse?"

"Cut the bull. I'm serious."

Alex said to Red, "Get the medic."

A moment later, a young doctor dressed in combat fatigues climbed into the back seat and attended to Ray's wound.

"How's it look?" Janis asked, noticing blood on the medic's pants.

"I've seen worse."

Janis asked Alex, "How'd you find us?"

"Curtis said you'd be on 55 with a pack of police on your tail. So we took a detour to see if we could help. You were easy to find. The Captain decided to drop the transport down in front of you, figuring you'd take the ramp rather than deal with those cops. What did you do, kill somebody?"

"Something like that." Janis looked at Lisa who was holding Ray's hand as the medic dressed his shoulder, her eyes still shiny with tears. The finality of killing Lawson hadn't yet struck her. For now she seemed concerned about her father's condition and attentive to the medic's work.

The intercom crackled. *"Ten minutes to touchdown."*

Payload specialists attached anchor straps to the car's axle.

Alex opened the driver's door. "Everybody out." The aircraft banked right. He braced himself on the door. "Find a seat and buckle in," he said as the plane rolled back to level flight.

Janis climbed out of the car. "I'm Dr. Mackey," he said to Alex.

"You had us worried there for a while, professor."

"It was one close call after another. I just don't understand why Devin was so hell-bent on stopping us."

"Beats me. But it cost him plenty." A wry smile formed on Alex's lips, but a turbulent bump of air jarred the aircraft and quickly changed his expression to a frown. "I hate when it does that."

After applying adhesive tape to a gauze bandage on

Ray's shoulder, the medic got out of the car and reported to Alex. "That'll hold him for now. Get the doc to pull the slug when we're on the ground."

Alex held his hand out to assist Lisa from the car but she refused it.

"Help my dad."

Alex helped Ray to a web seat and strapped him in. Lisa sat next to him.

Janis and Lo found seats among the troops and buckled in. Lo mumbled something in Chinese.

"What's the mumbo-jumbo, Lo?"

"We go now into jaws of tiger," he translated. "Bad feeling about this…" he pointed to his stomach, "…here."

Janis shrugged, but when he looked around and noticed sweaty soldiers and smelled the lingering odor of gunpowder, he wondered if Lo was right. Sooty M-16 barrels slung here and there made Janis suspect these troops had been in some kind of skirmish, probably for Curtis and probably against Devin. The gladiators had done battle.

He glanced around the cargo bay, trying not to be obvious as he took note of the men's faces. Some were stern and unfeeling. Others were blank and distant. None were happy. All were tired. Looking toward the cockpit, he suddenly realized Lo was right. Two soldiers lay wounded and bandaged on evacuation gurneys. Damn. Was Curtis just as dangerous as Devin? Was he equally capable of causing death and destruction? Could Janis trust him, or Alex, or any of these soldiers? He felt as though he couldn't see the snake pit for all the snakes.

The engines quieted and the aircraft pitched down for landing. Janis looked at Lo.

We go now into jaws of tiger.

Chapter 63

THE LONG BLACK EXECUTIVE CAR, flags flapping from the fenders, cruised through the airfield gate. Several black staff cars followed behind it. The procession headed for the tarmac where a staging area had been decorated with banners. Curtis sat in the back seat and scanned the sky for any sign of the approaching transport. He was elated when Alex radioed news of the successful rescue of his scientists. That, and Devin's defeat, brought him joy. "Today has been a great day," he said to himself, still looking skyward. His golden staff lay across his lap.

The plush luxury car came to a graceful halt, and the trailing staff cars fanned out on both sides. Like a choreographed precision driving team, they all stopped in formation. Staff car doors swung open, and top supervisors and department heads of Solartech Labs, dressed in dark suits, got out and padded toward the executive car. Jonathan opened the door for Curtis, who emerged into sunshine, donned his sunglasses and tipped a salute to his supervisors. Again, he turned his attention to the sky. Nothing.

He tapped his staff on the concrete. "Shall we?"

His men joined him as he made his way to a covered bandstand fronted by rows of folding chairs. As they walked, they talked and laughed among themselves. He was pleased to see everyone's excitement over the arrival of the project's new mathematician, the man who would fix all the calculations and formulas and guarantee success. Not smiling, he scampered up the steps to the shaded podium as the others found seats to their liking.

"Gentlemen," he spoke into the microphone. "Today is a proud day for Solartech Labs and for all of you, the men who made this possible. In a few minutes, Dr. Janis Mackey will be joining us. As you know, his help is vital to the 13th Power project. This is not new territory for him. Twenty-five years ago, he and Ray Crawford developed the hypothesis that you have been working with. Simply put, our reality is the world we live in. It's made up of atoms and surrounded by the universe. The magnitude of each of these things is dependent upon perspective."

He paused looking over his assembly, sweltering in the sunshine.

"The hypothesis proposes that since the earth is a ball so big that everywhere on its surface appears to be the top, then the same goes for the atom or the universe. As the perspective changes, the physics and math change, too. If we look at the earth from a different perspective, say from the moon, we can clearly see that we live on the side of the ball, not the top. So the hypothesis proposes there is a place inside the nucleus of an atom where the space around it appears as vast as the universe, a perspective we believe to be from the Higgs boson. Does that mean smaller equals larger? The hypothesis says it does. Can negative equal positive? The hypothesis says it could. Do the rules of physics and math as we know them apply in this realm of the Higgs, the 13th Power? The hypothesis says no."

The assembly stirred and talked among each other softly. Waiting for them to return their attention to the bandstand, he felt as if he had a whole school of suckers on his hook. If these brainards knew what he was really after, they'd all want a cut. No way. Milk them with their own science. Make them think big. Keep them on the hook.

"Think of the possibilities of the 13th Power. Without the rules of physics to shackle our technology, we can harness the speed of light, alter gravity, and tap the energy that generates the atomic force. E equals M C squared will be obsolete, gentlemen. The new math will be more powerful than we ever imagined."

He raised his fist and pulled it down forcefully. "Yes. Then we will have the power."

His audience stood and cheered. He smiled, raised his golden staff, and turned his back to the podium. The clamor behind him grew louder and louder, suddenly turning into a roar that stifled the applause.

Curtis whirled around and saw the huge form of a flaring C-130 transport. Massive belly-tires smoked on the concrete and, as the nose wheel gently settled to the runway, reverse thrusters roared the aircraft to braking speed. Vibrations of sound and power pounded the onlookers. Some of them turned their backs to the onslaught and covered their ears, but Curtis stood upright and took it all in like a junkie on a psychedelic trip.

The jungles of Borneo seemed a long way off. His dreams were now on his doorstep.

Chapter 64

From the perimeter fence twenty yards away, Steve stood with Susan, watching the spectacle played out on the bandstand. They hadn't been invited to this event, but when he saw the activity from the window of their suite, he decided they should take a walk.

As he listened to Curtis's speech, he recalled what Devin had told him about the impostor. Judging from Curtis's obsession with power, Steve figured Devin must have been right. Melvin Anderson was, indeed, a dangerous man. And as he listened to what sounded like another madman, Devin's warning didn't go entirely unheeded.

I need to be careful with this guy, Steve reminded himself. Curtis wouldn't want his real identity revealed because his followers wouldn't be so loyal if they knew they were working for an impostor. Keeping his secret had to be worth a fortune.

Steve spotted the C-130 transport approaching from the west, dark and eerie and seemingly gliding down an invisible string. The wing flaps were fully deployed, giving it the appearance of a giant aberration that somehow defied gravity. He pointed to the aircraft, turning Susan's attention away from the podium. A cold shiver ran down his spine when the quiet day suddenly turned into a roar of turboprop engines and screeching tires from the landing aircraft.

Susan gripped his arm.

Questions raced through his mind, questions about the raid and the men that went to stop the madman. The thought of Devin's death excited him even more. He couldn't wait to hear how it happened and see the cell phone pictures. His hate for Devin was unmoved by the madman's incredible insight of the impostor.

Susan watched the aircraft come to a stop on the tarmac. She had mixed feelings about Devin and didn't want to hear how he'd been killed.

A flight-line crew unrolled a gold carpet from the bandstand to the cargo ramp. Curtis came down from the podium and stood at the carpet's edge as if he'd practiced this ceremony a thousand times before.

Soldiers marched down the ramp to the cadence of their leader. When they cleared the aircraft, Red barked, "Column right, huh. Company, halt." They stood in formation and Curtis saluted them with the golden staff.

Red saluted back, proud as could be.

Two men made their way down the cargo ramp, followed by a woman and an Asian man. One of the men had a bandaged shoulder, his arm in a sling. Susan thought they looked important. Then she saw Alex walking behind them, long-faced. Why? Had something gone wrong? They all stopped at the gold carpet and faced Curtis.

"Those are the guys Devin was trying to kill," Steve told her.

"The girl, too?"

"I guess."

"Who are they?"

"I don't know. I wonder how they ended up on the plane." Steve took Susan's hand. "Come on. Let's find out."

At a full run, they headed for the gate.

Chapter 65

Janis Looked at Curtis, standing pompously at the other end of the gold carpet, and wondered what he'd gotten himself into. He complained to Ray. "This is ridiculous."

"Just humor the guy, Janis. For Christ's sake. He got us here alive, didn't he? So smile."

Janis gritted his teeth and forced a smile. The rich man seemed more interested in his stupid ceremony than the well being of his new arrivals. "Let's get this over with." He started walking without an invitation. Ray and the others followed him.

The assembly stood and applauded.

Curtis greeted them with his hand extended. He seemed especially delighted to meet Ray's daughter. Smiling at her, his gold tooth glistened in the sunlight. "Welcome to Solartech Labs." He took her hand and turned it palm down. Janis saw her tremble as Curtis kissed the back of her hand.

Janis sneered. *Pompous bastard.* He wanted to belt Curtis for being overly suave with Ray's daughter, but he had to chuckle when Lisa pulled her hand away and wiped it on the side of her shorts.

Seemingly unconcerned, Curtis turned his attention to Lo. "I hear you do computer consulting, Mr. Chin." He shook Lo's hand. "I hope you are planning to stay on with us. We could certainly use your help."

Lo bowed. "I have to see what help you need. Right now, we're tired. I would thank you very much to help us with that." Lo smiled but kept eye contact with Curtis.

"Very well." Curtis turned to Ray. "Looks like I need a damage report on you. Does it hurt?"

"Like hell, sir."

"I bet it does. We'll get that taken care of shortly."
Curtis looked at Janis. "And how are you, professor? Glad
to see you could make it."

As Curtis reached to shake his hand, Janis was quick
to protect it. "I've been nursing this cut since Devin blew
up Lo's house. It needs stitches."

"We'll have to fix that, too," Curtis said. "From the
looks of you all, I'd say you had a rough trip."

"That would be an understatement," Janis said.

Curtis turned to his security chief. "How did things go
for you and your men, Alex?"

"I need to brief you about last night in private, sir."

"Shall we get together on that later this afternoon?"

Alex nodded.

"Good. Now I'd like to introduce my staff to Dr.
Mackey."

Janis glowered. "Look, *Mister* Curtis. This is a bad
time for a party. So save it. We need medical attention,
food, and rest. Just point us in the right direction."

Curtis tapped his golden staff on the tarmac. "Alex
will take care of all the details, gentlemen…" He hesitated
and looked at Lisa. "…and my lady, of course. All in good
time." Curtis focused on a couple sprinting toward them.
"Alex, who are these intruders?"

"That's Steve and Susan," Alex said, waving to them.
"It's a long story. Let's just say they're your guests."

Curtis didn't look impressed. He turned to the
bandstand. "Ray, Dr. Mackey. Follow me." They went up
the steps to the podium. Lisa held Janis's arm, and Lo
followed them.

The assembly stood and applauded the newest
members of their team. Curtis raised the staff, but his
attention was not on his audience. He was watching Alex
intercept the approaching couple. Shaking hands, they
stood together talking. Steve clenched his fists. Curtis's

interest spiked. They were arguing about something.

The clamor from the crowd began to subside. Curtis pumped his staff in the air, prodding them to continue cheering, buying him a little more time to observe Alex and his guests.

Susan clasped her hands in front of her mouth and dropped her head. Was she praying? Or crying? Steve shoved Alex. They scuffled for a moment then embraced as if consoling each other. Alex took something from his pocket. It looked like a nameplate. He handed it to Susan. She, too, joined the embrace.

Curtis frowned. What was that all about? He made a mental note to ask Alex later. In fact, he had a lot of questions for his top security man. Alex had better have plenty of answers.

Janis noticed the soldiers marching up the cargo ramp with their leader. A tug had hooked onto the nose wheel of the massive aircraft. The broken-down sheriff's car had already been pushed down the ramp and was now hanging from the sling of a tow truck, which started driving away. "Hey, our stuff's in there," he yelled.

"Later." Curtis tapped the golden staff on the microphone. A clunking sound reverberated through the speakers, and the assembly came to order.

"Gentlemen," he began. "I present to you Dr. Janis Mackey from the University of Colorado."

Janis acknowledged the crowd with a slight wave of his hand.

As the applause began again, Curtis raised his hand to silence it. "Tomorrow we'll meet in Tech-Com Control at 0900 hours. In the meantime, our cafeteria personnel have prepared a big barbecue party for this afternoon. I suggest we celebrate today; there will be no time to play once we get this project back on track." He raised his staff once again, and the assembly responded with cheers.

Janis nudged Curtis aside and blew into the mike. "I

want you to know we are happy to be here." He paused and looked over the group. "Hell, we are happy to be alive."

The assembly laughed lightly.

"We're looking forward to working with you people. After tomorrow's meeting, we want a complete tour of Solartech Labs. But today we want to get cleaned up, rested, and fed. Any objections?"

'No' and 'no, sir' could be heard among the heightened applause. Janis stepped back beside Lisa.

Ray moved up to the microphone. "This is going to be the big one, boys," Ray trumpeted to his fellow workers. "My lifelong dream will become reality, and the Higgs will soon be ours." He raised both fists, and the crowd cheered wildly.

Janis tapped Ray on the shoulder. "Shut up and let's go."

Curtis led the way down from the bandstand. Everyone gathered at the bottom of the steps where they could mingle with the new arrivals. Janis kept Lisa tucked snuggly under his arm as they made their way through the crowd, shaking hands and patting shoulders as they went. Short greetings and quick introductions could not be avoided. The group conversed and moved slowly toward waiting staff cars.

Straining, the tug pushed the C-130 transport back onto the runway threshold. As Red stood in the jump-door, he saluted Alex and Steve. They saluted back, and Susan waved goodbye.

Four massive engines cranked, spewed smoke, and roared to life. Red swiveled the door shut. The prestigious crowd stopped to watch the giant aircraft poised for flight. A few moments later, the thundering aircraft rocketed down the runway and clambered into the midday sky.

Janis and Lisa watched their rescuers disappear in the distance. Ray and Lo joined them. As Janis made eye contact with Ray, he wondered if they had chosen the right direction in this. Many people had paid a high price for them to get here; many lost their lives.

"Is the 13th Power worth all the trouble?" he asked Ray.

"How was I to know it would come to this?"

"A caged tiger is never content," Lo said.

Janis nodded. "I'm afraid our troubles have just begun."

Chapter 66

Colonel Fallon PACED the floor in the control center at Nellis Air Force Base. His shiny black boots clunked on polished hardwood, and his jungle fatigues hung loosely on his stocky frame. He listened to radio transmissions coming over the ComLink. Beads of sweat trickled down from his balding temples. Removing thin wire-framed glasses, he wiped his brow with a handkerchief. His day had started with a disaster.

The ComLink crackled with static as his helicopter squadron neared the Atomtech compound. From the third floor control room in the Central Communications Building, Fallon was in constant contact with the mission specialists. He stopped pacing at the plate-glass window overlooking the flight line. They should've been there by now.

The radio on the ComLink squawked. *"We've got smoke, ten miles out. Towering black column."*

"Roger that, Green Leader," the controller answered. "Send in the remote Geigers."

"Sensors away."

Remote radioactivity sensors were rocketed into Atomtech's compound ahead of the advancing squadron. A few minutes later: *"We're not getting any signals. It's clean down there."*

Colonel Fallon felt instantly relieved. "Send them in."

"You're clear to land, Green Leader."

"ComLink, Red Leader," the speaker blared with a pilot's urgent voice. *"I've spotted a blue van speeding across the desert like hell's on fire. Request clearance to intercept."*

The controller looked at the Colonel.

Fallon had other priorities to deal with. "No."

"Negative, Red Leader. Stay with the mission."

"Put out an APB on the van," Fallon said.

"Yes, sir."

An airman breathlessly arrived holding a phone, the mouthpiece covered by the palm of his hand.

"It's the media again. What should I tell them?"

"No comment." Fallon knew he couldn't hold them off forever. He was still trying to ascertain the severity of the disaster. Until he had more answers than they had questions, he would keep the press in the dark.

"ComLink, Green Leader, we're on the ground. There are dead and wounded all over the place. Send in the Med-Evacs."

"Roger that."

Minutes later, as his staff collected statistics from his troops on scene, Fallon realized the staggering cost in human life. He dispatched another Med-Evac chopper to handle the flow of wounded. A triage team at the site was reporting injuries consistent with a battlefield scenario. Those reports made him think he was dealing with a terrorist strike rather than an accidental explosion. And the fate of his friend, Walter Devin, was also on his mind. Even though he thought of him as a cheat at cards, he still favored his friendship and was concerned about his well being. He could only hope Devin wasn't among the dead.

An airman handed him a decoded secret communiqué. "Get a load of this, sir."

"Now what!" The Colonel read the note aloud. "A decapitated corpse was found in a stairwell. The head had been bayoneted to a desktop."

He looked up, a chill running down his spine. "What are we dealing with here?"

The airman shrugged. "Something bizarre, that's for sure." He turned back to his terminal at the com-station.

Another airman signaled the Colonel's attention. "Sir,

report coming in. Munitions has discovered C4 residue…"
He paused to listen into his headset, his eyes on the ceiling.
"…M-16 shell casings scattered everywhere and…hand
grenade blast zones with shrapnel scoring." He looked at
the Colonel and frowned. "They say it looks like it was a
military operation, sir. They're interviewing survivors right
now." He jotted down more notes.

The Colonel walked back to the window and looked
out past the flight line, out into the vast span of desert to the
north. What evil had lurked beyond the horizon last night?
Who would have done such a thing?

The window rattled as a formation of F-16 fighters
flew over the runway, pitched upward, and banked
gracefully to the west. Its thunderous splendor only
sidetracked his attention for a moment. He returned to
pacing the floor.

A few hours passed before the final assessments were
compiled. The good news, no radiation had leaked from the
compound. The rest, all bad news: thirty-seven dead,
ninety-four injured, some seriously. Most of the injuries,
lethal or otherwise, were multiple gunshot wounds or
shrapnel trauma. One building was a total loss, along with
the sophisticated equipment that it housed. Most of the
other buildings were blast damaged. Someone familiar with
security circumvention had cut the perimeter fence. It had
been a professional operation. Colonel Fallon, standing at
the window again, decided he had enough information to
prepare a press release.

He watched the last Med-Evac chopper land on the
flight line below. Medical personnel transferred wounded
Atomtech workers to waiting ambulances that raced off
toward the base hospital, lights flashing and sirens wailing.
A makeshift morgue had been set up in Atomtech's
gymnasium. The dead would be evacuated later, after
autopsies and identifications were completed.

He rubbed his temples. This was going to be a long

day.

***

Sending up a plume of dust, a blue van rumbled down a road that cut its way across the desert. Though the midday heat had dried Devin's clothes, his boots and socks still sopped with water from the pit, but now he missed the coolness of a wet shirt.

For the past thirty miles, he had said nothing to Toothless. The terror of the raid ravaged his mind. Anger boiled inside. He was now more determined than ever to end Curtis's quest for the Higgs. Devin would rebuild his company after the imposter was put out of business. For that, Colonel Bruce Fallon was his only hope.

Devin wiped away a bead of sweat trickling down his cheek. Maybe the Colonel would believe him now, after what had happened at Atomtech.

Outside the window of the speeding van, cactus and sage streaked by. A dust devil swirled across the distant sandy flats. Devin thought about Colonel Fallon. A trusted friend, he was one of the few people with whom Devin socialized. Poker was their bond. On occasion, they'd head up to Reno for a few high-stake hands. During one of those all-nighters, he'd beaten the Colonel with the draw of an ace. Fallon accused him of cheating. The resultant fist fight landed them both on the sidewalk out front, nursing bloody noses. The casino had warned them to never come back again.

Devin lit up a rank cigar.

"Smoke that damn thing outside," Toothless shouted, batting at the smoke.

"Don't like it, don't breathe." Devin blew a puff of smoke in his face. "Just keep driving. Twenty miles to the highway, then go left. Got that?"

"Whatever you say, boss."

***

Toothless braked at the main gate to Indian Springs Air Force Base. The guard, a burly Security Policeman dressed in jungle fatigues, stood in front of a drawbar, signaling the dusty blue van to halt. Another guard with *SP* on his helmet approached the driver's window cautiously, as if expecting trouble. "What's your business here?"

Toothless just stared at him.

"I have to talk to Colonel Fallon," Devin said from the passenger seat.

"Let's see some IDs."

Toothless pulled a wet wallet out of his back pocket and fished out a soggy driver's license. "Flash flood."

The guard scrunched his brows, not amused.

Devin shrugged his shoulders. "I left home without it."

"Get out of the vehicle," the SP ordered, backing away from the van's door. His hand hovered over his holstered weapon.

Toothless heard the click of an M-16, a round from the clip sliding into the chamber. A guard, standing by the shack, brandished the weapon as if he intended to use it. Toothless snickered. Soldier Boy with the big gun didn't scare him. Shaking his head, he reached for the Luger tucked under his belt.

Devin held Toothless's arm down. "We'll play their silly game."

As they got out of the van, several more SPs ran toward them with weapons drawn.

"Hands on your head. Do it now."

At gunpoint, they were led around to the front of the van.

"Hit the ground, right here. Bellies down."

Toothless, trying to keep his chin off the hot pavement, glared at Devin. He should've let him shoot the bastards. Roughly, SPs slapped on handcuffs and frisked them. The Luger was quickly discovered.

"This has to be them," the guard said.

A siren wailed in the distance. Toothless craned his neck to look down the street. Flashing lights on a security Jeep sped toward them. He spit. Did all Devin's friends treat him this good?

"Keep 'em covered," the guard ordered as he turned to meet the approaching officer.

***

As Lieutenant Banks approached the main gate, he saw a group of guards surrounding two prisoners on the pavement. Some of his men were searching through a blue van. The squawk on the radio was barely audible over the wailing siren. *"We have them in custody."*

Banks exhaled a breath of relief. All bases in southern Nevada were on a full-scale security alert in response to the disaster at Atomtech. An APB had been posted for a blue van seen speeding from the area. Now the suspected terrorists were at his front door. He stopped at the drawbar and shut off the siren. Leaving the overheads flashing, he jumped out and ran to the waiting SPs. "What's their story?"

"One has no ID," the guard said as they walked toward the prisoners. "Says his name is Walter Devin. The ugly one was armed with this." He showed him a Luger.

"And the van?"

"Nothing in it, sir."

Banks stepped up to the subdued men. They looked uncomfortable with their hands cuffed behind them and lying on their considerable paunches. "Get 'em off the ground."

Several SPs grabbed the prisoners by their arms and lifted them to their feet. Devin's cold eyes and stern face caught Banks' attention immediately. A shiver went up his spine. "What do you people want?"

"I demand to see Colonel Fallon."

"What for?"

"My company was attacked this morning. We barely escaped with our lives."

"You're referring to the explosion at Atomtech?"

"That *explosion* was a military assault on my facility, commandos and all." Devin spit. "Now take me to the Colonel and stop wasting my time."

Banks stepped back and looked at his prisoners standing there shackled like criminals. They certainly looked like they'd had a bad day. Maybe Devin was telling the truth. Banks went back to his Jeep and keyed the radio mike. "We're taking them into custody until we talk to Colonel Fallon. Over."

***

Colonel Fallon sat at his desk, writing his report for the media. An airman summoned him to the phone. "Indian Springs, sir." He took the call.

"We've got two men here. They drove up in a blue van. One guy claims to be Walter Devin. Says he's a friend of yours."

"Is he all right?"

"Claims to have been attacked by a military force of some kind. Wouldn't elaborate any further. Insists on seeing you personally."

"Military?" A confirmation, Fallon thought.

"That's what he says."

"Put him on a chopper, ship him down here right away. Who's with him?"

"An ugly looking goon. Says he's Devin's aide."

"Send them both."

Fallon hung up and turned his attention to the flight

line outside his window. He crossed his arms over his chest and watched a Med-Evac helicopter rise from the pad. As it flew into the distance, he decided to hold off the press a while longer, at least until after he'd spoken with Devin. There had to be an accounting for the dead and wounded at Atomtech. A stranglehold of anger gripped him. Vowing to track down the marauders, he swore he'd bring them to justice.

The murderous military operation within his jurisdiction would be avenged.

Chapter 67

AT INDIAN SPRINGS, Devin's handcuffs were removed, and he was ushered into a holding cell with Toothless. Banks thought they weren't dangerous but elected to be cautious anyway. Devin's complaints about being locked up fell on deaf ears. Toothless didn't complain about anything, except the loss of his Luger. Chow was served on green metal trays. Devin wasn't hungry. Toothless ate enough for three men.

While they waited for the Colonel, they showered and shaved. Afterwards, Devin took a nap. The Lieutenant woke him. "Get up." He unlocked the cell. "You're going on a chopper ride."

Blackhawk helicopter engines whined and rotors slapped overhead as Devin climbed into the rear cabin seats with Toothless right behind him. A spotter gave the pilots an all-clear signal. The chopper lifted from the pad with the smoothness of an elevator.

Watching out his window as the flight line fell away, Devin thought about how he would expose the imposter to Fallon and derail Curtis's dangerous quest for the 13th Power. He would pay dearly for what he had done to Atomtech.

The twenty-minute flight was over quickly. Nellis AFB stretched out below him. As the chopper neared the landing pad, he spotted Colonel Fallon standing at the edge of the platform.

"Shit is going to hit the fan," Devin said under his breath as the ride came to a gentle end. The engines whined to a stop. He jumped to the sun-scorched pad and rushed to the Colonel. "Am I glad to see you." Devin shook the Colonel's hand exuberantly.

Toothless lowered his bulk to the pad and stood back.

The Colonel's greeting was more official. "What happened out there at your place?" He directed them toward the communications center.

"They tried to kill me—"

"And me," Toothless put in, pacing along behind them. "But they killed Little Man."

"Who?" The Colonel glared at Devin and then glanced back at Toothless.

"My friend."

"Let's talk about that inside," Devin said. "Say over a cold beer and a good cigar." Devin reached in his shirt pocket and plucked out a fat one to tempt the Colonel.

"Follow me."

Fallon pushed open the double doors to the Central Communications Building. Cool air-conditioning made the desert's heat seem far away. On the elevator, he said, "I have the body count, Walter. We've been processing them all morning. E-vac this afternoon."

"How many people did I lose?"

"Thirty-seven dead, ninety-four wounded, and some of those are critical."

The elevator door slid open, but Devin just stood there, anger and shock rooting him to the floor. *Thirty-seven dead?* If it weren't for Toothless and Little Man it would have been thirty-eight.

And if not for Susan's rescue of the aggravating private eye, the pit wouldn't have been an escape route, but only the death trap he'd intended it to be. Talk about fate...

He believed in fate. Move a single grain of sand on the shore and change the history of the world. He felt dizzy. This time fate was good to him, bad for thirty-seven of his people, and the ninety-four who were wounded. For their fate, Curtis was going to pay dearly.

Chapter 68

IN THE OFFICERS CLUB, Colonel Fallon lit the cigar Devin had given him. A foaming mug of beer slid along the bar and sloshed to a stop in front of Devin. Another slid to Toothless. He smiled his spacious grin and chugged the mug dry. Belching, he slammed the empty mug on the bar. "More."

The bartender worked a gurgling tap.

Toothless picked up a magazine.

Resolving the tragedy at Atomtech was Fallon's top priority. He stood beside Devin's barstool, unwilling to start drinking in the middle of the day. Though the officers' lounge wasn't his idea of an official meeting place, given the circumstances, it would have to do. He faked a smile and took in a rich drag of tobacco. "All right, Walter. You've got your beer and cigar. Now tell me what happened at Atomtech last night."

"I warned you about him, Bruce. But you wouldn't listen." Devin took a swig of beer.

"I'm listening now. Who did it?"

Smoke swirled from Devin's cigar. "I told you Curtis was up to no good. Now my people are dead and Atomtech is in ruins. This could have been avoided."

"How do you know Curtis had anything to do with it? Could've been terrorists trying to get their hands on some of your enriched uranium."

"They didn't take anything except my secretary's nameplate off her desk. This was personal, Colonel, damn personal."

"All right. I'll take your word for it and haul him in for questioning. Where is he?"

"Solartech Labs in Simi Valley, searching for the key

to the universe. The Higgs is at his fingertips."

Colonel Fallon took a drag on his cigar. Maybe he should've listened when Devin had warned him about Curtis, but there wasn't anything he could have done. Curtis hadn't broken any laws or caused any trouble, not that he knew about. Fallon couldn't beat down Curtis's door if he wasn't throwing a party. That had all changed now. His investigation into the Atomtech disaster gave him probable cause to look for answers anywhere he wanted. First, he had to get the facts. "What's the Higgs?"

Devin looked up, face pinched with concern. "The end of the world, Bruce."

An awkward silence permeated the officers' lounge as the Colonel pondered Devin's words: *the end of the world?* "That's a little hard to believe." Actually, he found it a lot hard to believe. He looked at Toothless for a reaction to Devin's claim but found the aide thumbing through a girly magazine, unconcerned.

Looking again at Devin, he saw a familiar dread in his eyes, one he'd seen before, in the eyes of a young bombardier over Hanoi, just before he pushed the bomb release button for the first time. The lieutenant seemed to be crying out for some way to stop what was about to happen. The dread in Devin's eyes was just as real, but Fallon couldn't comprehend the end of the world. That couldn't be real. He sat down on the bar stool next to Devin, his friend, the harbinger of doom. "Tell me about it, Walter."

Devin clasped his hands around the beer mug. "This goes back a long way, Bruce."

Toothless turned another page of his magazine.

"Einstein proved mathematically that matter could be converted into energy. Then Oppenheimer proved it. The Manhattan Project, Alamogordo, July 16th, 1945. The atom bomb changed the world. Missiles of death were pointed at everyone, just waiting for one lunatic to push a button. We built our bomb shelters and our missile silos and propelled the civilized world into a Cold War of threats and counter threats. Our only hope for survival was the promise of mutual annihilation. It's a miracle we survived."

A vein in Fallon's forehead throbbed.

"Now scientists are after the Higgs boson. It's the particle that gives matter mass. They even call it the God Particle."

"What could they do with it if they found it?"

Devin stared into his beer. "Who knows? Maybe they could develop some kind of doomsday weapon orbiting in space like Star Wars, or Buck Rogers' ray guns or something. The government's been trying to do that for years now. Since Reagan anyway."

"So the government could be involved."

"The Russians went after the Higgs first, then Fermilabs and CERN. It was like a race. The Russians dropped out after the Troitska disaster."

"Troitska?"

"The official report was that a meteor hit the area, left a big crater, but I'm not buying it. I think they loosed the Higgs, created a black hole, and a big chunk of Russia disappeared.

"Disappeared?"

"Disintegrated."

"Jesus. Can you prove that?"

"Of course not."

Fallon still wasn't any closer to solving the Atomtech tragedy. "Get to the point, Walter. What's all this science mumbo jumbo have to do with what happened last night?"

Devin took a breath. "I was trying to stop Curtis and his scientists from conducting the same experiments the Russians had botched. Curtis struck back."

Chapter 69

THE COLONEL STOOD and paced. Devin watched him for a moment, and then went back to his beer. He thought he'd let Fallon stew over the trouble the world was in.

Several minutes passed in silence. Except for the sound of Toothless flipping through pages of his magazine and the Colonel's footsteps, nothing else stirred in the officers' lounge. Anymore, Devin didn't care what Curtis wanted with the 13th Power. Now he was only concerned with settling the score, to destroy Curtis's precious project and snuff out his fucking life. Smiling at the thought, Devin took another swallow of beer.

Fallon walked up, frowning. "How could Curtis and a bunch of scientists orchestrate such a military assault on your company?"

"The use of military force tells me the government is involved. Somebody high up wants the 13th Power, and they'll do anything to protect the project."

"Then we have to stop him." Fallon rubbed his chin. "But how?"

Devin rotated the cigar in his fingertips, ashes dropping on the bar. "Military force, Bruce—just like he did to me last night."

Fallon sat on a barstool. "What did you do to Curtis to make him, or the government, strike back?"

Devin gulped. He knew he was in trouble now. People had been killed, property destroyed, all on his orders, but he had to do something to stop Curtis. The truth would surely make it look like Curtis had acted in self-defense. Still, the experiments had to be stopped, and to that end any means was justified. Now Devin had to think of a way to enlighten the Colonel without looking like some kind of homicidal maniac. Rule #1: always blame someone else. Devin put the mug on the bar.

"You wouldn't help me investigate Curtis, so when I found out Curtis was recruiting Janis Mackey from Colorado, I sent some men to delay his cab so he would miss his flight and miss a meeting with Curtis in San Francisco. My men got a bit overzealous and ended up dead."

Fallon scowled.

"So I sent some other guys to persuade Ray Crawford that he could get hurt. My men got a bit carried away, shot up his hotel room, but Ray's okay, just got shook up a bit is all.

"Then I sent three of my toughest bruisers to bring Janis to me for questioning. They got the shit beat out of 'em. So I told them to disable Janis's limo. The boneheads decided that blowing it up was a good way to do that. When they followed Janis to a mansion, I told them to send him a message. They sent him a bomb instead. I tell you, can't get good help these days."

Fallon didn't look sympathetic.

Undeterred, Devin continued with his tale. "I hired a private eye who discovered Curtis was after the Higgs, the 13ᵗʰ Power, the end of the world. From then on, I tracked his scientists by satellite, trying to neutralize them as they made their way to Simi Valley. I thought that eliminating his hired minds would derail his project."

"Don't play word games with me, Walter. *Neutralize* and *eliminate* sound like *kill* and *murder* to me. Say it isn't so."

"I was desperate, Bruce."

The Colonel glared. "Desperate enough to use your Cobra? Lieutenant Evans didn't go loony, did he? He was acting on your orders, wasn't he?"

"Burt went on a rampage. He never did like cops."

Devin gulped a swallow of beer. "That's my story and I'm sticking to it." The Colonel would play hell trying to prove otherwise.

"Your story stinks, Walter. I'm going to investigate your actions, as well."

"You can arrest me, you can jail me, you can execute me, but it doesn't change the facts. Curtis has to be stopped. His real name isn't Frank Curtis. It's Melvin Anderson. Check him out. You'll find he's a notorious grave robber who's supposed to be dead. He's a goddamned fraud."

The Colonel stared, his eyes disbelieving. "How did *you* get wind of all this?"

"I met Curtis during an official visit at Solartech Labs, right after he took over the place. I recognized him as Melvin Anderson from a carbon-dating seminar I attended in Zurich ten years ago. We sat across from each other at the conference table. Yeah, Melvin Anderson, a con man if ever I saw one. A grave robber. A murderer. The Malaysian authorities would have him in prison right now if his helicopter hadn't crashed. His appearance in California under an alias made me suspicious, so I had to find out what he was up to. The rest is history."

Fallon thought about that for a moment. Back home on the farm in Idaho, when a snake escaped into a hole, they'd flush it out with a gasoline fire and cut off its head with a shovel. Apparently Devin had opened a viper pit. Fallon could see it was going to take a lot of fire and a big shovel to deal with Curtis and his project, especially if the government was involved. Now was the time to start thinking about how to put an end to it.

He crushed his cigar in an ashtray. "Finish your beers, boys." He got up and headed toward the door. "I'll send someone to show you to your quarters. Get some rest. You're going to need it." He walked out of the officers' lounge, his footsteps fading down the hallway.

Devin looked at Toothless. "Like I said, shit is gonna fly."

Toothless tossed his magazine on the bar and grinned his ugly grin.

Chapter 70

FALLON SLAMMED the office door and walked past his desk to the window. As he looked out at rows of Apache helicopters parked on the tarmac, he mulled over what Devin had told him. How could Curtis have come up with enough firepower to launch a military attack against Atomtech? A civilian with military capability didn't seem possible. And the armament that was used: C4 explosives, M-16s, and hand grenades, made it all the more impossible. How many men had it taken? How had they gotten in and out? By land? By air? He picked up the telephone.

"Sergeant, connect me to the tower." The phone rang almost immediately.

"Tower. Airman Brown."

"Colonel Fallon, SP," he said. "I need the radar recordings for last night's air traffic. Who do I need to talk to?"

"I'll connect you with Las Vegas Center, sir."

"Very well." The phone clicked and rang again.

A woman answered. "Las Vegas Center, how may I help you?"

"This is Colonel Fallon calling from Nellis Air Force Base. I'm investigating the Atomtech disaster."

"Horrible."

"I need last night's radar recordings for southern Nevada."

"The FAA has them," she said.

"Why is the FAA interested?"

"Probably has something to do with a radar echo that disappeared from our screens about twenty-five miles southwest of Desert Rock this morning. Our controllers thought the aircraft had been destroyed in midair, but before they could initiate a search of the area, the echo returned, going the other direction. Just disappeared and reappeared, like magic."

"How long was the aircraft lost on radar?" The line was suddenly muffled, as though she had put her hand over the mouthpiece.

A moment later she replied, "I can't answer that, sir. You'll have to take your inquiries to the FAA. Sorry." The phone line clicked dead.

"The FAA, hell." He slammed the receiver down. That tape was important. It could help him determine the origin and destination of that aircraft. Maybe it wasn't significant, but then again, it might be a breakthrough. He grabbed the telephone again.

"Get me the FAA Regional Office."

"Right away, sir."

A recording came over the line. *"Thank you for calling the FAA Nevada office. The regional director wishes to convey to the traveling public that we are doing everything possible to ensure the safety of air traffic in this country."*

"Yeah, yeah."

"All of our agents are currently busy with other calls. Please stay on the line and we will answer your call as soon as possible."

"Shit." He pushed the speakerphone button. The music playing on hold annoyed him. He paced the floor while waiting for an agent to pick up. Excited about the discovery of a mysterious aircraft in the vicinity, he was impatient to get some answers. Too many people were awaiting his report. The music stopped and another recording came on.

"Thank you for holding. Someone will be with you shortly."

Colonel Fallon sighed in disgust and sat at his desk. On a pad, he began writing notes in an effort to piece together a timeline of events related to the Atomtech disaster. His outline had a lot of blanks to be filled in.

"Agent Lester, may I help you?" came from the speakerphone.

"This is Colonel Fallon at Nellis. I'm investigating the Atomtech tragedy last night, and I need a copy of the radar recordings from Las Vegas Center. Have one available for my courier."

"Sorry, sir. A malfunctioning player accidentally destroyed the tape you're referring to. Burned it to a crisp." The agent cleared his throat. "Is there anything else I can help you with?"

Without replying, Fallon hung up in disbelief. He flexed his jaw. A crucial piece of evidence destroyed? Or so they claimed.

Thinking of another possibility, he picked up the phone again. "Get me General Brigham at the Pentagon."

"I'll ring you when I get connected, sir."

"Very well." He went back to his outline of events and wrote *Curtis* and *Solartech Labs* on the top of the page. He drew an arrow between them. Below them he wrote *Melvin Anderson*. He drew an arrow to *Curtis*. The phone rang.

"General, how are you?"

"Late for my tee off, Bruce."

"I'll make this brief. I'm investigating the Atomtech tragedy—"

"It's all over the news," the General said. "What's going on out there, Colonel?"

"That's what I'm trying to find out, but my investigation has been stonewalled at every turn. I think the military is involved. Can you help me with that?"

The General coughed. "What are you suggesting, a United States military operation against its own citizens? Not out of this office, I tell you."

"Certainly not, General. But how about the Corbett

satellite? Could we get some reconnaissance information from it, radio transmissions, audio, video, anything?"

"The CIA commissioned it yesterday for something in Central America. You know how much trouble they're getting into down there."

"Then will you check with some of your CIA contacts, see what you can learn?"

"The CIA can *rot* as far as I'm concerned."

Colonel Fallon understood. General Brigham and the CIA had a falling out two years ago. He recalled the flack over it. In fact, the President had threatened to bust Brigham down to Corporal if he persisted with his accusations of a conspiracy between the White House and the CIA. A special committee, appointed by the Justice Department, convinced Congress the General was just pissed off because the President had taken Star Wars away from him. He was nearly imprisoned for misappropriation of funds. In the end, Brigham held no fondness for the President, either.

"Sorry, sir. Enjoy your golf game." The Colonel hung up with yet another dead end. Frustrated, he looked again at his outline, focusing on *Melvin Anderson*. Devin had been adamant about Curtis being his alias, an impostor. Fallon double underlined Melvin's name. What could the FBI dig up on this guy? He reached for the phone again.

Chapter 71

CURTIS WATCHED THE C-130 transport disappear over Simi Valley. He decided to concentrate his attention on the arrival of his scientists. They had made a grand entrance.

Scanning the crowd for Alex, Curtis noticed the newcomers huddled together, the bond between them obvious. He could only wonder what they had been through, but there would be time to get that story later. Ray and Janis needed medical attention, and they all needed food and rest. He would give them that much before pressing them for details.

For now, the California sun shined much too intensely to be standing around in a full-length black coat. The air-conditioned executive car beckoned him. He removed his sunglasses and ducked inside the car. The door closed and cool air surrounded him.

Jonathan got in. "That went well, sir."

"Very well, indeed. Let's go."

Jonathan motioned to the driver. The executive car accelerated and weaved its way through the lingering crowd toward the airfield gate.

***

Alex commandeered the nearest staff car and invited Susan and Steve to ride along. Sitting shotgun, Steve's gaze went to Curtis's car as it sped away. "There he goes."

Susan, sitting in the middle, squeezed his arm. "Don't do anything stupid. Please."

He didn't answer.

Alex asked, "Do what?"

"Nothing," Steve said. "You better get your boys some medical attention."

Alex saw Ray on the tarmac, holding his arm, and spoke into the wrist radio. "Station two, get the Doc ready. He's got customers."

The tiny speaker squawked. *"Roger."*

Alex drove around the crowd to where Ray stood with Janis, Lisa and Lo. "We gotta get you to the clinic, Ray. Everybody hop in."

Lisa opened the door and slid in after Ray. Janis and Lo squeezed in next to them.

Steve turned to the back seat. "I'm Steve Raven and this is Susan Rivers." He looked at the bandage on Ray's arm. "How did you catch that bullet, Ray?"

Ray looked at him for a moment, a deep frown across his brow. "How did you know my name?"

"I know a whole lot more than you think."

Susan patted his shoulder. "He's a private eye."

Steve smiled slyly. "I saw you at the Balli Club. You might have noticed me. I was disguised as a janitor."

"Disguised?"

"The beard makes me invisible. Devin hired me to find out what you brainards were up to. We've since had a falling out."

Janis shot him an angry glare. Alex wasn't sure if Janis was going to hit Steve or not. Driving on, Alex listened while watching Janis's expression get angrier in the rearview mirror.

"Now don't get the wrong idea, here," Steve said. "I had nothing to do with your problems."

Janis didn't look convinced.

Alex could feel the tension in the car, like a rubber band stretching beyond its limits. "He's on our side now," Alex said, hoping to relax Janis. "That's what counts."

Steve bobbed his head in agreement. "Who shot you, Ray?"

Ray recounted his brush with death as Janis glowered at the private eye. By the look on Janis's face, he didn't seem comfortable with Steve's loyalty. Nor did Lisa, but Alex wasn't sure if she felt uneasy about Steve or the story Ray was telling him.

Susan seemed especially interested in Ray's story. Her mouth hung open when he got to the part about Lawson's death. She looked at Lisa. "You shot him?"

Lisa nodded. Her taut lips gave Alex the impression she wasn't proud of herself, like she wished there had been another way to deal with the crooked cop.

Finishing his short rendition, Ray moved his shoulder to demonstrate his wound but grimaced in pain.

Steve said, "Damn. You're lucky to be alive." He looked at Alex. "Devin isn't going to let this thing go, you know that."

Alex ground his teeth, frustrated that the madman had escaped during the raid. He accelerated the staff car toward the airfield gate.

Solartech Field Road was paved and neatly striped, lined with swaying palm trees and well-groomed grass waysides. A sign directed traffic to go left for the main gate and Simi Valley, or right for the compound security checkpoint. Alex turned right.

The staff car slowed at a stone archway, where video cameras recorded their arrival. A heavily armed security officer saluted, and the car drove on. Alex activated his wrist radio. "Station two, ETA three minutes."

"They're waiting," came the reply.

Ray's heightened pulse rate made his shoulder ache. He just wanted to get this over with. Doctors, needles, and blood were nowhere on his list of favorite things. His stomach churned just thinking about the upcoming procedure to remove the bullet. He watched out the window to get that bloody mess out of his mind. Lisa held his hand. Though he found some comfort in that, he wished she wasn't attracted to Janis. The thought of those two together rekindled an anger he'd been harnessing, for her sake. Pain stung his shoulder again, this time with more intensity.

The staff car stopped in front of C-Wing. Steve and Susan got out.

"The cafeteria's inside," Alex said. "I'll catch up with you later. Save some food for us."

Janis moved to the front seat and closed the door. "I'm starving."

"Doc needs to look at your hand first." Alex drove away from C-Wing. At a stop sign, he turned right and headed up a ramp to an elevated viaduct between two stainless-steel buildings, five stories high. Tinted plate glass windows on both sides reflected images off each other, giving the illusion of driving through a kaleidoscope. Ray watched Janis's expression, his face beaming.

"Incredible place," Janis said.

The staff car passed under glass-enclosed pedestrian catwalks that bridged the gap between the two buildings high above the car. Up ahead, a huge steel arch spanned the viaduct, its facing inscribed with the words, *Welcome to Solartech Labs. Gateway to the Atomic Universe.*

"Oh, my God," Lisa said. "Will you look at that?"

Lo looked impressed in spite of his reservations about tigers and teeth.

"I told you, Janis," Ray said. "This place isn't like anything you've ever seen."

Alex cleared his throat. "The building on your left is administration. On your right is Tech Com, the main laboratory complex with Tech-Com Control, the heart of Solartech Labs. All the technical work is done within those walls. You'll get the grand tour tomorrow."

"Unbelievable," Janis said, looking back and forth out the windows.

The staff car sped under the archway and into a vehicle reception lobby. Centered in the lobby, an array of huge glass doors marked the entrance to this hi-tech facility. Chrome and black escalators moved up and down just inside the atrium where video cameras swept back and forth in ever-silent vigil. Ramps to an indoor parking garage extended up both sides of the vehicle lobby. A horn reverberated from somewhere within.

Alex hung a left. Squealing tires echoed through the steel-reinforced lobby as the staff car swung onto a ramp that spiraled upward. Around and around he drove higher and higher until the car broke out onto the sundrenched rooftop parking area.

Ray squinted.

To the right, a helicopter pad extended out from the roof, its windsock swaying lazily in the breeze. To the left, a fountain, which erupted every hour from a pool five stories below, gushed water higher than the roof. Ray was pleased with the amazed expression on Janis's face.

The staff car stopped in front of an elevator lobby. Double doors swung open. Several personnel in white gowns wheeled a gurney out.

Ray's stomach rolled over. They were coming for him.

Chapter 72

THE EXECUTIVE CAR SCREECHED to a stop under a carport in front of the presidential quarters. A little gray lizard darted across polished granite steps and scurried up a white marble pillar. From the safety of its lofty perch, it peered at an attendant who rushed out the revolving door to greet the CEO of Solartech Labs. A pop from the car door made the lizard cock his head sideways to get a better look. When Curtis emerged and donned his sunglasses, the light-footed little creature ran for cover under a shaded eve.

Curtis tapped the golden staff on the driveway. He had to maintain his façade even if he was at home. Jonathan followed him into the lobby, and they made their way to the Penthouse elevator. Curtis punched a code on a keypad mounted to the wall. The door opened with a ding and he stepped inside.

Jonathan didn't follow him. "See you at the barbecue party." He headed toward the elevators on the other side of the lobby.

The door closed, encasing Curtis in a chamber of mirrored walls draped in gold velvet. Soft lights around the ceiling made the golden draperies glimmer. Mirrors projected the light, giving the illusion of sparkling glitter floating in the air. The elevator ascended smoothly.

Removing his sunglasses, he wiped sweat from his brow with his coat sleeve. He was tired but too excited to care. As he leaned against the back wall, he caught a glimpse of his face in the mirror. Wrinkles on his forehead and cheeks reflected the wear and tear of time. Sagging skin under his eyes made him look older than he felt, but he grinned anyway. This would one day be the face of the Higgs Master.

When the elevator reached the Penthouse, the door opened into a spacious parlor. A large crystal chandelier hung from the ceiling. Golden light beams scintillated around the room. After hanging his coat on a rack by the elevator door, he walked briskly into the front room and headed straight for the bar.

He poured himself a glass of brandy, kicked off his boots, and settled into an easy-chair by the fireplace. He laid the golden staff across his lap and stroked its smooth, shiny surface, cautious of the eagle head's emerald eyes. After he propped his feet up on the hassock, he took a moment to savor the sweet vapor of his drink. Peach, his favorite. He loosened his tie, took one sip, then another, and began to relax. Enjoying the moment, his mind wandered as he settled lower into the chair. Another sip or two later, he felt himself slip into slumber.

A sudden crash of thunder rumbled through the room and jolted him from his seat. His golden staff fell to the floor. He threw up his arms, shielding himself from a blast of wind that whipped in through a shattered window. The broken sash flailed violently as the tempest blew in a torrent of rain.

Shards of glass littered the carpet and cut his feet as he struggled, step by step, to reach the window. Something was drawing him to look out. Whatever it was, terrified him. When he peered out the window, he saw a world that made his stomach twist in horror.

Lightning bolts cracked the dark sky and lit up the valley of boulder fields. The ground rolled like an ocean in a gale, an earthquake of a magnitude twenty on the Richter scale.

Thunder banged again. Wind blew in the rain, which pelted his face as he looked up at spinning clouds glowing red, then orange, then yellow, and then back to red. Rotating like a giant pinwheel, the storm spun off funnel clouds that twisted down and snaked across the ground.

Flashing blue streaks of lightning spit fingers earthward and made sinkholes appear. They gobbled up trees and rocks, filled with water, and froze over.

"What in God's name?" Curtis screamed.

Icy hail pummeled him, bounced across the room, and melted into sparkling fireballs. He spun away from the window, ducked and covered his head with his hands.

The sound of thunder rolled into the room. He watched in horror as jagged fingers of static electricity arched over the windowsill and wormed their way toward him, randomly forking to the ceiling and the walls. They crackled, sizzled, and hissed as they moved blindly about the ravaged room.

Heart pounding, he screamed and turned to run from the stormy window and its lethal electric tongue. He ran hard but he wasn't moving, like his feet were slogging through wet cement.

"Oh, shit, run, damn it. Run."

But he couldn't manage but a couple of steps. He felt a heavy weight on his back. It was more than he could carry. His knees bent under the strain. The room was going by in slow motion as the deadly electric limb arced closer and closer. There was no escape. With adrenaline rushing through his veins, he turned back into the tempest to face the approaching nemesis, but the arching death had disappeared, leaving behind the ionized smell of battery acid in the air.

He was suddenly looking out the window again. Through the jagged opening he could see the lab complex, Tech-Com Control, from where the storm was spawned. "Bastards," he yelled above the gale. "You started without me."

Janis and Ray stepped out into the gale and waved up at him, smiling like they were so proud they'd accomplished the impossible.

Without warning, the wind and rain stopped. The

storm held its bitter breath with the stillness of a funeral parlor.

"What the hell?"

Someone shoved him from behind. He tumbled out the window into thick, sulfur-laced air. The dizzy sensation of falling engulfed him. He looked up to the window. Jonathan was waving goodbye. The horror of his impending death swirled in his mind. He struck the ground, numbed by the impact.

His body jerked. Breaking glass ripped at his consciousness. He grabbed the golden staff and leaped from the chair. With his heart hammering in his chest, he looked around the room. Except for the brandy glass lying shattered on the fireplace hearth, nothing was broken. Everything was in place, including the ominous window. Gasping, he tried to shake the cloudy nightmare from his mind, but the terror lingered.

He was soaked in Brandy. A shower became a necessity.

Hot water stimulated his body, which still trembled in the wake of his terrifying dream. Had he seen a premonition? Though he knew that fooling around with the 13th Power was tricky, he wondered if his imagination was being fed by unfounded fears. Could mutated atoms spread like a cancer, changing natural events into bizarre phenomenon with catastrophic consequences? Would the rules of physics be changed...or nullified?

Steam fogged the shower stall glass, blurring his reflection. The hot water dissolved the tension in his back. With steamy mist swirling around him, he thought about other scientists who'd been splitting atoms for decades, attempting to study the building blocks of matter. They'd slammed nuclei together in super colliders without changing the basic nature of the universe. So what if he was going to do the same thing, only at higher speeds and in greater numbers. Nuclei would just be broken into much smaller pieces of short-lived particles. How was that supposed to create mini black holes as Boris had warned him about?

Even so, Curtis was prepared for that possibility. He'd fight fire with fire and build a black hole in a containment chamber from which the Higgs could not escape. He'd open up the 13th Power, pluck out the Higgs, and store it in a titanium cylinder where it would be used to rearrange lead atoms into gold atoms. The prize would be his and his alone.

He put his head under the shower spray. His father's words came back to him: *Risk nothing, gain nothing.*

He twisted the shower knobs closed and stepped out. Grabbing a towel, he thought about Ray and Janis. They weren't so smart. Interested only in the science of the 13th Power, they were completely unaware of the wealth they would give him. The only man who could have stopped him knew. Walter Devin.

And he was dead.

Chapter 73

Holding SUSAN'S HAND, Steve Raven strolled onto the patio behind the cafeteria at C-Wing where the barbeque party was in full swing. Smoke, rising from the barbecue pit, scented the air with the aroma of hickory and tangy sauce. His stomach churned with anticipation.

Several cooks wearing white aprons and towering chef's hats attended the grill, flipping steaks and burgers and chicken and skewers of shrimp and lobster. Other servers worked behind a long table of sides and fixings: hot wings, cold cuts, cubed cheeses, potato salad, coleslaw, baked beans, cut vegetables, and fresh baked cookies and breads and cakes. Curtis had spared no expense for this celebratory meal.

A light breeze rustled the canopy above the bar, shifting Steve's attention to Solartech Lab's employees and supervisors gathered around, drinks in hand, sipping and talking among themselves. Boisterous laughter rose above the hubbub. Hawaiian music drifted across the patio, giving the festivities a Polynesian flair.

Susan tugged on his shirt. "Over there." She pointed to the food tables.

"I'm coming." He scanned the crowd, looking for Curtis as she pulled him toward the buffet. Not seeing him around the bar, he quickly scanned the courtyard. Most of the patio tables scattered about the lawn were vacant, their gold umbrellas flapping lazily in the breeze. Swaying palm trees adorned the walkway that led to a swimming pool. Again, he didn't see Curtis.

As he followed Susan's persistent lead toward the food, he glanced down at the .45 holstered under his short-sleeve shirt. It wasn't concealed very well. He believed it was better to have a gun and not need one, than to need a gun and not have one. And this was no place to be caught without one. There must've been a dozen security goons hanging about, their suit coats unbuttoned and the butts of their guns visible.

Susan saw them, stopped abruptly, and pulled him in close, her eyes filled with concern. "Do you have to go through with this?"

"Don't worry."

"If I don't, who will?"

He pursed his lips and stared at her. Back in their suite, while dressing for the party, she had expressed concern for his safety. Not being used to dealing with someone else's feelings, he felt annoyed by her persistence. Hell, he'd been dealing with bad guys all his life. Now all of a sudden she thought he needed worrying about.

"I can take care of myself."

Her beautiful eyebrows arched. "Like you did in Devin's pit? You'll end up dead."

So…okay…she was right about the pit. He'd still be wallowing in the slop if she hadn't saved his neck. "But that was different."

"Dead is dead, Steve. There is *no* difference." Looking confident she had made her point, she started walking toward the food table again.

Steve followed her, thinking maybe he should be extra careful.

She looked over the selections at the table and handed him a plate. "Don't make this your last meal."

Feeling mothered, he scooped up some potato salad and coleslaw and grabbed a handful of hot wings as he walked down the buffet line behind her. She looked great. Her dress, a flowing silk gown brought up by housekeeping, accented her fluid motion. Smiling to the server, she requested a chicken breast. He set an especially plump one on her plate. She was good with people, not shy to talk frankly and with an air of confidence. He liked that. Her sweetness seemed contagious to those around her.

He looked over the menu on the chalkboard. The skewered shrimp kabob with green peppers and artichoke hearts looked good. "I'll have the shrimp thing."

The server looked at the board. "Sorry, we're all out of that, sir. You'll have to pick something else."

"What?" He was sure he read it right. Looking again, there it was in white on black. His jaw clamped in anger and embarrassment for ordering something that wasn't available. The solution seemed obvious. "Then why is it still on the chalkboard? You run out of something, you erase it. Don't make me out to look like an idiot." His angry voice boomed above the crowd. He pulled back his shirt panel, revealing the .45.

A spoon clanged on the floor. The server stepped back. The din of conversation went silent, everyone's attention now on Steve. Just the way he wanted it.

Susan tugged on his shirt. "Never mind, dear. Have a steak kabob instead." She forced a smile. Steve's tough-guy attitude and hair-trigger temper was probably the only reason he'd survived so long in his line of work. Could his anger go so far as blind rage? She didn't think so. She'd seen his softer side, but now he had the attention of the security people, a dangerous thing if someone were to take him seriously. She needed to defuse him before he got himself killed, so she pointed at the server. "Just don't shoot the poor guy 'til *after* dinner."

Steve covered up his gun and growled at the server. "Erase it before you piss off somebody who's not as nice as I am."

"Right away, sir." The server went to the chalkboard and rubbed off the shrimp selection with the palm of his hand. Another server took his place and held up a juicy skewer of steak adorned with plump mushrooms and green pepper slices. "Is this one satisfactory, sir?"

"Fine." Steve shot a menacing glance at the bar crowd.

They quickly went back to minding their own business, all but the security guards, that is.

#

Sitting alone at a patio table, dressed in a Hawaiian shirt and green Bermuda shorts, Judas slid sunglasses down his nose and watched the fracas in the serving line, just the kind of thing he was policing for, troublemakers within the organization. Because he was the kind of weasel who would rat on his own mother, he liked spying on the employees of Solartech Labs. His reputation had instilled fear in them. Fear meant control. Control meant power. And Curtis gave him a free rein. He took another sip of his iced tea, and crossing his legs, kept an eye on the irritating stranger with the gun under his shirt.

#

With heaping plates and napkins in hand, Steve led Susan to the courtyard and selected a shady table. He sat facing the patio, as he would never have his back to a crowd or the center of a room. It wasn't safe that way, especially after the show he'd just put on. Now everyone knew he had a mean streak. They knew he had a gun. They'd step aside for him. They wouldn't dare interfere with his plans.

He forked a chunk of steak off the skewer, keeping one eye on the patio. The rich impostor could appear at any time. Then it would be payday.

Chapter 74

JANIS STOOD WITH LISA in front of the rooftop entrance to Solartech Medical and waved goodbye to the staff car as it spun around and drove away. Alex and Lo were headed for the maintenance garage to get their luggage out of the 2885 car. They were going to take everything over to Tamarack Hall, the employee's quarters, a place with a soft bed, a place Janis longed to be, fast asleep. But not yet. He followed Ray into the clinic, the medical team leading the way.

Inside the atrium, large ferns grew to the ceiling on both sides of the elevators. A huge chrome-framed photo of a Rega air-ambulance helicopter hung over a waterfall that flowed down tiers of moss-rock and trickled into a shimmering pool. Coins, glittering reminders of wishes once made, reflected from the shallow bottom. Lisa knelt at the pool's edge and ran her fingers through the water. Janis wondered if she was silently wishing for something.

The elevator doors slid open. He reached for her hand, and they went in after Ray.

On the ride to the infirmary, an antiseptic smell permeated the elevator. Ray hugged Lisa, and with a nervous smile, looked at the nearest attendant who must have noticed his apprehension. "We'll have you fixed up in no time."

"I'm hungry enough to eat the damn bullet," Ray said.

"You'll be eating steak at the barbecue party before you know it."

The door opened into a brightly lit corridor.

"We'll be waiting," Lisa said as the medical team led Ray down the hall.

Another doctor approached Janis. "I'm Dr. Lucero.

Let me take a look at that hand, professor."

"Oh, this little cut?" He showed the doctor.

"This little cut needs cleaning and stitches."

Janis knew he was going to hate this doctor.

"Follow me."

They walked down the hall and turned into a small room.

"Sit right here." Dr. Lucero pointed to a folding chair next to a table. "And set your hand like this." He situated it precisely, palm up, fingers straight. "Now hold it right there." He turned to a drawer under the counter and started rummaging through stuff.

A nervous shudder trounced through Janis's stomach. The room shined bright white and smelled of alcohol, not his idea of a fun place.

"Let's see. I need this." Lucero held up a big hypodermic.

Janis grimaced.

Lucero chuckled.

From a brown glass jar on the counter, the doctor drew liquid into the syringe. "It's a peroxide and water solution, to clean the wound."

"Very funny," Janis said with a sigh of relief.

"You'll think *funny* until I start scrubbing that little cut." He stretched on a pair of latex gloves. "It'll feel like the Grand Canyon is on fire in the palm of your hand."

Janis gritted his teeth.

The doctor sat down at the table and began to wash the dried-up wound. Janis winced. He had to be tough. He didn't want Lisa to think he was a big baby.

As the doctor scrubbed away the scab, the wound came open and began to bleed. He squirted the solution from the syringe into the gaping cut and rubbed some more.

Janis meshed his teeth. Excruciating pain knifed up his arm. He almost didn't care *what* Lisa thought about how tough he was. Almost.

Satisfied the wound was clean, the doctor grabbed a small vile and another syringe, a smaller one with a skinny needle on it. "This will prick a little." He administered the Novocain.

The pain began to subside. Janis never thought he would be so happy to get a shot. He only wished it was a shot of Scotch. Double.

"Let that go to work for a few minutes," Lucero said then placed a clean gauze pad on the open wound. He popped the needle from the syringe, tossed it into the disposal chute, and patted Janis's shoulder. "I'll be right back." He walked out the door, closing it gently behind him.

Lisa strutted toward Janis, smiling. "Way to go, cowboy." She kneaded his shoulders.

Her fingers felt as soothing as the medication numbing his hand. "Lisa…?"

"Just, relax." She massaged him gently.

"You need to keep your guard up around here." He turned to face her. "I know this all looks like paradise…but I have my doubts."

She looked into his eyes. "But it's beautiful here."

"It's an illusion."

"What makes you say that?" She turned his head back around and resumed the massage.

"On the plane, did you notice the soldiers?"

"Smelly bunch, huh."

"They looked like they'd been in a war. Did you see the wounded men?"

"No."

"Lo said we were going into the jaws of the tiger by coming here. Those men were in a fight on behalf of Curtis, I'm sure, probably with Devin." He turned around to face her again. "Curtis isn't any better than Devin. We aren't safe here. Promise me you'll be careful."

"Of what?"

"I didn't like the way Curtis looked at you."

"He's just an old man, eccentric but old."

"He's dangerous."

"I think you worry too much."

"Maybe."

"Then I'll be careful." She said it like an annoyed child and pushed his head around more forcefully than before. "Are you going to relax now?"

Janis slumped in the chair and let Lisa's fingers work their magic on his shoulders. He closed his eyes. He'd never met anyone like her before. The women he'd encountered in his life had always been the snooty professional types. They were extremely educated and so driven to be better than their male counterparts that they regarded men as competition, not companions. There was no tenderness in their manner, no care giving, only care taking. Janis never had any success with women like that. Lisa was young enough that she hadn't developed any of those unattractive traits.

He opened his eyes and looked at her over the top of his glasses, her smile, her hair hanging down. She was a beautiful woman. His mother would approve, if she could, except maybe she'd say Lisa was too young for him. Or the California sunshine was warping his sense of reason. Lisa was Ray's daughter. And that alone was a deal-breaker.

Chapter 75

AFTER DR. LUCERO SECURED the bandage to Janis's hand, Lisa asked, "Can we see Ray now?"

Lucero examined his work, seemed satisfied. "Keep this dry for two days. I want you back here on Tuesday."

Janis tested the bandage, wiggled his fingers. "Nine stitches?"

"We'll take 'em out soon."

"I want to see my dad now, Doc." Lisa smiled at him as she hugged Janis's neck.

"I'll see if he's ready for visitors." Lucero slipped out the door.

She needed to talk to her father. If she wasn't going to hate him anymore, she needed to know why he'd sent her away.

***

Dr. Lucero walked down the hallway to the surgical area. When he pushed through the double doors, he spotted the *Occupied* light flashing over the door to operating room B. Taking note, he scrubbed up, donned a gray surgical robe and mask, and placed a cap on his head. He headed for the OR.

The bright light over the operating table silhouetted the team and their head surgeon who held up a pair of forceps. "There it is." Dr. Randolph released the slug from Ray's shoulder into a metal tray. A dull clang echoed through the room. "A few stitches and you'll be good as new."

"Thanks, Doc."

Lucero introduced himself.

"Mind if I don't shake your hand?" Ray said.

"Lisa wants to know how you're doing. She can be very persistent."

"Tell me about it."

"Looks as though you're in good hands here." Lucero picked up the metal tray and examined the bloody bullet, flattened like the head of a mushroom. "What bone did it hit?"

"The scapula," Randolph said. "Another inch, it would have passed clear through. We'd be eating barbecue by now."

"Dumb luck, huh." He set the tray on the instrument table. "What should I tell Lisa?"

"Send her in when they're done with me. Then I'd like to get some sleep. I'm beat."

Lucero nodded. "We'll put you on twenty-four hours bed rest."

"By then you'll be begging to get out of here," Dr. Randolph said.

"Don't bet on it." Ray closed his eyes.

Lucero patted Randolph on the shoulder. "See you at the barbecue party." He walked out.

Dr. Randolph sutured the wound and stepped back from the table. "Wrap him up, boys." He peeled off his latex gloves. "Put him in post-op. He can rest there."

Ray opened his eyes. "Thanks again, Doc."

"My pleasure, Ray. After all, you're the celebrity around here, and we are merely your humble servants, at least to hear Curtis explain it, that is."

"Do I detect a tone of sarcasm in your voice?" Ray asked, not sure why he was getting that impression.

"All we ever hear about anymore is this 13th Power project and how prioritized it is." The doctor pulled his surgical mask off. "Most of us dummies around here don't have a clue what the big deal is about. Personally, I think it has gotten way out of hand." He walked to the door.

"Wait." Ray turned on his side opposite the bad shoulder. "This experiment will be the greatest advancement in nuclear research since the Manhattan Project. Just because you people don't understand it doesn't mean you're dummies. It'll take all of us to succeed. It's a team project in which everyone here has an important part. We're going to make history, Doctor."

"History?" Randolph huffed. "Just what do you expect to find at the end of this experiment, Ray?"

"Fame," he answered and rolled onto his back again, smiling. "The Nobel Prize, at last."

"Maybe for you, but what about Curtis? You can bet he isn't in this for the glory. No way. That man runs on two things, power and money. He has more money than he knows what to do with. That leaves only power. Something tells me the Higgs boson will give him more power than he'll know how to handle." Dr. Randolph opened the door. "This 'history in the making' is big trouble for us all, if you ask me."

"Well, I didn't," Ray mumbled and turned his head away. He heard the door close and set his jaw. How dare the doctor question Curtis's intentions? He was a man of science. Ray had brushed off Janis's skepticism because he didn't want to hear it. He didn't want to hear what Dr. Randolph had to say either. Just because they were doctors didn't mean they were so smart. They lacked the vision that drove true scientists toward new discoveries.

The room light went out. Ray closed his eyes and stewed over their shortsightedness.

Chapter 76

Lisa FOLLOWED Dr. Lucero down the corridor toward the operating rooms. The hallways seemed to go on forever. Her head felt light, her heart heavy. She had to confront her father. During the harrowing trip to Simi Valley, she'd had no time to ask him why he'd sent her to Europe and Canada, why he'd alienated her in a big, scary world. But now, after saving his life, she had to know why she should stop hating him. That hate had been such a big part of her for a long time.

Dr. Lucero stopped in front of operating room B. "He's resting in there. Don't be long."

Lisa pushed the door open and walked into a dimly lit room. The smell of disinfectant was strong. She saw her father lying on a gurney, covered with a white sheet that draped to the floor. He looked helpless, nothing like the man she hated. She walked up to him. "Dad?"

He opened his eyes.

The unexpected motion startled her. "I thought you were sleeping."

"I'm glad you could come to see me." His voice was firm, like a father's.

She leaned against the gurney and took his hand. "Does it hurt?"

"No." But he nodded yes, contradicting his word. "Thanks to you, I'm still alive."

"I wish..."

"I know. I wish you didn't hate me so much either."

"I wasn't thinking that."

"I was."

"What did you expect?"

"Certainly not this." He scooted over on the gurney.

"Sit." He patted the pad. "Come on."

She sat next to him, looking down into his eyes. They were strong eyes, like a father's. She'd really missed having a father, all those years wasted. "Why?"

"What?"

She squeezed his hand, wanting to hurt him, but he didn't complain. "How could you send me away like that?"

"I had to."

"It was your damn job, wasn't it? I was in the way, so you got rid of me, like you did my mother." That familiar burn of anger coursed through her body. "Why?"

Ray lifted his head off the pillow. "You were too young to understand."

She let go of his hand and stood. "That's a lame excuse."

"It's the truth."

"The truth is I hated you for what you did to me and my mother." She turned her back to him. "But when I thought you were going to die today, I suddenly realized I had to stop hating you long enough to help you. If I hadn't helped you, I'd never have a chance to do anything *but* hate you, forever."

"Hating me was a small price to pay," Ray said. "You think I didn't want you? I ached for you. All those years, from the time you were six, I had to live without you...to keep you safe."

"Safe?" She turned to him, her heartbeat rising. "Safe from what?"

He reached out his hand. "Never ask a question you really don't want to hear the answer to."

She looked at his offered hand then turned her head away. "Tell me..."

"Please, Lisa. You don't want to hear it, and I don't want to tell it. Let's just start off fresh, with a clean slate."

"Why won't you tell me?"

"Because if I do, your image of your mother will be

destroyed. What you thought you had all those years will be gone. And then you'll hate me for that, too."

"What's my mother got to do with this? You cast her out just like you did me."

"I did not." He took a deep breath. "Kate left *us*."

Slowly, Lisa turned her head to her father, her chest tightening. "That's not true. You threw her out. Nanny Jean told me so."

"Nanny didn't know the truth. I never told her that your mother came back strung out on cocaine again; her umpteenth bender had left her dead broke."

"She was a junkie?" Lisa put her hand on her heart.

"Worse yet, she came back to get you."

"I don't understand."

"I told you you wouldn't."

"Then help me." She sat by his side on the gurney again and took his hand. "I don't even remember my mother. She has no face, no smile, no form. Why is that?"

Her father's eyes drooped.

"Why, Dad?"

He looked like a man about to confess to murder. "I knew it wouldn't last, Kate and I. We met on the strip in Las Vegas. She was a working girl."

Lisa felt a surge of fire in her bloodstream. "A hooker?"

"A working girl. I fell in love with her. She was so sweet, so much fun. And beautiful. But when I found out it was cocaine that made her happy, I decided to rescue her from herself. I convinced her to swear off drugs, prostitution, her seedy way of life on the street with the pimps and dealers. I tried to help her."

Lisa put her hands over her ears. "Daddy, I don't want to hear anymore!" She thought she'd rather die.

Ray continued anyway. "We got married. She said she was clean, drug free, but she'd lied and hid it very well. I found that out the day you were born. Your heart was racing. Your blood pressure was off the scale. The doctors thought you were going to die. Blood tests came back. You were high on cocaine. Your withdrawal was agonizing."

Lisa clenched her fists. "Oh God, no!"

"She addicted her baby. My baby. You."

"No."

Like a man obsessed with freeing his soul, he went on with the seamy story. "After you were born, she tried to quit. For two years she fought the battle, we fought the battle of her addiction. The sober Kate was a basket case. I often thought something was tormenting her, something she wouldn't talk about. She'd run off in the middle of the night, leaving me to lie awake and listen to every car that drove by. Was this one hers? No. Maybe the next one. All night long, worried to death.

"When she finally came home, she was a mess, throwing up drunk, crying, saying she was sorry, promising to never do it again, promising to get professional help. I'd forgive her and she'd do it again anyway, pulling tricks for dope and not giving a rat's ass about us, the ones who loved her, the ones she was supposed to love. Finally, she gave up. She left and didn't come back until you were five."

"When she came back for me?"

"That's when I divorced her. Enough was enough. The custody battle was bitterly fought, Lisa. Her higher-ups in the drug world went to bat for her. I spent a fortune, but she lost. You were safe from growing up like her."

Lisa sniffled. "So why did you send me away?"

"Kate was a sore loser. In the middle of the night, she took you away. By God, I was never so afraid in my life. I got up and you were gone."

"Gone?" She felt like she would faint.

"For eight agonizing months I was on the verge of insanity, not knowing where you were, where she'd taken you. I hired a private investigator who specialized in the underground world of missing and exploited children. He tracked Kate to a little trailer town in the desert outside North Las Vegas, plying her trade while you wallowed in filth, underfed and abused."

"Abused? How?"

"Remember what I told you about questions you don't really want the answers to?"

An unknown terror engulfed her. What had her mother done to her? Had she given her to the men who came to the trailer? Why couldn't she remember? Had it been so horrible that she'd blocked it from her memory? She fell on her father's chest. Tears burned her eyes. He stroked her hair, soothing strokes, like a father's.

"When she was released from jail, I swore she'd never find you again, even if it meant I'd have to live without you. With the pain of a thousand daggers in my heart, I sent you away, like I said, to keep you safe."

"Where is she now?"

"Back in prison. Bad habits are hard to break."

"Why didn't you tell me about her?"

"Like I said, you were too young to understand. Besides, I didn't want to risk jarring any memories you had of your time with her. The things you've forgotten are best forgotten. Besides, every child deserves a loving mother, even if it's only an illusion."

"And all this time I thought I had a father who didn't care about me."

"The price I had to pay to keep you out of her clutches."

She looked into his eyes. "The price *we* had to pay."

"I'll be damned if I'll lose you again."

"Is that why you disapprove of Janis?"

His chest rose. "Not entirely. But don't you see? You deserve a man in your life you can plan and build a future with, not a man living in a future he'd planned for himself decades ago."

"But I think I love him." She ached for her father to understand.

"I know you think you do, but you don't. He's a father figure to you, to replace the father you never had."

"A father who loved me?"

"More than anything."

Lisa smiled, intent on lapping up this new love she'd found. "Like more than the whole world?"

"More than the whole world."

She hoped he'd never have to prove that.

Chapter 77

SUSAN FINISHED THE LAST bite of her potato salad. A flurry of activity on the patio caught her attention. She glanced at Steve who was already concentrating on the commotion.

Dignitaries emerged from the cafeteria doors with an entourage of security personnel. A smile crossed Steve's lips as he reached for a napkin and wiped away barbecue sauce. She knew he was headed for trouble; that look was unmistakable. He had the searing glare of an eagle as he scanned the scene, taking mental notes and calculating his next move. She put her hand on his arm, but he didn't take his attention off the patio.

Curtis emerged, dressed in his long black coat and dark sunglasses. The golden Pharaoh's staff thudded on the patio deck with every step he took.

"Soon," Steve said with a crafty smile. "Very soon."

\#

Judas noticed the stranger's sudden interest in Curtis's arrival. He repositioned his sunglasses, uncrossed his legs, and sat upright. Not knowing the man's intentions, he wanted to be ready for anything. His hand closed over the cold butt of his Glock .45 stuffed under his shirt, just in case, but the stranger didn't make a move. He just sat there, staring at Curtis.

Glancing at the woman seated with him, Judas took note of the worried expression on her face. He'd been trained to read those expressions when he was with the Secret Service. The stranger had more than a casual interest in Curtis, who stood on the patio, taking note of how many people had gathered for the festivities.

\#

Pleased by the large crowd, Curtis smiled at Jonathan.

A young waitress wearing a short black skirt approached the new arrivals. "Drinks, anyone?"

"I'll have a Margarita," Curtis said. "On the rocks with salt."

"Yummy." She turned to Jonathan. "And for you?"

"A red beer will be fine."

Curtis led the way to the head table. He enjoyed being treated like royalty, and his table especially pleased him. As if for a king's feast, the places were set with gold tableware and delicate china. A red satin tablecloth fluttered in the breeze. In the center, an ice sculpture of an atom with a key inserted into the nucleus, slowly dripped into a champagne bowl. He couldn't resist touching it. The chill reassured him it was real ice.

Tipping his head to the waiters standing ready, he claimed his seat at the end of the table. Jonathan sat to his right. His Margarita and Jonathan's beer were delivered with a smile. All around him, the atmosphere was light and jovial, and he soon became engrossed in petty conversation.

#

Steve tossed his napkin on his plate. Now was as good a time as any. He stood and walked toward the head table.

Payday.

Susan ran up behind him, tugging on his arm. "No, Steve. Not now."

"I just want to introduce myself," he said with a huff. "Don't get all..."

A nauseating dizziness suddenly engulfed him. His knees buckled. The sound of Susan screaming was the last thing he heard before a black silence cloaked his consciousness.

He never felt his body hit the ground.

Chapter 78

J UDAS, holding the butt of his Glock in one hand and Susan, struggling and screaming in the other, stood over the man he had just knocked unconscious. Susan fought to slip from the hold he had on her arm, but he wouldn't let go. She kicked him in the leg.

He squeezed her arm tighter. "Cool it, lady, or I'll send you to never-never land with your boyfriend."

"Go ahead, tough guy."

The party fell silent. Two other security men ran up. Judas shoved her at them and knelt down, frisked Steve, found the .45, and held it up for everyone to see. "I got the bastard," he yelled. "He made a move on Curtis, and I got him."

Curtis stood, and staff in hand, padded toward Judas. Jonathan followed behind.

"Are you people nuts?" Susan cried. "He didn't do anything."

"Get her out of here," Curtis ordered.

They dragged her away, screaming. She couldn't fight them off. They wouldn't listen to her. They were all crazy.

"What's with this guy?" Curtis poked at Steve's body with his golden staff.

Judas handed Curtis the .45. "He was acting suspicious."

"Who is he?" Bending down, Curtis grabbed the man's hair and turned his face up. Anger gripped him. "I've seen this guy earlier, at the ceremony." He dropped Steve's head to the turf and stepped away.

"Alex knows him," Jonathan said.

"I thought that screaming broad looked familiar." Curtis pointed his golden staff at Steve. "Toss this fool in the rat cellar. And his girlfriend, too."

Judas smiled.

Curtis walked back to the head table. "And get Alex up here right away." He opened his coat and tucked the doomed man's .45 under his belt. "Now, where were we?" he said to the men gathered around.

#

While Curtis made light of the matter, Judas signaled for help from his security personnel. He knew his boss wasn't going to let this incident overshadow the celebration at hand. The 13th Power project was not going to be upstaged by a stranger with a gun.

Security struggled with Steve's limp body as they dragged him out of C-Wing and tossed him into the back of an all-terrain vehicle. Judas pushed the rear hatch shut, which slammed with the bang of a Dumpster lid. He climbed into the driver's seat. Two of his men jumped on the running boards and grabbed the suicide rails.

The diesel engine clattered to life. Black smoke puffed out the vertical exhaust stack. A security car, with overheads flashing, passed the ATV, and Judas accelerated after it. He could see the woman in the back seat flanked by two men. It looked like they were still struggling with her. He grabbed the communications headset from the dash and positioned it over his ears. Adjusting the mouthpiece close to his lips, he pressed the mike switch mounted on the steering wheel. "Salvo, just knock her out."

"No fun that way," came the response.

"Morons." He switched the channel to *Supervisor.* "Alex. Report to me at once."

"What is it?" Alex's voice sounded tinny through his wrist radio.

"Curtis wants to see you right away. Trouble's brewing big time."

"What happened?" The radio squelched.

"We're taking your buddy to the rat cellar. Got his

girlfriend, too."

The radio went silent for a moment. *"Steve and Susan? Don't do it! I'll meet you there in fifteen minutes."*

"No you won't. Go see Curtis right now. He insists. Besides, we can take care of these two just fine." He held the mike switch just long enough to broadcast a moment of cynical laughter.

"Touch them and you'll have me to deal with, Judas! Fifteen minutes! Got that?"

"You don't scare me, Alex. I could have you swimmin' in concrete by morning." He released the mike button. Just who did Alex think he was dealing with anyway?

Judas careened the six-wheeled ATV onto a dirt road running east toward the valley flats. As the diesel growled under the hood, he choked in the tail of dust kicked up by the security car in front of him. He spit. Enough of this shit. He wasn't following them a moment longer.

He glanced at both big rearview mirrors attached to each side of the ATV. The men clinging to the suicide rails were hanging on, their hair and clothes lashing in the wind.

Slamming the throttle to the floor, he swerved off the road, crashed over a drainage ditch and down an embankment, and after plowing through a clump of bushes, raced past the security car.

"Yahoo!" Judas yelled as he veered back onto the road in front of them. "Now you morons can eat my dust." Again, he checked the rearview mirrors. Both his riders were gone.

He pressed onward, unconcerned.

Two miles down the dusty road, the turnoff to Morrison Ridge wound past several abandoned gold mines and ended in a town that had long been left to rot in the sun. The ATV slid to a stop in front of a dilapidated hotel. Judas pulled the fuel valve closed. The diesel engine rattled to silence. He jumped off the ATV and smiled at the thought of what awaited Steve and Susan inside.

The security car slid to a stop alongside the ATV, and the doors flew open. Susan was still struggling with her captors as they pulled her out of the car. From the look on her face, he could tell she was concerned for her safety, and rightly so. He opened the rear hatch of the ATV.

"Salvo. Get 'em inside."

***

"Damn it." Alex switched off the wrist radio, hit the brakes, swung the car into a spin, downshifted and accelerated in the opposite direction. Tire smoke clouded the air.

Lo coughed and tightened his seatbelt. "What's a rat cellar?"

"Under an old hotel at Morrison Ridge there's a large cellar, once used by the local vineyards to store and age their wines. Now it's in ruins. The only inhabitants are vicious Kangaroo rats.

"Kangaroo rats aren't vicious."

Alex aimed the car toward the valley flats. "These rats are. A hundred fifty years ago their ancestors roamed the valley floor and were drawn to the cool cellar. Wine kegs were easy pickings and the drunken orgies that followed spanned thousands of rat generations. Their young were genetically altered. Deranged. They became vicious and insane, hunting in packs, feeding on carrion and even taking a farmer's cow now and then."

Lo made a sour face.

"During the morning and evening hours they hunt in the valley, but when the day heats up, they travel back to the cellar where they nap and breed some more, a living sea of undulating fur. Scared me half to death when I first saw the little bastards. Their lethal nest is no place for man or beast."

"So Curtis found a use for the rats?"

"When he took over Solartech Labs, he discovered the rat's peculiar behavior. The rat cellar became the last stop for people Curtis wanted to get rid of. Rats left no remains."

No remains echoed in Lo's head. "Steve. Susan. Go faster!" A bad feeling churned in his stomach. Jaws of tiger. Jaws of rats. Insanity. He felt helpless to do anything but hang on for the ride.

The staff car careened onto a dirt road.

***

Salvo and his men pulled Steve out of the ATV and carried him into the old hotel. They dragged Susan along, kicking and screaming. Before Judas went in behind them, he looked to the west and spotted a plume of dust rising from the dirt road in the distance. Alex's staff car.

You're too late, ya dumb bastard.

"Toss 'em in now," he ordered his men.

Chapter 79

SUSAN RECOILED IN HORROR. The opening to the cellar looked like a black hole into hell. The stairs must've rotted away decades ago, leaving no escape from the dark depths below. Salvo the thug dropped Steve's limp body in. He hit the floor with a solid thump.

"You bastards." Susan screamed.

She fought to free herself from the men who dragged her to the edge of the abyss.

Salvo stepped up and grabbed her arm. "You're next, bitch." He shoved her.

She felt herself falling and clung to Salvo's arm. He tumbled into the darkness with her. They hit the bottom together.

Stunned from the impact, she fought off a surge of terror that rippled through her body. It was cold and damp and dark, and a musty fecal smell assailed her nostrils. The heavy air made her nauseous. Bile burned the back of her throat. She was about to start screaming when Salvo's antics distracted her.

He'd started running in circles, stomping his feet, and screaming to his goon buddies upstairs, "Get me out of here. Get me out of here."

The terror in his voice frightened her more than the unbelievable stench. She felt around for Steve. The floor was crumbs in her hands like she was plying a thick layer of Rice Krispies. The more she groped around, the worse the smell.

In spite of all the noise Salvo was making, she heard Steve gasping. Guided by the sound, she groped her way to him. "Steve."

A sudden stinging pain shot up her leg. She yelped.

Salvo had tripped over her ankle and fallen on the floor, and now screaming in terror, he scrambled back to his feet. "Judas, get me out of here."

She thought he was going insane. The tough guy was afraid of the dark.

"Steve." She shook him.

He coughed.

"Steve?"

Slowly, he became aware of her.

She shook him again. "Steve."

He grabbed her arm and pulled her close, sucking in large breaths of air like he'd had the wind knocked out of him. "What…happened?"

"Steve. You're all right."

"I don't know about that."

A flickering light killed the darkness. She turned and saw Salvo's face lit up by the flame of his lighter. His wide-open eyes revealed unimaginable terror. He glared into the darkness beyond the dancing light.

Steve hacked. "W-what's there?"

"Nothing." Salvo laughed out loud. "Not a damn thing." He looked up to the cellar opening. "Judas, there ain't no stinking rats down here."

"Rats?" Susan put her hand on her mouth. "What rats?"

A light scratching sound echoed through the cellar. Susan's stomach tightened. The scratching sound came again.

"T-those rats," Steve said, pointing to a commotion in the corner, eerily lit by the flickering lighter.

From crevices in the walls, one, then two small rats wiggled through and fell to the floor. A few more followed them and several more after that. And more after that. An eerie chitter began to echo within the cellar walls. She froze with fear as more and more rats poured in through the cracks, like a living waterfall cascading into a growing pool of rats. Susan thought her heart had quit. *My God.*

"Judas," Salvo shouted again. "They're coming. Get me out of here."

Judas just stood at the opening and looked down on the doomed and laughed. "Sorry, Salvo. Looks like you're gonna have a really bad day."

Susan watched in horror as the horde of rats spilled toward her. She tried to pull herself to her feet, but Steve held her down. "Stay still," he whispered softly. "Don't do anything to piss them off." He reached into his shirt. "Shit! My gun's gone."

"Curtis took it after Judas clobbered you." She cocked her head toward the man silhouetted in the light above. "What do you think you're going to do, shoot every rat in here? Better have a lot of bullets."

"Just one rat, up there." He pointed at Judas.

Salvo kept screaming for help, but no one made a move to help him. He trembled with fear as wave after wave of rats flooded the cellar floor. On large back feet, they hopped around each other like little kangaroos. Bushy hair on the tips of their tails made them look cute; their numbers made them look horrendous, an army of distorted shadows now dancing on the walls to the rhythm of Salvo's lighter flame.

Salvo made a running leap for the opening.

"No, don't," Susan yelled.

He missed and landed in the mass of teeming rats. Holding the lighter at arm's length, he ran in circles, stomping rats, kicking rats, and screaming. The chitter became deafening as the pack hunters attacked him, jaws snapping, teeth gnashing. His screams changed from fearful to painful, eerily mingling with the chitter and bouncing off the cellar walls.

Steve clung to her arm as she watched in horror. The gnawing horde forced Salvo to his knees. Screaming, he fell backward into the sea of crazed rats. Only his rigid arm stuck up from the writhing mob, still holding the lit lighter. His screams became muffled, as if someone had shoved a sock into his mouth. Then he started gagging as the rodents infested him. A moment later, the lighter went out and darkness hid the hideous feast.

Susan buried her face into Steve's chest. He held her tight. Not knowing how long before the rats would turn their attention to them, she tried to calm the terror welling up inside. More so now than in Devin's pit of horror, she feared for Steve's life, and hers. Dear God, now she would pay the price for Steve's get-rich-quick scheme.

It wasn't supposed to turn out this way.

Chapter 80

THE STAFF CAR FISHTAILED down the dirt road as Alex raced toward the old mining town. He clutched the steering wheel so tight his knuckles turned white. Anger was an axe grinding on the stone wheel of his stomach. The existence of the rat cellar had never bothered him before, as long as it didn't interfere with his mission for *The Ark*, he didn't care what Curtis used it for, but Judas had just changed all that. "Damn you, Judas."

"Who's Judas?" Lo asked.

"A snake in the grass, that's who. I should've known it would come to this. We've had bad blood between us ever since Curtis hired him. He was supposed to provide security against threats from within Solartech Labs, where as I'm responsible for external threats to the project. Judas turned his job into a sneaky underhanded crusade against anyone he didn't like personally."

"Hard to make friends that way."

"The brown-noser reports directly to Curtis. Every time I complained about him, Curtis exemplified him. *A valuable asset to Solartech Labs*, he told me. The menace was untouchable. But this time he's gone too far."

The staff car rounded a curve. Alex saw two men walking in the middle of the road. He slammed on the brakes and swerved to miss them. The car skidded out of control, careened off the road, and ended up sideways in a drainage ditch, suspended by the bumpers. The engine roared. The rear wheels spun uselessly.

"Shit. Where the hell did they come from?" Dust lingered thickly around the staff car. Alex couldn't see the men he'd almost run over. He threw open the door. The men ran up to the car. They were his security men. What were they doing in the middle of the road? They looked like they'd already been run over once.

"That was close," one of the haggard men said. "You all right?"

"What are you doing out here?"

"Judas, the crazy bastard, bounced us off the ATV."

Alex groaned then rushed to the front of the car. "Let's get this thing out of the ditch." He signaled Lo to get behind the wheel.

Together, they pushed and pulled and dug in the choking dust to free the car. A few minutes later, it lurched back onto the dirt road.

"Hurry," Lo yelled. "We waste too much time already."

Alex jumped in the passenger side. The two men climbed in back, and Lo hit the gas.

A few minutes later, Lo slid the car to a stop in front of an old hotel and cut off the engine. An eerie chitter echoed from within the rotting walls. He turned to Alex. "What's that?"

Alex looked like he'd just seen a ghost. "We're too late." He turned to his men in the back seat. "Stay here." Raising his Glock .40, he pulled back the breach. A round chambered with a click. "Judas is mine." He kicked open the door and jumped out.

Lo watched him walk up creaky steps to a porch and disappear inside the hotel. Without turning his attention from the doorway, Lo said, "I can't sit here and do nothing." He got out of the car and tailed Alex.

Floorboards creaked beneath Lo's feet. Sunshine beamed in through cracks in the wall timbers and ceiling boards, splitting the darkness with razor-thin lines of light. A chittering sound filled the air, raising the hackles on the back of Lo's neck. As he moved deeper into the old hotel, the chittering got louder. He tiptoed down a hallway of doors, some open, some closed, some missing from their hinges. Approaching what might have been the kitchen at one time, he felt a twinge of panic. The chitter was coming from somewhere below his feet. The rats were feeding.

No Remains.

He thought about running outside and all the way back to San Francisco, but he had to press on.

#

Alex ran to the kitchen above the rat cellar, his neck hairs tingling from the chitter of the rats. At the door, he put his back against the frame, held his Glock in both hands and pointed at the ceiling. Carefully, he peered into the room. He saw Judas standing at the opening above the rat cellar and looking down, probably admiring his handiwork. The smile on his face sent a burst of rage through Alex. The thought of Susan covered by those gnawing rats turned his rage into vengeance. He stepped into the room, aimed the Glock at Judas's head, and tightened his finger on the trigger. "Judas—"

A sudden flash of black boot leather sent a blunt-force-trauma pain rifling up his right arm. The Glock flew from his grasp, slid across the floor, and flipped over the edge of the rat cellar. Down it went. Gone. His arm throbbing, he realized too late his anger had made him careless. The maniac he stalked was not unguarded.

Before he could react, another kick slammed into his left kidney, arching his back and sending him to the floor. Pain blasted through his guts. Wind rushed from his lungs. He tried to gulp air. Another kick rocked the side of his head, numbing his senses. He rolled on his back. The blurred images of two men circled above him. He tightened his muscles against the pain.

Get up! Fight back!

He rolled to his right. An adrenaline rush fueled his defense and, with a scissor kick, he snared one of his assailant's legs and tripped him. He hit the floor.

In a dusty brawl, he grappled with the two men. He

recognized Harold Petty. Pitiful Petty they called him, a longhaired-hippie-brown-noser of the first degree. He smelled of old sweat. The other puke looked like Jeff Tillman. Someone said he had sold his sister to the Mexicans. Judas had shit for friends.

Alex peered under a smelly armpit to see what Judas was doing. The smile on the bastard's face made anger dynamite through Alex's chest. He connected an elbow to the jaw of one of his attackers. Must have been Tillman. He squealed like a stuck pig.

Out the corner of his eye, a motion at the door caught his attention. Lo? Alex tried to yell, to tell Lo to get back, but took a left hook in the nose. His head buzzed with stars. This was no place for Lo. He could get hurt. Alex shifted his leg from under the pile of bad guys and kicked the door shut in Lo's face. Maybe he got the hint. Alex grabbed a handful of long hair. An elbow caught him in the eye.

He shook off the blur in his mind and fought harder.

Chapter 81

L O RAN BACK OUTSIDE to recruit the help of the security men waiting in the staff car. Shit! The car was gone. He looked down the road. A plume of dust rose in the wake of the speeding car.

"Not good."

The security car was still there, overheads still flashing. His first thought was to jump in it and chase the staff car down, force it to stop, and plead with the chicken-shit security men to come back and help him. That would take too much time.

His second thought was to run back into the hotel. A little karate lesson would do the bad guys some good. Three against one was no big deal. It was all those guns that bothered him. Bullets always won. With the chitter echoing in his brain, he spun a full circle, looking for a better idea.

The ATV caught his eye, a six-wheel drive, steel-reinforced off-road-monster truck. It reminded him of his training in the National Guard. He climbed aboard, turned on the fuel valve, and fired up the engine.

"Like ride bike, no forget."

He slammed the transmission into low range and powered toward the old hotel. Six knobby tires ripped at the porch steps, tearing away boards and cracking joists. The front tires crashed through rotting porch planks, but the trailing wheels drove the ATV forward. Diesel engine roaring, the ATV plowed through the front door, ripping the doorframe from the wall.

Driving through the lobby at full throttle, Lo turned on the flood lamps and hit the back wall head-on. Wood planks and wallboards exploded, flying in all directions.

The ceiling buckled and sagged. Dust choked the air.

The old hotel shuddered.

The chittering stopped.

***

Steve heard the gun hit the rat cellar floor, somewhere nearby in the darkness. He reached out, groping, patting the feces-littered ground until he found it. Salvation had fallen from heaven. The cold steel gave him a new hope. He could hear a fistfight knuckling above him, cursing and swearing.

Suddenly, the old hotel shook, as if from an earthquake. The rats went eerily silent.

Susan flinched. "What was that?"

The building rumbled above them.

Steve sensed a change in the rats. The horde began moving in waves, first to the left, then to the right, as if in a panic and not knowing which way to run. Now they were coming toward him, a thousand little footsteps scampering in the dark, getting closer and closer. He clutched Susan in his arms. At least he could try to protect her. Terror gripped his mind. To be eaten alive, what a horrible way to die. He held his breath, tightened every muscle in his body. And then they were on him.

Like a furry carpet being dragged over him, he felt the lightness of their lethal touch. He thought he would go insane. As the wave of rats bounded over him, he suddenly realized there was no pain, no attack. The rats were scrambling to escape something that had frightened them. In a few seconds that seemed like eternity, they were gone, the last of them scratching their way back into the cracks from which they had come.

He glanced up to the cellar opening. It sounded like the place was falling apart up there: a diesel engine roaring, lumber cracking, voices yelling and then the familiar sound of gunfire.

"What the hell is going on?" He got up and pulled Susan to her feet.

"Whatever it is—"

An explosive shower of splinters and debris rained down into the cellar. Steve pulled Susan away from the opening and pressed her against a wall. He could feel her shaking and closed his eyes. Behind him, a horrendous crashing sound shook the walls.

Then silence.

Susan trembled in his arms. "What was that?"

He opened his eyes. The cellar was ablaze with light. He squinted and turned around, completely dumbfounded at what he saw. An ATV had crashed nose-first into the cellar. Lo was hanging onto the steering wheel. Floodlights illuminated a smile on his face. "Need a lift?"

Susan shrieked and clung to Steve's arm. He followed her eyes. Not far from the ATV, now visible through the dusty haze, lay Salvo, or what was left of him: a yellowish ribcage protruded from half-eaten flesh, pink intestines spilled on the floor, shiny strands of tendons glistened, and one eyeball still intact, stared out from a faceless skull.

Steve's stomach clutched. The rats would be back to finish their meal. He had no intention of being around for dessert. "Come on." Steve lifted Susan up to the ATV's suicide rails, and as she began to climb, he grabbed her foot and stopped her. "Wait."

"Who's up there?" he asked Lo, checking the clip in the Glock from heaven.

"Alex and one man he called Judas. The other two guys I ran over, squish. Sorry."

"One bad guy left, huh." He looked up at Susan. "I'll go get the bastard. You stay here."

"But he'll kill you."

"He tried that already." Steve climbed up the ATV to the room above and spotted Alex and Judas fighting on the floor, Judas on top, fists swinging, apparently beating the crap out of Alex. Steve rushed up behind Judas and put the Glock's muzzle against the back of his head.

"Enough!" Steve yelled.

Judas took another swing at Alex.

"You don't listen too good." Steve jabbed the muzzle again.

"All right, damn it. All right!" Judas let go of Alex and raised his hands.

"Get up." Steve forced Judas to his feet and pushed him against the wall, pressing his face into the wallboards. Steve ached to pull the trigger, to kill the bastard for what he'd done to Susan, to him, but without a second thought, he raised the Glock and slammed the butt down hard on the back of Judas's head. He hit the floor like a wet towel. "See how you like it, prick."

Alex, still sitting on the floor and panting, looked at Steve. "Thanks."

Steve gave him a helping hand to his feet.

Looking at Lo, "The ATV was brilliant," Alex said. "Those piles over there…" He pointed to the crushed remains of Petty and Tillman, "…were about to tear me apart when all the noise distracted them." He turned to Steve. "You should've seen it. Before they could open the door to see what was going on, wham-o. The door and the ATV flattened the bastards. Judas started shooting at the ATV, but I tackled him."

"Bullets fly everywhere," Lo put in.

Alex brushed the dust off his pants and went over to Judas, lying motionless on the floor. "Help me with this piece of shit." They dragged him to the opening above the rat cellar, his limp body leaving a trail in the dust.

"Turnabout is fair play." Steve kicked Judas over the edge. "If he's lucky, he'll wake up *before* the rats come back."

"Sleep tight, you cockroach," Alex yelled down and

helped Susan scale the ATV.

Steve handed the Glock to Alex. "Thanks for the loaner."

As they stood above the rat cellar, Susan peered down into her would-be tomb. In the floodlights' glow, Judas lay sprawled on the fecal floor not far from Salvo's haunting remains. "Nighty-night," she said and walked away.

Lo picked up the gun that Judas had dropped when Alex tackled him. He handed it to Steve who ejected the clip and took inventory of the rounds. "Well, it's not my .45, but it's better than nothing." He slammed the clip into the grip. "Let's get back to the party."

They made their way through the wrecked hotel and into the sunlit afternoon. The security car overheads were still flashing. Alex shut them off.

Susan leaned against the fender. "These people are crazy, Steve. Let's fly out of here right away."

"I'm not done with Curtis."

"Don't you get it?" she shouted. "Curtis was the one who told Judas to throw us in there." She pointed to the hotel. "Don't piss him off anymore than you already have."

Steve huffed. "He's a wimp. But there's something he needs to know. Right, Alex?"

"What?"

"Have you told him that Devin is still alive?"

"Not yet."

"Good," Steve said. "I want to be there to see the look on his face." He kicked at the dirt. "Better yet, I have some bad news for him, too."

Alex frowned. "Such as?"

"Let's just say it'll rattle Curtis's cage."

Glaring into Steve's eyes, Alex saw a man that had been pushed to the limit, but Alex's first priority was to protect Curtis from *any* kind of interference, including cage rattling. It was his job, his mission for *The Ark*. "What are you going to tell him?"

The 13th Power Quest

"And spoil the surprise? No way. I'm not giving up my ace in the hole. You'll find out *after* I talk to Curtis."

Alex grabbed Steve's arm. "Don't be confused about where my loyalty lies, Steve. Mess with Curtis, and I'll put you down."

Steve pulled his arm away. "You'll find your loyalty is misplaced, pal. So don't get cocky with me. You don't know all the facts." He turned and walked around the car, paused and glowered at Alex over the roof. "Are we going or not?"

Alex just stared at Steve, wondering what it was that the private eye knew about Curtis. One thing was certain, Steve wasn't the kind of man who could be bullied into doing anything he didn't want to do. The only way to find out what he was up to was to play along.

"Have it your way, Steve. Get in."

Chapter 82

Back at the barbecue party, Janis led Lisa out to the patio, hand in hand. He quickly drew the attention of those milling around Curtis and his table of dignitaries. Janis held Lisa a little closer as a group of well-wishers and avid conversationalists flocked toward them. He held his bandaged hand up to thwart off the onslaught. "Give us a break, you guys," he shouted above the loud Hawaiian music. "Don't interrupt your meals on our account. Just carry on as you were. The 13th Power can wait until tomorrow." To his surprise, they returned to their frivolities.

Curtis nodded to Lisa then returned his attention to his guests.

"Impressive, darling," Lisa said with a May West accent and smile.

"Curtis must've given me a lot of clout with his people."

"I wonder how long *that* will last."

"Let's eat."

Janis carried a pitcher of iced tea and two cups, while Lisa juggled several heaping plates and followed him to a table in the courtyard. Seated, he scanned the area for any sign of Lo.

As Lisa arranged the table, Janis took a moment to admire her again. His mind replayed the events of the past three days since they'd met. Seemed more like three years, for all they'd been through together.

She caught him staring. "Penny for your thoughts, cowboy."

Janis blinked. "Just looking, girl."

"Then just look at this." She slid a plate of barbecued

chicken at him.

He picked up a plump thigh. The jailhouse food from King City had long since worn off.

Lisa sighed and selected a wing.

"What is it?" Janis asked, concerned.

"I was just thinking about my father. He really loves me, you know."

"I'm sure."

"But he's not ready to let me date you. He's overprotective. On account of my mother, and that won't change overnight."

Janis forked some potato salad. "He must realize you're a grown woman."

"To him I'll always be six years old. That's how he remembers me, when he sent me away."

"That'll have to change before you two will ever get along."

"I don't know. At least I understand him now."

"So you don't hate him anymore?"

"Foolish of me, huh?" She looked around. "I wonder where Lo is."

"No telling."

A gentle breeze rustled the palm trees lining the courtyard. Shade from the patio crept motionlessly across the lawn as California's sun settled westward.

"The pool looks good. Want to go for a dip?"

He showed her his bandaged hand. His fingers were free enough for typing, but swimming? "I really shouldn't."

"Maybe a hot bath then." She plucked a thigh from the pile on the plate.

Janis sipped his iced tea and watched the patio party progress. The music had escalated to loud rock and roll. A little country wouldn't hurt these people. Shrill guitars and pounding drums overpowered the words of the song, but the beat incited Curtis's guests to bump and grind and gyrate. They humped around each other like spastic lovers with their clothes on. Many of the women looked like they'd been hired-out from Los Angeles, not looking like the professionals from *this* community. The men, groping and flirting, were enjoying their company.

Lisa rubbed his shoulder. "I really like the music, but I'm too tired to get into it. The meal made me sleepy."

"How can anyone sleep with all this noise?"

"Let's go anyway." She tugged on his arm.

Janis didn't get up. Even though their staff car was waiting out front, he took a moment to watch the revelers, basking in their pseudo-glory over a hypothetical intrusion of the atomic cosmos. They couldn't have been more joyous at a wedding reception. He occasionally glanced at Curtis, who wasn't any better behaved than the rest of his band of lunatics. Janis huffed. They were all idiots. But for a million bucks, he'd tolerate them. He tossed his napkin on his chicken bones. "I'm ready."

Scrambling down the concrete steps from C-Wing, he spotted their staff car, its driver leaning against a front fender and leisurely smoking a cigarette. When the driver saw them approaching, he tossed the butt and opened the car door. But before they got in, the sound of squealing tires filled the air.

"Now what?"

A security car screeched to a stop. The doors flew open. Steve and Alex jumped out, arguing about something. "I'll tell him about Devin first," Alex was saying. "So keep your pie hole shut 'til I say it's okay, got that?" Without so much as a nod of recognition, they stomped up the steps to C-Wing. "But I'm talking to him in private." Steve returned. "Don't screw me up on this, damn it." They disappeared inside. Janis thought everyone had gone crazy.

Lo got out of the car, shaking his head.

Lisa rushed up to him but hesitated to give him a hug. He was dusty and sweaty. "Where have you been?"

"Long story. I'm going to eat now."

"What happened?" Janis asked.

Walking backwards toward C-Wing, Lo said, "Tiger really pissed off." He turned and tromped up the steps, mumbling something in Chinese.

Lisa spotted Susan sitting in the back seat. Her dress was all dirty, her face smudged, and she sat with her chin down. "I wonder what happened to her."

"Find out," Janis said, holding his bandaged hand. The Novocain was wearing off. "I'll wait in the car."

\#

Sliding in next to Susan, "What's all this?" Lisa asked, pointing at her dirty dress.

Susan threw her arms around Lisa's neck. "Oh God, it was horrible."

Lisa patted Susan's back. "What was horrible?"

"J-Judas…and…the rats. They were everywhere."

"What rats?"

"Now they're…they're both going to get themselves killed. These people…they're animals, I tell you. We have to get out of here."

"You're not making any sense."

Susan sat back in the seat. "Steve and Alex are going in there to confront Curtis. They're both angry as hell. Somebody's going to get killed, I tell you." Her chin quivered. She looked terrified.

"They're big boys," Lisa said. "They can take care of themselves."

The look in Susan's eyes didn't soften. "They're in over their heads, Lisa."

Lisa recalled Janis's warning while they were waiting at Solartech Medical. He must've been right; they weren't safe here. An ominous feeling swirled in her stomach. Susan's fear was real. Lisa couldn't find any words to comfort her, but from the looks of her, a hot bath and clean clothes would be a good start.

Terry Wright

"Let's get you back to your room."

Chapter 83

SUSAN CLUTCHED A FISTFUL of dirty dress as the staff car headed toward the executive suites. Why did men have to be so bullheaded? Whenever they got a hair-brained notion, they'd run off half-cocked. And Steve took the prize. Didn't he know there were people's lives at stake here? Didn't he care? Why was the money so damned important to him? Or was it the winning? Was it a game to him? *The tough-guy wins; nice guys finish last.*

It was all macho bullshit.

Now she had to figure out why she cared so damn much for him. If he got himself killed, she'd never speak to him again. That'd teach him. She felt the urge to cry, but didn't.

The car stopped in front of the executive suites. Susan followed Lisa through the front doors. Janis and Lo trailed behind. The driver drove off in a cloud of dust.

Upstairs in Tamarack Hall, Sheila, the housekeeping supervisor, used her cardkey to open the door to Susan's room. A wave of relief rushed over her. The room felt cool, and safe. She plopped on the bed, exhausted. Sheila closed the curtains and left. Janis walked in and handed Lisa a cardkey. "Your room is 319."

Taking the card, she sat next to Susan. "Steve will be all right. You'll see."

Susan didn't find Lisa's words reassuring. "You don't realize what Curtis is capable of." Susan sat up. "I do. I was there. I saw it. They're killers and they don't care who lives or dies. Christ, Lisa. Steve's not the least bit afraid of Curtis."

"What does he want with Curtis that's worth risking his life for?"

"Money, what else? Devin ripped him off so he came here to collect from Curtis. I tried to stop him...before...at the barbecue."

"How does Steve figure Curtis is going to give him any money?"

"He wouldn't tell me." Susan trembled. Not knowing was the hardest part.

Janis walked to the window, parted the curtains, and looked out, his glasses riding low on his nose. "It's apparent there's bad blood between Steve and Curtis. I suggest we let them settle it." He looked at Susan. "One thing's for sure, you're lucky to be alive."

She dropped her chin to her chest.

"Let's round up our luggage and get some rest," Janis said. "My hand aches." He looked at the bandage, scowled, and walked out.

Lisa stood. "Steve will be back soon. Get cleaned up for him." She patted Susan's knee and walked toward the door.

Susan said goodbye while fighting back tears. When the door closed, she fell back on the bed and stared at the ceiling. This trip to Simi Valley had turned into a nightmare.

An uninvited tear trickled down her cheek. At first, she'd hoped Steve would abandon his scheme and take her away from this awful place. But now, as she thought about the situation her new friends were in, she'd have to do something to prove they were in grave danger.

The horror of the rat cellar came back. She closed her eyes. The room spun. She tried to ward off the dizziness, but it was too strong. In submission, she rolled over and cried for Steve, hoping he'd make it back to her alive.

Chapter 84

THE CAFETERIA DOOR to the patio swung open. Alex went outside first; Steve followed close behind. Rock and roll dancers took up most of the floor, so he had to weave a path through them to get to the tables on the other side. No one paid the intrusion any mind.

Alex spotted Curtis sitting at the head table, talking with a lab-tech supervisor. "We have to talk." Alex interrupted their conversation.

Looking annoyed, Curtis growled. "I told Judas to summon you more than two hours ago. What took you so…?" He stopped talking. His wide eyes had locked on Steve, standing beside Alex now. Eyes shifting between the two men, Curtis scrunched up his eyebrows as if he didn't know what to expect. "I'm a little busy right now. We'll talk later."

"We'll talk now."

"It can wait," Curtis demanded.

"No it can't."

Curtis addressed his guests. "Excuse me, folks. It appears I have some urgent business to attend to." He got up from his chair. "This way, gentleman, if you will."

#

Steve followed Curtis and Alex through the cafeteria and down a hallway, his pulse racing with anticipation.

Payday.

The tapping of Curtis's golden staff and their footsteps echoed down the corridor. Music from the patio faded. Stopping at a conference room door, Curtis pushed it open. "This should do nicely." He turned on the ceiling lights and set his staff on a long table.

Steve looked around the lavishly appointed room.

"Very impressive—"

Curtis turned suddenly, grabbed him by the shirt, and slammed him against a wall. The wind rushed from his lungs. "Just who the hell do you think you are?" Curtis snarled in his face.

Steve gulped air, searching for a good answer. He didn't want to overreact and escalate the situation, but before he could say anything, Curtis threw him to the floor and pressed a knee into his chest. He could hardly breathe under Curtis's weight. The old man was a lot tougher than he looked. Steve could see Alex standing spread-legged, arms folded across his chest. He was obviously serious about his loyalty to Curtis. Diplomacy was no longer an option.

Curtis sneered. "I should kill you...huh?" His face twisted in pain.

"Get off me," Steve rasped. "Or I'll blow your balls back to Dallas, you bastard." Judas's .45 had come in handy. "And then I'll kill you." Steve jabbed the gun into Curtis's groin a little harder.

Curtis slowly released his grip on Steve's shirt, rose cautiously, hands raised.

Alex saw the gun and drew his own. "Drop it, Steve."

"*You* drop it, Alex." Steve got up off the floor, still aiming at Curtis. "I don't want to kill him. It'd be kind of like killing the goose that laid the golden egg. But I will if I have to."

Alex pulled back the breach of his gun. "Have you forgotten where my loyalty lies?"

Steve forced a smile. Why did Alex have to make this so damn difficult? "Tell him about Devin, Alex. Go ahead, tell him. See how far your loyalty gets you."

Curtis glared at Alex. "What about Devin?" he bellowed and put his hands on his hips. His black coat fell open as he stared at his security officer.

"Well..." Alex looked back and forth between Steve

and Curtis. "We had a problem at Atomtech."

"Tell him."

"We couldn't find Devin anywhere," Alex said. "He disappeared right in the middle of a gunfight."

Steve glanced back to catch Curtis's reaction to the bad news. Unfortunately, he got some bad news of his own. Curtis had him sighted in, point blank down the barrel of Steve's own .45. He flinched instinctively but held his gun on Curtis, whose eyes were throwing daggers at Alex. "Are you telling me Devin is alive?"

"You better believe it, bozo." Steve put in. "And he's really pissed off at you guys. How do you like them apples, asshole?"

"Who the hell is this guy?" Curtis barked and pointed the .45 at Alex. "What is he doing here, damn it?" He looked as if he ached to pull the trigger on both of them.

Alex took a step backwards. "Now, everybody calm down." Sweat suddenly appeared on his forehead. He held his gun on Steve and his eyes on Curtis.

"Shoot him, Alex," Curtis ordered. "Or I'll put a bullet in you."

"Go ahead, Alex," Steve said. "I'll put three rounds into your boss before I hit the floor."

"Don't bet on it," Curtis said, now aiming at Steve.

"Try me," Steve shouted. "I'm waiting. Go ahead, shoot him. I'll blow you away before he hits the floor. Either way, Curtis, you die."

"This is ridiculous," Alex said. "Nobody is shooting anybody." He paused a moment, and then tossed his weapon down.

"Nice move," Steve said and turned to Curtis. "Now you. Throw the gun down or shoot me. I'm ready either way."

"I should shoot both of you," Curtis said, showing teeth.

"Go for it."

Curtis raised the gun to Steve's head.

His heartbeat went up a notch.

"He just wants to talk to you," Alex said.

"I don't want to hear what he has to say." Curtis pulled the trigger. The gun resounded a harmless click. He pulled the trigger again. Two more times. Nothing.

Steve lunged forward and grabbed the gun from Curtis's hand. "You're a dumb bastard." He pushed Curtis backwards.

"It was empty?" Curtis yelled.

"Secret safety," Steve said. "I made it myself." He slid a slider on the barrel back. "Never know when some dumbass might take my gun away. Hell, he might even be stupid enough to try to shoot me with it." He pointed the gun at the floor and pulled the trigger. The report was deafening.

Point made.

Curtis stood dazed, his mouth hanging open, cheeks mottled with rage. "You knew all along, I couldn't have shot anyone. Who the hell are you, anyway?"

"Your worst nightmare." Steve grinned and faced Alex. "It's my turn to talk to him."

Shaking his head, Alex didn't move.

"I need to be alone with him."

"I'm not going anywhere," Alex said.

"We made a deal."

"Screw the deal."

Steve pointed the .45 at Alex. "Get out."

Curtis glowered. "Go ahead, Alex, but I'm not through with you on the Devin matter."

"Yes you are," Alex said and left the room, slamming the door.

"Never mind him." Steve reached into his pocket. He pulled out a folded piece of paper and handed it to Curtis. "Read it."

Curtis unfolded the paper. A look of confusion crossed his face. "What's this?"

"My bank account number. Feel free to transfer a million dollars into it. In fact, I insist."

"Oh, do you?" Curtis sneered. "Suppose I tell you to go to hell?"

"Suppose I blow the lid off your charade?"

"Who are you?"

"Steve Raven, private eye." He crossed his arms. "Your good friend Walter Devin hired me to keep tabs on your little shenanigans around here."

Curtis didn't look impressed.

"The bastard stiffed me for my fee, but not before I learned something from him, something much more valuable."

"Like what?"

"Something you would want kept quiet."

"Sounds like blackmail," Curtis growled. "Are you loony?"

Steve looked Curtis in the eyes. "Loony enough to mess up your little science project here, put an end to it real quick like." He turned his back on Curtis, took two steps.

"I'll have you killed. Five grand, you're out of the picture."

"Then the Singapore authorities will get a letter."

Curtis took a step back. "What did you say?"

Steve turned around. "Transfer the million dollars or kiss your phony ass goodbye, Melvin Anderson."

Chapter 85

Janis WENT TO THE LOBBY where he found their luggage neatly sorted. After picking up his bags, he headed down the hall and spotted Lisa gently closing her door. Good, she was going to get some rest.

He looked at the cardkey in his hand. Room 317. That should be right over here. No. Over here? Something wasn't right. He swore his room was the same door Lisa had just closed.

Sheila brushed by him, smiling slyly. What was that all about? He slid the cardkey into the slot. It clicked and he went inside.

Hearing water running, he walked toward the bedroom where he tripped over a sandal. A pair of denim shorts lay on the floor, and a white blouse not far away. What the hell was Lisa up to?

He threw his bags on the bed next to a black lace bra and silk panties. Shaking his head, he pulled the knob on the bathroom door. Inside, the lights were dim, and steam clouded his view, but he found her lying in the tub, up to her neck in bubbles, smiling at him.

"Hello, cowboy," she said breathily and raised a handful of bubbles. "Come on in." She puckered her lips and blew the bubbles at him.

His heart skipped with surprise, not by how beautiful she looked, but by how inapprehensive he felt. Her being here like this wasn't right. She was Ray's daughter, for Christ's sake. Janis's accelerated heart rate made his hand throb. "I gotta get some ice for my hand."

"Don't be long, cowboy. The water's fine." She leaned forward and shut off the faucets. The bubbles barely covered her breasts.

Janis got out of there as fast as he could. He ran down the hall to the ice machine, hardly able to keep up with his feet. They wouldn't slow down. What did they think he was going to do with Lisa? He couldn't believe he was even considering it. He and Lisa. Lovers. No way in hell.

Why not? He imagined the devil on one shoulder, an angel on the other, both badgering him to make a decision.

Ray would never stand for his daughter being intimately involved. Not with him, maybe not with any man, especially an older man. That would be asking for trouble, and God knew they'd had enough of that already.

Ice bucket in hand, Janis made his way back down the hall, driven onward by the thought of Lisa's bubbly body.

The elevator doors slid open. Steve and Alex bolted out, pushing each other. "Just like that?" Alex shouted. Steve shoved him. "You can't stop me!"

Janis dropped the ice bucket, trying to get out of the way. He felt invisible.

Alex grabbed Steve's arm. "Watch me."

Steve showed him a fist. "I'll knock you into next week."

"Just try it." They went face-to-face in the middle of the hall, neither looking like he'd back down to the other.

"We're out of here tomorrow," Steve growled.

"Like hell," Alex yelled. "What kind of deal did you make with Curtis? I saw him leave. He was fuming mad. What did you tell him?" He shook Steve. "I have to know."

"None of your damn business. How many times do I have to tell you?" Steve pushed him. In the shoving match that followed, they fell against the wall and Alex clamped Steve in a headlock. Cursing, they tumbled to the floor.

Janis stepped in. "Knock it off."

Susan ran out of her room. "Steve. Oh, thank God. Steve." She jumped onto the pile. "Let him go," she shrieked, pounding on Alex's back.

Janis stepped back to assess the new complication as

the three of them grappled with each other on the floor.

Lo was standing beside him now. "What? You don't want to play with them?"

"You first," Janis replied.

Lo chuckled, and as if assured no harm was being done, he walked back into the library, mumbling something in Chinese. He'd been doing a lot of that lately.

Stepping in again, Janis shouted, "That's enough." He grabbed Susan around the waist and lifted her off the pile, kicking and screaming. He tossed her to the carpet and again tried to separate the men. "Alex. Steve. What's the matter with you guys?"

"He's got something on Curtis," Alex said. "The shit told me I didn't know all the facts."

Steve punched Alex in the stomach. Susan ran back to the pile. "Stay out of this," Steve warned her.

Standing with her hands on her hips, her eyes tense and angry, she seemed unaware of the rip in her nightgown, which revealed more than she would have wanted Janis to see.

Alex looked up at him. "He said he would tell me what he told Curtis afterwards, if I let them talk in private."

Steve elbowed Alex in the ribs.

"He lied. I kept *my* end of the deal, but he reneged." Alex balled a fist and hit Steve in the jaw.

"Get this, you piece of shit," Steve yelled. "I can't tell you. I promised Curtis I'd keep my mouth shut, so back off." Steve belted him in a kidney. "You're his hot-shot security chief. Go ask him yourself. We're getting out of here tomorrow—"

"Tomorrow?" Susan said. "Steve, are you serious?"

"Serious as a heart attack. If this shit-ass ever lets go of me." He slugged Alex again.

"Stop it," Janis yelled and yanked on Alex's arm. Steve broke loose, kicked Alex in the shin, and sat up against the wall, gasping.

Alex yanked his arm from Janis's grasp and sat next to Steve. The private eye was a hard head. A shit. Alex had a hunch that Steve knew something about Curtis, maybe even his real name. Who could have told him, and how much did he know? Was the mission at risk? If he detained Steve for questioning, it could blow Alex's cover, blow the whole operation. *The Ark* would have his ass. It wasn't worth the risk. Besides, Steve had said he was leaving tomorrow, maybe that would be the end of it. Alex got up, straightened his shirt collar, and walked to the elevator. "I hope you haven't done anything stupid this time, Steve." He turned and left Tamarack Hall.

As the elevator door slid shut, Susan ran to Steve and hugged him, her eyes filled with tears. "You made it back."

"What else did you expect?" He held her warm body, which trembled in his arms. He was beginning to like how she cared about him. The rip in her nightgown was rather sexy, too.

Janis picked up the spilled ice bucket and walked away, grumbling.

"We're leaving tomorrow," Steve said.

"But Steve," she whispered in his ear. "We can't go."

Steve saw a flash in his brain. "Like hell we can't. You've been bugging me about leaving ever since we got here."

"These people are in trouble. We have to help them. We can't just leave. Look around. There's something horribly wrong here. Don't you see?"

Steve looked at the ceiling. "So what if I do?"

"Then help them."

He stood and pulled Susan to her feet. "I know what I'm doing."

Chapter 86

IN JANIS'S ROOM, music was coming from the bathroom. He removed the luggage and underwear from the bed and pulled down the sheets, an apprehension in his chest as heavy as a parked truck. What was he going to do about Lisa? Why was she tempting him: to get back at her father, to piss him off some more? Janis didn't want any trouble from Ray; they had to work together. He undressed to his boxer shorts. At the bathroom door, he stopped and sighed. It wasn't going to happen. Not today. Not ever.

Now all he had to do was break the news to her.

Slowly, he swung the door open and walked into the steamy bathroom. *Love is Blue* played from the radio, the instrumental version, the sexy one. It made him feel all mushy inside.

A floral fragrance drifted in the bubble bath mist. Lisa was lying in the tub, her head on a water pillow, fast asleep. Bubbles floated all around her. She looked beautiful, even with her hair wet.

Reaching into the water, he gently lifted her from the tub. The bubbles cascaded off her body like a foamy waterfall. As he wrapped her in a fluffy bath towel, she sleepily put her arms around his neck and moaned. His heart raced. He carried her to the bed, his mind swimming in emotions and desires. *Could* he make love to Lisa? Yes. Certainly she'd be willing. But *should* he make love to Lisa? No. She was Ray's daughter, goddamn it.

He felt like his insides were being torn to pieces by wild horses.

Laying her on the bed, he covered her with a sheet. He stood there a moment and watched her sleep. She was too young for him. They had nothing in common. But more so, she was a California girl with a lifestyle far different from his quiet existence in the university community of Colorado. If they got together, she'd soon become bored with him, wander off, and break his heart. Love wouldn't be enough to keep them together. In this complicated world, it took more than love, much more.

Sadly, he returned to the bathroom and showered. The water felt wonderful, made him sleepy. As he dried off, he felt relieved; he'd made up his mind about Lisa. At the window, he looked out over Simi Valley and up at a star-lit sky. Somewhere in the universe, the woman he was meant to love still waited undiscovered, as elusive as the 13th Power itself.

After donning a new pair of boxer shorts, he slid under the sheet next to Lisa. She rolled over. The towel fell away. In the darkness she cuddled into him, the warmth of her body like torture, but he was sure he'd made the right decision.

"Good night, my cowboy," she murmured.

They slept in each other's arms.

Chapter 87

STEVE ROLLED OVER and picked up the phone that seemed to be ringing in his dream. The damn racket was real. He shook off sleep. "Yeah?"

"Steve Raven?" The voice on the phone sounded harsh and cold.

"What?"

"You've got your money. I suggest you get the hell out of here before Curtis changes his mind about letting you live."

"Who is this?"

The phone went dead.

Steve rubbed his eyes. Was that good news or bad? Didn't sound good. Dazed, he held the buzzing receiver and glanced across the bed. Susan was lying on her stomach, her bare back uncovered. He hung up the phone, not taking his eyes off her. Unbroken by tan lines, her sun-kissed skin looked smooth and inviting. He scooted next to her and wrapped her in his arms. She stirred sleepily. He wondered if last night's passion fires were still burning embers, waiting to be rekindled.

\#

Susan opened her eyes, pleased to see his face. His warm, strong arms around her felt like heaven. He smelled of Stetson. Clean. Sexy. Last night's ecstasy drifted in her mind like a hazy dream. He'd survived the confrontation with Curtis. Relieved, she left no doubt about her feelings for him. Never before had she been attracted to a man so strongly. Last night she wanted all of him. She took all of him. It was a night she'd long remember.

And this morning, as she kissed him, she hoped that nothing would ever change the way she felt right now. The warmth, the love, the strength: last night he gave it all to her. She moaned and held him tighter. He responded to her touch. She kissed him from his lips to his ear and hugged him. She couldn't get close enough. As the bed sheet shifted and fell to the floor, the damn phone rang again.

#

Steve picked it up. "What do you want?"

"Mr. Raven?"

"It's your quarter."

Susan rolled over on top of him, the teasing smile of a naughty girl on her lips. With her long black hair hanging down in his face, he tried to divide his attention between her foreplay and what the man on the phone was saying.

"Mr. Olson, here. First National Bank."

Steve blinked. "First National, yes?"

"You requested we notify you when a transfer into your account had been completed. I am happy to report it came through this morning. Looks like you finally got a decent paycheck."

"How many zeros?"

"Six."

"I'll be damned."

"May I make a suggestion?" the banker said. "I think this might be a good time to settle up on those bad checks you have in collections. We'd certainly like to have them off our backs. And let's get your airplane out of hock, too."

"Handle it, Mr. Olson." He tossed down the phone, smiling. He was a goddamn millionaire. Rolling over, he put Susan on her back. "Six big ones, baby. Let's get out of this dump." He kissed her and jumped up from the bed. As he pulled his trousers on, he looked at her lying there, uncovered and beautiful...and not moving. What the hell? She wasn't getting up. "Come on. We're leaving. Get your clothes on." He gave her a wink. "Or are you flying naked this morning?"

She smiled and stretched out her arms, beckoning him

to come to her.

"Not now. We've gotta go, Susie Baby."

She sat up, frowning. "We're not going, Steve."

He ignored her, zipped his pants, and reached for his holster. Of course they were going, fast as a couple rats fleeing a barn fire.

"I wasn't kidding last night. We can't go."

He put his shirt on over his .45 and tucked in the tails without buttoning the buttons. He wasn't kidding, either. They were going. And they were going now.

Definitely she wasn't getting the message loud and clear.

He dropped to his knees in front of her and stared into her eyes. For several moments, he didn't say anything, but searched for the words she'd understand. This was important; it meant life or death. He couldn't risk her life any longer. The rat cellar was a close call. Too close. How many more of those would she survive? The first phone call lingered in his mind: the threat against his life.

"I need to get you out of here," he said. "Trust me to do the right thing."

"Blind trust is a lot to ask of someone."

"You have to."

"Then you have to take them with us."

"Ray won't go. You heard his speech. He's all fat in the head about this 13th Power malarkey."

"Janis and Lisa will. And Lo."

"The plane can't carry everyone."

"Steal a staff car. I'll even drive it. Lisa can go with me. You take Lo in the plane."

"They'll just run you down. Take you hostage. Make me come back for you. We'll get caught. The only way to survive is to run."

Tears shined in her eyes. She *had* to understand; she *had* to trust him. "We have to go now." He got up and held his hand out to her. Slowly, she grasped his fingers, and he pulled her to her feet. For a few moments, he held her. Then she dressed quietly and they slipped out of Tamarack Hall.

Steve hailed the first staff car he saw. "Airfield," he said. The driver seemed happy to have somewhere to go.

As they raced toward the main gate, the ominous phone call lingered in Steve's mind. He knew these people didn't make idle threats. And Curtis was as stable as a one-winged airplane. Eyes keen for trouble, Steve tensed as the car approached the security checkpoint. The driver stopped and talked with a guard.

Looking into the back seat, the guard asked, "What's your business at the airfield?"

Steve was about to snarl that it was none of his damn business when Susan jumped in.

"Officer," she said with a wink. "My friend here," she hung on Steve's shoulder, "is taking me up in his air-o-plane. He promised to get me higher than anyone else ever had. I suspect, though, it'll be the other way around." She slowly pulled her dress above her knees, adding to the effect.

The security guard touched his helmet. "I'll bet you're right about that, pretty lady. Have a nice flight." The draw bar went up, and he waved the car through.

Steve couldn't believe it. Susan was truly amazing. She smiled at him, and they both started laughing.

On the tarmac, the Cessna had been parked next to Curtis's gold and white Learjet, its turbine intakes covered with gleaming gold caps to keep out the birds. His little blue and white airplane looked so unimpressive next to the sleek jet, but he didn't care. Flying was flying. Little planes and big jets all flew by the same rules: pitch was airspeed, power was altitude, and any landing he walked away from was a *good* landing.

He unlocked the door of his plane.

Susan buckled in.

The engine cranked and fired with a puff of smoke, the propeller's drone filling the California morning air. Steve taxied to the runway threshold where he performed his run-up and pre-flight checklist. Satisfied, he set the *Com-One* radio to 121.3 and dropped the flaps ten degrees. He looked at Susan. "Ready to get high, baby?"

She gave him the thumbs-up sign.

He pushed the throttle all the way in. The knob vibrated in his hand as the engine revved to full power. He released the brakes. The cool morning air was perfect for flying. The airplane quickly accelerated to sixty knots, and he pulled back on the yoke. Holding the nose high, the Cessna rose from the runway. Easing the nose over to gain airspeed, he slowly retracted the flaps. As he turned south, and still climbing, he picked up the radio mike. "So-Cal Approach, Cessna niner-four-niner, twenty-four miles north. Request radar vector to Orange County."

"Cessna niner-four-niner, squawk three-three-two-seven, ident," came the reply over the ceiling speaker.

Steve reached down and turned the transponder dials to the requested frequency. "Three-three-two-seven coming at you." He pressed the *Ident* button. A little yellow light glowed on the console. A few minutes passed as the controller talked with another pilot.

"Niner-four-niner, radar contact, two-one miles northwest. Turn to heading one-two-zero and maintain one-five-hundred. Clear to Orange County. Maintain VFR."

"Niner-four-niner on one-two-zero at one-five-hundred. Thank you." Steve put the mike back into its holder on the panel.

"What was all that?" Susan asked, shouting above the engine drone.

"He told me to fly a compass heading of 120 degrees at 1500 feet above sea level." He pointed to the instruments. "And here," he pointed to the transponder. "I'm squawking this number, which identifies our bleep on their radar screens. Now they know who we are up here."

"So we won't run into anyone else?"

"True to a point, but he said to maintain VFR, or visual flight rules, which means I am ultimately responsible for the safe separation of aircraft, visually."

"Why didn't you do all this on the flight from Nevada to Simi Valley?"

"We didn't need to." He looked around. "But now we're entering the most congested airspace in Southern California. Up here, we all have to work together to make it safe for everyone. It's amazing though, the number of people working down there to make this flight possible." Steve spotted a 737, off to his right, dropping through his altitude. A United emblem adorned the tail.

"*Niner-four-niner,*" the speaker blared. "*Traffic, three o'clock, descending to LAX through one-five-hundred.*"

Steve grabbed the mike. "I have the traffic in sight, niner-four-niner." He put the mike in his lap. "See how they can help? But not always. We have to keep our eyes open all the time."

Susan looked out the window at the city below. Los Angeles skyscrapers reflected off the underside of the wing. It was a beautiful morning to leave Solartech Labs, but thinking of those they had left behind tainted her excitement over this flight to Orange County. She had no idea what Steve was up to. That worried her even more.

"Why are we going to Orange County?"

He pulled a piece of paper out of his pocket and handed it to her. "If we should get separated for any reason, this is where you'll be safe. Tom and I go way back." He checked his airspace with a visual sweep and picked up the mike again. "So-Cal Approach, niner-four-niner still with you."

"*Niner-four-niner, stay on course,*" the controller answered. "*In four miles expect heading zero-niner-zero and one-thousand. John Wayne tower is on frequency one-*

one-niner-point-niner."

"Call my turn."

"Roger."

Steve set the tower's frequency on the *Com-Two* radio. "When we're on the ground, we'll rent a car, and I'll take you to Tom's. You'll stay there 'til I get back."

"Get back? From where?"

"Just some unfinished business I need to attend to."

She didn't like him leaving her in the dark and was about to voice a protest when the speaker crackled. *"Niner-four-niner, turn to heading zero-niner-zero and begin your descent to Orange County. Contact tower. Frequency change approved. Have a good day."*

"Thank you," Steve replied. He switched to *Com-Two*. "John Wayne tower, niner-four-niner with you." The engine drone subsided as Steve pulled back on the power, and the airplane began to sink toward the airport that seemed to appear magically in front of them.

"Niner-four-niner, welcome to Orange County. Winds light and variable. Make right traffic. Clear to land, one-niner right."

"Roger," Steve radioed. "One-niner right, clear to land."

Susan tightened her seatbelt and wondered when this would really be over.

Chapter 88

THE MORINGING SUN BEAMED down from a misty California sky. Janis, having left Lisa sleeping, followed Lo out of Tamarack Hall to a staff car idling under the carport. An attendant opened the door. "Good morning, gentlemen."

Janis got in. "Smile," he said to Lo. "It's a beautiful day."

"So you say. I'm not so sure this day is any better than last three." He looked at his watch. "They called meeting for 9:00 AM. We already late."

"Relax. Half of them are probably wrecked with hangovers. They won't mind the delay."

"Maybe not the workers, but Curtis different story." Lo touched his nose. "Something stinky about rich man, Janis. Nothing on the Internet about him. I look for hours. It's a mystery to me."

"Nothing?"

Shaking his head, Lo looked out the window as they raced toward the lab. "Tiger jaws clamp tight," he said and mumbled something else in Chinese.

"Will you quit that?" Janis was in no mood for Lo's soothsaying. Besides, the Internet didn't have information about everyone. He fidgeted in his seat. All he knew for sure was the sooner he got this project started, the sooner he'd be finished and on his way home. He leaned forward and tapped the driver's shoulder. "Step on it."

The car barreled up the ramp between the towering stainless steel buildings and under the steel archway to the vehicle reception lobby. The driver stopped in front of the glass-encased entrance. Janis got out after Lo, and the staff car drove away.

Lo held open the atrium door. "Enter tiger's lair."

Janis smirked. They rode the escalator and got off at the lobby. His shoes ticked on the marble floor, which was inlaid with gold atomic symbols that spanned the foyer. Walking toward the reception counter, he looked up at the ceiling some five stories high, supported by six gold pillars. At least they looked like real gold.

Under the *SECURITY* sign at the end of the counter, a bank of video screens lined the wall. Monitoring various areas within the building, they were under the watchful eye of a security officer dressed in a white shirt and black tie. A smile lit his face as they approached. "Dr. Mackey," he said then turned to Lo. "Mr. Chin. Nice to meet you."

Lo bowed.

From behind the counter, a woman with silver hair brought them two folded white lab coats. Squinting behind her spectacles, she helped Janis into his coat, wrestled with a stubborn button, and inspected the fit.

Janis thought it felt stiff from too much starch.

"Very nice." The woman turned to Lo and helped him with his coat. "Such a handsome man."

Lo gave her a funny look.

Smiling, she shuffled away.

The security officer opened a folder, shuffled through some papers, and removed two ID tags. "You'll need these." He clipped an ID tag to each of their coat pockets. Lo inspected his. He didn't seem impressed. There was no picture, just a black-on-white barcode under a Solartech Labs insignia, a gold shield and a blue atom pierced by a yellow lightning bolt. Janis noticed the security officer didn't have an ID tag clipped to his pocket.

"Where's yours?"

Displaying a proud smile, he pulled up his left sleeve and showed him a twenty-four-pin microchip that had been surgically implanted in his arm, complete with a flashing red LED. The black-on-white barcode was sealed in clear plastic. "Never leave home without it. The halls and labs are blanket laser scanned. Our main computers track the whereabouts of everyone in this building." He pulled his sleeve down. "This one is electronically encoded. Yours have to be in plain view, so don't be sticking them in your pocket or under a lab coat. We don't like false alarms. Got that?"

As Lo patted his tag, Janis quickly rechecked the position of his, making sure it was clearly visible.

"We're ready," the officer said. "They're waiting for you in Tech-Com Control."

Chapter 89

JANIS FOLLOWED THE GUARD down a long hallway and into the depths of Solartech Labs.

"Mr. Chin," the guard said to Lo as they walked. "Weren't you on the Polaris programming team a couple years back?"

Lo nodded.

"I read somewhere that you debugged the transcription program single-handed. Pretty impressive feat considering the number of brainards who had tried it."

"Thank you. But please, all in a day's work." He looked at Janis. "Magazine make big deal over nothing."

"Maybe to you," Janis said. "I'm impressed."

At an intersection in the corridor, they entered a glass-enclosed catwalk that connected the two buildings. Janis looked down to the ramp. A car went by. He looked up at the steel archway with its engraved message towering above. *Gateway to the Atomic Universe.*

At the end of the catwalk, he followed the security guard into a room skirted by electronic control panels and dozens of monitors stacked floor to ceiling. Several video screens hung from the rafters. Technicians, wearing white lab coats, sat on swivel chairs in front of their stations. A bank of windows overlooked a room where six rows of super computers hummed in servitude to the technicians.

Janis saw another window like no window he'd ever seen before. He crossed the control room to get a closer look. About eighteen inches high and six feet long, the window was made of glass a foot thick with rounded corners. A light beyond the ominous window blinked on and off in one-second intervals. When the light came on, he saw a steel-ribbed chamber with tunnel-like walls laced with piping. When the light went off, he saw a red glow coming from somewhere beyond his view. The contraption looked like something out of a horror movie.

Lo stood next to him, staring into the strange window. "Eye of tiger," he said hauntingly.

His words sent a chill down Janis's spine. As his mind tried to calculate the meaning of all this technology, a voice from above broke the silence.

"Dr. Mackey."

Curtis stood on a landing above the control room, an office window and door behind him. He made his way down the steel stairs, tapping the golden staff with each step. The metallic twang reverberated around the room. Several other personnel emerged from the office and followed him down. "Glad you could join us this morning. We've been waiting for this moment for a long time."

Reaching the control-room floor, the technicians fanned out around Curtis. Dressed in his long black coat and wearing sunglasses, he looked out of place among the men in their white lab coats, ID tags dangling from their pockets. But Curtis didn't have an ID tag. Janis got goose bumps, recalling the security officer's implant, and shook Curtis's hand.

The others went to their stations.

"Before I show you around, I'd like to introduce my staff." Curtis walked up to the first man sitting at the console. "This is Roger Deadford."

Roger smiled, his black hair slicked back with a greasy shine. He looked about thirty. Clean-shaven.

"Our electrical engineer," Curtis said. "Power plant and distribution. Keeps us plugged in, so to speak."

Janis scanned all the meters and dials on the console then smiled at Roger. "How are you?"

Roger nodded.

Curtis patted him on the back and walked to the next station.

"Good morning, sir," the longhaired young man at the monitor said.

Curtis rested a hand on his shoulder. "This is Stan Burton. Mechanical engineer, Harvard grad, and a genius at keeping the nuts and bolts tight around here. Nothing he can't build or repair."

"With a little help from my team, sir."

"Ah, yes. Your team. Of course." He moved to the next station.

Janis lagged behind to acknowledge Stan, who looked more like a hippy than a mechanical engineer. Probably smoked dope 'til he was forty.

Lo stayed one step behind Janis.

The man at the next station was much older than Stan, mid sixties Janis figured, thin gray hair and wrinkled cheeks. Curtis shook the man's hand. "Robert. How are you this morning?"

"Tired, sir."

"Sorry to hear that." He turned to Janis. "Best damn synchrotron operator in the business. Goes way back, 1952, wasn't it? He worked with Glasser on the Brookhaven Cosmotron. The man's busted a lot of atoms in his time. Right, Robert?"

"A smashing career, sir."

Curtis laughed lightly and moved on.

"And this, gentlemen, is Dr. Tracy McClarence. She joins us all the way from Cavendish Labs at Cambridge, Great Britain."

Janis's mouth fell open. The redhead was stunning to look at. Sparkling green eyes, little freckles on her nose, not too many, but just enough to be interesting, and behind those thin pink lips, a perfect set of teeth bedazzled him. She sat at a keyboard, returning his smile. He almost didn't hear Curtis explain that she was a laser physicist, tops in her field. As Curtis moved on to the next station, Janis followed him but continued smiling at Tracy as he walked backwards, his heart in a flutter. Every line. Every curve. She was gorgeous. More his age than Lisa. He hoped Tracy didn't turn out to be the snooty type.

"This is Ray's station," Curtis explained as he placed his hands on the back of an empty chair. "From here, he controls the hydrogen atoms. He'll be joining us later."

"How's he doing?" Janis asked.

"Rested well last night, or so Doc tells me." Curtis moved to the next man seated at the console. The monitor at this station grabbed Janis's attention because it was the most beautiful thing in the place, except Tracy. A computer-generated funnel rotated like a tornado, color coded in green, yellow, and red. Mesmerized, Janis watched in awe as it whirled and twisted.

Lo leaned forward as if to inspect it more closely. "Gravity generator?"

"That's right!" Curtis said. "We call it the MIGGS. Johnson here is our expert."

Johnson smiled. His straight brown hair hung down past his shoulders, another hippy, and he wore black-rimmed glasses. He looked like he'd eaten too many Twinkies. "The MIGGS is our Mass Imitation Gravity Generating Simulator," Johnson explained as he pointed to the strange window in the far wall, the one with the thick glass. "She's capable of simulating a 3M star mass rotating at the speed of light." He turned back to the monitor. "This is a rerun of the last test...let's see...14 July last month. Got her up to full speed. We can identify the event horizon on the monitor, right here, in red. Escape velocity 186,000 miles per second. Nothing will get past her."

"An artificial black hole?" Lo asked with a mix of curiosity and disbelief etched on his face.

"Mathematically, yes," Johnson explained. "The Supers work the numbers." He pointed to the super computer bay window. "They don't know the difference between a real black hole and a digital one."

"What's it for?" Lo asked.

"Containment," Curtis said.

"What has to be contained?" Janis asked.

"Later," Curtis barked.

Janis flinched, puzzled at the harsh reaction to a simple question.

"This way." Curtis motioned them on to the next station. It had two swivel chairs, twin monitors, and dual keyboards. "And this, Janis, is where you will work your mathematical magic. We've modified this station to accommodate both of you." He wagged his finger between Janis and Lo.

As Janis inspected his terminal, his eyes caught the motion of an old man entering the control room. He wore a white lab coat with the familiar ID tag dangling from a pocket. The old guy looked like the mad scientist in a Frankenstein movie. Maybe it was because of his scraggly gray hair and bushy eyebrows.

Curtis pointed to the old man. "Ah, yes, gentlemen. Last, but not least. I'd like you to meet our Tech Com Director of Operations, Mr. Ted Benning."

Slightly hunched over, Ted limped up to Janis, shook his hand and smiled, showing off his perfect white teeth. "You we welcome."

"Russian?" Janis asked him.

"American," Ted replied. "Thanks to permanent resident visa and this job I have here."

"It doesn't get any better than this," Curtis proclaimed as he stood in front of the windows overlooking the Supers. He raised his arms and held the golden staff above his head. The black coat spread open, making him seem larger than life against the glare of the glass. Wearing sunglasses indoors made him look ridiculous. "Together, we'll crack the 13th Power and claim the Higgs." His words echoed through the control room.

Janis looked at Tracy, checking her reaction to

Curtis's theatrics. She just shook her head and went back to her keyboard, typing. Janis pushed his glasses up. He wanted to get close to her, get to know her, but she could be the type of woman he'd never had any luck with before. The competition. He was sure to find out soon enough.

Lo sat down at his workstation and began typing. The monitor blinked on. Numbers and symbols began scrolling down the screen.

"Leave him to play with his new toy," Curtis said to Janis. "Follow me. There's more to see."

With Curtis at his side, Janis walked out of Tech-Com Control through a set of swinging doors that opened to a long hallway. Windows lined the wall overlooking the Supers below. Several technicians passed by. They seemed preoccupied with their duties and managed only cordial nods in passing.

Curtis motioned a turn down a hallway to the left. At the end, a set of huge steel doors blocked their way. Curtis gained admittance by placing his hand on a scanner. A light beam traversed his palm, and a buzzer sounded. Door locks clicked. He pushed the doors open and let Janis enter first. It seemed to him as though he'd entered a world straight out of Star Wars.

"The heartbeat of Tech-Com Control," Curtis yelled over the loud drone of machinery. A technician driving an electric cart whizzed by, another passed from the other direction, towing a trailer full of workers wearing gray jumpsuits and white hard hats. The place buzzed with activity.

Janis looked up to a brightly lit ceiling some three stories above him, skirted by steel catwalks and supported by I-beam pillars. Pipes, electrical cords, and air ducts snaked throughout the massive room. Huge steel-encased machines towered up the walls. High up, welders spewed molten flack down to the floor while several men held a beam in place with the help of two cranes that did the heavy lifting. A man standing on a ladder must've been their supervisor.

Hauling a large wooden crate, a forklift whined by; the driver waved. Several men dressed in white lab coats and holding clipboards were standing around a cylindrical tank. They seemed concerned about vapor escaping from a valve on top of the tank. Another electric cart went by with a diesel generator in tow. The whole place smelled like wet cement.

"What's all this?" Janis yelled to Curtis over the drone.

"This is where it all begins, the race to the Higgs boson." Tucking the golden staff under his arm, Curtis directed Janis's attention to a group of men wearing thick gloves and stacking silver cylinders that were covered with frost. "Liquid hydrogen for the 13th Power experiment," Curtis explained at the top of his voice. "They go in the ionizer, that rust colored machine with round doors. It reverses the polarity of atoms, strips off electrons, and injects them into the synchrotron, over there."

He pointed to a twenty-foot high steel ribbed tube that seemed to end at a concrete wall. "It's sixteen miles in diameter and can accelerate protons to damn near the speed of light." Curtis turned. "See that glass tube? It's a linear accelerator, four miles long. It directs laser boosted protons into the MIGGS."

Janis noticed submarine hatch-like doors painted with hazard stripes mounted in the walls next to the glass and steel tubes. "Where do those doors go?" he hollered over all the noise.

"Service access tunnels," Curtis shouted. "Fifty miles worth honeycombing the valley floor, with dozens of access doors like that, some from inside this building and others from outside locations throughout the compound. Makes it easy for us to service the synchrotron and laser resonator."

Janis looked around. "So where *is* the laser?"

"At the other end of the glass tube four miles away. It shoots a beam into the linear accelerator. In a millisecond, it can boost a stream of protons to the speed of light."

"A particle beam," Janis shouted.

"If it works right." Curtis looked up at the ceiling and pointed to a chrome-plated pipeline. "Up there," he yelled. "Electrons stripped from the atoms are directed into the MIGGS going in opposite directions and electro-magnetically aligned to collide with an electron target suspended in the titanium cylinder. Call the protons the nuts and the electrons the nut crackers. The more protons packed into the opposing beams, the more collisions are possible. We should get fission and containment in a titanium cylinder, specially designed to operate at these high speeds." Curtis smiled. His gold tooth glistened. "Wham-o." He slammed a fist into his hand. "That's where you come in."

"How's that?"

"Get with Ray. He'll tell you what he needs." Curtis looked around, his hands outstretched. "All this is for naught if you guys fail to reach the 13th Power. We've got the equipment but we don't have the formulas to make it work. Don't let me down on this, Janis."

He followed Curtis out through the steel doors, the silence a welcome relief. Gave him a chance to think, and all he could think about was how impossible a task Curtis had undertaken. And the fact that success rode on his mathematical abilities didn't make Janis feel comfortable. He now realized the huge investment Curtis had in the project. Was he chasing a fantasy? Could Janis help him catch it? He guessed it didn't matter. Succeed or fail, Janis was getting paid to try. One question lingered.

"What about containment?" he asked as he walked with Curtis toward Tech-Com Control. "What needs to be contained?"

Curtis stopped in the middle of the hall. "The MIGGS is no bubble chamber, Janis. We're not going to smash atoms into tiny particles, take pictures, and name the debris before it burns out. No, sir. We're going to contain the debris."

"You mean trap the Higgs bosons."

"It's never been done before." Curtis began walking.

"What are you going to do with them?"

He stopped and turned back to Janis. "Yes, the million dollar question."

Janis decided to be blunt. "There's got to be something in it for you. I mean, Ray wants to be famous. That's no mystery. But you, an archeologist turned atomic scientist, you're not doing this for your health."

"Never mind what's in it for me, Dr. Mackey." He shook his golden staff. "Just do your job and we'll get along just fine." He started walking away.

Janis ground his molars. Curtis and his damn attitude problem. He certainly didn't have all his cards on the table. He could be holding jokers or an ace up his sleeve. Whatever the case, this wasn't the time to force his hand or call his bluff. Janis didn't want to blow his million-dollar deal. He hurried to catch up to Curtis.

As they walked through the doors into Tech-Com Control, Janis decided to cooperate, for now. See where the project was headed. Besides, it had just become very interesting.

He was looking at the redhead.

#

The doors closed behind Curtis as he walked into Tech-Com Control. He went up the metal stairs to his office above the control room, wondering if Janis was being stubborn or careful. Would he perform to the caliber required for the project? He'd better.

Inside, Jonathan sat waiting for him, his face long.

Curtis laid his staff on the desk. "Why the look?"

"I transferred the money, as you requested."

Curtis didn't answer. He poured a cup of coffee to keep from screaming obscenities at the top of his lungs.

"The P. I. has been notified. He's gone."

"Good riddance." Curtis stirred sugar into his coffee. His mind raced back to the jungles of Borneo. Memories of Fred Jenkins' death sent a cold chill down his spine. Not the killing, the punishment: a Sumatra prison and death by hanging or beheading. Should the Malaysian authorities ever find out he was still alive, they'd stop at nothing to get him back. His life wouldn't be worth a nickel. He couldn't afford to take the chance that Steve Raven was bluffing about turning him in to the authorities in Singapore. It had been a long time since he left Borneo, and he had a lot invested in this project, too much to let a greedy P. I. ruin him. Killing him seemed like a good idea, but they'd tried that, and failed. Steve had guts and luck, the kind of man who was hard to kill. He had to be dealt with wisely.

"I can have Judas track him down, if you want. Kill him."

"Steve Raven is like a bad dream," Curtis said. "He keeps coming back. Just let him go." He took a sip of coffee. "He acts like a tough guy, but right now his tail is tucked between his legs, and he's running like the chickenshit that he really is."

Jonathan walked to the window overlooking Tech-Com Control. "I don't know, boss. The bad dream may come back to haunt you."

"Then we'll get Judas to kill him." Curtis looked into his coffee cup. "Speaking of which, have you seen him lately?"

"Judas?" Jonathan shook his head. "Can't say I have."

"I wonder where he is." Curtis stood beside Jonathan, looking out the window that overlooked Tech-Com Control below. A commotion caught his eye. Lo seemed excited, waving at Janis who ran to Lo's terminal and leaned over his shoulder. Lo pointed to something on the monitor.

#

"What is it?" Janis asked.

"Run file checks here, get feel for system."

"It's all Greek to me."

"But look." Lo scrolled down a list of files. "All these reside in upper memory. Most are program files in directories like this." He clicked on one for demonstration. An error flag appeared: *No Application Associated.* "See. It's okay to do that." He clicked on several more with the same result.

"So?"

"Now look here. Mixed up with files I found these." He pointed to one. "File extension *w-m.* I've not seen anything like that before."

"Is that bad?"

"Look what happens." He clicked on a *w-m* file and got: *Access Denied.* He clicked on several more with the same result. "See?"

"What does that mean?"

"System bugged. And I bet..." He worked the keyboard. The monitor flashed to a program manager called the Worm. All the information for the program appeared.

Janis said, "What does it do?"

"Spies on data and reports to a host computer, off site somewhere. Very complicated but not intrusive, so it can go undetected, unless stumbled on like me."

"Who's bugging the system?" he asked as Lo clicked through several windows.

"No telling. Worm has read-only files. Changes locked out. Can't break into program."

"Then delete the damn thing and be done with it."

Lo closed the program manager for the Worm and went back to the list of files. He typed the command to delete them. *Access Denied* flashed on the screen. He looked at Janis, shaking his head. "No can do."

Janis swallowed hard. "We better tell Curtis about this." He turned, found Ted at the MIGGS console with Johnson. It looked like they were busy with something. Tracy was with them. Not one to miss an opportunity to get close to her, Janis walked over to the huddle.

"Hi," Tracy said with a smile.

Janis said, "Hello," and quickly turned his attention to Ted. He didn't want to seem overly anxious to talk to her. Tapping the old man on the shoulder, "Ted, get Curtis down here."

"Wait one minute." He didn't turn his attention away from the MIGGS monitor.

Janis looked at Tracy. She shrugged. He tapped the old man's shoulder again. "Now."

Ted handed Janis a cell phone. "Dial *G-O-L-D,* 4-6-5-3."

"Thanks." He dialed. The phone rang. Gold? How pompous.

"Curtis." His voice sounded harsh, as if the interruption annoyed him.

"You better get down here right away," Janis said. "The Supers are bugged."

The phone clicked. A moment later, the sound of Curtis's voice filled the control room as he stormed down the stairs. "What are you talking about?" He ran to Lo's station. "Bugged? Bugged how?"

"Memory resident program," Lo said. "The Worm."

"A virus?"

"A bug. A spy." Lo pointed to the monitor. "Every time something happens in computer, the Worm analyzes the data and sends report out on Modem2, secondary device running in upper memory. Main modem not used so computer not report to terminal. Very sneaky."

"Can you get rid of it?"

Lo thought a moment. "Aside from pull plug, no."

Curtis picked up the phone, dialed quickly and groaned. "Get Alex up here. Now." As he put the phone down, Ray stormed into the control room, arm in a sling and eyes on fire.

"Ray, how are you feeling?" Janis said. He was still smiling when Ray pushed him against the console. "What the...?"

"You think I don't know, you bastard."

"Know what?" Janis put up his guard.

"She wasn't in her room all night!" Ray grabbed Janis by the lab coat. "I tried to call her." Curtis and two technicians jumped in to restrain Ray. During the scuffle, he kept yelling, "That's my daughter, you bastard. My daughter. How could you sleep with her?"

Janis, seething, pulled free of Ray's grip. The others held him back. After straightening his ruffled lab coat, Janis clutched his throbbing hand. Ray was going to make this job impossible. How could anybody work with a raving lunatic? He was going to ruin everything. "What's with you?" Janis glared at the maniac.

"So I called your room this morning. Guess what? Lisa answered, you son of a bitch."

"She was sleeping."

"In your bed!"

"Nothing happened!"

"That's what you say."

Janis felt like beating some sense into Ray though it probably wouldn't do any good. Lisa was right, her father was overprotective. An understatement. "Did you ask her? You said she answered the phone. Did you ask *her*, damn it?"

"No." Ray looked down to the floor.

"Why not?"

"I hung up and assumed the worst." He readjusted the sling on his arm. "Maybe I was wrong. I'm-I'm sorry."

"Sorry? You're obsessed. Accuse me of having my

way with your daughter...is there nothing you won't do?"

"Nothing."

"That's what you've given her. Nothing. No love. No happiness. No freedom. Nothing."

"That's not true. I've sacrificed a lot for her. And I'd sacrifice a lot more. My life, even the whole world if I had to."

"Stop talking like an idiot."

The room fell silent.

Ray's shoulders slouched. "All right, I said I was sorry. I lost my head. But you know how I feel about her. Why do you have to push it?"

"I pushed nothing. She fell asleep in my tub, so I put her to bed and left her there when I went to work this morning. She's not six years old any more, Ray. Let her make her own choices. She's really quite capable—"

Alex stormed into the control room, followed by two of his security men. "What's going on in here?"

"It's the computers," Curtis said. "They're bugged. What do you think?"

Alex looked at Lo's monitor, still flashing: *Access Denied*. "What do you expect me to do about it?"

"I want a full investigation," Curtis bellowed. "Find out who put the bug in here, who it's reporting to, and how to kill it. I suggest you start with Devin. Get on it right away." Curtis climbed the stairs to his office, cursing.

#

Ray rubbed his throbbing shoulder and thought there was no end to Devin's interference. "How could anyone plant a bug in here?" he asked Alex.

"Stranger things have happened."

"What about the private eye? Could he have penetrated security this deep?"

Alex furrowed his brow. "I doubt it."

"Well, go get him, find out."

"He left this morning."

Looking at the door, Ray said, "So we'll never know."

Alex shrugged and walked out.

Ray blinked. Steve couldn't have had anything to do with the message flashing on Lo's monitor. The P. I. may have been cunning and resourceful, but he wasn't knowledgeable enough to access the Supers, much less plant a bug.

Seemed odd to Ray that Alex had been satisfied with that flimsy explanation so quickly.

Turning to Janis, who looked disgusted with him, Ray said, "Lisa will always be my little girl. I can't help it. Kate forced me to do things you'd never understand. You've never been a father. "

Janis sat down, stared at the monitor like he wasn't even listening.

Ray went on anyway. "I've been overprotective, I know it. Lisa's never had a mother, Janis. She has no recollection of Kate. We talked about that yesterday. She understands why I sent her away. She'll forgive me. I'm all she's got."

"But not all she'll ever have."

#

Janis, still boiling with anger, looked at Tracy. She was shaking her head as if unimpressed with the madness around her. *Great first impression.* Maybe she wouldn't be any different than the other women he'd known, but he wished Ray hadn't made him look like a womanizer. Tracy walked back to her station, her red hair swaying, her green skirt worn tight at her knees. She was perfect: perfectly professional, perfectly wrong for him.

Janis swiveled his chair toward Ray who had leaned against the console and was now futzing with his sling. "Are you done with your temper tantrum?"

"I told you I was sorry."

"What's on the agenda for today?"

"A test fire," he said.

"What's that?"

"A full-systems run. Go over the math first, check the formulas. Lo can reprogram the Supers. How long will it take you?"

"I don't know how much needs fixing. Give me six hours to check it out."

"Let's go with that." He turned to Ted at the main control console. "Start the clock."

Ted pushed a button on his panel. Above the window overlooking the Supers, a black digital clock with red numbers started running backwards, one second at a time. A program schedule appeared on all the monitors. "Let's keep the countdown on schedule," Ray said. "Six hours."

Was he nuts? "I didn't say I'd be ready in six hours. What's the matter with you?"

"We've got to start somewhere. If we're not a go in six hours, we'll abort and restart the clock over again."

"You've done this before?"

"Not the entire program."

"What if the formulas are still wrong?"

"Then we'll have to fix them and try again until we get them right."

Janis adjusted his glasses. "So what makes this experiment any different than the hundreds of atom-smashing projects going on around the world every day?"

"First of all," Ray said. "We're using a carbon dioxide laser to boost accelerated protons to the speed of light. At least that's the plan. This high-speed collision will produce the smallest subatomic particles ever. Secondly, we're going to contain the fission in a gravity chamber. No one else has ever done that. Two particle beams and a multiple-collision strategy increase our odds of success, but it's dangerous. Without the MIGGS, the atomic reaction could level the place. Nothing like Hiroshima, of course. But we're still at ground zero."

"Curtis said you couldn't get the math right. What

problems am I looking for?"

"We have some formulas the Supers keep spitting out as errors. When we couldn't reformulate them properly, I thought of you. I'm hoping you can correct the formulas so the programming accepts them. Then the Supers will be able to examine the particles, measure them, compute the 13th Power, and isolate the Higgs instead of bleeping out a bunch of errors."

Lo cut in. "When we calculate and measure the 13th Power, how do we see what we find there?"

"The monitors will display a computer-enhanced nucleus. It will appear to be expanding, and you'll get the illusion of traveling into its core."

"How?" Janis asked.

"Colliding at high speeds, things happen pretty fast, so we're using a triangulation of electron microscopes and blue lights to transmit a 3-D image of each event, each collision, to the Supers. As the protons come apart, the MIGGS will contain the particles in the titanium cylinder where the CEI, the Computer Enhanced Imaging program, will record it in slow motion. When we play it back, it should be quite a show."

Janis rubbed his chin. "So why is it necessary to contain the Higgs?"

"Curtis wants to one-up the scientists at CERN and Fermilabs." Ray touched his mustache. "We got one chance in every collision to contain the Higgs in the titanium cylinder."

"What's he going to do with it then?"

"Who cares?"

"The God Particle must mean something to a man like Curtis. What can it be?"

Ray wrinkled his brow, thinking. Then his eyes widened, and he snapped his fingers. "That's it!" Excitement lit up his face. "Nuclear reconstruction."

"What's that?" Janis asked.

"It's been theorized for decades. If you can control the number of protons and electrons in an atom, you'd end up with something different than you started with." Ray ran to the MIGGS window and tapped on the thick glass. "He's going to do the reconstruction in the titanium cylinder. Curtis is going to make history."

"History?" Tracy asked, walking up to their conversation.

"That's right. If the Higgs boson is at the 13th Power, it makes sense to contain it, not because he wants to outdo the other guys, not just to prove it exists, but to...to... Oh, God." Ray gasped. "He can make anything he wants."

Janis got the idea. "And judging from his affinity for gold, I'd say that's what he's going to do. Make gold."

"Make gold?" Tracy said. "He's loony." She turned back to her monitor.

"The possibilities are endless," Ray assured her.

"What are we going to do about it?" Janis asked him. They couldn't let him get away with it.

Ray didn't answer. He was staring into the MIGGS window as if mesmerized by the blinking light.

"Come on, Ray. What do you think?"

He turned from the window. "We better get cracking on those formulas."

"What about Worm?" Lo asked.

"It's Alex's problem."

Tracy smiled.

Janis wondered why she seemed so pleased.

Chapter 90

AT FBI HEADQUARTERS, an elevator door opened. Agent Lou Marston stepped out with another passenger who was folding a copy of the *Washington Post*. The disaster in Nevada had taken the headlines. Lou walked to his reception desk where his secretary greeted him with a smile.

"Good morning, Lou."

"For a Monday, I guess." He set his sunglasses on top of his pepper-gray hair. "Anything for me?"

"Your wife called, told me to tell you, and I quote, 'Don't even try it.' What do you suppose that's all about?"

"She must have heard from my lawyer." Lou loosened his tie.

"And this." She handed him a memo. "Answering service faxed it over this morning."

He read the note. "Hmm. Atomtech. Get this Colonel Fallon on the line. I'll be in my office."

"Right away."

He closed the door, removed his suit coat, and tossed it over a chair. Straightening his vest, he walked to his desk and picked up a silver framed picture of a beautiful woman hugging a young girl dressed in their Sunday best. His eyes stung with fresh tears. "Sorry, Sandy," he said to the photo. "Somebody has to end this madness." He hoped his lawyer hadn't been too hard on her.

He replaced the picture, walked to the window, and opened the blinds. The Capitol building stood majestically before him, a sight that inspired him every morning. But he felt sad today. He was missing her already. The phone rang.

"I have Colonel Fallon on line one."

He picked up the phone and walked back to the

window. "How can I help you, Colonel?"

"The Atomtech tragedy, Lou. I'm sure you've heard about it."

"I read you're heading up the investigation." He paced in front of the window. "How's it going?"

"The FAA and the Pentagon have been jerking me around. I'm hoping you'll check out a lead I have."

"Depends."

"Some dead guy from Malaysia, he went by the name of Melvin Anderson. I have sources telling me he's alive and going by the name of Frank Curtis, an archeologist turned atomic researcher. Can you help me with that?"

"This kind of thing is out of my jurisdiction, more down your alley, don't you think?"

"Thirty-seven Americans are dead, Lou."

"I thought it was an accident."

"I have reason to believe they were murdered by government soldiers."

Lou swallowed. "Outrageous."

"Get your nose out of the reg book and help me nail the bastards."

"You got any proof?" Lou went to his desk, pushed aside some paperwork, and grabbed a pad and pen.

"First of all, the dead and wounded sustained battlefield injuries. Military!" the Colonel said with a sting. "Second, the place was littered with M-16 shell casings and hand grenade shrapnel. Military! And third, C4 explosives leveled one of the buildings. Military! Better yet, survivors said they saw heavily armed soldiers, equipped for war. Military! And get this, Air Traffic Control recorded an aircraft in the area that mysteriously disappeared at altitude then reappeared some time later going the other direction."

"How much later?" Lou asked, jotting notes on his pad.

"They won't say. Claim the tape was accidentally destroyed."

"You suspect a cover up?"

"Something big."

"What's that name again? Marvin Anderson?"

"Melvin. Melvin Anderson."

"How does he fit in?"

"He may have ordered the assault against Atomtech in a defensive move to protect his project at Solartech Labs in Simi Valley."

"What project?" Lou asked after he finished writing.

"The 13th Power project."

He wrote it down, not having a clue what it meant. "Defensive, you say. Had Atomtech been on the offensive?"

"That's the way I understand it. Regardless, I need to know about Anderson. If he's a bad guy, like my information suggests, we need to shut down his project and lock him up."

"What about this project?"

"I've been told it's a dangerous experiment in sub-nuclear technology, atomic particle stuff."

"Dangerous?"

"Something about disintegrating the world. Black holes. I don't know."

"Pretty scary."

"Or alarmist banter, yet Atomtech's people tried to stop Anderson from conducting the experiments. The guy may have struck back."

"You're saying a civilian with military capability?"

The line went silent for a moment. "Check on Melvin Anderson. We may find out how he did it."

"I'll do that. And I'll send a task force to Nellis. Brief them on all the facts."

Lou ended the call, jotted down some instructions, and grabbed his coat on the way out the door.

He handed his secretary his notes. "Type this up with a case number and fax it to the field office in Las Vegas. I want them at Nellis within the hour and here with their report by six PM. I'll be downstairs."

Before she could reply, he stepped into the elevator, and the doors closed.

The basement housed master files, stored on magnetic tape and managed by a mainframe computer. Here, fingerprint and identification records were safeguarded for use in FBI investigations worldwide. With Internet connections to the databases of Interpol, Tokyo, Sidney, Singapore, and Scotland Yard, the system was the most complete record of the population ever compiled. Lou Marston hoped it knew something about Melvin Anderson.

The elevator stopped and a buzzer sounded as the door opened. Lou flashed his badge to the clerk in a steel cage. The door clicked and unlocked.

Inside, he sat at a computer terminal. Though the room was brightly lit, the air smelled stale. He was alone.

"Let's see." He typed *Control Q*. A search form appeared on the monitor. He filled in the blanks: name: Melvin Anderson. Occupation: archeologist. *Enter*.

A few moments later the monitor flashed: *MATCH - Singapore System,* then, *Standby for Download* scrolled across the screen.

"Bingo!"

Within moments an empty picture frame appeared with blank information boxes under it. The computer bleeped. *Record Deleted* flashed in red on the monitor.

"What? How?"

He pressed *reload* and got the same result. Lou bit his lower lip. Somebody had tampered with this file. But who? He left the basement, disappointed and concerned.

Back in his office, he sat at his desk, this problem rolling around in his brain. A pile of paperwork sat unattended, his caseload already burdensome enough without this addition, but the deleted record was more important. Ominous. There had to be another way to find out about Melvin Anderson, the ex-archeologist turned nuclear scientist.

He stood and paced in front of the window. The Capitol building glistened in the sunlight. He wondered if archeologists had a union or an organization where members of the profession could congregate or contact one another. Sitting at his computer, he searched online and came up with The World Society of Archeologists. They even had a toll-free number. He picked up the phone.

Dr. Benjamin Church, whom his secretary had said was a leading archeologist in the United States, answered the call.

"Sorry to bother you this morning," Lou started, "but it's urgent. I'm Agent Lou Marston from the FBI, and I'm wondering if you could tell me about a colleague of yours, a Melvin Anderson. Does that name ring a bell?"

Silence.

"Dr. Church?"

"I'm sorry," he finally said. "You caught me by surprise, you did. It's been a long time since that name's been mentioned around here."

"What can you tell me about him?" Lou held his pen in hand, ready to write.

"He was a bad apple, I tell you. Heard he died in Indonesia some years back. In Borneo, I believe. What do you need to know?"

"You say he was a bad apple?"

"In the ninety-seven years of this organization, he's the only archeologist we publicly banned from digging. Black listed him."

"Why?"

"The man was a good digger, all right. Trouble was, he was a better thief. Robbed the host countries blind, more than a half billion from Malaysia alone." He grunted. "Spawned a lot of hostility and killing. Did some killing of his own, too. Funny thing about greed, there's no satisfying it. Never enough. Feeds on a man's soul." The doctor paused, blew his nose. "Devil's got him now, I'm sure. So why the questions?"

"I heard his name from a friend. Can you tell me how he died?"

"Helicopter crash in the jungle. Ended up crocodile fodder. A fitting end to the scoundrel, just the same."

A fitting end to the scoundrel. Lou could hear Church's words long after the conversation ended. One fact was clear. Melvin Anderson had lived and died, but his record had been erased. Maybe someone didn't want anyone to know he was still alive. Lou pushed the intercom button.

"Sir?"

"Help me with something. I searched for a file downstairs. The computer downloaded an empty form with the information fields blank. How's that possible?"

"Somebody must've deleted the data file but not the index file."

"Who would do something like that?"

"Someone unfamiliar with our system and its safeguards."

"Safeguards?"

"Index files not only keep track of data files, they also record every user. Lets us keep track of who's interested in who, how many hits a file gets."

"Hits?"

"Inquiries."

"Can you get me that information? Who hit the file last?"

"Sure," she said. "What's the file name?"

"Melvin Anderson, archeologist. Came up on the Singapore system."

"Right away, Lou."

Curbing his impatience, he picked up the picture of his wife and child again. God, what was he doing? He'd spent his whole life solving problems, sometimes big problems, but this one, his marriage, was bigger than he could manage. Married at 40, life was simple at first, but before long it became the most complicated project of his life. Between *his* job, *her* alcohol, and the constant bickering over both, after nine years, he believed only divorce could bring them peace.

He looked into the hazel eyes of his little girl, his baby. Trisha would bear the brunt of the pain. If only there was a way to spare her from it. He set the picture back down. Carefully.

His secretary knocked and opened the door. "Here it is."

She handed him the printout. It showed the record of his inquiry into Melvin Anderson this morning. The only other entry was two years ago, logged on by *The Ark*, the CIA operative with White House authority. Untouchable. Lou couldn't breathe. The White House and the CIA had an interest in the goings on in Simi Valley. Colonel Fallon was right. The civilian could have had military capability, as only the CIA would be so bold to orchestrate.

Lou got a sick feeling in his stomach. The government had killed its own citizens for the sake of a science project. Why would they do such a thing? And who the hell was this guy, Melvin Anderson? Certainly, he was dangerous, the 13th Power project was dangerous, and *The Ark* was backing them both. Why?

He again paced in front of the window.

The Capitol building didn't look so majestic anymore.

Chapter 91

In TECH-COM CONTROL, the digital clock counted down the seconds from ten minutes to laser firing. *9:59, 9:58, 9:57.* The MIGGS hummed to life, sounding distant at first then getting louder with each passing moment. Janis pushed up his glasses and looked into the thick window. The blinking green light went out, and a crimson glow now flooded the interior.

Ted worked a lever on his terminal, opening a panel in the ceiling of the MIGGS. The high-pitched whine of electrically driven gears echoed through the control room. A shiny titanium cylinder, bullet-shaped, slowly descended into the chamber on a single folding arm with little hydraulic muscles.

"Sighting beam," Ted said.

Tracy typed on her keyboard. A thin yellow beam of light appeared in the MIGGS, running horizontally from inlet to outlet.

Looking at Ray's monitor, Janis saw a gun-sight, which Ray maneuvered with a joystick at his terminal. Moving it left and right and up and down, he aligned the titanium cylinder with the sighting beam of the laser. *Laser Locked* displayed on the monitor, flashing in red. Janis thought that didn't look too hard.

Satisfied, Ray clicked off his sighting screen and brought up the scheduler from the Supers. He adjusted his arm in the sling and looked at Lo's monitor, hoping Janis's new formulas would make the programming statements work. There was only one way to find out, put them to the test.

A bead of sweat trickled down Ray's cheek. *Ready* scrolled across the screen. He clicked on the *Load* button.

A status window on the monitors opened. The Supers charged the Ionizer with liquid hydrogen. The clock above the window read *7:15*.

Load Time remaining: three minutes, scrolled across the monitors. Ray glanced up to the office window above Tech-Com Control. He saw Curtis looking down at them. Jonathan handed him a tall glass. Ray bet it wasn't iced tea and looked at Ted. The old man's face shined with sweat. He looked like a nervous father in a delivery room. Ray hoped the Russian wouldn't crack under the strain.

Load Time remaining: two minutes. Ray looked at Robert. He seemed calm, waiting for the Supers to verify ionization and request access to the synchrotron. Ray turned to Johnson. His eyes were on the monitor where a faint wisp of a vortex was beginning to form, the gravity generator building its artificial black hole, humming louder and louder. Ray looked at Tracy. She scrolled through formulas on her monitor, which displayed the laser firing sequence.

Load Time remaining: one minute. Ray glanced at Roger who was adjusting the main power dial, increasing the supply as the machinery demanded more. Meters were steadily rising. Stan was on the phone with one of his team members at the Ionizer, verifying a tight seal on the injection tubes. He typed something as he held the phone to his ear with his shoulder.

Ionizer ready. As a fail-safe, the load program stopped automatically and a new window opened indicating: *Ionizer Command Sequence Start / Abort*. The countdown clock read *4:15*. The scheduling program showed *3:38*.

ERROR.

"Damn!" Ray shouted. "Hold the scheduler, Lo." Something wasn't programmed right. Wiping sweat from his forehead, Ray waited for the countdown to catch up, a thirty-seven second hold. His shoulder ached. The temperature of the liquid hydrogen was rising. In thirty-one seconds it could be a useless gas. With precious seconds ticking off the clock, Ray glanced at Lo, whose monitor began flashing errors.

Lo looked at Ray, concerned. "What do we do now?"

"Abort," Ted shouted.

Curtis tapped the golden staff on his office window. "Proceed." His voice echoed over the intercom.

Ray entered the *Start* command seven seconds too soon.

The Ionizer buzzed. Inside the hyper-cold machine, the hydrogen atoms were now stripped of their electrons and vacuum sealed in their respective injection tubes.

Across Lo's monitor, the Supers started flagging errors faster and faster. He went to work, frantically clicking the *Ignore* buttons as fast as they came up.

Ray's mouth went dry. The program was falling apart. "Stay with it, Lo…Johnson. MIGGS ready?"

"I need those seven seconds, Ray."

Ray turned to Ted. "Can we run seven seconds over in the synchrotron?"

Ted shook like his nerves were on mass-overload. "Seven seconds, seven minutes, what's the difference? It's all wrong. We must abort."

"No," Curtis yelled. "Proceed."

Robert's monitor bleeped: *Request Synchrotron Now / Abort.*

"Now," Curtis bellowed.

Without another second passing, Robert clicked *Now*.

The Ionizer injected hydrogen protons into the synchrotron going in opposite directions and electrons into the MIGGS target, which suspended them in an electromagnetic field, its generating magnets now rumbling like an oncoming freight train. Tech-Com Control began to tremble.

The Supers engaged the RMS, Refractive Measuring System, and the electron microscopes and blue light strobes, which would triangulate the collision events and digitize them back to the Supers. At least that was working properly, Ray thought and looked at Johnson's monitor where a vortex swirled wildly, greens and yellows, but no red event-horizon had yet formed. The dial was at full power. He needed more time.

As the synchrotron accelerated the protons toward light speed and their eventual doom, Ray's monitor switched to the targeting window. The Supers made the electron target in the MIGGS appear as a disk of quivering little spheres suspended inside the titanium cylinder's blunt-nose nozzle. Janis's monitor switched to the CEI, the Computer Enhanced Imaging program that would record the collisions and hopefully reveal the Higgs bosons at the 13th Power. Janis was crosschecking the formulas scrolling down his screen.

Ray turned to Robert at the synchrotron controls. "Give me seven seconds."

"I can't. We hit 14 trillion electron volts at two seconds before laser firing. Seven more seconds will put us over 16 TEV. The electromagnets won't hold the protons on target. We'll be shooting blanks in seven seconds."

"Then give me two seconds."

"You got it." Robert brought up the configuration window and added two seconds.

Ray turned to the MIGGS terminal. "Johnson?"

"No good, Ray. I'm at full power."

Janis looked up from the CEI program. "Roger? Can you give him more power?"

"A hundred-sixteen percent is all Tech Com can handle without blowing the breakers. It's a long shot. Everything will get a voltage spike so be prepared for some weird responses."

Ted yelled across the room at Roger. "No more power. It's too dangerous."

"Do it!" Curtis shouted.

Ray pointed to Roger. He twisted the big voltage dial. The ceiling lights brightened; the electromagnets roared like a diesel locomotive on steroids, now shaking the consoles, the monitors, and the windows above the Supers.

A red band finally appeared on Johnson's screen.

"That's it," he announced. "We've got an event horizon."

Ray rushed to the MIGGS window. A swirling black mist grew inside the gravity chamber, expanding like a Texas tornado, swallowing up the titanium cylinder and snuffing out the crimson glow, dowsing the MIGGS in total darkness. The roaring magnets hurt his ears. He couldn't help but think they were about to unleash some sort of other worldly aberration.

The clock ticked down to *ZERO*.

The laser fired with amplified intensity. As thick as a flashlight beam, bright as the sun, and saturated with accelerated protons from the linear accelerator tube, four miles long, the laser buzzed into the MIGGS and collided with the electron target, smashing atoms and hurling the debris into the titanium cylinder.

The Supers began to display the spectacular results.

However, error flags kept popping up on the screens all over Tech-Com Control. The measurement status table began to falter. Janis and the rest of the team rushed to the MIGGS window and crowded around Ray.

Inside the gravity chamber, the thick black mist rotated like a dark typhoon where no light penetrated and no light escaped. The steel-reinforced walls vibrated, and the floor shook from its fury. Flashes of light began flickering in the black mist, like lightning in a distant storm cloud on a moonless night.

Johnson ran back to his MIGGS monitor. "She can't hold it," he yelled over the roar.

Ted screamed in terror. "You, I told. You, I told. What more I can do? We are all going to die!"

Ray spun around to look at Janis's monitor. The measurement status bar had shut down.

Power = 12.90 flashed on the screen.

Sparks flew from a bank of Supers. Ray ducked instinctively, but the shower of sparks bounced off the glass window bays. "Damn."

Tech-Com Control shook. The MIGGS roared.

Ray slowly turned his eyes back to the ominous window, his heart now pounding from a fear he'd never known. Light waves were arching across the chamber now, swirling and twisting like the angry snakes of Medusa's hair, lashing out at the walls of the MIGGS, leaping up from the black mist and plunging back down into it like captured beasts fighting to be free of the gravity field. The light pulsed and surged brighter and brighter becoming painfully hard to watch, like the blinding glow of a welding torch. Ray squinted, thankful for the protection of the thick glass window.

The pulsating light expanded and burst into billions of tiny specs that now sparkled in the darkness like glitter. For what seemed only a second, Ray thought he saw the universe expanding endlessly beyond the vibrating window. Millions of star clusters, swirling galaxies, and pulsing supernovas streaked by the glass. He blinked in disbelief. The Big Bang. How the hell was that possible? The beginning of all creation? The universe born?

With a crack like thunder, it all went black. The MIGGS stopped vibrating, and the roaring subsided to a hum. Tech-Com Control stopped shaking.

Inside the MIGGS, the black mist broke into smaller vortexes and twisted down floor grates as the gravity equalized. The green light started blinking again, one second on, one second off.

Ray couldn't believe his eyes. The titanium cylinder was gone; part of its suspension arm was left dangling from the ceiling. "Where did it go?"

A loud buzzer sounded, echoing through Tech-Com Control. He looked at the countdown clock. It was stopped at zero and still flashing red. The air tasted like tin.

"Gone," Johnson said. "The Higgs consumed the gravity that would have contained it." He sat in his chair and looked blankly at his monitor. *Fault* scrolled across the screen. He turned the power dial off and looked at Ray with wide eyes. "What was that?"

"Soul of tiger," Lo said. "It almost got loose."

Chapter 92

Janis TURNED AWAY FROM the MIGGS window and its blinking green light. What had he seen? Where did the titanium cylinder go? Why was Ted yelling like a crazy man? He looked at the Russian leaning on his console, shaking, his face flushed. Why? What did he know?

Turning to confront Ted, Janis noticed Tracy at her keyboard, typing feverishly. Eyes intense, she didn't look happy. Her red bangs stuck to the sweat on her forehead. Formulas and calculations scrolled down her screen. Janis didn't recognize any of them.

He did recognize all the error flags, though. She stopped typing, put her elbows on the console, and cradled her chin in the palms of her hands, still staring at her monitor. Obviously, she had a problem that she wasn't sharing with anyone else. She went back to typing. Janis returned his attention to Ted. He was gone.

"Damn!"

Frustrated and confused about what had just happened, Janis rushed back to his station where Lo and Ray were working with the Supers. *Programming Replay. Please Wait* flashed on Lo's monitor. A drop-window read: *CEI Engaged.* Janis sat down, checked the bandage on his hand, and glanced up to the office window. Curtis was nowhere in sight.

Ray rubbed his shoulder and looked at Janis. "Next time we'll get it right."

"You think it's that easy?"

"The Supers report every error to *MOM*, a monitoring program that will give us a detailed printout of every point in the experiment that failed, every formula that miscalculated. All we need to do is make the corrections on the list, and we'll be ready for a rerun."

"That doesn't sound easy to me."

Lo nudged Ray. "Coming up." The monitor displayed the Solartech Labs insignia over a screen titled: *Replay Ready.*

"Let's see it," Ray said.

Lo clicked the *GO* button.

A computer-enhanced image of the electron target and the titanium cylinder appeared on the monitor. Running backwards in the upper left corner, a digital clock spun off seconds in hundredths. Electron microscopes zoomed in on their quivering target, which was suspended inside the titanium cylinder's nozzle. A white tracking scale, it looked like a vertical ruler, came up on the right side of the screen; it was divided into thirteen increments depicting each calculation to the 13th Power.

The clock hit *ZERO.*

A flash of light arced across the screen.

"Laser firing," Ray said.

Janis winced, startled by the sudden brightness of the particle beam. The glare subsided quickly and depicted a proton as a shiny gray sphere smooth as polished agate, expanding on the monitor, getting bigger and bigger as it approached the electron target. The particles collided at incredible speed, and the CEI recreated the splitting of the atom in a sort of slow-motion virtual tour.

In the upper right corner, the formula, "Power = 1.0" appeared as the particles shattered. The Supers made the calculations, and the CEI made it all look like some kind of journey into the tiniest place in nature. The tracking scale turned red on the bottom and began to rise like a thermometer as the measurements were mapped.

Janis watched, amazed, yet the hairs on the back of his neck prickled with dread.

The *Power* numbers changed: 1.10 to 3.25 to 5.38. As

the red scale edged upward toward the 13th Power, the illusion of speed increased with each calculation.

"Look," Ray said, pointing at the expanding image. "A meson of quarks. There should be six of them: the up, down, and strange and their antiquarks."

"Antiquarks?" Janis said.

"Antimatter. They have the same mass as their partners but an opposite charge. When the two meet, they disintegrate."

"Amazing," Janis said as the colors changed inside the cylinder. Reds and blues, reds and greens, reds and yellows, abstract art was never so brilliant.

The *Power* numbers climbed higher: 7.69 changed to 9.70, as the particles broke into smaller and smaller pieces. The CEI went faster and faster.

Someone standing behind Janis said, "Wow."

The *Power* number hit 11.80, and the monitor went suddenly black.

Janis leaned forward, not knowing what to expect.

A tiny spot of light appeared in the center of the screen. It seemed far in the distance and pulsated, growing larger and larger as it neared.

The *Power* number climbed to 12.50.

Light beams emanated from the expanding glow, which bent and twisted like the tentacles of some kind of luminous squid that exuded rippling rays like the Aurora Borealis.

Ray gasped. "It's the Higgs, the Higgs boson."

"My God, will you look at that thing," Janis said, staring, mesmerized by its beauty.

Streaking toward them at breathtaking speed, the Higgs suddenly broke apart and disappeared, returning the monitor to black again. The *Power* numbers hit 12.90 and stopped rising.

Then the blackness on the screen slowly opened up like the iris of an eye.

Janis felt a chill. He couldn't take his eyes from the monitor now, as if it had cast a spell on him. Icy sweat trickled down between his shoulders. He couldn't believe what he was seeing beyond the optical opening. The CEI revealed a galaxy rotating in the star-studded blackness of space, its middle bulging, glowing fat with white and yellow clusters of supernovas, and its stellar plane swirling tails of sparkling stars in its wake. Billions of stars speckled the darkness around it.

Ray couldn't contain his excitement. "Is that us? Is that ours? Is that the Milky Way?"

ERROR flagged diagonally across the screen.

The CEI switched to the view of a giant Nebula with three pulsars glowing around it. A comet trailing an icy tail streaked through a swirling mass of colorful gasses.

"Where's that? Anybody know what it is?"

ERROR.

The opening snapped closed, and the monitor went black. *End Rerun* scrolled across the screen.

"Is that it? That's all?"

Nobody answered Ray. The control room fell silent as a cemetery.

Janis sat stunned, breathless, his mind trying to sort out rampant confusion. He didn't know what to think; the mathematics didn't make sense. How could the universe reside inside a proton? It was as if the smallest place in nature was equal to the largest place in nature.

He turned to Ray. "We shouldn't be messing with this."

Ray didn't even look at him. He seemed to be in a daze, his eyes still focused on the dark monitor, staring.

"There's something wrong here," Janis said. "Light travels in a straight line. It doesn't bend and twist like that." He wiped sweat from his forehead. "It would only do that in a place where the rules of physics don't apply. At least our rules, as we know them. The Higgs was trying to get out of the gravity field. When it disappeared, it took the titanium cylinder with it. Could've taken us, too. Maybe even the whole world."

"Thank God the MIGGS held up long enough," Johnson said, patting his monitor like a proud father would pat his son after hitting a homerun.

Lo rubbed his eyes. "13th Power dangerous as pissed off tiger."

Ray finally looked at Janis. "You guys don't get it, do you? We've just discovered the key to the universe, a doorway, a portal to the galaxy. We saw the Higgs field, how it encompasses the entire universe. It's put the universe at our fingertips. This is bigger than anything we could have ever imagined."

"This is a disaster, Ray," Janis shouted. "We were one tenth of a power away from disintegration."

"Jesus Christ, Janis. The titanium cylinder isn't gone. It isn't disintegrated. It's somewhere out there." He pointed to the ceiling, "Across the Milky Way, maybe 100,000 light years from here. Maybe farther, in a split second—"

"You don't know that."

"Then let's prove it. Or let's disprove it. Either way, we've got something here that no one has ever seen before."

"It was disintegrated, Ray."

"Hell, I'll be more famous than Einstein."

"You'll be dead, along with the rest of us."

"Just think of it, Janis, space flight without liftoff, interstellar transition in seconds."

"Are you even listening to me?"

"We might even find other planets, other life, other civilizations." Rays eyes went big around. "The age-old question will finally be answered: *Are we alone?*"

"We can't risk disintegrating the whole world to prove a nonsensical theory, Ray. It's too dangerous."

"I'm with Curtis. Risk nothing, gain nothing. It has a

ring to it, don't it."

"Lisa could die, Ray."

That shut him up. His face turned sullen. "My God, you're right. What am I thinking? I wouldn't risk her life…But…but couldn't we—"

Janis snapped his fingers, like he was trying to snap Ray out of a trance. "Sorry, Ray. We can't risk everything."

"But what about my place in history? The Nobel Prize? Is it gone, poof, like the titanium cylinder?"

"Write a book." Janis turned off his monitor. "We're done."

"Now wait a minute." Tracy got up from her station and stomped across the control room. "We're not done. We didn't get to the 13th Power, twelve point nine, that's it, and the Higgs boson wasn't contained. You can't be serious about quitting now."

"Didn't you see what almost happened?" Janis asked, thinking maybe she wasn't so bright after all. "We could have been sucked out of existence. If we'd reached the 13th Power, you can bet we wouldn't be here right now. There's no way the MIGGS could have saved us."

"That's ridiculous," she said. "You have no proof of that?"

"Show her the rerun, Lo."

\#

Tracy watched the rerun. Her pulse pounded in her temples, but she couldn't let them see her fear. She had to convince them to try one more time. The power setting for the laser resonator was too high. The data she got didn't make any sense. She needed another firing at the correct power setting. If not, her particle beam technology would be lost, Directive Number 119 would be dead, and *The Ark* would blame her for failing the President.

End Rerun.

She hugged herself. *Quick, Trace.* She always called herself Trace when she felt frustrated or lost, when things seemed hopeless. Think of something; keep this project alive.

"The CEI made a mistake," she said to the team. "It was flagging errors like crazy. You saw them. The test fire was a failure from the start." She started pacing. "The countdown was wrong, the scheduler was programmed wrong, the hydrogen was too hot, the synchrotron was pumping 15 TEV. Hell, everything was running at sixteen percent overpowered. Even the laser was too intense." She turned to Roger at the power station. "Didn't you say to be ready for some weird responses?"

"But not that weird."

"See? We have to try again. Take the fail-safes out of the scheduler and let the Supers run the countdown. It'll work, I tell you."

Janis and Ray looked at each other and shook their heads.

"The fail-safes are what saved us," Janis said. "Our mistakes created the errors that truncated the test fire."

"Okay, no mistakes next time."

"A perfect firing *is* a mistake. The final errors were inevitable because the computers were multiplying by negative tens, expecting a smaller number in the end, a smaller measurement at the 13th Power, but they came up with the universe, a bigger number, a bigger measurement, as if the calculations had been made in the positive instead of negative. It's mathematically impossible, so the computers flagged the errors."

"How do you figure the answer was positive?"

"You saw it, the galaxy. The universe. These are positive distances. 100,000 light years or farther. The CEI was racing through the negative distance inside the atom toward the 13th Power. We saw the Higgs boson at the threshold and got a glimpse of what lies beyond it. A doorway. We almost opened it. The universe almost rushed in."

"Like turn sock inside out," Lo said.

"It's too dangerous."

"Now you're starting to sound like Boris…" she stumbled. "I-I mean Ted. The old man is paranoid."

Janis's eyes narrowed. "I think the old man knows what we're up against here. He knows, doesn't he?"

Tracy turned away from the conversation and sat at her terminal. She felt Janis's stare. But now she understood why the Russians had abandoned their experiments. They *were* scared to death. Boris was right; *The Ark* should've stopped Curtis. Now her sense of duty and her moral convictions began to tug at her conscience. She needed one more laser firing, but one more might be one too many. They were working too close to the 13th Power, too close to disaster.

"I have to find Curtis," Janis said. "His precious 13th Power project is finished."

"I'm going with you," Ray said.

She didn't envy them for their task as they walked out of Tech-Com Control. Flicking a lock of hair from her cheek, she began typing again. *The Ark* was counting on her. There had to be another way to get that particle beam for Directive 119.

Chapter 93

AFTER A SILENT WALK to the lobby with Ray right behind him, Janis approached a guard at the security station. The wall behind him glowed with monitors displaying activities in the halls and labs throughout the building. He was watching them closely.

"Where's Curtis?"

The guard looked up. "C-Wing, I think."

"You think? I thought all these fancy computers kept track of everyone around here."

"Only inside this building." He pointed to the escalators. "I saw him go that way, with Jonathan. They usually go to the cafeteria at lunchtime. Don't need no stinking computers to figure that out."

Janis turned to Ray. "I'm hungry, how about you?"

"Famished." They headed for the escalators. On the ride down to the atrium, Ray put his hand on Janis's shoulder. "What about the money?"

Janis thought about that. The money. A million bucks. Curtis would probably back out of the deal. He had every right to, now that they were quitting. Janis would have to move his mother to a state run nursing home. He'd have to keep driving that clunker of a Subaru and continue living in that dump of an apartment, at least until his raise came through, if ever... At least he wasn't dead. "It's not important anymore."

In the parking garage, he hailed a staff car.

Tires squealing, the car accelerated toward C-Wing. After passing under the towering archway, Ray looked back and read aloud the words inscribed on its steel facing. "Welcome to Solartech Labs. Gateway to the Atomic Universe. Sounds like Curtis knew all along."

"How could he have known?"

"Ted Benning," Ray said. "The Russian could have told him."

Janis thought about the Russian. "Did you see him?"

"He about went crazy with fear."

"Tracy mistakenly called him Boris."

Ray looked at Janis. "Ted Benning doesn't sound very Russian to me, but Boris on the other hand, that's a common Russian name. Maybe Ted isn't who we think he is."

Janis looked out the window and the rocky hillside sliding by. "And obviously Tracy knows that."

"She's playin' us, Janis."

"Not the first time a woman has conned me."

The line of employees in the cafeteria was long and moving slowly when Janis and Ray walked in. The air, filled with conversations, smelled of roast beef and apple pie. Looking around for Curtis, Janis spotted Jonathan at a table across the room, sitting alone. After working through the maze of people, Janis sat down across from him without an invitation.

Ray grabbed the chair next to Jonathan.

Jonathan looked back and forth at Ray and Janis disdainfully then put down his fork. "What can I do for you guys?"

"Where is he?" Ray demanded.

Janis snatched the dinner roll from Jonathan's plate, took a big bite, and tossed the remains into the potatoes and gravy then swallowed a gulp of Jonathan's milk. "Where's Curtis?"

"You guys better leave him be," Jonathan said flatly. "He's not in a good mood."

"Neither are we," Ray replied, his voice gruff, serious.

Jonathan groaned. "In his private room, down at the end of the corridor." He pointed. "Now leave me eat my dinner in peace."

Ray stood without another word. He fixed his sling and Janis followed him, their footsteps echoing down the hallway. At the far end, Ray stopped in front of a room with double oak doors. He didn't bother knocking, just pushed his way in.

Curtis's private dining room was lavishly decorated in royal décor, purple curtains, stained wood, gold chandelier, and a floor to ceiling bookcase against the back wall. Cell phone to his ear, he glanced up from his seat at the table. Janis was surprised at how ordinary he looked without his usual sunglasses on. His long coat lay neatly across the back of a chair. Snapping the phone shut, Curtis yelled, "What's the meaning of this intrusion?" He stood and put his hands on his hips. "Get the hell out of here."

"Funny thing," Ray said. "That's exactly what we intend to do." He leaned on the table and glared into Curtis's face. "But first, there's the matter of Janis's money."

"What are you getting at?"

"We're done," Janis put in. "The experiment is finished." He said the words calmly because he meant them.

Curtis frowned. "Finished? What the hell are you talking about? The test fire today was a huge success. We're almost there."

"Not so," Ray said. "We could've ended up in oblivion along with your titanium cylinder."

Curtis glowered.

"Do you understand what you're messing with here?" Janis asked.

Curtis didn't answer.

"Then let me explain it to you in five simple words: the-end-of-the-world." Janis clicked them off, one at a time with his fingers.

Curtis shook his fist. "Just like that?" His cheeks turned red, his eyes bulging. "You come in here blowing smoke up my ass because you think you saw something. Truth is you big-shot brainards don't know what you saw. You turn chicken shit and run to Mommy because you're afraid of the dark. You're pathetic."

"This project is dangerous," Janis said. "Pathetic is not recognizing it for what it is."

Curtis sneered. "I'll tell you about pathetic, Dr. Smart-Ass." He hit the desk with his fist. "I bought you Janis, with money, a million bucks worth. And you, Ray, I bought with the promise of fame. How feeble is that? I exploited your weaknesses to get what I wanted. You didn't even know it. You think you're so smart. I think you both *define* the word pathetic."

Ray looked as if he would explode. Blood vessels in his neck started growing, and his eyes narrowed. "All this time, I believed your intentions were strictly scientific. Now, I wonder what those intentions really were." His mustache quivered. "You're going to dabble in nuclear reconstruction, aren't you."

"So you figured it out." Curtis curled his upper lip.

"Gold? Right?"

"Riches beyond my wildest imagination," Curtis said. "Janis will get his measly million while I control the financial markets of the world."

"How do you figure?"

"He who has the gold has the power." Curtis gleamed as if in ecstasy just talking about it.

"Now look who's blowing smoke," Janis said. "Too much gold on the market drops the value."

Rays eyes went wide. "No, Janis." His voice was almost a whisper. "He knows that already. Curtis has something else in mind."

Curtis grinned.

"I'll be damned," Janis said. "He's going to wreck the gold market while his fortune is invested elsewhere."

"Diamonds? Platinum?" Ray speculated. "Genius."

Curtis looked impressed with that word.

Janis scowled at Curtis. "Genius or not, you're finished, *Mister* Curtis. You'll get nothing more from us pathetic brainards." Janis headed for the door. "Come on, Ray, let's get the hell out of here."

"Not so fast, boys." Curtis came around from behind his desk, staff in hand. "You have another firing tomorrow at noon. Not another test fire, but the real thing this time. I—"

"You haven't been listening," Janis cut in. "You're finished. We're leaving."

"You're staying!" Curtis snapped. "Tomorrow at noon." He paced the floor, tapping the staff with each step. "As we speak, Stan Burton is installing a new titanium cylinder. Ray, you'll reprogram the Supers to run the scheduler without the fail-safes. Janis, your formulas worked until the Higgs appeared, one-tenth of a second before the void opened. All you need to do now is reformulate the programming to contain it. But you must shut the experiment down before the 13th Power is attained."

"That's impossible," Ray said. "The programming expands time into a measureable scale, you know, slow motion. In real time, hell, we'd have to snatch the Higgs in a micro-second."

"You're out of your mind, Curtis," Janis said.

"Try. I insist." Curtis stopped pacing in front of a door by the bookcases. "I have confidence in you. Besides, it's your opportunity to save the world."

"Why are you being so bullheaded about this?" Janis asked. "You know the dangers."

Curtis smiled wide. "Risk nothing; gain nothing." His gold tooth glistened.

Janis turned to Ray. "He's insane. Come on, we're leaving. What makes him think he can make us fire that thing again anyway?"

"Wait," Curtis shouted. "I was afraid you lightweights would turn tail and run. So you might say I took out a little insurance. Before you go, I'd like to show you why you *will* do it." He moved to the bookcase against the back wall. One touch and it began to swing open like a door. "I think you'll be highly motivated."

From out of the darkness behind the bookcase, Lisa stumbled into the room as if shoved from behind. She was nearly naked in bra and panties and bound in chains, struggling to stay on her feet. Her mouth was gagged, her hair tousled, her wide eyes ringed in white.

Ray's face turned pale with disbelief and horror. "Lisa."

Janis felt his heart turn over in his chest. He stepped backward, staring, first at Lisa and then at the man now standing behind her, his face and hands bloody, his clothes ripped and shredded. He looked as though he'd been nearly eaten alive.

"I'd like you to meet Judas," Curtis said and laughed. "He's had a really bad day."

In one hand, Judas held the end of a leash, which was attached to a dog collar around Lisa's neck. In the other hand, he held a small gray box with a big red button and a black antenna. Quick to demonstrate its purpose, Judas pushed the red button. Lisa let out a throaty scream and fell to the floor, writhing in pain as blue electrostatic sparks lashed out from the chains and stabbed her body in a million places. The smell of singed hair filled the room.

"Don't anybody get any dumbass ideas about being a hero," Judas warned. "I'll zap her if I even think you're gonna get brave."

Ignoring Judas, Ray clenched his fists and lunged at him. "You bastard!"

Judas pushed the button again.

Lisa screamed in guttural agony.

"Back off," Judas yelled.

With teeth bared, Ray stepped back. "I'll kill you for this."

"I doubt it." Judas pushed the button again, this time just for fun.

The terror in Lisa's screams tore at Janis's sanity. Filled with anger and frozen with fear, he felt helpless to do anything to rescue her. Any move toward Judas would only cause her more pain and anguish.

"Okay. Okay. No more," Ray pleaded.

Curtis raised the golden staff. "We've made our point, Judas. You may leave us now."

Judas snarled and yanked on the leash, pulling Lisa to her feet. They disappeared through the opening behind the bookcase. The rattling of chains quickly faded away.

Curtis closed the bookcase and walked back to his table. He looked at Janis and Ray as if he'd just won a bet, obviously pleased by their horrified expressions. Sitting down, he laid the staff across his lap and, still looking at his pathetic scientists, he smiled.

"I suggest you boys get to work. It's going to be a long night."

Chapter 94

AGENT LOU MARSTON STOOD on the tarmac at Andrews Air Force Base, his black FBI squad car idling behind him and his gaze on landing lights approaching the runway. Tires squawked as the Hawker jet touched down. After the nose gear settled to the concrete, reverse thrusters roared. He looked at his watch: 8:30. They were late.

Day had turned to dusk, but for Lou, it wasn't nearly over. He had spent the afternoon compiling his report on Melvin Anderson and *The Ark*, while his task force met with Devin and Colonel Fallon at Nellis. They had gathered information about Curtis, his 13th Power project, and the Atomtech disaster. Lou was anxious to put all their information together into one report. Then he'd have enough evidence to get Grand Jury indictments against *The Ark* and operatives from the CIA to the White House. The bastards weren't going to get away with domestic espionage and terrorism. Problem was he didn't know who *The Ark* was, but he knew who would, CIA Chief Bret Lawrence. A hot rush pumped through his veins. His confrontation with the CIA boss was fast approaching.

He watched the Hawker negotiate the taxiway toward him, the shrill whine of its engines getting louder as the glaring lights came closer. The jet pulled up into floodlight beams that illuminated an FBI seal on its tail. A soaring Bald Eagle spanned the fuselage.

The door opened, steps descended, and the engine whine subsided. Turbine-fans rotated slowly as Lou climbed the stairs and stepped into the plane where the air was tainted with cigarette smoke. His men were shuffling papers and compiling reports on a laptop computer, testimony they'd taken from Colonel Fallon and Walter

Devin.

Lou removed a flash drive from his pocket, the evidence he'd gathered against *The Ark* and Melvin Anderson, and handed it to Agent DeSoto, a young man with thick glasses. "Add this to your report."

"No problem." DeSoto inserted the drive. The laptop copied and merged the files. "Almost finished." He copied the new file back onto the flash drive, a complete record of the 13th Power case, enough evidence to send some hi-powered operatives to the death chamber, a record that would avenge the deaths of thirty-seven Americans. It only lacked one thing: *The Ark's* name. He gave the drive back to Lou.

Lou pocketed it, looked over the other task force agents on the plane, and saw a familiar face. "Carmichael. What are *you* doing here?"

"Transferred from the LA office." His muscular frame made up for his short stature. He finished reorganizing an overhead compartment then rubbed his stubbly chin. "Just in time for some excitement. We heard an incredible story from Colonel Fallon."

"Just wait 'til you hear it, Lou," Agent Bell added, a young black man with pearly teeth.

"I can imagine." Lou looked into the cockpit and saw the pilot and copilot completing their checklists. "Captain Connors, good to see you again."

The pilot glanced up from his clipboard. "Hey, Lou." He motioned to his copilot. "My first officer, Maggie Collins." They exchanged smiles.

"You're on for tomorrow," Lou said. "0900. Better get some rest."

Nodding, the pilots returned to their post-flight chores.

"What's up tomorrow?" Carmichael asked, approaching with an outstretched hand.

"Listen up, men," Lou announced as he accepted

Carmichael's handshake. "It appears this 13th Power project has the backing of the CIA and is connected to the Atomtech disaster. I have evidence *The Ark* is involved."

"No way," Agent Bell said.

"It's all in my report," Lou assured his men. "Tomorrow we're going to shut down Solartech Labs. Tonight, Judge Freeman is waiting for us in his chambers. He's agreed to take our testimony and issue a Federal warrant for Melvin Anderson. He'll be up against a Grand Jury next week."

Agent DeSoto removed a second flash drive from his computer. "Then let's get to it." He closed the laptop and handed the drive to Agent Bell. "Lock it up."

"It's a copy for the Colonel," Bell explained. "We promised him."

"That's fine," Lou said. "He's really pissed about what happened at Atomtech."

"He wants the culprits caught," Carmichael put in.

"There's enough evidence on that flash drive to indict and prosecute *The Ark*, whoever the hell he is," Lou said. "I hope to find out tonight."

"Only the President knows who *The Ark* is," Agent Bell said as he put the drive into a small air-safe, closed its thick fireproof door, and spun the dial. "How are we going to ID him?"

"Before we see the judge, we're going to pay a visit to CIA Chief Lawrence. He's at the Marriott, attending a campaign fundraiser. I think he knows about *The Ark* and Dr. Curtis…or Anderson…or whatever his name is."

"Why should Lawrence know?" Bell asked, wiping dust off the FBI seal on the air-safe's door.

"He's the chief, top dog, but if *The Ark* is activated, he drops to Number Two in the CIA's hierarchy. He'll know."

"I bet he doesn't," Agent Bell said and secured the panel covering the air-safe. Colonel Fallon's copy of the report was safely stowed for tomorrow's flight.

"We're ready," Carmichael said.

Lou turned to the pilots. "9:00, sharp." He ducked out the door and down the steps, his task force following behind him.

Chapter 95

IN THE MARRIOT HOTEL, at the entrance to the banquet room, Lou and his men flashed their FBI badges to the maître d' and walked in. This formal affair had attracted the rich and famous of Washington. The room was filled with the din of their conversations.

Lou led the way between rows of tables draped in white linen and set with polished silver, crystal, and china. His men marched behind him. The aroma of prime rib and lemon meringue drifted in the air. Lou's stomach fluttered. The tuna fish sandwich he'd had for dinner seemed so mundane, but he'd been eating a lot of tuna fish sandwiches lately.

Red, white, and blue banners hung from rafters above a podium at the front of the room. In a corner, a twelve-piece band played softly, and several couples were dancing.

Near the center of the room, Lou spotted the CIA Chief, sitting with his wife, daughter, and two Congressmen. They all looked so formal in their fancy eveningwear. Lou wondered if Lawrence used some kind of wax to make his bald head shine so brightly.

Task force in tow, Lou marched toward the table. Lawrence looked up, put his fork down, and wiped his mouth with a napkin. His wife, in mid sentence, stopped talking, her gaze now on the approaching FBI agents.

"We need to talk, Lawrence," Lou said with an official tone.

"Agent Marston," the CIA Chief said, his voice festive and without concern. "You remember my wife, Beverly." She smiled. He indicated an unoccupied chair. "Have a seat."

"No, thanks." Lou looked over the party. "Excuse us.

We have to go to the men's room."

"Come to think of it," Lawrence said. "I'll be right back, dear." He left his guests and led the way through the maze of tables and dignitaries.

In the men's room, a man backed away from a urinal, zipping his trousers. As he walked to a sink, the door burst open and FBI agents rushed in. They fanned out, checking under the stall doors for unwanted company.

"Out," agent Carmichael ordered the man at the sink.

He held up the palms of his hands. "But, I—"

"Wash 'em later." Carmichael grabbed the man's collar and threw him out. As the task force agents stood guard, the top Feds stepped up to adjacent urinals.

"What's on your mind, Lou?" Chief Lawrence asked and unzipped his pants.

"Tell me about Melvin Anderson and the 13th Power experiments at Solartech Labs," Lou said, urinating.

"You've been playing super cop, have you?" Lawrence spit into his urinal. "Take my advice and walk away from this one, Lou. It's way over your head."

"Atomtech was destroyed, Americans were murdered, and the smell of it drifts all the way up to the White House. I suggest you either prepare to explain it to a Grand Jury or come clean right now."

"You're nuts."

"The President assigned *The Ark* to someone. Who is he?"

"Have you been drinking? There's no boogieman."

"I'm willing to cut you a deal, minimum prison time."

"A word of advice, Lou. You're messing with the wrong people. I seriously suggest you boys go back to bank robbers and leave this one alone."

Lou backed away from the urinal, zipped his pants, and leaned into the CIA Chief's ear. "Listen real good, you bastard. Judge Freeman is issuing the warrant tonight. Our jet is ready at Andrews. Tomorrow we're goin' in.

Solartech Labs is goin' down and Melvin Anderson will be in chains. With a murder rap hanging over his head, he *will* talk and I guarantee you'll be put to sleep right along with your buddy, *The Ark*. Are you clear on that?"

"You're wrong." The CIA chief zipped up his pants with a jerk. "You don't know what you're dealing with here, damn it. Anderson can tell you nothing. It's a covert operation. We're untouchable."

"We'll see about that."

"Don't be stupid, Lou." He pointed his finger at the task force agents posted around the men's room. "Walk away from this. All of you."

"Tomorrow," Lou said with finality. He turned to his men and signaled an exit.

"Don't do it," Lawrence shouted.

Lou stopped at the door, slowly turned around and jabbed a stiff finger at Lawrence. "You should've said that to the Atomtech assault, *before* thirty-seven Americans were executed."

"You got it all wrong," Lawrence said. "Let it go."

"Not on your life." Lou led his men out.

"Don't say I didn't warn you."

Chapter 96

Early morning sunlight knifed through the office window and woke Agent Marston. He opened his eyes but didn't move. His arms were folded on his desktop, his head resting on his forearms. He blinked. His mouth tasted like glue. The picture of his wife and daughter caught his eye, propped on top of the Federal Marshal's warrant for the search and seizure of Solartech Labs. Lou wanted to talk to his wife; he ached to see his daughter, but he had to wait until the 13th Power case was closed. Again, his personal needs were put on hold for the sake of his job, and as usual, his job dragged him into the late hours of the night. They hadn't gotten out of Judge Freeman's chambers until after midnight.

Licking his lips with a cottony tongue, he looked at the clock: 7:05. His task force men were downstairs in temporary quarters for transient agents. He had chosen to be alone in his office, his life. Stretching, he got up and walked out. His secretary was sitting at her desk, as usual.

"Get Colonel Fallon on the line for me, please."

She reached for the phone.

Lou went into the locker room, showered, and shaved. After jamming yesterday's clothes into the bottom of his locker, he put on a fresh shirt and slacks. After years of never knowing from one day to the next whether he'd make it home or not, he was already accustomed to being separated from his wife. He spent most of his time without her, anyway. That bothered him. He hadn't been the best husband to her, either.

Over his vest he slung his holster and locked in the .38. What a way to travel to California. He made a final check in the mirror and turned to leave.

As he walked out into the lobby, elevator doors slid open and his task force agents stepped out.

"They're trying to locate the Colonel, Lou," his secretary reported.

"Thanks." He turned to his men. "In here."

They followed him into his office.

The picture of his wife and daughter on the desk attracted agent Carmichael's attention. "Sandy, how is she?" he asked as he picked up the picture. "And look at Trisha. What is she, seven now?"

Lou smiled. "Eight and just a living doll."

The other agents looked over Carmichael's shoulder. "How long have you and Marston known each other?" agent DeSoto asked.

"Thirty years." Carmichael set the picture down. "I was best man at their wedding."

Memories of that day came crashing back. Lou stood at the window, grappling with the anguish of his decision to divorce Sandy. Somehow, deep down, he knew her drinking was his fault. If he'd only spent more time with her, more time with his family, maybe she wouldn't have turned to the bottle to fill the loneliness he had left her to deal with.

Guilt tore at his soul like a bullet to the heart.

He wanted to make his marriage work. She deserved better than what he'd been giving her. Excuses: the FBI *this* and the FBI *that*. The reality of this impending divorce was forcing him to see his mistakes more clearly. He'd let her down. Was it too late to change? Could he make it up to her? God, he should try. After this assignment, he'd call her then. He'd promise to change.

The phone rang.

"Colonel Fallon?"

His task force agents gathered around.

"What's the plan, Lou?"

"We're going into Solartech Labs to arrest Melvin

Anderson."

"On whose authority?"

"Judge Freeman issued the Federal Marshal's Warrant."

"I want Anderson first."

Lou thought about that. "You can have him after we're done with him."

"Do you have my copy of the report?"

"It's on a flash drive, in a safe on the plane."

"What did you find out?"

"It's all on the report, enough to hang the bastard."

"Who?" the Colonel growled.

"I don't have his name yet, but we'll get it out of Anderson."

"Let me know when you've got him."

"I'll call you."

Lou hung up, grabbed the warrant off the desk, and spoke softly to the picture of his wife and daughter. "I'll call you, too, as soon as I get back." He grabbed his coat off the chair and turned to his men. "Let's go get him."

Chapter 97

SECURITY WAVED THE FBI car through the gate at Andrews Air Force Base. Up ahead, Lou saw the Hawker parked on the tarmac, a scaffold-like ladder rolled up by its tail, an engine cover open. He wondered if something was wrong with the jet. That was all he needed. A delay.

As the car came to a stop, he spotted Captain Connors and his copilot standing off to the side, watching a man work on the left engine. He wore navy blue coveralls and a matching ball cap.

"What's the problem?" he asked the Captain.

"Just a final check on an Airworthiness Directive they performed some time back. I don't know, came up rather sudden. He's about finished."

\#

Leaning into the dark engine compartment, the man dressed like an aircraft mechanic checked each of the devices he'd attached to the fuel lines and the main hydraulic pressure hose. The LEDs glowed faintly, as they should. He knew that these magnesium chips, once ignited, would burn white hot and were not extinguishable, not even under water. They could burn through anything. The size of the chip determined the amount of heat exposed to the fuel and oil inside the targeted lines. He'd selected large chips for this assignment.

Satisfied that everything was in proper working order, he closed the engine cover, climbed down the ladder, and rolled it to the side. "All set." He handed the Captain an official-looking FAA form. "Sign right here."

Captain Connors looked over the form. "Paperwork is a pain." He scribbled his signature, and smiling, handed it back to the mechanic. "There you go."

"Have a nice flight." The man walked away.

Agent Marston called to his task force. "Get aboard."

#

The pilots began their pre-flight checklists as the task force agents, armed with their Federal Marshal's Warrant, seated themselves and buckled in. The engines whined to life and the stairs retracted. Hooking up to the nose wheel, a tug operator pushed the Hawker onto the taxi ramp.

First Officer Maggie Collins radioed ground control. "Andrews Ground, Hawker November-zero-four-seven-Echo at Delta-niner request taxi to active. Awaiting clearance to LA Center."

"Hawker four-seven-Echo," the ground controller said. *"Taxi to zero-one-left. Standby for clearance."*

The Hawker's engines revved and the jet began to roll toward the runway.

"Hawker four-seven-Echo," the ground controller came back, *"you are cleared to the Kirby VOR. Expect eight thousand in ten. Departure frequency one-one-seven-point-two-five. Squawk five-three-niner-niner. Awaiting read-back."*

Maggie repeated her instrument flight instructions and set the dials for the flight out of Washington DC. Captain Connors prepared his aircraft for takeoff.

"Hawker four-seven-Echo—read-back correct. Clear for takeoff on zero-one-left. Have a nice flight."

Within moments, the jet turned onto the runway and the engines revved to full power, jetting the FBI task force into the sky over Washington, D.C.

#

As the aircraft climbed to altitude and turned on course, the FBI agents sat quietly, glancing back and forth at one another. Lou didn't know what to expect when they arrived at Solartech Labs. He could only hope the seizure would be executed peacefully.

Lou's cell phone rang. Caller ID revealed it was his

secretary calling. "Marston."

"Just breaking news, Lou," she said. "When the Justice Department opened at nine this morning, they found Judge Freeman in a pool of blood on the floor of his chambers. The place had been ransacked. Isn't he the judge you were with 'til all hours last night?"

Lou's throat seized. "He's dead?"

"What?" Agent Carmichael asked.

Lou thought his chest would burst. He couldn't find the words to thank his secretary. Hanging up, he realized he'd sentenced the judge to death just by mentioning his name to Lawrence. Would the CIA go so far as to assassinate a Federal judge to protect the 13th Power project? His mouth went dry. Was there nothing they wouldn't do..? "Oh shit."

"What?" Carmichael again, and Bell.

"The mechanic." Lou shot out of his seat and ran to the cockpit. "Get this plane on the ground. Now."

"What's wrong?" Conners asked.

"Declare an emergency and land. I don't give a shit where."

"What happened?" agent Carmichael demanded, his face white with fear.

Lou turned back to the cabin to relay the bad news to his men. "Judge Freeman was murdered in his chambers last night, and I'll bet that mechanic was no mechanic. God damn it." He returned to his seat and buckled in. "*The Ark* is out to kill us—"

An explosion jolted the jet.

#

In the cockpit, an alarm rang out. "Fire on number two," Captain Connors announced. He hit the extinguisher switch, which would flood the engine compartment with fire-retardant foam. The *FIRE* light didn't go out. It wasn't working. He scanned his instruments. Fuel pressure to number two was dropping. Number one: dropping. He must've blown a fuel line. He shut down the pumps in hopes of starving the fire. The downside was both engines flamed out.

"Shit." He turned to Maggie. "Call a May Day."

With the loss of power, the altimeter started winding down. Keeping his cool, he trimmed the jet for landing, anywhere, maybe that parking lot down there, no, too small, too many buildings, the interstate, no, too many cars. Where? Check airspeed, okay. Flaps. He moved the lever for ten degrees.

Another alarm sounded. He scanned the instruments. The flap indicator hadn't moved. "Flaps? What's wrong with the flaps?"

"They're not extended," Maggie said, checking out the window to get a visual on the flaps' position. "Try again."

He worked the flaps lever again and again but nothing happened. Another alarm sounded. The hydraulic pressure gauge had dropped to zero. "Damn. We've lost the hydraulics."

The descending Hawker began to roll to the left. Captain Connors turned the yoke to the right. Sluggishly, the jet rolled right. He turned back toward level flight, but the jet continued to roll right. His stomach clutched. Terror gripped him as the nose started to pitch down and his aircraft continued to roll right.

Flying on its right side, the jet side-slipped toward the ground, and the nose pitched farther down. Stomping on the left rudder peddle yielded no results. "Backup hydraulics," he shouted, fighting for control of his aircraft.

Maggie was already working the switches. "Nothing, sir." She tried them several times.

As the altimeter needle spun downward and the vertical speed indicator showed 2,000 feet per minute, smoke began to fill the cabin. The crippled Hawker was in gravity's grip of death.

Captain Connors yanked and twisted his useless controls. He looked at Maggie who was desperately trying to restore the hydraulics. When he looked back, the horizon was no longer in view out the windshield, only the ground.

"God help us all."

#

Heavy G-forces pressed on Lou Marston's chest. He clung to the armrests as the Hawker plunged toward the ground. He gagged on acrid smoke filling the cabin. Looking at his task force agents, he could see the terror on their faces, each man locked in his own helpless mortality.

"*The Ark* won, damn it."

His men didn't respond, now hanging upside down in their seats. The nose dropped into a steep dive. Lou closed his eyes and fought tears, an ache in his chest, and a sudden sadness in his soul. He swallowed hard. "Sorry, Sandy."

When the plane hit the ground, it felt like he'd suddenly stepped into a dark room and someone hit him with a pillow.

Chapter 98

OVERRIDING THE COVERAGE of Federal Judge Freeman's murder, wire services picked up the news of the plane crash in Washington. Video of the carnage quickly hit the airways as local television news teams rushed to the scene to cash in on the catastrophe.

FAA phone lines lit up with calls from investigative reporters attempting to get information on the plane and its ill-fated passengers. A television news helicopter beamed back live pictures of the horrible accident scene. Dozens of fire trucks pumped water on the raging fire that consumed a jet and the shopping mall it had struck. Not far away, in a cluttered parking lot, lay rows of blanket-covered bodies, some still smoldering underneath.

Rescue workers and firemen went about their gruesome duties. A steady stream of ambulances, laden with people who'd been wounded on the ground, negotiated congested streets toward hospitals throughout the city.

There were no survivors onboard the jet.

***

Nathan walked into the Oval Office just as the news about Freeman flashed across the television screen. His office had been ransacked and nobody knew what, if anything, was missing. But *The Ark* knew what was missing, the evidence linking him to Solartech Labs.

A bulletin interrupted the news report. *Breaking News.* An aircraft had crashed just minutes after takeoff from Andrews Air Force Base.

Nathan sat with the President and watched in horror as

the ugly turn of events unfolded. A terrible sense of loss shadowed him. How many people were killed in yet another commercial airliner crash?

The newscaster adjusted the knot on his tie as he came on-screen. "We've just learned through unconfirmed sources that the downed plane was an FBI Hawker jet destined for the Los Angeles area with four agents and two crew members aboard."

Nathan took a shot of adrenaline to the chest. What the hell had Lawrence done? This time the son of a bitch had gone too far.

"Excuse me, sir," he told the President. "I have a phone call to make."

***

From his desk at CIA headquarters, Lawrence answered the ringing phone. It was the red phone, a secure line between the White House and his office.

"Lawrence, what the hell are you doing?"

"Relax, John. For Christ's sake." Lawrence stood at the window, blinds parted, peering out at the smoky sky in the distance. "Look at it as a confirmed kill."

"It's a needle in our arms," Nathan said. "Damn it. Why wasn't it rigged to crash over Colorado like we planned? Now this mess is in our backyard."

"That pea-brain Marston threatened Grand Jury indictments against us. I wanted to watch his plans go up in smoke. Couldn't have done that in Colorado, now could I?" He let the blind go with a snap and walked back to his desk. "I saved both our asses, John."

"You better have a tight lid on this thing, Lawrence. No slip-ups."

"We're the CIA, goddamnit. We play for keeps. Besides, Alex says the 13th Power project is on schedule. They're going for broke this afternoon."

"Will the particle beam work?"

"Tracy's had some problems."

"But we're close?"

"She's expressed doubts about the safety of the project, but she's a trooper. She'll hang in there. With any luck we'll be heroes tomorrow."

"I wish there'd been another way."

"There's always been another way, John. It's called diplomacy. Your White House agenda put peace in the hands of technology. Not a good substitute for a nuclear arms treaty and a handshake. But who am I to tell you guys?"

"The President wants it this way."

"As long as he does, *The Ark* will always be a necessity."

"The same goes for the CIA."

"Job security," Lawerence replied. "We did what had to be done. For the country. It was a horrible accident. That's all anyone needs to know."

"What about the judge?"

"We got the flash drive. I destroyed it myself. Other than that, it was a burglary gone bad."

"Make it official." Nathan hung up.

Lawrence put the receiver down and returned his attention to the television. The graphic images of the disaster sent a shiver through him, a good kind of shiver.

Chapter 99

COLONEL FALLON PLUNGED a fork into his pancakes. An airman rushed into the Officers' Mess and switched on the TV. "Get a load of this, sir."

A newscaster came into focus, talking about the murder of Judge Freeman. Fallon felt a sick feeling churn in his stomach, like the pancakes he'd eaten had swelled up and ran out of room. Marston had told him that Freeman had issued the warrant for Anderson's arrest.

Now the judge was dead. That was too much of a coincidence to be believable.

Just as he was digesting that information, news of a plane crash took center stage. He watched intently as a helicopter circled the crash scene.

Devin and Toothless bounded in. "What happened?" Devin asked and sat down.

Toothless grabbed the Frosted Flakes and began eating them out of the box.

"I'm not sure." Fallon didn't take his eyes from the newscast. "A few minutes ago they were talking about Judge Freeman being murdered, and then this plane crash came up."

"Wasn't Freeman the judge who—"

"I got that connection, too."

"But how could he wind up dead over that? Curtis isn't that powerful."

"They say it was a burglary gone bad."

"I don't believe it."

"Me either." Fallon took a sip of coffee, thinking. "What if Curtis is just a pawn on a bigger chess board?"

Devin made a face as if he didn't agree.

"Marston and I figured that Curtis didn't have the

resources to conduct a military assault on Atomtech. So he had to have a connection to a government source with a military agenda, whether he knew it or not. Marston was checking into that scenario."

"I wonder if he found something." Devin pointed to the TV. A picture of an FBI jet appeared, offset in a window next to the newscaster.

"It has been confirmed," the newsman announced. *"The plane that crashed into the Dreamland Mall was an FBI jet en route to Los Angeles. It had just taken off from Andrews Air Force Base when the pilot reported engine failure. On board, a task force from the Las Vegas bureau perished along with an agent from the D.C. office of special investigations. There were two crew members."*

Colonel Fallon dropped his cup. It shattered and coffee splashed everywhere. The connection was solid. Curtis was the common element, but he had a powerful protector. Who? Fallon looked at Devin. "I talked with Marston only an hour ago. It was all set." He made a fist. "Now this. I don't get it, Walter. What's going on?"

Devin poured himself a cup of coffee. "Now we're the only ones left who know about Curtis and his fuckn' project."

"You're right. Everyone else is dead, the task force, the judge, agent Marston. My copy of the report was probably destroyed, too."

"Report?"

"A flash drive with the FBI's report and the evidence against someone, they didn't have a name. Marston said it was safe on the plane. Hell, it's toast by now. We're in this thing alone."

"Except for the bastards who did that." Devin indicated the TV with a nod.

"Someone high up knows what's going on at Solartech Labs." Fallon rubbed his forehead. "Someone with enough clout to derail every attempt to intervene, someone who doesn't want any public attention and has a vested interest in Curtis's Simi Valley enterprise."

"Who?"

"I don't know but it's time we flush the snake out of its hole. God knows there's no one else left to do it." He threw his napkin on the coffee spill and stood.

"What are you going to do?"

"Take the Apaches into Solartech on an MPA."

"MPA?"

"Military Police Action."

"You can do that?"

"In an emergency, I can do that. And believe me, this *is* an emergency. Meet me in the com-center at 1100 hours. Be ready to go." He headed for the door.

Devin smiled.

Toothless chucked another handful of Frosted Flakes.

Chapter 100

JANIS PEELED OFF his glasses, tossed them on the console, and rubbed his aching eyeballs. He'd been working with Ray and Lo through the night reformulating the event program, feeding new formulas into the Supers, and rerunning the CEI. The results were bizarre imitations of the possibilities of the 13th Power. The Higgs was elusive, always producing an error message. Then it was back to the drawing board.

Their only hope was the right calculations to achieve containment. Curtis would get his Higgs and let everybody go home.

"How long do we have?" Ray asked, frustrated with another error message.

"Maybe lucky, six hours," Lo said. "But time goes fast when we have fun."

Pushing the keyboard aside, Janis laid his face down on his arms. Fighting sleep, he feared for Lisa's horrible predicament. Seeing her in chains and tortured like that had made him push his mathematical skills to the limit, hoping beyond hope he could save her with a stroke of genius.

Janis shuddered, thought about the aberration, the Higgs boson, the God Particle. It permeated the universe like a magnetic field saturates the area round a magnet. It was inside every atom with mass, everywhere but nowhere to be found, except at the 13th Power where it appeared that negative equaled positive. Reciting that equation over and over in his mind, he understood why the Supers spit out the errors; they knew the answer was wrong. Negative never equals positive. Negative two and positive two are two different numbers. The computers knew that.

The computers knew that? The computers knew

nothing they weren't told to know. Nothing they weren't programmed to know. Janis sat up. "That's it!" He nearly toppled from his chair in excitement.

Ray stopped typing. "What's it?"

"We're going about this all wrong." Janis threw his glasses on. "The Supers know the formulas won't work because they've been programmed with the mathematics we know and use everyday. But we're dealing with a realm so small, so tiny, that our rules of physics and math don't apply."

"Physics and math are universal, Janis."

"You saw the light bending and twisting. It didn't travel in a straight line. That's proof that things are different at the 13th Power. Positive and negative are equal. All we have to do is program that into the Supers."

"Oh, sure," Lo said. "If I program Supers that way, it'll make big mess of everything."

"Not exactly. We need the math to work by our rules up to the moment of laser firing. At that exact instant we need a reprogramming statement telling the Supers that negative and positive are equal, just before they clock out."

"But the space-time continuum will be mathematically impossible," Ray said. "Time will stop."

"Dead," Janis said.

Lo squinted. "What time will stop? In MIGGS or in real world?"

Janis didn't know for sure but he had a theory, actually more of a hope. "Long enough to contain the Higgs and bail out before the void opens up and sucks the earth down a black hole. Punch in the numbers at laser firing, then run a test on it."

Lo typed and the CEI engaged. The monitors displayed the scheduler with the new formula, negative equals positive. At laser firing, no error message appeared.

"Yes," Ray exclaimed, his face beaming under the stubble of a new beard. "Bring up *MOM* and the list of errors from the test fire. Delete the time sensitive ones. What are we left with?"

Punching the keyboard, Lo brought up the list.

"Get to work on those."

"We've got it, Janis," Ray said, patting him on the back.

Janis forced a smile. He might have been too hasty. Something felt wrong with that approach, but he couldn't put his pencil on it. Containment had to take place in the gravity simulator where the event horizon was critical. If positive equaled negative, would the escape velocity still be 186,000 miles per second? A lapse in the MIGGS would mean certain disaster. The Higgs and the void would not be contained. The thought of being sucked out of existence sent a chill down his back. He had to be sure that wouldn't happen.

After opening the scheduler, Ray deleted the fail-safe messages, giving the Supers total control over the sequencing of the MIGGS, ionizer, synchrotron, and laser. With a few more keystrokes, the Supers tapped into the power station to control the power, as well.

"You sure about that?" Janis said over his shoulder.

"Without a glitch, it'll work."

"I don't know," Janis winced. "There're so damn many glitches in this thing."

Giving the Supers control of everything made his stomach hurt. He needed an insurance policy. "Lo—put a back door in both the scheduler and laser sequencer. If anything even looks like it's going wrong we'll be able to get in and shut the experiment down."

Lo went to work.

Janis saw Ted limp toward the coffee pot. It was time to have a little talk with the old man.

Chapter 101

JANIS GRABBED A COFFEE cup. "Good morning, Ted. I'll take a splash of that."

He poured Janis's coffee but didn't seem talkative.

Janis waited while Ted filled a mug of his own and set the pot on a burner. He began to walk away. Janis stopped him. "The test fire yesterday, Ted, you kept saying you told us. Told us what?"

Ted didn't answer.

"What were you afraid of?"

"Nothing." Ted turned toward his console.

Janis blocked his way. "Don't bullshit me. You were horrified, and I want to know why."

Ted sidestepped but Janis checked his move. "My guess is you know something you're not telling us."

"So what if I do?"

"Let's have it, Ted."

"I can't talk about it."

"Why not?"

Ted's eyes darted around the control room. "Where's Curtis?"

"He's not here."

Ted leaned in toward Janis's ear. "In Mother Russia…" he whispered, "…we discover 13th Power very dangerous." He took a swig of coffee and stared over the brim of his cup, looking as if he anticipated more questions he didn't want to answer.

Janis didn't make him wait long. "What did you think was going to happen?"

"It happened in Russia. The Troitska. Gone." He limped to his station and Janis followed him, listening. "Leave big crater in ground. I nearly not escape death."

Janis felt his mouth fall open. He clamped it shut, then said, "Does Curtis know about this?"

Ted set his cup down on his console. "I tell Curtis, I tell CIA. Too dangerous I tell them both. Nobody listen."

"The CIA? What do they have to do with this?"

"Ask I did not."

Janis put a hand on the old man's shoulder. "If it's any consolation, we believe you, Ted."

"Boris," he said with a toothy smile. "Real name Boris."

Janis's heart stuttered. He was right about Tracy's verbal slip. She knew Ted wasn't Ted all along. What else did she know? He looked at the vacant chair at her station and wondered what she was up to.

"Thanks for being straight with me, Boris."

"Boris, yes, but for you I am Ted. I don't want crazy bastard Curtis to know I let bag get off of cat."

"What do you know about Tracy?"

"Pretty. That's all."

"Yeah." Sipping coffee, Janis walked back to his station. He saw Lo working through an error message. Leaning over his shoulder, Janis whispered, "Can you get into Tracy's database?"

"For what?"

"I need to find out what she's been doing at her terminal."

He stopped typing. "First I need her terminal access number, but if I find it, and if I use it, can't be secret about it. The Worm will know we log on and report to someone."

"Screw the Worm, Lo. If this thing goes bad this afternoon, the snoop program will be with us in oblivion anyway. Try to find her access number."

Lo resumed typing.

Janis started pacing.

Matching his stride, Ray joined him. "Now what?"

"Nothing," Janis answered gruffly, reacting to lack of

sleep more than annoyance. "Is the scheduling program set?"

"Yes."

"I've still got some problems to work out."

"What kind of problems?" Ray asked.

"When I figure it out, you'll be the first to know."

Ray went to his station and slumped in his chair, obviously exhausted.

Lo signaled Janis. "Access number."

"Let's see it."

The display opened a *WELCOME* window and asked for a password. "Wait." Lo returned to his hacking.

Janis stared at the monitor. "Why the double security on her terminal?"

Lo shrugged, his display changing windows as he worked his magic. "Ah ha!" he said with a grin. "She like Irish Tea."

"How do you know?"

"Password." Tracy's desktop appeared on Lo's screen, scrolling formulas and equations. Janis recognized those related to the speed of light, but the others he hadn't seen before. She'd programmed a spreadsheet of some kind, capable of running several scenarios simultaneously. Janis couldn't make any sense of it, but he was sure of one thing, Tracy had an agenda that had nothing to do with the 13th Power. "What is she looking for?"

"The particle beam," Tracy said over his shoulder.

Janis started, nearly spilling his coffee, the unexpected sound of her voice sending a shiver through him. *Busted.*

Lo sat upright. "So, this s-stuff yours?" he stammered. "Just pop on screen, like magic."

"Like hell." She looked Janis in the eyes. "All you had to do was ask. Day before yesterday I'd have told you nothing, but today is different. Since the test fire, I'm scared."

"Why?"

"I'm not convinced the particle beam technology is worth the risks we're taking."

"What about the particle beam?"

She touched his hand. "It's too complicated to explain right now but listen to me. We've got to stop Curtis. You were right. A perfect test fire would have been a disaster."

Janis led her to the MIGGS window, away from the others. "I don't know how many agendas this project has, but I can tell you I'm sick of them all. Still, we can't stop now. The Supers are set to run the 13th Power experiment without the fail-safes. Curtis wants us to snatch the Higgs before the black hole overpowers the MIGGS. We believe we've made that possible."

Tracy's eyes widened. "N-no. You shouldn't have taken my advice."

"We had no choice. Curtis is holding Lisa hostage and he'll kill her if we don't cooperate."

"Lisa?"

"Ray's daughter." He left it at that.

"Curtis never fails to surprise me. He's a man to be wary of." Her voice was almost a whisper.

Janis gave her a baleful glare. "You also know that Ted is really Boris."

Tracy pursed her lips. Speechless, she turned away.

Janis wasn't going to let her avoid him. He yanked her around. "Right now I don't have time to give a damn about what you know or why you're here. We're in trouble and I need your help."

"What can I do?"

"That lunatic Curtis expects us to contain the Higgs in a millisecond after the laser fires. We've been working all night trying to get the Supers to run the scheduler without error messages. Nothing worked until I added the formula, *negative equals positive* at laser firing."

"You didn't."

"It fixed the error messages."

A look of panic came over Tracy's face. "But what about the MIGGS?"

"We may have a problem there."

"I can think of two problems right off the top. Did you cross-formulate it?"

"I can't come up with the equations to double check the programming statement against the escape velocity. The MIGGS is a simulator, math makes it work. One wrong formula and it's nothing but an illusion. I'm afraid I've overlooked something."

"If the escape velocity is wrong, the MIGGS won't contain the black hole. It'll expand without restraint." Tracy looked around the control room. "You're talking goodbye Solartech Labs, Simi Valley, California, and who knows what else. Stopping time was a tricky way to try to make it work."

"It sounds impossible, I know. It can't be cross-formulated with standard mathematics. We need new formulas. Maybe between the two of us, working together, just maybe we can come up with the answers." He squeezed her hand. "We have to know for sure. If this thing goes bad, no one will survive."

"Then we better start working on those formulas." She headed for her station. "If this doesn't work, we're all going to die today."

The video monitors around the room suddenly flickered on and slowly came into focus. Like a horror movie coming to life in the living room, a vivid image of Lisa appeared. She was struggling against shackles that anchored her arms and legs to a stone wall. Her body was wrapped in chains. She cursed at Judas who was quick to push the transmitter button. Blue sparks crackled. Her screams filled Tech-Com Control.

Janis felt a chill, cold as the growing urge to murder Curtis filled his chest.

Tracy turned her head away.

Knowing he was on the air, Judas put his rat-gnawed face in front of the camera lens and pushed the button again. He laughed as if he were having the time of his life.

Janis couldn't breathe. Lisa's agonizing screams pierced him like arrows.

"Judas," Ray yelled and threw his sling to the floor. "I'll kill the son of a bitch."

A light came on above the control room, and Curtis emerged from his office. He leaned on the metal railing and tapped his staff on the landing. "I thought a little motivation might be in order here. Anybody screw up and Judas will kill her, right before your eyes. Not quickly mind you, but slowly. Painfully. He'll fry her, a little at a time."

"Curtis, you bastard," Ray yelled. "You'll have your Higgs. I hope you choke on it."

"I'd better have it or you'll choke on Lisa's memory." He turned with a flourish and stepped back into his office.

Lo sat at his station, staring at the video monitor, his face clouded with fear. "Poor Lisa. Tiger claws slash deep."

Boris limped up to Janis and put a hand on his shoulder. "I not know what more dangerous, 13th Power or asshole up there. Sorry I ever met him. We now must do best we can to save the lady." He turned back to his console and picked up his coffee cup, his hand trembling.

Janis went back to Tracy's station where her monitor lit up with equations and formulas on a spreadsheet of lettered rows and numbered columns. "Try 47-D," he suggested.

She was intensely focused on her screen. Her pretty face and sexy hair didn't matter now. He needed her expertise with the spreadsheet she'd developed. Never before had he counted on a woman so much. There was no time for competition. They had to work together to get out of this mess. Her fingers danced over the keyboard.

The Supers made the calculations.

ERROR

Lisa's screams shrieked through Tech-Com Control.

Ray rushed over. "We've got to start this experiment before they kill her, damn it. What's the problem now?"

"There's a good possibility the MIGGS won't work with my new formula," Janis said.

"It *has* to work—our lives depend on it."

"The escape velocity might be wrong," Tracy explained.

"Try 44-B," Janis said to Tracy, leaning on the back of her chair.

Tracy typed.

"How are we going to know?" Ray asked, looking at his daughter's horrible condition on the video screen.

"We're cross-formulating it now."

ERROR

"Take out the new formula," Ray said. "It's too dangerous."

"It's our only hope to contain the Higgs before the black hole gets away from us. We just need to prove it won't screw up the MIGGS."

"If it does, everything's gone."

"We have to keep trying," Tracy said. "There's no time to lose." She typed in *46-D*.

ERROR

Janis returned his attention to the formulas. Somewhere in that jumble of numbers the answer lurked elusively. "Try 45-C."

Tracy typed.

Ray went back to Lo's station where his monitor scrolled the errors from *MOM*.

Tech-Com Control was silent, except for Lisa's bone-chilling screams.

ERROR

Chapter 102

FROM THE CURB, Steve kissed Susan goodbye and waved to Tom. "Take care of her."

Tom gave him a two-fingered salute.

Susan held onto Steve's arm, not wanting to let him go. Doubts flooded her mind. Maybe she shouldn't have made such a big deal over leaving the others at Solartech Labs. Maybe she was sending him to his death in a valiant effort to appease her. Maybe she would never see him again.

Steve gently pulled her tight fingers from around his arm. "Don't worry. I'll be back. Just stay here like we planned."

"But—"

Steve placed his fingers over her lips. "I know what I'm doing."

She stood helplessly, tears flowing down her cheeks as Steve's red Lebaron disappeared into traffic on Balboa Boulevard. An empty feeling enveloped her.

#

Stopped at a traffic light, Steve checked the case on the seat. In it was the gadgetry he needed to circumvent Solartech Lab's security. It had worked when he breached the perimeter at South Gate. He felt confident he could pull it off again. The light turned green.

He accelerated onto the freeway toward Simi Valley.

***

A squadron of Apache helicopters sat poised for flight on the tarmac at Nellis; the noise of roaring engines and thumping rotors filled the air. Devin stood with Toothless just outside the communications building's front door, waiting for Fallon's signal. Twelve Hueys approached from the north. Within moments they were hovering overhead, loud as floating jackhammers. Devin felt the sound waves pound his chest. Fifty-caliber machineguns, each armed with heavy ribbons of shiny ammunition, protruded from open side doors. Men seated inside wore white armbands with *SP* printed in bold blue letters. They were ready to put an end to the experiments at Solartech Labs and capture Curtis. Finally, the bastard was gonna pay.

Colonel Fallon ducked under the rotating blades of his Blackhawk helicopter and waved Devin and Toothless to climb aboard. Devin led him headlong into the bruising rush of wind. He jumped aboard, helped fat-ass Toothless get in, and then took the nearest seat.

The pilot radioed the tower. "Alpha Bravo ready."

Devin buckled up. Toothless too.

The shiny black chopper lifted off and headed west.

Cleared by the tower, the formation of Hueys followed the Blackhawk. Devin watched the Apaches rise from the tarmac in unison and join the armada now hammering over the city. From the north, he saw another squadron of Apaches flying an intercept course toward them. Dispatched twenty minutes earlier from Indian Springs, they would fortify the Nellis assault force.

The Colonel nodded to his pilot who returned him a thumbs-up signal. They were right on schedule.

Over downtown Las Vegas, the squadrons merged and flew toward Simi Valley, their chopper blades beating to a rhythm unlike anything Devin had ever heard before.

***

Inside Tamarack Hall, Steve slapped dust off his jeans. After breaching the perimeter at South Gate again, he thought he'd start his search for Janis and Lisa at their quarters. As he walked down the hallway, a scream came from a room up ahead. Sheila had just opened the door to Janis's room. Steve ran to her side. A wave of panic swept over him.

"What a mess." He walked into the room and righted the couch. As he picked up the phone from the floor and placed the receiver back on its hook, he noticed the cord had been ripped from the wall. The place looked like the aftermath of a barroom brawl. When he spotted a smear of blood on the bedroom door, he knew someone had put up one hell of a fight. He turned to Sheila. "Janis must be in big trouble."

"No, Señor. I don't think so. I saw him leave with Lo this morning. Lisa was here, still sleeping."

"Oh, damn." That was Lisa's blood. Steve ran out. "Don't touch anything."

She shook her head and closed the door.

As Steve rode the elevator down to the lobby, he realized that Susan was right. He shouldn't have left without them.

Outside, he hailed a passing staff car. "Run me by the labs, will ya?"

"Hop in."

At the entrance to the lab buildings, Steve thanked the driver and sprinted up the glass-encased escalator to the lobby where a guard sat watching the monitors on the wall.

"How may I help you?" he said evenly.

"I'm looking for Alex," Steve said, his eyes scanning the monitors behind the guard. "Is he around here...?" He spotted Lisa on one of the screens, chained to a stone wall, struggling and screaming.

"He should be at C-Wing—"

Steve put his .45 in the guard's face.

"What the fuck?"

"Your gun. Give it to me. Slowly." The guard handed over the pistol, grip first. Steve tucked it under his belt.

"There, on monitor 27. Where is that video feed coming from?"

"D-Block, in the basement on the right." He pointed to a gold elevator door.

"Why is she in chains?"

"Mackey and Crawford tried to back out of the project. Curtis is using her for leverage." The guard shook his head. "None of us are backing him on this, but we have no choice. He's threatened to kill our families if we don't cooperate. The man is a tyrant, and so is his henchman there." He pointed to the monitor.

Steve looked again and saw Judas. "Son of a bitch." Thoughts of revenge raced through his mind, like blowing the bastard's brains out for starters, but he wasn't looking too good: his face all gouged and bloody, one ear about gone. "The rats damn near killed him."

"He's really pissed off, too."

With a swift stroke of his .45, Steve knocked the guard unconscious. "About as pissed off as you're going to be when you wake up with that knot on your head."

Rummaging through the drawers behind the counter, he found a roll of duct tape and a guest ID tag. He clipped the tag to his shirt, dragged the guard into a men's room, and taped him to a toilet.

As he placed tape over the guard's mouth, he suddenly became aware of a noise outside. Faint at first, it was getting louder and louder. He had trouble placing the sound, but finally it came to him.

Choppers?

He ran out of the men's room and headed for the gold elevator, his .45 in one hand, the guard's revolver in the other.

Chapter 103

ALEX CLOSED HIS OFFICE door and logged on to the CIA website, typing his password for *The Ark*. Things had gotten out of hand...way beyond his control.

The instant message window came up with a flashing cursor. He typed: *Apache assault choppers approaching from the north. Curtis is torturing a female hostage to force the scientists to continue the experiment. They're due to fire the laser within minutes. Request permission to terminate mission immediately. Mole.*

He waited. How could the military have gotten involved? It must have been Devin. The computer flashed a return message: *Arrest Melvin Anderson. That'll give the military credible evidence that the CIA was on top of this thing. Then eliminate the Russian and Dr. McClarence. They're the only ones who can implicate us. The Ark.*

Alex typed back: *Implicate us? In what?*

You don't have much time, so get on it.

From the top drawer of his desk, Alex picked up his Glock. The thought of using it on Tracy and Boris settled in his stomach like a rock. But he'd do it; such was his loyalty to *The Ark*. Though Alex wasn't looking forward to arresting Anderson without backup, he knew he had to, before the military arrived. Grabbing a pair of handcuffs, he closed the drawer.

Melvin Anderson would be on a plane to Sumatra by morning.

***

Tracy sat at her station in Tech-Com Control. Her monitor scrolled formulas across the screen with error messages following each calculation. Janis had helped her program the spreadsheet, which now worked through the variables automatically. The escape velocity of the MIGGS eluded her. Over her shoulder she saw Janis pacing, occasionally glancing at the video monitor where Lisa was being tortured. Judas was enjoying himself, laughing every time he hit the red button, screaming every time she screamed.

Made Tracy feel ill. She'd need a hot shower after this was over, to get the creepy off her skin, though she worried she'd never be able to scrub hard enough.

The technicians reported to their stations. They too appeared tense and uncomfortable with Lisa's situation. As if in shock, they went about their jobs in silence.

Boris stood at the main console, working the controls. With the whir of electric motors, the new titanium cylinder came down from the MIGGS ceiling; its shiny chrome finish glistened in the blinking green light. With the joystick, Ray maneuvered the gun sight on his monitor. The titanium cylinder swiveled right and left until *Laser Locked* flashed on the screen. Janis and Ray looked at each other, their eyes red and puffy from lack of sleep. Tracy thought hers probably looked just as bad. How had she ever let *The Ark* talk her into this?

She glanced up to the office window where Curtis stood, a pleased look on his face. Her stomach felt sick. Alex walked into the room. He looked nervous, his golf shirt soaked with sweat. Without a word, he headed up the stairs. Curtis backed away from the window as Alex went into his office. She looked at Janis. He was sweating.

It was almost noon.

***

Inside the office, Alex wasted no time. He pulled the Glock out of his waistband and pointed it at Melvin, straight-armed. "CIA, Anderson. You're under arrest."

Melvin just stood upright, holding his golden staff and staring at him from behind those ridiculous sunglasses. "You don't say."

"Drop the stick, hands up and turn around."

"This is no stick," he protested. "It's a pharaoh's staff."

With his left hand, Alex took the handcuffs from his back pocket. "Drop it, I said. And turn around."

"You think you can just waltz in here and blow my deal behind a CIA smoke screen? Who the hell do you think you are anyway, a hero or something? You're a nobody, a nothing, a bug I'm going to crush under my shoe."

"Make it hard, make it easy, Anderson. It's your choice. Either way, you're going back to Sumatra. They'd love to know you're still available for immediate tenancy. Or maybe they'll just throw you a hanging party, right off. I'm sure they haven't forgotten about Fred Jenkins. Personally, I don't give a damn. Now assume the position and quit wasting my time. I've got two other fish to fry."

Curtis turned his back to Alex and outstretched his arms, raising the staff in the air like Moses about to part the Red Sea. His coat spread open making him look twice his size.

"Don't be stupid, Melvin. Drop—"

Suddenly, the sound of a toilet flushing and a door opening jerked Alex's attention to Jonathan coming out of the bathroom. "Okay, boss. I'm ready to—"

Alex pointed the gun at Jonathan. "Get over—" A sudden wrenching pain stung Alex's arm. His Glock hit the floor. He grabbed his forearm. It bent in the wrong place. Curtis had struck him with that fuckin' staff and broke his arm. In the heartbeat that it took him to figure it out, Alex found himself slammed against the wall, the tip of the golden staff now pressed hard into his throat. Grabbing the staff with one hand, Alex tried to wrench it away but it was caught under his Adam's apple, cutting off his air.

"CIA my ass." Anderson pressed the golden eagle's emerald eye. With a shrill sound, spring steel ejected a dagger into Alex's neck, and with a thunk, the blade embedded in the wall behind him.

Impaled with his eyes wide open, he could still see Anderson sneering at him. Alex tried to take a breath. It was no use. He tried to kick. His legs wouldn't obey. Lungs burning, he dropped the handcuffs. The last sound he heard was the clink as they hit the floor.

Chapter 104

CURTIS STEPPED OUT of his office, brandishing Alex's Glock, and yelled down to Tech-Com Control. "Proceed."

It was noon.

Ray looked at Janis. Janis looked at Tracy.

"Not yet," she said. The escape velocity had still not been computed.

On the video monitor, Judas pushed the shocker button. Sparks crackled. Lisa's cries grew more intense as he cranked up the power of his torture machine.

"Let her go first," Ray demanded.

"And ruin all the fun?" Curtis quipped.

"I'll do anything."

"Then start the computer sequence."

"Give us more time," Ray said.

"You've had enough time."

"But we're not ready."

Curtis grinned slyly. "All right. I'll set her free. All you have to do is start the experiment."

Lisa screamed. Judas laughed.

"Okay," Ray shouted.

Janis yelled, "No."

Tracy shouted. "You're going to destroy the world."

"No. You are."

"You think we're not serious?"

Curtis huffed. "Destroy the world? Give me a break. You're stalling."

Lisa's torment pained Ray more than he could stand. If they were all going to die anyway, shouldn't they die together? He couldn't bear the thought of his daughter taking her last breath chained to a stone wall, Judas's face the last face she would see. He felt faint with fear. The room spun around him. It was the only way...the only way...the only...

He pressed the button.

Instantly, the Supers began to run the scheduler. The digital clock above the windows showed 4:10 and began counting down each second.

"Now you've gone and done it," Janis yelled. "We were going to stall him. We're not ready."

Ray turned to Janis, whose face was sour with anger, but Ray didn't care. "It's time to earn your money, you hotshot mathematician." Ray pointed to the clock. "You have four minutes." Then Ray yelled up at Curtis. "Are you happy now?"

Curtis just smiled.

"I did what you asked. Now let Lisa go."

Curtis leaned over the railing. "I like her just fine where she is."

"Bastard."

The MIGGS began to rumble, to vibrate.

"Ray," Janis shouted. "We have to go through with this now, so screw your head on straight and start thinking about how we're going to survive it."

"Is he suicidal?" Ray asked.

Janis nodded. "His motto, risk nothing, gain nothing doesn't have that same ring to it anymore, does it, Ray."

"Look," Tracy shouted.

A red glow emanated from the MIGGS window as the black swirling mist began to form. The monitor at Johnson's station displayed a swirling funnel of colors. All they could do now was watch and wait: the fail-safes were gone. This could be the end.

The clock hit 4:00 and the ionizer charged automatically. An electronic female voice announced: *"Three minutes to synchrotron."*

Judas's harsh voice shouted from the video monitors.

"Get back or I'll kill her."

Ray shifted his attention from his computer to the video screen. Judas had his back to the wall, holding the transmitter in front of him with both hands, like a gun. "You think I'm shittin' you?" Judas twisted the button on the transmitter to full power.

Steve Raven stepped into the picture. "Go straight to hell!" He opened fire on Judas with both guns blazing. The transmitter clunked on the floor. Judas keeled over. In the flash of an instant, he was on his way to eternity.

Steve frisked through the dead man's pockets, pulled out a key, and unlocked Lisa's chains. She collapsed in his arms. Steve put his face in the camera. "Choppers coming in, Janis. Let's blow this pop stand."

The clock hit 2:49.

"All right," Ray cheered. Relief felt like a Fourth of July fireworks display going off in his head. Lisa was safe. It was over. He hit the Abort button.

CHANGES LOCKED OUT flashed on his monitor in bright red letters.

Another wave of terror rippled through him. "Damn it." His elation turned to despair.

"Two minutes to synchrotron."

"What's wrong?" Janis asked. "It didn't shut down."

"We're locked out. There's no stopping it."

Janis just smiled and put his hand on Ray's shoulder. "Is that all?" He turned to Lo. "Shut her down, Lo." The clock hit 2:21.

"Put tiger in cage." Lo started typing.

"What's he doing?" Ray asked.

"Opening a back door to the scheduler. We put it in, just in case."

"Thank God," Ray said.

ACCESS DENIED flashed on the screen in a window labeled *Worm Security*. Lo's face twisted in disbelief. "Worm took out back door. We're screwed."

Janis turned to Tracy. "Where do we stand?"

"I don't know yet, Janis." Her fingers worked the keyboard.

"One minute to synchrotron."

"Oh God, I just don't know."

Lo typed. "Try back door to the laser sequencer."

ACCESS DENIED.

"Shit!" Ray shouted. "There has to be a way to stop this damn thing."

"Shut down the power," Janis said. "Roger, pull the plug."

"I can't. The Supers have complete control. My panel is useless."

Johnson stood, pointing at the MIGGS monitor. "We've got a bright red event horizon, Ray. Escape velocity 186,000 miles per second. We'll be all right."

Janis asked Tracy, "Is it real or an illusion?"

"God, I'm trying…." Tracy typed feverishly.

The targeting electromagnets switched on; their roar shook Tech-Com Control.

The clock hit *1:00.*

The ionizer injected protons into the synchrotron, a million, trillion, billion of them. The RMS electron microscopes focused on the electron target now awash in a blue light.

The CEI engaged.

"One minute to laser firing."

The synchrotron picked up speed, accelerating protons to the speed of light. They spun faster and faster in their magnetic sling, the meters rising higher and higher. Ray took a step back from his console. Everything was working perfectly. They'd be okay.

"It's wrong," Tracy yelled, pointing at her monitor. *FAULT* flashed across the screen. "The MIGGS is just a swirling shadow."

"Everybody out," Boris yelled and ran for the exit.

Ray hit the intercom mike. "Attention all personnel." His voice echoed through Solartech Labs. "Evacuate the building. Tech-Com Control is going to blow in forty-seven seconds."

An emergency horn resonated throughout the compound, sending workers scrambling for exits. Ray was headed for the door when Janis grabbed his arm.

"Where do you think you're going, damn it? You got us into this mess. What are we missing here?"

"I gotta find Lisa."

The clock flashed 0:25.

Tracy sat at her station as if choosing to die at her terminal. "The damn Supers should know this isn't going to work," she said. "They're supposed to control everything."

Janis turned to Ray. "They're supposed to, but they don't. They don't control the titanium cylinder."

The clock showed fifteen seconds. "For Christ's sake, Janis, there's no time for this conversation."

"Do they, Ray?" Janis shook him.

"Taking the cylinder out of the MIGGS won't stop the particle beam."

Janis looked at the clock. ...Nine seconds, 0:08, 0:07... "But we can sure as hell redirect it." He ran to Ray's station, grabbed the joystick, and yanked it to the left. The titanium cylinder rotated sideways in the MIGGS.

0:00. The laser fired.

From out of the linear accelerator, four miles long, came a beam of intense light, buzzing with accelerated particles. The power of sunlight was fused and focused on a single point, which struck the shiny side of the titanium cylinder and reflected back into the particle accelerator. Traveling at the speed of light, the beam reached the laser resonator four miles away in a fraction of a millisecond. Released Higgs bosons gave mass to the light photons creating a particle beam with the punch of a missile. It disintegrated the laser resonator and a large portion of the synchrotron along with every atom within the bubble of destruction.

Janis heard the boom deep under Simi Valley. And the shock wave rumbled in the distance, resonating out from the center, getting louder as it rolled toward Tech-Com Control.

Now the entire building started to shake.

"Tracy," Janis yelled, stumbling toward her station.

Video screens crashed to the floor. Windows cracked. Terminals spewed popping sparks. Plaster rained down.

Hanging on to her trembling console, she stood staring, open-mouthed and wide-eyed at her screen. "It worked. I can't believe it. The particle beam worked."

Janis grabbed her arm. "Run."

He pulled her out of Tech-Com Control and into the hall. "This way."

Running down the glass-enclosed catwalk toward the adjacent Admin building, he saw windows blowing out at the far end of the Tech-Com building. Like a tidal waving crashing to shore, getting closer and closer, one at a time, the blown out windows showered the vehicle ramp below with shattered glass. The deafening noise thundered through the halls behind him.

Under his feet, the floor twisted, cracking the glass walls, the fracture lines racing him toward Admin as he ran pulling Tracy along. They stumbled and tripped on the writhing floor and almost reached safety when, with a horrendous bang, the catwalk buckled, broke loose, and fell.

"Jump!"

Chapter 105

Janis and Tracy leaped just as the catwalk broke away from its anchors. Hitting the corridor floor together, they slid on the tile and slammed to a stop against a wall. Breathing hard, he looked back. In a shower of glass and twisted steel, the catwalk crashed down to the ramp below. Through a gaping hole left in the building, he could see the steel archway with its ominous greeting teeter back and forth. Creaking eerily, it twisted and plummeted to the ground. He wiped sweat from his forehead. That was too close.

Dust and smoke billowed from the debris and swirled up into the corridor. Janis pulled Tracy to her feet. She held his hand so tight it hurt. At least they were safe. Hand in hand, he led her toward the lobby. In silence, he turned to look at her. A light smile graced her lips and their eyes met. He felt warm inside. They had worked together and won.

Suddenly, from a dark office, Jonathan leaped out, brandishing a Colt revolver and blocking their way. His eyes glittered with fury.

Janis pulled Tracy close as he calculated his next move. Jonathan wouldn't shoot them; Janis was sure of it. But his confidence changed abruptly when Curtis stepped from behind his aide. Janis tried to swallow a lump in his throat. "What do you want?"

Curtis walked forward, tapping his golden staff. His menacing glare escalated Janis's concern for their safety. Curtis stood in front of him, the staff at his side, a gun tucked behind his belt. "We made a deal, Dr. Mackey. A deal we sealed with a handshake. In the performance of my part, I transferred the balance of the agreed-upon fee into your bank account in Colorado."

"You shouldn't have."

"I don't feel as if I got my money's worth, Dr. Mackey. Where's my Higgs boson?"

Janis released Tracy and went nose to nose with Curtis. "It doesn't belong to you, *Mister* Curtis. It's not yours for the taking. It belongs to the cosmos, safeguarding the rules of physics and math that make our known universe possible. Our galaxy is bound to the universe by those rules, the same rules that bind our earth to our sun and the tiniest atom's electron to its proton. Even you can't break those rules, though your greed made you think you had the right to try."

Curtis didn't answer, just stared into Janis's eyes, looking like he could explode with anger any second. He clutched his golden staff so tightly his knuckles bulged.

Janis held his ground. "Take the time to look up at the sky tonight. When you see the stars stretching across the heavens, be glad you're still here to see it." He pulled on Tracy's arm. "Come on. It smells bad in here."

Stepping in front of them, Curtis raised the golden staff, his thumb hovering over an emerald eye on the eagle-head handle. "You're pathetic."

"You're the one who risked everything and gained nothing."

Running footsteps and yelling voices echoed from somewhere down the corridor.

Curtis whipped around.

Devin and Colonel Fallon rounded the corner, followed by several SPs.

"That's him!" Devin yelled, pointing at Curtis.

A gunshot rang out.

Janis dove to the floor, pulling Tracy down with him, shielding her with his body and looking back up at Curtis. He had a gun in his hand, and along with smiling Jonathan and a stunned Colonel, he was looking at Devin, who was now lying in a pool of blood on the floor. The round had struck him in the heart.

Curtis smiled. His gold tooth glinted.

"You're under arrest," the Colonel yelled.

Curtis started shooting.

The SPs opened fire.

Jonathan and Curtis dove back into the dark office.

Janis sheltered Tracy in his arms, hoping a stray bullet wouldn't end their lives. When the gunfire stopped, he glanced up. SPs rushed the office doorway, but sensing a trap, they hesitated to go in after Curtis. "Throw down your weapons," the Colonel ordered. "Come out with your hands up."

Silence.

The golden staff lay on the hallway floor, alone.

Fallon stooped to pick it up.

Janis stood and helped Tracy to her feet. "Come on."

Outside, he squinted against the hazy afternoon sunshine. Whining turbine engines filled the air. There were choppers everywhere, some hovering overhead while others had landed on lawns, streets, parking lots, and rooftops. The Air Force had invaded every part of Solartech Labs. SPs were posted all around, their rifles held at the ready. Solartech Labs' security force had surrendered without a fight. The incursion appeared to have been swift.

Stepping over fire hoses, which were running every-which-way across the lawn, between fire trucks, hydrants, and the building, he led Tracy through a maze of men and machines, looking for the others. He saw a security guard kneeling on the grass, pulling duct tape off his clothes.

A team of medics emerged from the building, rolling a gurney. Janis stopped them. Carefully, he lifted the sheet covering a body. It was Alex. A golden dagger pierced his throat. Tracy quickly turned away. Shaking his head, Janis dropped the sheet and motioned the medics to move on.

"We have to find the others," he said to Tracy. "Let's keep moving."

They made their way to the fountain where Janis scooped up a handful of water and splashed it on his face and neck. Tracy patted water on her forehead.

Boris found them. "Dr. Janis. Dr. Tracy. You are very smart under pressure. I thank you for saving my life." He shook their hands and smiled through those perfectly white teeth. "I go now."

"Not so fast." Janis grabbed the old man's collar. "You and Tracy have some explaining to do."

They sat by the fountain as valves opened and water shot skyward. The cool spray was as refreshing as it was magnificent. Tracy and Boris explained their involvement with the CIA, the 13th Power project, and the President's Directive Number 119. The roar of the fountain overpowered their voices, so Janis was sure no one else heard what they said or the advice he gave them. "Be careful where you tell this story. The CIA isn't going to want it made public. I think they'd sooner kill you."

Ray rushed up. "Brilliant, Janis, using the joystick like that."

"Sometimes it's the simplest things that are most important."

"You guys all right?"

Janis nodded. "How about the others?"

"Shaken is all, thanks to you."

"And Lisa?"

"Steve took her to Tamarack Hall to get some clothes. Doc says she's okay, considering."

The Colonel and his men caught Janis's attention as they emerged from the building with Devin's body. Fallon carried the golden staff in one hand. He told his men to lay Devin on the grass.

The sight sent a shiver down Janis's spine. He and Ray ran over to Colonel Fallon, who summoned a medic to bring a gurney. "And a clean sheet, too."

Toothless scrambled from a nearby chopper and

kneeled beside his boss. "Why?" he wailed. "I should've gone in with him."

Janis lowered his head, not wanting to watch the big goon cry.

Ray stood stunned with his mouth hanging open, obviously distressed by the sight of Devin lying there dead. "Why couldn't he have just left us alone?"

The Colonel was quick to answer. "He's the only one who knew that Curtis was about to destroy the world. Even I didn't believe him at first."

"So where *is* Curtis?" Janis asked.

"Gone," the Colonel replied.

"He got away?"

"Disappeared down a stairway that led to hell for all we know. We found a maze of tunnels going every which way."

"Son of a bitch," Janis said. "The service access tunnels."

"We searched what we could, but it was obvious, the snake escaped into his hole. He's probably headed to Mexico by now."

"But he's no coward. He'll be back."

"And I'll be waiting," Fallon said.

Disappointed in the fact that justice wouldn't be served, Janis headed back toward the fountain.

Ray rubbed his stubbly chin as he walked alongside Janis. "You know what I'm thinking?"

"I can't imagine."

"This place needs someone like us to get it up and running again. I'm going to stay on here, and Lisa, too. How about you? And let's ask Tracy and Boris. We all make a great team."

"Sounds like a good idea, Ray. Count me out. I miss my quiet life in Colorado."

"Won't you even think about it? It'll be just like old times. Only better."

"When was the last time I heard that?"

"Janis." His name floated in the air with the sweetness of Lisa's voice. He whipped around and saw her running toward him from the open door of a staff car where Lo leaned against the fender and beamed a bright smile.

"Janis," she called out as she ran. Golden hair flowed behind her like silk.

She threw her arms around his neck and hugged him. Her body felt warm.

"Don't ever let me go, cowboy," she whispered in his ear.

"Lisa. I'm going home."

"No." She hugged his neck tighter.

"My mother needs me and your place is here with your father. He risked the world for you. He needs you and you need him."

Her sparkling eyes met his. "It feels so good not to hate him anymore."

"I'm happy for both of you."

She hugged him one last time and whispered softly in his ear. "Thanks for the ride, cowboy."

He tipped an invisible hat. "You're welcome, ma'am."

As she ran to her father's side, Janis thought he would miss being her cowboy.

A red Lebaron pulled up to the curb. Steve Raven was at the wheel.

Janis walked toward Tracy. She was as smart and courageous as she was beautiful. He took her hand. Her eyes looked sad. "Goodbye, Tracy. If you'd like to see the peaceful side of life, call me at the University of Colorado. We could use a brilliant scientist like you."

"I just might do that," she said with a warm smile that lit up her eyes.

Janis walked to the Lebaron without looking back. He got in, shut the door, and Steve accelerated toward the main gate, leaving a cloud of dust in their wake.

Chapter 106

IN THE CIA OFFICE, the red phone on the desk rang. Chief Lawrence let it ring longer than he had to. It was Nathan calling to bitch about something. Finally he picked it up. "Lawrence."

"What happened in Simi Valley? My communications are down."

"Look, John, we've lost Alex. I've pulled the rest of my men out. It's over."

"Did we get the particle beam for the President?"

"The Worm's transmissions were cut off by an explosion."

"Damn it, Lawrence. What am I going to do now?"

"Guess it's back to old-fashioned diplomacy," Lawrence said. "Now I'd like to get back to my guest list for the party."

"Party? What about our involvement in this thing? Are we covered?"

"Quit worrying, I tell you. There's no evidence to link us to the 13th Power project, Atomtech, Judge Freeman or the Hawker crash. I've covered our tracks. So, relax. We're home free."

"What about the 'black box'?"

"I've got a team at the crash site," Lawrence said, annoyed that Nathan would even think the CIA Chief could forget such a thing. "They're going to transport it for quick analysis. Nobody will ever see it again."

"And Tracy and Boris, are they still alive?"

"For now, but we'll get them."

"You sure?"

"It's all arranged."

"It better be." Nathan hung up.

Lawrence huffed. *The Ark* worried too damn much.

***

Joe Rose sat on a flatbed trailer hitched to a cab-over semi and scanned the black scene of the Hawker jet crash. Acrid smoke wisped from small pockets of smoldering debris, carrying with it that same rancid smell of every crash site he'd seen: a mix of charred flesh and burned jet fuel. The air stunk of death. And though he'd seen worse in his twelve years with the NTSB's crash investigating team, this crash fell into his one-size-fits-all category of air disasters: Bad.

Arching his back to relieve the stiffness in his muscles, he realized the endless hours of waiting were taking their toll. Affectionately known as *The Scrappers*, his team had the last and hardest job to do. It sometimes took hours, sometimes days. This mess didn't look too tough, not much of it was over waist high.

For the past two hours, he had watched recovery teams scour through tangled aluminum and twisted metal. Their orange fire suits and helmets glowed in the blackness of the charred wreckage around them. With small yellow flags, they marked the locations of the grisly remains of passengers and crew. Large yellow body bags were laid out among the flags. He didn't understand how they knew which pieces went into which bags. Or did it really matter?

Flash bulbs popped, giving the crash site an eerie contrast of grays, blacks, and shadows. After the photographers finished, a coroner's team went in to do the gruesome task of body removal. While they worked their way through the rubble, filling their yellow bags, investigators stood off to one side, huddled in conversation. The I-team, with their neatly pressed white lab coats, looked too sterile for this bleak environment. Joe glanced down at his dusty blue jeans and black rubber boots. He was dressed for the dirty work.

Day turned to dusk by the time the investigators finished. Joe pulled a roast beef sandwich from his lunch box as the recovery team tagged mangled pieces of the wrecked Hawker: red for the scrap yard, green for the hanger for closer inspection. The red ones would go on his flatbed.

A sudden commotion near the twisted tail caught his attention. An I-team member was carrying something. It was bright orange and sooty. Several others gathered around him. Joe raised his eyebrows. They'd found the prize, the *black box* containing the flight data and cockpit voice recorders, all vital clues to the demise of the Hawker.

A group of dark-suited men, Joe counted four of them, approached the I-team members. This was unusual, and Joe wondered who they were. He ate the last of his sandwich and watched them converse. After what appeared to be a lengthy discussion, the I-team gave the *black box* to the suits who rushed it away in a black sedan. Joe bit his lower lip. Must have been something really important about that flight.

A diesel generator rattled to life. With a thunk, huge floodlights came on, the brightness making him squint. He chucked a cookie and closed his lunch box. It was time to go to work.

"Let's go, boys," he said into his two-way.

His men worked through the night under floodlights. With blazing torches they cut up the jet and loaded his flatbed. A chunk of wing and the tail section were already secured with tie-downs. Joe thought the job was coming along just fine. As the early rays of dawn began to penetrate the sky, one of his men called him over.

"What is it, Al?"

"Look what I found." He yanked on a steel box, half covered by debris and scorched black. "Help me with this."

Working together, they freed it from the rubble.

"It's an air-safe, boss."

"And a heavy one." Joe groaned, rolling it over. The dial on the door was broken off but the hinges were still intact. "These air-safes are pretty much fire, bomb, and impact proof. This one survived the crash."

Joe pulled a rag from his pocket and rubbed soot off the door, revealing a seal and inscription. "It's the FBI's, all right."

Al rubbed his prickly chin. "Do you think there's any money in it?"

"I doubt it. These things are used to protect important documents, maybe critical evidence in their investigations, in files or on computer drives."

"Maybe they stashed somethin' in this one."

"Who knows?" Joe stood and stuffed the rag in his back pocket.

Al gave the air-safe a kick. "What should we do, boss, scrap it?"

"No. Let's return it to the FBI. They'll know what to do with it."

Next up "The 13Power Journey"

In the second book of The 13th Power Trilogy, Ray Crawford, having failed to achieve fame, has formulated a new plan: reprogram the Supercomputers, build a bigger gravity chamber, and degenerate NASA's prototype Inter Space Station Transporter into the 13th Power. He will discover that fame carries a terrible price.

Since the undercover operation in Simi Valley failed, *The Ark* is under more pressure from the President to fulfill Directive 119, the Strategic Defense Initiative, and deploy at network of proton laser beams in orbit. He captures the fugitive murderer Dr. Curtis, aka Melvin Anderson, and offers him a deal he can't refuse.

Just when Janis Mackey is settled into a peaceful life with Tracy in Boulder, the CIA calls on him to help them steal the 13th Power technology for Star Wars. Of course, he refuses, so acting on orders from *The Ark*, they take Tracy into custody and threaten to kill her if Janis doesn't deliver the goods.

Janis's return to Simi Valley is not the joyous reunion Lisa expected. She's heartbroken over his devotion to Tracy, but she's determined to win him back. And Lisa has a new problem: her mother. Kate returns after her release from prison. She's looking for forgiveness from a daughter she'd abandoned and a husband she'd betrayed. Good luck with that.

In this stunning sequel to The 13th Power Quest, humanity is at the mercy of technology, and a family's love for each other is put to a brutal test.

About the Author

There's nothing mundane in the writing world of **Terry Wright**. Tension, conflict and suspense propel his readers through the pages as if they were on fire. Published in Science Fiction, Supernatural, and Horror, his mastery of the action thriller has won him International acclaim as an accomplished screenplay writer. A longtime member of the Rocky Mountain Fiction Writers, he coordinated their annual Colorado Gold Writing Contest for six years, received their highest award for service, The Jasmine Award, and was nominated for the Writer of the Year in 2014.

Terry is a Vietnam Veteran (USAF – Red Horse - SAC), a certified pilot of light aircraft, and an avid Harley Davidson motorcycle enthusiast. He's a member of the Harley Owners Group (HOG), the American Legion Post 178, and the American Legion Riders. He lives in Lakewood, Colorado, with his wife, Bobette, and their Yorkie, Taz.

www.terrywrightbooks.com

Enjoy other fine short stories and novels by Terry Wright

The 13th Power Journey, Book 2 (TWB Press, 2011)

The 13th Power War, Book 3 (TWB Press, 2013))

The Grief Syndrome (TWB Press, 2011)

The Duplication Factor (TWB Press, 2011)

The Pearl of Death (TWB Press, 2013)

Black Jack (TWB Press, 2014)

Z-motors, The Job From Hell (TWB Press, 2011)

Street Beat (TWB Press, 2011)

The Gates of Hell, Justin Graves Series (TWB Press, 2010)

Return me to Mistwillow – (TWB Press, 2013)

Wilderness Rampage (TWB Press, 2014)

www.twbpress.com